Frederick Saunders

A Festival of Song

a series of evenings with the greatest poets of the English language

Frederick Saunders

A Festival of Song
a series of evenings with the greatest poets of the English language

ISBN/EAN: 9783337850531

Printed in Europe, USA, Canada, Australia, Japan

Cover: Foto ©Andreas Hilbeck / pixelio.de

More available books at **www.hansebooks.com**

A
FESTIVAL OF SONG.

A SERIES OF EVENINGS WITH

The Greatest Poets of the English Language.

BY

FREDERICK SAUNDERS,

AUTHOR OF " SALAD FOR THE SOLITARY AND THE SOCIAL,"
" EVENINGS WITH THE SACRED POETS," ETC.

ILLUSTRATED

WITH SEVENTY-THREE ORIGINAL PICTURES BY MEMBERS OF THE NATIONAL ACADEMY
OF DESIGN, AND NUMEROUS PORTRAITS AND AUTOGRAPH
POEMS IN *FAC-SIMILE.*

ST. LOUIS, CHICAGO, AND CINCINNATI:

SCAMMELL & COMPANY.

1876.

PRESENTATION.

R IGHT welcome, gentle dames, and ye, worthy gal-
lants, to this our festive banqueting. And sith, as
" rare Ben" saith,

> " 'Tis the fair acceptance that creates
> The entertainment perfect, not the cates,"

come to it joyously, with hearts elate, and all a-glow
with sweet expectancies and kindly thoughts. The feast
itself, select and choice, and enriched with multitudinous
dainties to tempt the taste and please the fancy, now but
awaits the generous gusto of the guests. There is, for-
sooth, a rare and prodigal diversitie of delicacies outspread
—a most Epicurean and pleasurable repast: I pray ye,
my masters, of your courtesy, look—there is wherewith
to regale both soul and sense; to wit, delicious Melodies
to charm the listening ear, and glowing Pictures to fasci-
nate the kindling eye withal. In fine, you shall share
much joyaunce and delectation from the costly spoils here
garnered from our own and divers other times.

Moreover, trusty friends, note well the noble folk who

grace this festival. Among them are the "kings of thought," ay, "heirs of more than royal race,"—a rare companie of most renowned wits and worthies, with whom it is our privilege to hold quiet colloquy, or listen, delighted, to their high discourse. Meanwhile, from their *ardentia verba*, we may, perchance, catch somewhat of their inspiration; since, in order thereto (if I trow aright), it needeth that our ear be but attent to the unfolding of

> " Whate'er in rhapsody, or strain most holy,
> The hoary minstrels sang in times of old,"

as well as to the sweet melodies of bards of later days. Nay, of your clemency, look not askance at the mention of ancient minstrels and sages, nor urge that their mouldy tomes are rife with quaint conceits and rugged rhymes. Go to; certes, they are as delightsome as odoriferous herbs, and as voiceful of rich melody as their own loved lyre. Rather let us render rightful homage to these "magnates of the mind," forasmuch as, by their sweet sentiment and song, the tedium of life's prosaic routine hath oft-times been beguiled : whilst their concentrated wit hath, not seldom, unwittingly seduced us into the pleasant places of wisdom and virtue.

I beseech ye then, my singular good friends, let us forget the turbulent world awhile, and surrender ourselves to the high enjoyment that now awaits us.

FREDERICK SAUNDERS.

POETS.

PAGE

FIRST EVENING.—CHAUCER, SURREY, SIDNEY, RALEIGH, SPENSER, SHAK-
SPEARE, JONSON, BEAUMONT, SHIRLEY, CAREW, LOVELACE, LYLY,
TITCHBOURNE, MARLOWE, DANIEL, LODGE, HERRICK, KING, WOT-
TON, SUCKLING 3

SECOND EVENING.—DRUMMOND, HABINGTON, QUARLES, WALLER,
AYTON, COWLEY, MILTON, BYRD, CHAMBERLAYNE, HERBERT, DEN-
HAM, MARVELL, DRYDEN, ADDISON, POPE, PARNELL, THOMSON,
COLLINS, SHENSTONE, YOUNG 55

THIRD EVENING.—GRAY, AKENSIDE, JONES, BERKELEY, IRVING, ALL-
STON, DANA, PERCIVAL, SIGOURNEY, PIERPONT, DRAKE, SPRAGUE,
BROOKS, PAYNE, BURGOYNE, DARWIN, WOODWORTH, GOLDSMITH,
COWPER, BURNS, DARLEY, SHERIDAN, LOGAN, LEYDEN, BEATTIE,
CHATTERTON, WOLFE, WILDE, HALLECK 109

FOURTH EVENING.—BRAINARD, PINKNEY, READ, CUTTER, PRENTICE,
CIST, GALLAGHER, PERKINS, BYRON, CRABBE, SCOTT, HOGG, LAMB,
WHITE, MONTGOMERY, COLERIDGE, POE, HEMANS, SOUTHEY, MOORE,
BRYANT, HUNT, WELBY, NICHOLS, BOTTA.................................. 163

B   ix

FIFTH EVENING. — POLLOK, MORRIS, ROGERS, BOIES, CAMPBELL, OSGOOD, HOOD, MACLEAN, EASTMAN, ELLIOTT, BLANCHARD, MOIR, SPENCER, WORDSWORTH, SHELLEY, KEATS, WHITTIER, KEBLE, BURBIDGE, ELIZA COOK, MILMAN, SWAIN, MRS. NORTON, HERVEY, TUCKERMAN, BOWLES, PRAED, LINEN, MOTHERWELL, MRS. BROWNING, MRS. BARBAULD, LOVER, PEABODY, STERLING, JONES, WILSON, MACKAY, VEDDER, COOKE, WILLIS, CLARKE, SMITH 237

SIXTH EVENING. — LONGFELLOW, CHADWICK, FIELDS, MASSEY, BULWER-LYTTON, HOLMES, EMERSON, R. BROWN, E. ARNOLD, C. YOUNG, STREET, H. COLERIDGE, FRANCES BROWN, PROCTOR, R. BROWNING, A. PROCTOR, BAILEY, A. SMITH, SAXE, HINXMAN, KINGSLEY, B. TAYLOR, ROBERT LOWELL, THACKERAY, MACAULAY, WESTWOOD, J. R. LOWELL, R. B. LYTTON, A. C. COXE, ALDRICH, TENNYSON, STODDARD, STEDMAN, CRANCH, DICKENS, F. TENNYSON, ALLINGHAM, WINTER, BOKER, INGELOW 315

PAINTERS.

		Page
ALFRED FREDERICKS, A.	INITIAL—" FIRST EVENING "	1
" "	INTERIOR OF THE TABARD	3
JAMES HART, N. A.	DEER—SPRING	8
WILLIAM HART, N. A.	SPRING—LANDSCAPE	13
" "	SUMMER—LANDSCAPE	14
" "	AUTUMN—LANDSCAPE	14
" "	WINTER—LANDSCAPE	15
J. F. CROPSEY, N. A.	ANNE HATHAWAY'S COTTAGE	18
ALFRED FREDERICKS, A.	JULIET TAKING THE OPIATE	23
" "	ARIEL AND FERDINAND	28
" "	LOVE'S CHALLENGE	33
J. F. KENSETT, N. A.	SUMMER SEA	37
A. D. SHATTUCK, N. A.	PRIMROSES	43
S. COLMAN, N. A.	STARLIGHT	50
ALFRED FREDERICKS, A.	INITIAL—" SECOND EVENING "	53
JAMES HART, N. A.	LANDSCAPE—SPRING	55

		Page
J. A. SUYDAM, N. A.	QUIET SEAS	59
EASTMAN JOHNSON, N. A.	PENSIVE NUN	65
C. PARSONS, A.	EVENING	69
A. F. BELLOWS, N. A.	SUMMER MORN	73
V. NEHLIG, N. A.	ALEXANDER'S FEAST	77
J. McENTEE, N. A.	TWILIGHT	82
W. WHITTREDGE, N. A.	THE WESTERN WILD	86
V. NEHLIG, N. A.	THE HERMIT	90
G. H. SMILLIE, A.	EARLY DAWN	94
W. J. HENNESSY, N. A.	THE SCHOOLMISTRESS	101
ALFRED FREDERICKS, A.	INITIAL—" THIRD EVENING"	107
V. NEHLIG, N. A.	THE WELSH BARD	109
S. COLMAN, N. A.	NORMAN TOWER	116
J. A. HOWS, A.	LANGUAGE OF FLOWERS	121
ALFRED FREDERICKS, A.	THE CULPRIT FAY	126
A. D. SHATTUCK, N. A.	THE OLD OAKEN BUCKET	130
W. WHITTREDGE, N. A.	RURAL PASTIMES	134
J. McENTEE, N. A.	WINTER SCENE	139
WILLIAM HART, N. A.	SCOTTISH COTTAGE	143
W. HOMER, N. A.	BOYHOOD'S SPORTS	149
G. H. SMILLIE, A.	NATURE—MORNING	154
J. A. HOWS, A.	THE MOCKING-BIRD	158
ALFRED FREDERICKS, A.	INITIAL—" FOURTH EVENING"	161

		Page
F. E. CHURCH, N. A.	Niagara—Table-Rock	163
C. T. DIX, A.	Iceberg	169
M. F. H. DE HAAS, A.	Ocean—Storm	174
S. COLMAN, N. A.	Spanish Bull-fight	180
ALFRED FREDERICKS, A.	Allen-a-Dale	186
M. WATERMAN, A.	Harvest Moon	193
V. NEHLIG, N. A.	Arnold de Winkelried	199
D. HUNTINGTON, P. N. A.	Girl's Head	207
R. GIGNOUX, N. A.	The Dismal Swamp	216
C. PARSONS, A.	The Waterfowl	223
A. BIERSTADT, N. A.	The Prairie Hunter	228
ALFRED FREDERICKS, A.	Initial—"Fifth Evening"	235
J. A. HOWS, A.	Primeval Nature	237
H. P. GRAY, V. P. N. A.	Joyousness	251
ALFRED FREDERICKS, A.	The Haunted Chamber	257
A. B. DURAND, N. A.	Nutting	266
S. COLMAN, N. A.	Moonlight	273
ALFRED FREDERICKS, A.	Nature	281
W. J. HENNESSY, N. A.	Mother and Child	285
R. S. GIFFORD, N. A.	The Adirondack Mountains	292
W. J. HENNESSY, N. A.	Child Sleeping	297
JAMES HART, N. A.	Moonrise	303
J. D. SMILLIE, A.	Morning Breeze	309

xiii

Page

ALFRED FREDERICKS, A................... INITIAL—" SIXTH EVENING"............ 313

F. O. C. DARLEY, N. A..................... THE VILLAGE BLACKSMITH 315

  "   "   .... WEARINESS................................... 318

J. D. SMILLIE. A. .... THE PLOUGHMAN........................... 325

S. R. GIFFORD, N. A........................ THE WOODPATH............................ 333

E. BENSON, A................................... AMONG THE ROCKS....................... 339

A. F. BELLOWS, N. A........................ THE CHURCH-GATE....................... 350

J. D. SMILLIE, A.............................. THE FOUNTAIN 357

ALFRED FREDERICKS, A................ ANNIE'S DREAM............................ 362

J. R. BREVOORT, N. A..................... NOVEMBER.................................... 366

M. WATERMAN, A........................... CATTLE IN STREAM 373

xiv

" Now, stir the fire, and close the shutters fast,
Let fall the curtains, wheel the sofa round,—
So let us welcome peaceful Evening in."

FIRST
EVENING.

Chaucer,

Surrey, Sidney,

Raleigh, Spenser, Shakspeare, Jonson,

Beaumont, Shirley, Carew, Lovelace, Lyly, Titchbourne.

Marlow, Daniel, Lodge, Herrick,

King, Wotton,

Suckling.

GEOFFREY CHAUCER, that
worthy minstrel-monk, first in the
order of Anglican poets, thus prefaces his *Canterbury Tales* :—

Befelle, that, in that seson on a day,
In Southwerk at the Tabard as I lay,
Redy to wenden on my pilgrimage
To Canterbury with devoute corage,

3

At nighte was come into that hostelrie
Wel nine and twenty in a compagnie
Of sondry folk, by aventure yfalle
In felawship, and pilgrimes were they alle,
That toward Canterbury wolden ride.
The chambres and the stables weren wide,
And wel we weren esèd attè beste.

Although written nearly five centuries ago, this work, notwith-standing its obsoleteness of style, has never been more popular among scholars than it is at this time. There is, indeed, to us of the present day, a charm in its very antiquity, as Campbell remarks,—"something picturesque in it,—like the moss and ivy on some majestic ruin."

This noble production of the early English muse, which was probably suggested by the *Decameron of Boccaccio*, supposes a com-pany to have convened at the Tabard,[1] Southwark, where they are entertained by the host, on the evening prior to their commencing pilgrimage to the shrine of St. Thomas à Becket, at Canterbury Cathedral; and that these "nine and twenty sondry folk," by way of beguiling time, agree amongst themselves to contribute each a tale for the entertainment of the company. The old "hostelrie," or rather part of it, is yet extant, under the name of "The Talbot;" where may be seen a sign-post bearing the inscription,—"*This is the Inne where Sir Geoffrey Chaucer and the twenty-nine pilgrims lodged in their journey to Canterbury, anno* 1383." Chaucer was given to the world in the year 1328; and he wrote his *Canterbury Tales* in the full maturity of his genius, when he had passed his sixtieth year. He was undoubtedly a laborious student, for, according to his own confession, he preferred reading to every other amusement, with the exception of "a morning walke in Maytide." He was fond of retirement, temperate in diet, "rose with the larke and lay

---

[1] *Tabard*, a sleeveless coat, worn by nobles in early times, now by heralds only.

down with the lambe." He seems to have surrendered himself to
the inspiring influences of nature, and to have revelled, as at a
festival, amid birds and flowers : hence the rich arabesque character
of his poetry, and the marvellous freshness and bloom of his pastoral pictures : witness the following :—

> The busy larke, the messenger of day,
> Saluteth in her song, the morwe gray ;
> And fiery Phœbus riseth up so bright,
> That all the Orient laugheth at the sight !
> And with his streamès dryeth in the greves,
> The silver droppès hanginge on the leves.

Chaucer is said to have been one of the handsomest personages
attached to the gallant court of the Plantagenets. As a court
ecclesiastic he became involved in the controversies of his times,
having espoused the doctrines of Wicliff ; and he was, for a season,
obliged to leave his native land. He afterwards returned, married
Philippa, sister of the renowned John of Gaunt, Duke of Lancaster,
and closed his career in the year 1400. His tomb is one of the
earliest of the illustrious dead in Poets' Corner, Westminster Abbey.

Now let us bear him company in one of his morning rambles in
" Maytide," and mark how observant he is of all that is delicious
to soul and sense :—

> I rose anone, and thought I wouldè gone
> Into the woode to hear the birdès sing,
> Whan that the misty vapour was agone,
> And cleare and faire was the morrowing ;
> The dewe also, like silver in shining
> Upon the leves, as any baumè swete,
> Till fiery Titan with his persant hete
> Had dried up the lusty licour newe,
> Upon the herbès in the grenè mede,

5

And that the floures of many divers hewe,
Upon hir stalkès gon for to sprede,
And for to splaye out hir leves in brede
Againe the sunne, gold-burned in his spere,
That dounè to hem cast his beamès clere.

Here is that most charming of descriptions and pictures, *Emelie in the Garden* :—

Thus passeth yere by yere, and day by day,
Till it felle onès in a morwe of May,
That Emelie, that fayrer was to sene
Than is the lilie upon his stalkè grene,
And fresher than the May with flourès newe,
For with the rose-colour strof hir hewe :
I n'ot which was the finer of hem two.
Ere it was day, as she was wont to do,
She was arisen, and alle redy dight,
For May will have no sluggardy a-night ;
The seson pricketh every gentle herte,
And maketh him out of his sleepe to start,
And sayth, Arise ! and do thine óbservance.

The great charm of Chaucer consists in his simplicity of detail, combined with dramatic effect, and his love of rural sights and sounds. We find the following estimate of his genius in the *British Quarterly Review* :—" He is, perhaps, the most picturesque poet we possess : his paintings are fresh, glittering and off-hand, done to the life. His love of nature resembles an intoxication of spirit : his sketches are bright with perpetual sunshine,—his flowers are always in bloom, fragrant with odoriferous perfumes, and gemmed with sparkling dew-drops. From mere narrative and playful humor, up to the heights of imaginative and impassioned song, his genius has exercised itself in nearly all styles of poetry, and won imperishable

6

laurels in all." Need we wonder, then, that Coleridge, like many others in the line of the Muses' priesthood, took such especial delight in poring over his beautiful living pictures and vivid sketches of character? We might, indeed, rather marvel, with another noted poet, that the bard should have seen so distinctly in that gray, misty morning of literature, and that his landscapes should still look green in the very dews of Spring. Tennyson beautifully styles him—

> The first warbler, whose sweet breath
> Preluded those melodious bursts, that fill
> The spacious times of great Elizabeth
> With sounds that echo still.

Campbell, with all a poet's appreciation, has thus beautifully expressed our obligations to the great pioneer poet :—

> Chaucer! our Helicon's first fountain-stream,
> Our morning Star of song, that led the way
> To welcome the long-after coming beam
> Of Spenser's lights and Shakspeare's perfect day.
> Old England's fathers live in Chaucer's lay,
> As if they ne'er had died: he grouped and drew
> Their likeness with a spirit of life so gay,
> That still they live and breathe in fancy's view,
> Fresh beings fraught with truth's imperishable hue

The evils of the protracted civil war in England, prevented not only the progress of literature, but even prostrated its very existence for upwards of a century after the death of Chaucer. With the exceptions of Gower, Wyatt, Raleigh, and Surrey, we meet with no great poet till the age of Spenser. The brilliant character of the EARL OF SURREY,—both as to his military career and scholastic attainments, as well as his sad end,—alike endear him to memory. His celebrated poem, written during his unjust imprisonment at Windsor, is universally admired ; and some of his sonnets are no less beautiful. Here is one :—

The sootè seson, that bud and bloom forth brings,
　With green hath clad the hill, and eke the vale;
The nightingale with feathers new she sings;
　The turtle to her make hath told her tale.
Summer is come, for every spray now springs;
　The hart hath hung his old head on the pale;

The buck in brake his winter coat he flings;
　The fishes flete, with new repaired scale;
The adder all her slough away she flings;
　The swift swallow pursueth the flies smale;
The busy bee her honey now she mings;
　Winter is worn that was the flowers' bale.
And thus I see among these pleasant things
Each care decays, and yet my sorrow springs.

Of Sir Philip Sidney, it has been said, that his literary renown
rests more upon his prose than his verse; Cowper indeed refers to
him as "warbler of poetic prose;"—yet he has his eminent place

among the poets, and here is an effusion of his muse : it is styled
Wooing Stuffe :—

> Faint amorist,—what, dost thou think
> To taste love's honey, and not drink
> One drachm of gall ;—or to devour
> A world of swete, and taste no sour ?
> Dost thou e'er think to enter
> Th' Elysian fields, that durst not venture
> In Charon's barge ?   A lover's mind
> Must use to sail with every wind.
> He that loves, and fears to try,
> Learns his mistress to deny.
> Doth she chide thee ?   'Tis to show it,
> That thy coldness makes her doe it :
> Is she silent—is she mute ?
> Silence fully grants thy suit :
> Doth she pout, and leave the room ?
> Then she goes to bid thee come :
> Is she sicke ?   Why, then, be sure
> She invites thee to the cure :
> Doth she cross thy sute with no ?
> Tush—she loves to hear thee woo :
> Doth she call the faith of man
> Into question ?   Nay, forsooth, she loves thee than :
> He that after ten denials,
> Dares attempt no further tryals,
> Hath no warrant to acquire
> The dainties of his chast desire.

Sidney's *Defence of Poesie* has long been a favorite with scholars.
Professor Marsh characterizes it as "the best secular specimen
of prose yet written in England :" and adds, that "it is destined
to maintain its high place in æsthetical literature."   The *Arcadia*

is the other prose production by which he is most known, although it is now but seldom read. Recently was exhibited before the Archæological Society at Salisbury, a copy of this production, between the leaves of which was found wrapped up a lock of Queen Elizabeth's hair, and some complimentary lines addressed by Sidney, when very young, to the maiden queen. The hair was soft and bright, of a light-brown color, inclining to red, and on the paper enclosing it was written :—" This lock of Queen Elizabeth's own hair was presented to Sir Philip Sidney by her majesty's owne faire hands, on which he made these verses, and gave them to the queen on his bended knee, A. D. 1573." And pinned to this was another paper on which was written, in a different hand—said to be Sidney's own—these lines :—

> Her inward worth all outward show transcends,
> Envy her merits with regret commends;
> Like sparkling gems her virtues draw the sight,
> And in her conduct she is alwaies bright.
> When she imparts her thoughts, her words have force,
> And sense and wisdom flow in sweet discourse.

The gentle Sidney was one of the especial favorites of the queen, whom she styled " her Jewel of the times," for the noble virtues he illustrated by his heroic life. Every one remembers his brave words, when, fallen on the battle-field, and suffering from thirst caused by loss of blood, as he ordered the cup presented to him to be given to the wounded soldier, saying, " Thy necessity is yet greater than mine." All England mourned his loss, for every one revered and loved him. Hear Shakspeare's tribute to his memory :—

> His honour stuck upon him as the sun
> In the gray vault of heaven,—and by his light
> Did all the chivalry of England move
> To do brave acts !

A scarcely less interesting character is that of the gallant SIR WALTER RALEIGH, who, after having brought a new world to light, wrote the history of the old in a prison. In his wonderful versatility of genius, and in all departments of his remarkable life, it may truly be said, he was equally illustrious. " He was honored by England's greatest queen, and was sacrificed to the caprice of the meanest of her kings." Probably the last words ever traced by his pen were the following, written in his Bible on the evening preceding his execution :—

E'en such is time, that takes on trust
   Our youth, our joys, our all we have,
And pays us but with earth and dust ;
   Who in the dark and silent grave—
When we have wandered all our ways—
Shuts up the story of our days :
But from this earth, this grave, this dust,
My God shall raise me up, I trust !

That "bold and spirited poem," as Campbell styles the " *Soul's Errand*," is now generally admitted to be from the pen of Raleigh, since it has been traced in manuscript to the year 1593 ; and two answers to it, written in his lifetime, ascribe its authorship to Sir Walter. It was originally designated thus :—" *Sir Walter Raleigh, his Lie.*" Campbell tells us that its perusal always deeply affected him ; and he adds,—" It places the last and inexpressibly awful hour of existence before my view, and sounds like a sentence of vanity on the things of this world, pronounced by a dying man, whose eye glares on eternity, and whose voice is raised by strength from another world."

Listen to a few of the strong stanzas :—

Goe, soule, the bodies guest, upon a thanklesse arrant ;
Feare not to touch the best ;—the truth shall be thy warrant :

Goe, since I needs must dye,
And give the world the lye.

Say to the Court, it glowes, and shines like rotten wood ;
Say to the Church, it shewes what's good, and doth no good ;
    If Church and Court reply,
    Then give them both the lye.

      *   *   *   *

Tell Zeale it wants devotion ; tell Love it is but lust ;
Tell Time it is but motion ; tell Flesh it is but dust ;
    And wish them not reply,
    For thou must give the lye.

Tell Age it daily wasteth ; tell Honour how it alters ;
Tell Beauty how she blasteth ; tell Fauour how it falters :
    And as they shall reply,
    Give every one the lye.

      *   *

Tell Fortune of her blindnesse ; tell Nature of decay ;
Tell Friendship of unkindnesse ; tell Justice of delay ;
    And if they will reply,
    Then give them all the lie.

      *   *   *   *

So when thou hast, as I commanded thee, done blabbing ;
Although to give the lie deserves no less than stabbing ;
    Yet stabb at thee who will,
    No stabb the soul can kill.

The author of one of the most romantic poems in the English
language, EDMUND SPENSER, was born near the Tower of London,
in 1553. To affirm that his *Faerie Queene* is replete with brilliant

and luxurious imagery, enriched with wondrous sweetness of versification, is but to echo the universal verdict of critics. Campbell styles Spenser the "Rubens of English poetry," while Charles Lamb refers to him as "the Poets' poet;" and such, indeed, he is: for not only was he the special favourite of Milton, Dryden, Pope, and Gray, but there has scarcely been any eminent poet since his day who has not delighted to peruse, if not to pilfer from, his prolific productions. Leigh Hunt considers him, in the imaginative faculty, superior even to Milton; his grand characteristic is poetic luxury. Another of our noted bards speaks of him as "steeped in romance;" and as "the prince of magicians." Glance at his group of the Seasons; how daintily his allegorical impersonations are decked with flowers, and redolent with perfume :—

So forth issew'd the seasons of the yeare :
First, lusty Spring all dight in leaves of flowres
That freshly budded and new bloosmes did beare,
In which a thousand birds had built their bowres
That sweetly sung to call forth paramours ;
And in his hand a iavelin he did beare,
And on his head (as fit for warlike stoures)
A guilt engraven morion he did weare ;
That as some did him love, so others did him feare.

Then came the iolly Sommer, being dight
  In a thin silken cassock colored greene,
That was unlyned all, to be more light :
  And on his head a girlond well beseene
  He wore, from which as he had chauffed been

The sweat did drop ; and in his hand he bore
  A bowe and shaftes, as he in forrest greene
Had hunted late the libbard or the bore,
And now would bathe his limbes with labor heated sore.

Then came the Autumne all in yellow clad,
  As though he ioyed in his plentious store,

14

Laden with fruits that made him laugh, full glad
    That he had banisht hunger, which to-fore
    Had by the belly oft him pinchèd sore :
Upon his head a wreath, that was enrold
    With eares of corne of every sort, he bore ;
    And in his hand a sickle he did holde,
To reape the ripened fruits the which the earth had yold.

Lastly came Winter cloathed all in frize,
    Chattering his teeth for cold that did him chill ;
Whilst on his hoary beard his breath did freese,
    And the dull drops, that from his purpled bill
    As from a limbeck did adown distil :
In his right hand a tipped staffe he held,
    With which his feeble steps he stayed still ;
For he was faint with cold, and weak with eld,
That scarce his loosèd limbes he able was to weld.

In these glowing lines, Spenser pays beautiful tribute to the floral
month of May :—

Then came faire May, the fairest maid on ground,
    Deck'd all with dainties of her season's pride,
    And throwing flowres out of her lap around ;

Upon two brethren's shoulders she did ride,
The twins of Leda ; which, on either side,
Supported her like to their sovereign queene.
Lord ! how all creatures laugh'd when her they spied,
And leap'd and danced as they had ravisht been ;
And Cupid's self about her flutter'd all in greene.

Here is another choice stanza from the *Faerie Queene*, descriptive of Una (the impersonation of Faith)—"radiant with beauty beaming through her tears :"—

One day, nigh wearie of the yrkesome waye,
From her unhastie beaste she did alight :
And on the grasse her daintie limbes did laye
In secrete shadow, far from all mens sight :
From her fayre head her fillet she undight
And layd her stole aside : her angels-face,
As the great eye of heaven, shyned bright,
And made a sunshine in the shady place :
Did ever mortall eye behold such heavenly grace ?

The original plan of this work contemplated twelve books, " fashioning twelve moral virtues ;" of these, however, we have only six ; the others, if ever written, were probably destroyed with the rest of his property, and, it is said, his child, in the burning of his castle in Ireland during the rebellion.   There is a story on record, but generally discredited, to the effect that when Spenser took his manuscript of the *Faerie Queene* to the Earl of Southampton,— the great patron of the poets of his day,—that after reading a few pages, his lordship ordered his servant to carry to the author twenty pounds.   Reading further, he cried out in a rapture, " Give him twenty more :" proceeding still with the perusal, he soon again stopped, and added another twenty pounds : but at length, checking his enthusiasm, he told his servant to " put him out of his house or he should be ruined." Sad to state, the close of our gentle poet's career was full of sorrow. He died at an inn in London, it is said, in poverty, and of a broken heart for his loss. Ben Jonson affirms that he died " for lack of bread," and that when Lord Essex sent him (too late) twenty guineas, Spenser refused the gift, saying, " He was sorry he had no time to spend them." He was the friend of Sidney, at whose estate, Penshurst, these gifted sons of genius consecrated many happy hours to friendship and the muse. In 1580 the poets separated, one to the service of the camp, the other to his estate in Ireland, where he became acquainted with another master-spirit, Sir Walter Raleigh, by whom he was introduced to Queen Elizabeth. " When we conceive," says Campbell, " Spenser reciting his compositions to Raleigh, in a scene so beautifully appropriate, the mind casts a pleasing retrospect over that influence which the enterprise of the discoverer of Virginia, and the genius of the author of the 'Faerie Queene,' have respectively produced on the fortune and language of England. The fancy might even be pardoned for a momentary superstition, that the genius of their country hovered unseen over their meeting, casting her first look of regard on the poet that was destined to inspire her future Milton, and the other on the maritime hero who paved the way for colonizing distant regions of the earth, where the language of England was to be spoken, and the poetry of Spenser to be admired."

SHAKSPEARE, whom Bunsen styles "the great prophet of human destinies on the awakening of a new world," was, in his fifteenth year, withdrawn from the " free school," where, in the words of Ben Jonson, "he had acquired small Latin and less Greek," for the purpose of aiding his father's business, which, according to Aubrey, was then that of a butcher; and that "when he killed a calf, he would do it in a high style, and make a speeche." A pursuit so uncongenial naturally tended to pervert his taste, and we soon find him among the roystering fraternities, known as "the topers and sippers" of Stratford, "so renowned for the excellence of its beer and the unquenchable thirst of its inhabitants." The lady of his love, as all the world knows, was *Anne Hathaway*, the dark-eyed maiden of the adjacent hamlet of Shottery; at whose picturesque cottage, worthy Master William was, doubtless, not an unfrequent visitor.

The traditionary charge of deer-stealing preferred against our embryo bard, and the indignities he suffered in consequence thereof, are supposed to have caused him to leave his native town, and seek his fortune in the British metropolis, where, after being seventeen years a player, he at length became proprietor of the " Globe" and other theatres, from which he derived an ample income. In 1612 he returned to Stratford, after having written most of his dramas. It was not till seven years after his death that the first collective edition of his plays appeared; and it is no less remarkable that it should have omitted *Pericles*, and included seven dramas since rejected as apocryphal. We all regret our ignorance of the " sayings and doings," and personal history of the great poet, who himself seemed to be so well acquainted with our common humanity. Even the walls of that rendezvous of rollicking wits,

WILLIAM SHAKSPEARE.

the " Boar's-Head Inn," Eastcheap, or the " Mermaid," Blackfriars, no longer echo with the jubilant mirth and pleasantries once fabled of Jack Falstaff and his merry men ; or with the " wise saws" of the illustrious author of those creations. Let us, then, leave the fictitious and turn to the real—let us accompany the genial author of *The Sketch-Book*, and seek the grave of Shakspeare :—" The place is solemn and sepulchral : tall elms wave before the pointed windows, and the Avon, which runs at a short distance from the walls, keeps up a low, perpetual murmur. A flat stone marks the spot where the bard is buried, upon which are inscribed the following lines :—

GOOD FREND, FOR IESVS SAKE FORBEARE,

TO DIGG THE DVST ENCLOASED HEARE;

BLESE BE Y MAN Y SPARES THES STONES,

AND CVRST BE HE Y MOVES MY BONES.

Just over the grave, in a niche of the wall, is a bust of Shakspeare, put up shortly after his death, and considered as a resemblance. The aspect is pleasant and serene, with a finely arched forehead." The bust is said to be life-size, and was originally painted over, in imitation of nature : the eyes were light hazel ; the hair and beard, auburn ; the doublet or coat, scarlet ; the loose gown or tabard, black. Malone, however, caused the bust to be painted over white, in 1793. " The inscription on the tombstone has not been without its effect : it has prevented the removal of his remains from the bosom of his native place to Westminster Abbey, which was at one time contemplated. A few years since, also, as some laborers were digging to make an adjoining vault, the earth caved in, so as to leave a vacant space almost like an arch, through which one might have reached into his grave. No one, however, presumed to meddle with his remains, so awfully guarded by a malediction ; and lest any of the idle or curious, or any collector of relics, should be tempted to commit depredations, the old sexton kept watch over the place for two days, until the vault was finished and the aperture closed again. He told me that he had made bold to look in at the hole, but could see neither coffin nor bones—nothing but dust. It was something, I thought, to have seen the dust of Shakspeare !"

But, leaving to its silent repose all that is mortal of the great poet, let us seek communion with the spirit that lives immortal in his pages—pages all aglow with clustered brilliants and gems of thought. Dr. Johnson, referring to the difficulty of exhibiting the genius of Shakspeare by quotation, says : "He that attempts it will succeed like the pedant in Hierocles, who, when he offered his house to sale, carried a brick in his pocket as a specimen." Nevertheless, as we are not restricted to a single specimen, we will make the most of our privilege. Had the great bard given us but these four dramas— *Hamlet*, *Macbeth*, *Lear*, and *Othello*, he would have yet been decked with the laurel-crown as Prince of Poets. What an affluence of imagery and splendor of diction signalize the first act of *Hamlet !* Familiar though it may be to us, yet it never can become trite,— that matchless soliloquy of the royal Dane :—

> To be, or not to be, that is the question :
> Whether 'tis nobler in the mind, to suffer
> The slings and arrows of outrageous fortune,
> Or to take arms against a sea of troubles,
> And, by opposing, end them ? To die,—to sleep,—
> No more ; and by a sleep to say we end
> The heart-ache, and the thousand natural shocks
> That flesh is heir to,—'tis a consummation
> Devoutly to be wish'd. To die ;—to sleep ;—
> To sleep ! perchance to dream ;—ay, there's the rub ;
> For in that sleep of death what dreams may come,
> When we have shuffled off this mortal coil,
> Must give us pause :—there's the respect
> That makes calamity of so long life :

For who would bear the whips and scorns of time,
The oppressor's wrong, the proud man's contumely,
The pangs of dispriz'd love, the law's delay,
The insolence of office, and the spurns
That patient merit of the unworthy takes,
When he himself might his quietus make
With a bare bodkin? who would these[1] fardels bear,
To grunt and sweat under a weary life;
But that the dread of something after death,
The undiscovered country, from whose bourn
No traveller returns, puzzles the will;
And makes us rather bear those ills we have,
Than fly to others that we know not of?
Thus conscience does make cowards of us all;
And thus the native hue of resolution
Is sicklied o'er with the pale cast of thought;
And enterprizes of great pith and moment,
With this regard, their currents turn away,[2]
And lose the name of action.

From this noble reach of philosophy, turn we to the fine impassioned burst of Romeo in the garden :—

But, soft! what light through yonder window breaks!
It is the east, and Juliet is the sun!
Arise, fair sun, and kill the envious moon,
Who is already sick and pale with grief,
That thou, her maid, art far more fair than she;
Be not her maid, since she is envious;
Her vestal livery is but sick and green,
And none but fools do wear it; cast it off.—
It is my lady; O! it is my love.
  *   *   *   *   *

---

[1] *These*, in first folio, but not in quartos.   [2] *Away*, in folio; in quartos, *awry*.

The brightness of her cheek would shame those stars,
As daylight doth a lamp: her eye in heaven
Would through the airy region stream so bright,
That birds would sing, and think it were not night.

What other poet has so felicitously portrayed all that is picturesque and lovely in a summer's dawn;—pouring on our souls all
the freshness and cheerfulness of the returning sunlight?

Look, love! what envious streaks
Do lace the severing clouds in yonder east:
Night's candles are burnt out,—and jocund day
Stands tiptoe on the misty mountains' tops!

Among the masterly passages of the great dramatist may be classed
the soliloquy of Juliet, on drinking the opiate :—

Farewell! God knows when we shall meet again.
I have a faint cold fear thrills through my veins,
That almost freezes up the heat of life:
I'll call them back again to comfort me.—
Nurse!—What should she do here?
My dismal scene I needs must act alone.—
Come, phial.—
What if this mixture do not work at all?
Shall I be married, then, to-morrow morning?
No, no;—this shall forbid it: lie thou there.—
                    [*Laying down the dagger.*
What if it be a poison, which the friar
Subtly hath ministered to have me dead;
Lest in this marriage he should be dishonoured,
Because he married me before to Romeo?
I fear, it is: and yet, methinks, it should not,
For he hath still been tried a holy man:

I will not entertain so bad a thought.—
How if, when I am laid into the tomb,
I wake before the time that Romeo

Come to redeem me? there's a fearful point!
Shall I not, then, be stifled in the vault,

To whose foul mouth no healthsome air breathes in,
And there die strangled ere my Romeo comes?
Or, if I live, is it not very like,
The horrible conceit of death and night,
Together with the terror of the place,—
As in a vault, an ancient receptacle,
Where, for these many hundred years, the bones
Of all my buried ancestors are pack'd;
Where bloody Tybalt, yet but green in earth,
Lies festering in his shroud; where, as they say,
At some hours in the night spirits resort :—
Alack, alack! is it not like, that I,
So early waking,—what with loathsome smells;
And shrieks like mandrakes torn out of the earth,
That living mortals, hearing them, run mad;—
O! if I wake, shall I not be distraught,
Environed with all these hideous fears,
And madly play with my forefathers' joints,
And pluck the mangled Tybalt from his shroud?
And, in this rage, with some great kinsman's bone,
As with a club, dash out my desperate brains?
O, look! methinks I see my cousin's ghost
Seeking out Romeo, that did spit his body
Upon a rapier's point—Stay, Tybalt, stay!
Romeo, I come! this do I drink to thee.

> [*She throws herself on the bed.*

In *Othello* we have many gems of thought : here is one :—

Good name in man and woman, dear my lord,
Is the immediate jewel of their souls :
Who steals my purse steals trash; 'tis something, nothing;
'Twas mine, 'tis his, and has been slave to thousands :
But he that filches from me my good name,

Robs me of that which not enriches him,
And makes me poor indeed.

We all remember these admirable lines :—

The quality of mercy is not strained ; ˎ
It droppeth, as the gentle rain from heaven
Upon the place beneath : it is twice bless'd ;
It blesseth him that gives, and him that takes ;
'Tis mightiest in the mightiest ; it becomes
The throned monarch better than his crown.

What a sublime passage is that on the end of all earthly glo-ries :—

The cloud-capp'd towers, the gorgeous palaces,
The solemn temples, the great globe itself,
Yea, all which it inherit, shall dissolve ;
And, like this insubstantial pageant faded,
Leave not a rack behind !

What can be finer in structure of words than the speech of Mark Antony over the body of Cæsar ? Or, take another variety—Othello's relation of his courtship, to the Senate ; or, still another familiar, yet exquisite passage, from *Romeo and Juliet*, on Dreams, commencing :—

O then, I see Queen Mab hath been with you.

For wonderful condensation and vigor, it has been thought that the passage in *As You Like It*, on the world being compared to a stage, is one of the greatest gems of Shakspeare : but we have the authority of Bunsen for assigning the highest merit to the description of a moonlight night with music, in *The Merchant of Venice :*—

25

How sweet the moonlight sleeps upon this bank !
Here will we sit, and let the sounds of music
Creep into our ears : soft stillness, and the night,
Become the touches of sweet harmony.
Sit, Jessica : look how the floor of heaven
Is thick inlaid with patines of bright gold ;
There's not the smallest orb which thou behold'st,
But in his motion like an angel sings,
Still quiring to the young-eyed cherubins :
Such harmony is in immortal souls ;
But, whilst this muddy vesture of decay
Doth grossly close it in, we cannot hear it.

Now for a cluster of little brilliants, rich and rare :—

From *Two Gentlemen of Verona :*—

Who is Silvia ? what is she,
   That all our swains commend her ?
Holy, fair, and wise is she :
   The heavens such grace did lend her,
That she might admired be.

Is she kind, as she is fair ?
   For beauty lives with kindness :
Love doth to her eyes repair,
   To help him of his blindness ;
And being help'd, inhabits there.

Then to Silvia let us sing,
   That Silvia is excelling :
She excels each mortal thing
   Upon the dull earth dwelling :
To her let us garlands bring.

From *Measure for Measure* :—

> Take, oh take those lips away,
>   That so sweetly are forsworn ;
> And those eyes, the break of day,
>   Lights that do mislead the morn :
> But my kisses bring again,
>   Bring again,
> Seals of love, but seal'd in vain,
>   Seal'd in vain !

From *The Merchant of Venice* :—

> Tell me, where is Fancy[1] bred,
> Or in the heart, or in the head ?
> How begot, how nourished ?
>   Reply, reply.
>
> It is engender'd in the eyes,
> With gazing fed ; and Fancy dies
> In the cradle where it lies :
>   Let us all ring Fancy's knell :
> I'll begin it,—Ding, dong, bell.
>   Ding, dong, bell.

From *As You Like It* :—

> Blow, blow, thou winter wind,
> Thou art not so unkind
>   As man's ingratitude :
> Thy tooth is not so keen,
> Because thou art not seen,
>   Although thy breath be rude.
> Heigh, ho ! sing heigh, ho ! unto the green holly ;
> Most friendship is feigning, most loving mere folly.

*   *   *   *

---

[1] Frequently used by this poet in the sense of Love.

27

From *The Tempest* :—

> Come unto these yellow sands,
> And then take hands :

Court'sied when you have, and kissed,
(The wild waves whist !)

28

Foot it featly here and there ;
And, sweet sprites, the burden bear.
The watch-dogs bark—bowgh, bowgh.
Hark ! hark ! I hear
The strain of strutting chanticlere
Cry cock-a-doodle do.

Where the bee sucks, there suck I ;
In a cowslip's bell I lie ;
There I couch, when owls do cry.
On the bat's back do I fly,
After summer, merrily :
Merrily, merrily, shall I live now,
Under the blossom that hangs on the bough.

From *Cymbeline* :—

Hark ! hark ! the lark at heaven's gate sings,
    And Phœbus 'gins arise,
His steeds to water at those springs
    On chaliced flowers that lies ;
And winking mary-buds begin
    To ope their golden eyes :
With every thing that pretty bin ;
    My lady sweet, arise ;
        Arise, arise !

From *Midsummer Night's Dream*.   The fine song of Oberon :—

I know a bank whereon the wild thyme blows,
Where ox-lips and the nodding violet grows ;
Quite over-canopied with lush woodbine,
With sweet musk-roses and with eglantine :
There sleeps Titania, some time of the night,
Lulled in these flowers with dances and delight ;

And there the snake throws her enamelled skin,
Weed-wide enough to wrap a fairy in:
And with the juice of this I'll streak her eyes,
And make her full of hateful fantasies.

Here is a magnificent apostrophe to Sleep :—

———— O sleep! O gentle sleep!
Nature's soft nurse, how have I frighted thee,
That thou no more wilt weigh my eyelids down,
And steep my senses in forgetfulness?
Why rather, sleep, liest thou in smoky cribs,
Upon uneasy pallets stretching thee,
And hush'd with buzzing night-flies to thy slumber;
Than in the perfum'd chambers of the great,
Under the canopies of costly state,
And lull'd with sounds of sweetest melody?
O thou dull god! why liest thou with the vile,
In loathsome beds; and leav'st the kingly couch,
A watch-case, or a common 'larum-bell?
Wilt thou upon the high and giddy mast
Seal up the ship-boy's eyes, and rock his brains
In cradle of the rude imperious surge,
And in the visitation of the winds,
Who take the ruffian billows by the top,
Curling their monstrous heads, and hanging them
With deaf'ning clamours in the slippery clouds,
That, with the hurly, death itself awakes?
Canst thou, O partial sleep! give thy repose
To the wet sea-boy in an hour so rude;
And in the calmest and most stillest night,
With all appliances and means to boot,
Deny it to a king? Then, happy low, lie down!
Uneasy lies the head that wears a crown.

In *Timon of Athens*, is this humorous passage on stealing :—

> I'll example you with thievery;
> The sun's a thief, and with his great attraction
> Robs the vast sea ; the moon's an arrant thief,
> For her pale fire she snatches from the sun ;
> The sea's a thief, whose liquid surge resolves
> The moon into salt tears ; the earth's a thief,
> That feeds and breeds by a composture stolen
> From general excrement ; each thing's a thief;
> The law, your curb and whip, in their rough power
> Have unchecked theft.

We have but space for one of Shakspeare's fine sonnets ; but we think this one of the best :—

> Let me not to the marriage of true minds
>   Admit impediments : love is not love
> Which alters when it alteration finds,
>   Or bends with the remover to remove :
> O no ! it is an ever-fixed mark
>   That looks on tempests, and is never shaken ;
> It is the star to every wandering bark
>   Whose worth's unknown, although his height be taken.
> Love's not Time's fool, though rosy lips and cheeks
>   Within his bending sickle's compass come ;
> Love alters not with his brief hours and weeks,
>   But bears it out even to the edge of doom ;—
> If this be error, and upon me proved,
> I never writ, nor no man ever loved.

In *Othello*, Desdemona says: "My mother had a maid called Barbara ; she was in love ; and he she loved proved mad, and did forsake her : she had a song of willow, an old thing 'twas, but it expressed her fortune, and she died singing it : that song to-night will not go from my mind ; I have much to do, but to go hang **my** head all at one side, and sing it like poor Barbara :—

> The poor soul sat sighing by a sycamore tree,
>   Sing all a green willow ;
> Her hand on her bosom, her head on her knee,
>   Sing willow, willow, willow :
> The fresh streams ran by her, and murmured her moans ;
>   Sing willow, willow, willow.
> Her salt tears fell from her, and softened the stones,
>   Sing willow, willow, willow—
> Sing all a green willow must be my garland."

Reluctantly as we leave the almost unexplored wealth of thought and imagery which cluster the pages of this magician of the pen, we yet must pass on to some of his contemporaries :—

> " Those shining stars that run
> Their glorious course round Shakspeare's golden sun."

Among these were BEN JONSON, BEAUMONT and FLETCHER, and others. Glancing over the life-records of these gifted, but, for the most part, erratic sons of genius, who can trace their checkered career without tender sympathy for their misfortunes, while cherishing reverence and admiration of their exalted endowments ! BEN JONSON's proud fame was allied with suffering and sorrow, for we find at his closing days the poet thanking his patron, the Earl of Newcastle, for bounties which, he says, had "fallen like the dew of heaven on his necessities."

The classic beauty of the following lyric of JONSON has ever been the admiration of all critics :—

> Drink to me only with thine eyes, and I will pledge with mine ;
> Or leave a kiss but in the cup, and I'll not look for wine.
> The thirst that from the soul doth rise doth ask a drink divine ;
> But might I of Jove's nectar sup, I would not change for thine.

I sent thee late a rosy wreath, not so much honouring thee,
As giving it a hope that there it could not wither'd be ;
But thou thereon didst only breathe, and sent'st it back to me ;
Since when it grows, and smells, I swear, not of itself, but thee.

His song, entitled *The Grace of Simplicity*, is one of the most
characteristic of its author :—

> Still to be neat, still to be drest,
> As you were going to a feast ;
> Still to be powder'd, still perfum'd ;
> Lady, it is to be presum'd,
> Though art's hid causes are not found,
> All is not sweet, all is not sound.
>
> Give me a look, give me a face,
> That makes simplicity a grace ;
> Robes loosely flowing, hair as free ;
> Such sweet neglect more taketh me,
> Than all the adulteries of art :
> They strike mine eyes, but not my heart.

Another of his exquisite songs is the well-known *Hymn to Diana*,[1]

---

[1] Diana is here addressed as the moon, rather than the goddess of hunting.

in which the spirit of the classic lyre is beautifully illustrated. It is
supposed to be derived from Philostratus :—

> Queen and huntress, chaste and fair,
> Now the sun is laid to sleep,
> Seated in thy silver chair,
> State in wonted manner keep:
>   Hesperus entreats thy light,
>   Goddess, excellently bright !
>
> Earth, let not thy envious shade
> Dare itself to interpose ;
> Cynthia's shining orb was made
> Heaven to clear, when day did close ;
>   Bless us then with wishèd sight,
>   Goddess excellently bright !
>
> Lay thy bow of pearl apart,
> And thy crystal shining quiver ;
> Give unto the flying hart
> Space to breathe, how short soever ;
>   Thou that mak'st a day of night,
>   Goddess excellently bright !

There is such a fulness of inspiration about the old poets, such
prodigality of fancy and imagery, that their chief difficulty appears
to have been to find place for their thick-coming fancies. For instance, take BEAUMONT's fine *Ode to Melancholy* :—

> Hence, all you vain delights,
> As short as are the nights
>   Wherein you spend your folly !
> There's naught in this life sweet,
> If man were wise to see't,
>   But only melancholy ;
>   Oh, sweetest melancholy !

Welcome, folded arms and fixèd eyes,
A sight that piercing mortifies,
A look that's fastened to the ground,
A tongue chained up without a sound ;
Fountain heads, and pathless groves,
Places which pale passion loves,—
Moonlight walks, when all the fowls
Are warmly housed, save bats and owls ;
A midnight bell, a passing groan,
These are the sounds we feed upon :
Then stretch our bones in a still gloomy valley,
Nothing's so dainty sweet as lovely melancholy.

Here is a delicious lyric from the same source :—

Look out, bright eyes, and bless the air !
Even in shadows you are fair.
Shut-up beauty is like fire,
That breaks out clearer still and higher.
Though your beauty be confin'd,
And soft Love a prisoner bound,
Yet the beauty of your mind
Neither check nor chain hath found ;
Look out nobly, then, and dare
E'en the fetters that you wear !

What a fine figure has BEAUMONT employed in the following
lines to illustrate the influence of woman :—

The bleakest rock upon the loneliest heath,
Feels in its barrenness some touch of Spring ;
And in the April dew, or beam of May,
Its moss and lichen freshen and revive ;
And thus the heart, most sear'd to human pleasure,
Melts at the tear,—joys in the smile of woman.

SHIRLEY, the latest of the Elizabethan dramatists, wrote the following :—

> Woodmen, shepherds, come away,
>   This is Pan's great holiday;
> Throw off cares, with your heaven-aspiring airs—
>   Help us to sing,
> While valleys with your echoes ring.
>   Nymphs that dwell within these groves,
>   Leave your arbours, bring your loves,
> Gather posies, crown your golden hair with roses :
>   As you pass,
> Foot like Fairies on the grass.

*   *   *   *

What stateliness and vigor of expression characterize his celebrated Dirge :—

> The glories of our blood and state,
>   Are shadows, not substantial things ;
> There is no armour against fate :
>   Death lays his icy hand on kings ;
> Sceptre and crown must tumble down,
>   And in the dust be equal made
>   With the poor crooked scythe and spade !
> Some men with swords may reap the field,
>   And plant fresh laurels where they kill ;
> But their strong nerves at last must yield,
>   They tame but one another still :
> Early or late, they stoop to fate,
>   And must give up their murmuring breath,
>   When they, pale captives, creep to death !
> The garlands wither on your brow,
>   Then boast no more your mighty deeds ;
> Upon death's purple altar, now,
>   See, where the victor-victim bleeds :

36

All heads must come to the cold tomb ;
   Only the actions of the just
   Smell sweet, and blossom in the dust.

Listen to the sweet music and melancholy flow of this fine old
song :—

Go sit by the summer sea, thou whom scorn wasteth,
And let thy musing be where the flood hasteth ;
Mark, how o'er ocean's breast rolls the hoar billow's crest,—
Such is his heart's unrest who of love tasteth.

Griev'st thou that hearts should change ? Lo, where life reigneth,
Or the free sight doth range, what long remaineth ?
Spring, with her flowers, doth die, fast fades the gilded sky,
And the full moon on high ceaselessly waneth !

Smile, then, ye sage and wise, and if love sever
Bards which thy soul doth prize, such does it ever.
Deep as the rolling seas, soft as the twilight breeze,
But of *more* than these—boast could it never !

       *   *   *   *

CAREW, the " sprightly, polished, and perspicuous," wrote sundry
love-ditties : one of his most popular begins—

Ask me no more where Jove bestows,
When June is past, the fading rose ;
For, in your beauties, orient deep,
Those flowers, as in their causes, sleep.

       *   *   *   *

His other noted song commences thus :—

He that loves a rosy cheek, or a coral lip admires,
Or from star-like eyes doth seek fuel to maintain his fires ;
As old Time makes these decay,
So his flames must waste away.

But a smooth and steadfast mind, gentle thoughts and calm desires ;
Hearts with equal love combined, kindle never-dying fires.
Where these are not, I despise
Lovely cheeks, or lips, or eyes.

       *   *   *   *

Here, also, we have some terse lines of his, touching things
terrene :—

Fame's but a hollow echo—gold, pure clay,—
Honour, the darling but of one short day ;
Beauty, the eye's idol—but a damask skin ;
State, but a golden prison to live in
And torture free-born minds,—embroidered trains,
Merely but pageants for proud swelling veins :

And blood allied to greatness, is alone
Inherited—not purchased, nor our own.
Fame, honour, beauty, state, train, blood, and birth,
Are but the fading blossoms of the earth.

The "gallant and accomplished" LOVELACE wrote this beautiful song to his mistress, on joining the army of the King:—

Tell me not, sweet, I am unkind, that from the nunnery
Of thy chaste breast and quiet mind to war and arms I fly.
True, a new mistress now I chase, the first foe in the field ;
And with a stronger faith embrace a sword, a horse, a shield.
Yet this inconstancy is such as you, too, shall adore ;
I could not love thee, dear, so much, loved I not honour more.

His fine lines written during his incarceration, *To Althea*, commence :—

When Love, with unconfinèd wings, hovers within my gates,
And my divine Althea brings to whisper at my grates :
When I lie tangled in her hair, and fettered to her eye,
The birds that wanton in the air know no such liberty.

His last is the finest stanza :—

Stone walls do not a prison make, nor iron bars a cage ;
Minds innocent and quiet, take that for an hermitage :
If I have freedom in my love, and in my soul am free,
Angels alone, that soar above, enjoy such liberty.

Love, the great theme of the poets, has been in these pages presented in most of its Protean aspects; but as it is classed among the noblest virtues, we can hardly have too much of it from the poets. Dr. Johnson once remarked, that "we need not ridicule a passion, which he who never felt, never was happy ; and he who laughs at, never deserves to feel—a passion which has caused the change of empires and the loss of worlds—a passion which has inspired heroism and subdued avarice."

Here is an airy, bird-like lyric, by HEYWOOD :—

Pack, clouds, away, and welcome day ;
　　With night we banish sorrow ;
Sweet air, blow soft ; mount, lark, aloft,
　　To give my love good-morrow !
Wings from the wind to please her mind,
　　Notes from the lark I'll borrow ;
Bird, prune thy wing, nightingale, sing,
　　To give my love good-morrow.
　　To give my love good-morrow,
　　Notes from them both I'll borrow.

Wake from thy nest, robin redbreast :
　　Sing, birds, in every furrow ;
And from each bill let music shrill
　　Give my fair love good-morrow.
Blackbird and thrush, in every bush—
　　Stare, linnet, and cock-sparrow—
You pretty elves, amongst yourselves,
　　Sing my fair love good-morrow.
　　To give my love good-morrow,
　　Sing, birds, in every furrow

O fly, make haste !　See, see, she falls
　　Into a pretty slumber ;
Sing round about her rosy bed,
　　That, waking, she may wonder.
Say to her, 'tis her lover true
That sendeth love to you ; to you !
And when you hear her kind reply,
　　Return with pleasant warblings.

LYLY's genius for lyric verse is seen in the following little *Song of the Fairies :*—

> By the moon we sport and play ;
> With the night begins our day :
> As we dance, the dew doth fall,
> Trip it, little urchins all.
> Lightly as the little bee,
> Two by two, and three by three,
> And about go we, and about go we.

The following exquisitely sportive lines are also by this noted dramatist :—

> Cupid and my Campaspe play'd
> At cards for kisses : Cupid paid.
> He stakes his quiver, bow, and arrows ;
> His mother's doves and team of sparrows ;
> Loses them too, then down he throws
> The coral of his lip—the rose
> Growing on's cheek, but none knows how,
> With these the crystal on his brow,
> And then the dimple of his chin ;
> All these did my Campaspe win :
> At last he set her both his eyes ;
> She won, and Cupid blind did rise.
> O Love, hath she done this to thee ?
> What shall, alas ! become of me ?

TITCHBOURNE, who was one of the victims of political despotism in 1568, wrote these quaint and touching lines the night preceding his execution :—

> My prime of youth is but a frost of cares ;
> My feast of joy is but a dish of pain ;

My crop of corn is but a field of tares,
　And all my goods are but vain hopes of gain.
The day is fled, and yet I saw no sun,
And now I live, and now my life is done!

My Spring is past, and yet it hath not sprung;
　My fruit is dead, and yet the leaves are green;
My youth is past, and yet I am but young;
　I saw the world, and yet I was not seen;
My thread is cut, and yet it is not spun,
And now I live, and now my life is done!

HERRICK'S lyrics are among the most sprightly and picturesque
that we possess; they are fragrant with the aroma of Spring flowers.
Listen to his lines addressed to " Primroses filled with morning
dew :"—

Why do ye weep, sweet babes?　Can tears
　　　Speak grief in you,
　　　Who were but born
　　Just as the modest morn
　　　Teem'd her refreshing dew?
Alas! you have not known that shower
　　　That mars a flower,
　　　Nor felt the unkind
　　Breath of a blasting wind;
　　Nor are ye worn with years,
　　　Or warp'd, as we,
　　Who think it strange to see
Such pretty flowers, like to orphans young,
Speaking by tears before ye have a tongue.

Speak, whimp'ring younglings, and make known
　　　The reason why
　　　Ye droop and weep:

42

Is it for want of sleep,
        Or childish lullaby ?
Or, that ye have not seen as yet
            The violet ?
            Or brought a kiss
        From that sweetheart to this ?
    No, no ; this sorrow, shown
            By your tears shed,
        Would have this lecture read,—
" That things of greatest, so of meanest worth,
Conceived with grief are, and with tears brought forth."

43

Here are two more of HERRICK's sweet songs :—

Fair daffodils ! we weep to see
  You haste away so soon ;
As yet the early-rising sun
  Has not attained his noon :
    Stay, stay,
Until the hastening day
    Has run
  But to the even-song ;
And having prayed together, we
  Will go with you along.

We have short time to stay as you,
  We have as short a Spring ;
As quick a growth to meet decay,
  As you, or any thing :
    We die,
As your hours do ; and dry
    Away
Like to the summer's rain,
Or as the pearls of morning dew,
  Ne'er to be found again.

———

To *Blossoms* :—

Fair pledges of a fruitful tree,
  Why do ye fall so fast ?
  Your date is not so past,
But you may stay yet here awhile
To blush and gently smile,
    And go at last.

What, were ye born to be
   An hour or half's delight,
   And so to bid good-night?
'Tis pity nature brought ye forth,
Merely to show your worth,
   And lose you quite.

But you are lovely leaves, where we
   May read how soon things have
   Their end, though ne'er so brave;
And after they have shown their pride,
Like you, awhile, they glide
   Into the grave.

Now let us rehearse that famous old song of MARLOWE, the favorite of that honest philosopher, angler, and right worthy gentleman, Izaac Walton :—

Come live with me and be my love,
And we will all the pleasures prove,
That hill and valley, dale and field,
And all the craggy mountains yield.

There will we sit upon the rocks,
And see the shepherds feed their flocks,
By shallow rivers, to whose falls
Melodious birds sing madrigals.

There I will make thee beds of roses,
And a thousand fragrant posies;
A cap of flowers, and a kirtle,
Embroider'd all with leaves of myrtle;

A gown made of the finest wool,
Which from our pretty lambs we pull;

65

Fair lined slippers for the cold,
With buckles of the purest gold ,

A belt of straw and ivy buds,
With coral clasps and amber studs :
And if these pleasures may thee move,
Come live with me, and be my love.

* * *

Here is the opening passage of a poem by DANIEL, who, for
the vigor of his verse, was styled the Atticus of his day :—

He that of such a height hath built his mind,
And rear'd the dwelling of his thoughts so strong,
As neither fear nor hope can shake the frame
Of his resolved powers ; nor all the wind
Of vanity or malice pierce to wrong
His settled peace, or to disturb the same ;
What a fair seat hath he, from whence he may
The boundless wastes and wilds of man survey !

He also wrote the following sprightly song :—

Love is a sickness full of woes,
All remedies refusing ;
A plant that most with cutting, grows ;
Most barren, with best using :
Why so ?
More we enjoy it, more it dies ;
If not enjoyed, it sighing cries—
Heigh-ho !

Love is a torment of the mind,
A tempest everlasting ;
And Jove hath made it of a kind
Not well, nor full, nor fasting :
Why so ?

More we enjoy it, more it dies ;
If not enjoyed, it sighing cries—
Heigh-ho !

Among favorite love-lyrics of the olden time, is that entitled
Rosalind's Madrigal, by LODGE.   Here it is :—

Love in my bosom, like a bee,
Doth suck his sweet ;
Now with his wings he plays with me,
Now with his feet.
Within mine eyes he makes his nest,
His bed amidst my tender breast ;
My kisses are his daily feast,
And yet he robs me of my rest :
Ah, wanton, will ye ?

And if I sleep, there percheth he
With pretty flight,
And makes his pillow of my knee,
The livelong night.
Strike I my lute, he turns the string ;
He music plays if so I sing ;
He lends me every lovely thing,
Yet cruel he my heart doth sting :
Whist, wanton, still ye,

Else I, with roses, every day
Will whip you hence,
And bind you, when you long to play,
For your offence :
I'll shut mine eyes to keep you in ;
I'll make you fast it for your sin ;
I'll count your power not worth a pin ;
Alas ! what hereby shall I win,
If he gainsay me ?

47

What if I beat the wanton boy
    With many a rod ?
He will repay me with annoy,
    Because a god.
Then sit thou safely on my knee,
And let thy bower my bosom be ;
Lurk in mine eyes, I like of thee,
O Cupid ! so thou pity me,
    Spare not, but play thee.

The following impassioned and beautiful lines are the commencement of a poem, entitled *The Exequy*, written by Dr. King :—

Accept, thou shrine of my dead saint,
Instead of dirges, this complaint ;
And for sweet flowers to crown thy hearse,
Receive a strew of weeping verse,
From thy grieved friend, whom thou might'st see
Quite melted into tears for thee !
Dear loss ! since thy untimely fate,
My task hath been to meditate
On thee, on thee ; thou art the book,
The library whereon I look,
Though almost blind ; for thee (loved clay)
I languish out, not live, the day,
Using no other exercise
But what I practise with mine eyes :
By which wet glasses I find out
How lazily Time creeps about
To one that mourns : this, only this,
My exercise and business is :
So I compute the weary hours
With sighs dissolved into showers.

His terse lines on *Life* are more familiar :—

> Like to the falling of a star,
> Or as the flights of eagles are ;
> Or like the fresh Spring's gaudy hue,
> Or silver drops of morning dew :
> Or like a wind that chafes the flood,
> Or bubbles which on water stood—
> E'en such is man, whose borrowed light
> Is straight called in and paid to-night :
> The wind blows out, the bubble dies,
> The Spring entombed in Autumn lies ;
> The dew dries up, the star is shot,
> The flight is past—and man forgot !

SIR H. WOTTON's admired lines, entitled *The Happy Life*, are well worthy of a place among the most perfect passages of our English poetry :—

> How happy is he born and taught
>   That serveth not another's will ;
> Whose armour is his honest thought,
>   And simple truth his utmost skill !
> Whose passions not his masters are,
>   Whose soul is still prepared for death—
> Untied unto the worldly care
>   Of public fame or private breath !
> *   *   *   *
> Who God doth late and early pray
>   More of His grace than gifts to lend ;
> And entertains the harmless day
>   With a religious book or friend :
> This man is freed from servile bands
>   Of hope to rise or fear to fall ;
> Lord of himself—though not of lands ;
>   And having nothing, yet hath all.

WOTTON is also justly celebrated for his brilliant stanzas addressed to the Princess Elizabeth, daughter of James I. :—

> You meaner beauties of the night,
>   That poorly satisfy our eyes
> More by your numbers than your light,—
>   You common people of the skies,
>   What are you when the moon shall rise?

> Ye violets, that first appear,
>   By your pure, purple mantles known,—
> Like the proud virgins of the year,
>   As if the Spring were all your own,—
>   What are you when the rose is blown?
>
> Ye curious chanters of the wood,
>   That warble forth dame Nature's lays,
> Thinking your passions understood
>   By your weak accents; what's your praise
>   When Philomel her voice shall raise?

So, when my mistress shall be seen,
 In sweetness of her looks and mind;
By virtue first, then choice, a queen—
 Tell me, if she was not designed
 Th' eclipse and glory of her kind?

Another of those courtly minstrels was SIR JOHN SUCKLING; and here, with some of his graceful contributions to our poetic anthology, we conclude the first of our evening studies :—

Why so pale and wan, fond lover?
 Pr'ythee, why so pale?
Will, when looking well can't move her,
 Looking ill prevail?
 Pr'ythee, why so pale?

Why so pale and mute, young sinner?
 Pr'ythee, why so mute?
Will, when speaking well can't move her,
 Saying nothing do't?
 Pr'ythee, why so mute?

Quit, quit, for shame; this will not move,
 This cannot take her;
If of herself she will not love,
 Nothing can make her;
 The devil take her!

His most celebrated piece is *The Wedding*, written in honour of the beautiful daughter of the Earl of Suffolk. Here are a few of the sparkling stanzas :—

Her finger was so small, the ring
Would not stay on which they did bring,
 It was too wide a peck:

And to say truth, for out it must,
It looked like the great collar, just,
    About our young colt's neck.

       *   *   *

Her feet beneath her petticoat,
Like little mice, stole in and out,
    As if they feared the light.
But, oh ! she dances such a way—
No sun upon an Easter day
    Is half so fine a sight.

Her cheeks so rare a white was on,
No daisy makes comparison
    (Who sees them is undone) ;
For streaks of red were mingled there,
Such as are on a Catharine pear
    (The side that's next the sun).

Her lips were red, and one was thin,
Compared to that was next her chin
    (Some bee had stung it newly) ;
But, Dick, her eyes so guard her face,
I durst no more upon them gaze
    Than on the sun in Júly.

       *   *   *

SECOND
EVENING

Drummond,

Habington, Quarles,

Waller, Ayton, Cowley, Milton.

Byrd, Chamberlayne, Herbert, Denham, Marvell, Dryden,

Addison, Pope, Parnell, Thomson,

Collins, Shenstone,

Young.

DRUMMOND OF HAWTHORN-
DEN,—the singular sweetness
and harmony of whose poetry re-
minds us of Spenser,—wrote some
touching sonnets in memory of his
lost love, whose sudden death occurred just prior to their appointed
nuptials. The poet was of noble lineage, and lived amidst the most
romantic scenery, at his fine castle on the banks of the Esk. The
following are his beautiful sonnets on Spring :—

Sweet Spring ! thou turn'st with all thy goodly train,
    Thy head with flames, thy mantle bright with flowers;
The zephyrs curl the green locks of the plain,
    The clouds, for joy, in pearls weep down their showers
    Thou turn'st, sweet youth, but, ah ! my pleasant hours
And happy days with thee come not again ;
The sad memorials only of my pain
    Do with thee turn, which turn my sweets in sours !
Thou art the same which still thou wast before,
    Delicious, wanton, amiable, fair ;
    But she, whose breath embalmed thy wholesome air,
Is gone ; nor gold, nor gems her can restore.
    Neglected virtue, seasons go and come,
    While thine forgot, lie closèd in a tomb !

    What doth it serve to see sun's burning face ?
And skies enamell'd with both Indies' gold ?
Or moon at night in jetty chariot roll'd,
    And all the glory of that starry place ?
What doth it serve earth's beauty to behold,
    The mountain's pride, the meadow's flowery grace ;
The stately comeliness of forests old,
    The sport of floods which would themselves embrace ?
What doth it serve to hear the sylvan's songs,
    The wanton merle, the nightingale's sad strains,
Which in dark shades seem to deplore my wrongs ?
    For what doth serve all that this world contains,
Sith she, for whom these once to me were dear,
No part of them can have now with me here ?

Hazlitt thought Drummond's sonnets approached as near almost
as any others to the perfection of this kind of writing.   Here is his
Address to the Nightingale :—

Sweet bird! that sing'st away the early hours,
Of winter's past or coming, void of care,
Well pleasèd with delights which present are,
    Fair seasons, budding sprays, sweet-smelling flowers:
    To rocks, to springs, to rills, from leafy bowers
Thou thy Creator's goodness dost declare,
And what dear gifts on thee He did not spare,
    A stain to human sense in sin that lowers.
What soul can be so sick, which by thy songs
    (Attired in sweetness) sweetly is not driven
Quite to forget earth's turmoils, spites, and wrongs,
    And lift a reverent eye and thought to heaven?
Sweet, artless songster, thou my mind dost raise
To airs of spheres, yes, and to angel's lays.

HABINGTON'S poem on *The Firmament* opens with these grand
lines :—

    When I survey the bright celestial sphere,
      So rich with jewels hung, that night
    Doth like an Ethiop bride appear;
      My soul her wings doth spread,
    And heavenward flies,
      The Almighty's mysteries to read
    In the large volumes of the skies.

The grave and eccentric QUARLES has written some remarkable
poems, equally quaint in conceit and curious in structure: for
example :—

    Behold
    How short a span
    Was long enough of old
    To measure out the life of man:
In those well-tempered days, his time was then
Surveyed, cast-up, and found—but threescore years and ten!

How soon
Our new-born light
Attains to full-aged noon !
And this—how soon to gray-haired night !
We spring, we bud, we blossom, and we blast :—
Ere we can count our days—our days they flee so fast !

And what's a life ? A weary pilgrimage,
Whose glory in the day doth fill the stage—
With childhood, manhood, and decrepid age.
And what's a life ? The flourishing array
Of the proud summer-meadow, which to-day—
Wears her green plush—and is to-morrow—hay !

False world, thou ly'st : thou canst not lend
    The least delight :
Thy favours cannot gain a friend,
    They are so slight !
Thy morning's pleasures make an end
    To please at night :
Poor are the wants that thou supply'st,
And yet thou vaunt'st, and yet thou vy'st
With heaven ! Fond earth, thou boast'st—false world, thou ly'st !

Here are some of his lines, gilded with a little more sunshine :—

As when a lady, walking Flora's bower,
Picks here a pink, and there a gilly-flower,
Now plucks a violet from her purple bed,
And then a primrose,—the year's maidenhead ;
There nips the brier, here the lover's pansy,
Shifting her dainty pleasures with her fancy ;

This on her arm, and that she lists to wear
Upon the borders of her curious hair ;
At length, a rose-bud (passing all the rest)
She plucks, and bosoms in her lily breast.

   *   *   *

WALLER, whose life has been thought to possess more romance than his poetry, is, however, the author of these striking stanzas, among the last he wrote :—

The seas are quiet when the winds give o'er ;
So calm are we when passions are no more.
For then we know how vain it was to boast
Of fleeting things so certain to be lost.

Clouds of affection from our younger eyes
Conceal that emptiness which age descries :

The soul's dark cottage, battered and decayed,
Lets in new light through chinks that time has made.

Stronger by weakness, wiser, men become,
As they draw near to their eternal home :
Leaving the old, both worlds at once they view,
That stand upon the threshold of the new.

For harmony and elegance of fancy, these verses, by AYTON,
have rarely been surpassed :—

I loved thee once, I'll love no more,
  Thine be the grief, as is the blame ;
Thou art not what thou wast before,
  What reason I should be the same ?
He that can love, unloved again,
Hath better store of love than brain.
  God send me love my debts to pay,
  While unthrifts fool their love away.

Nothing could have my love o'erthrown
  If thou hadst still continued mine ;
Yea, if thou hadst remained thy own,
  I might, perchance, have yet been thine ;
But thou thy freedom didst recall,
That if thou might'st elsewhere inthral,
  And then, how could I but disdain
  A captive's captive to remain ?

The " melancholy COWLEY," as that poet styles himself, was yet
the writer of this paraphrastic version of one of Anacreon's sparkling lyrics :—

The thirsty earth soaks up the rain,
And drinks, and gapes for drink again :

The plants suck in the earth, and are,
With constant drinking, fresh and fair.
The sea itself, which one would think
Should have but little need of drink,
Drinks ten thousand rivers up,
So filled that they o'erflow the cup.
The busy sun—and one would guess,
By his drunken, fiery face, no less—
Drinks up the sea ; and when he's done,
The moon and stars drink up the sun :
They drink and dance by their own light,—
They drink and revel all the night !
Nothing in nature's sober found,
But an eternal " health" goes round :
Should every creature drink but I—
Why—men of morals, tell me why ?

Cowley's deep love of rural retirement is exhibited in the sub-joined lines :—

Hail, old patrician trees, so great and good !
Hail, ye plebeian underwood !
   Where the poetic birds rejoice,
And for their quiet nests and plenteous food
   Pay with their grateful voice.
    *   *   *
Here nature does a house for me erect—
Nature ! the wisest architect,
   Who those fond artists does despise,
That can the fair and living trees neglect,
   Yet the dead timber prize

If, in the verse of Chaucer, the muse lisped her early numbers with the artless simplicity and grace of infancy, she may be said to have attained to her full-voiced maturity and glory in the august and matchless creations of Shakspeare, and the "magnificent sphere-harmonies" of MILTON. The latter, indeed, as it has been beautifully expressed, like the nightingale, sang his sublime song in the night : for not only was he deprived of the glad light of day, but the dark clouds of sorrow cast their added shadows on his pathway. Yet this noble man stood erect in his integrity and exemplary in his patience, amidst all adverse circumstances. Beautifully has he been likened to the bird of Paradise, which, flying against the wind, best displays the splendour of its golden plumage; so the bard of Paradise, in his sublime excursions amid the beings of light, bursts upon us with a more supernal grandeur, as he emerges from the darkness with which he was environed. Gray thus refers to him, as one—

> Who rode sublime
> Upon the seraph-wings of ecstasy;
> The Secret of the abyss to spy
> Who passed the flaming bounds of space and time,—
> The living throne, the sapphire's blaze,
> Where angels tremble while they gaze!
> He saw : but, blasted with excess of light,
> Closèd his eyes in endless night.

Milton did not commence the composition of his grand epic until he was forty-seven years of age; although he had matured its plan in his mind several years before. When he visited the Continent, he met Galileo, then a prisoner of the Inquisition : he also became acquainted with Hugo Grotius. It is a curious fact, that Grotius had then written a tragedy of which the leading subject was the *Fall of Man;* and Milton's epic was formed out of the first draught of a tragedy to which he had given the title of *Adam Unparadised.* No evidence has been adduced, however, to prove that Milton borrowed his design from Grotius; or from Du Bartas' *Divine Weekes,* as has been by some persons supposed. One of his earliest compositions, the *Hymn to the Nativity,* was written when he was but

JOHN MILTON.

twenty-one years old; yet it has been pronounced by critics as unsurpassed by any production of its class since the age of Pindar. Here is a splendid stanza :—

> No war, or battle's sound, was heard the world around;
>   The idle spear and shield were high uphung;
> The hookèd chariot stood unstain'd with hostile blood;
>   The trumpet spake not to the armèd throng;
>   And kings sat still with awful eye,
> As if they surely knew their sovereign Lord was by.

How fine is that passage referring to the silencing of the heathen oracles :—

> The oracles are dumb; no voice or hideous hum
> Runs through the archèd roof in words deceiving;
>   Apollo from his shrine can no more divine,
> With hollow shriek the steep of Delphos leaving;
>   No nightly trance, or breathèd spell,
> Inspires the pale-eyed priest from the prophetic cell.

The village of Horton is associated with the earlier portion of the poet's life; it was there that he wrote his *Comus*, *Lycidas*, and *Il Penseroso*. At Chalfont St. Giles he wrote his great epic. Fuseli thought the second book of *Paradise Lost* the grandest effort of the human mind we possess. How splendid is his *Invocation to Light*— how touchingly it closes !—

> Thus with the year
> Seasons return; but not to me returns
> Day, or the sweet approach of even or morn,
> Or sight of vernal bloom, or summer's rose,
> Or flocks, or herds, or human face divine:
> But cloud instead, and ever-during dark

63

Surrounds me, from the cheerful ways of men
Cut off, and for the book of knowledge fair,
Presented with a universal blank
Of nature's works, to me expunged and razed,
And wisdom at one entrance quite shut out.

*   *   *

According to Sir Egerton Brydges, Milton's sonnet on his loss of
sight, is unequalled by any composition of its class in the language :

When I consider how my light is spent
   Ere half my days, in this dark world and wide,
   And that one talent, which is death to hide,
Lodged with me useless, though my soul more bent
To serve therewith my Maker, and present
   My true account, lest He returning, chide :
   " Doth God exact day-labour, light denied ?"
I fondly ask : but Patience, to prevent
   That murmur, soon replies—" God doth not need
Either man's work, or His own gifts ; who best
Bear His mild yoke, they serve Him best ; His state
   Is kingly : thousands at His bidding speed,
And post o'er land and ocean without rest :
They also serve who only stand and wait !"

Il Penseroso abounds with striking passages ; such as the following,
to *Contemplation* :—

Come, pensive nun, devout and pure,
Sober, steadfast, and demure,
All in a robe of darkest grain,
Flowing with majestic train,
And sable state of cypress lawn,
On thy decent shoulders drawn !

6;

Come! but keep thy wonted state,
With even step and musing gait,
And looks commercing with the skies,
Thy rapt soul sitting in thine eyes:
There, held in holy passion still,
Forget thyself to warble, till

With a sad, leaden, downward cast,
Thou fix them on the earth as fast:
And join with thee calm peace and quiet—
Spare fast, that oft with gods doth diet,
And hears the muses in a ring
Aye round about Jove's altar sing:
And add to these retired leisure,
That in trim gardens takes his pleasure;

But first and chiefest, with thee bring
Him that yon soars on golden wing,
Guiding the fairy-wheelèd throne,
The cherub Contemplation.

*　　*　　*

What pen but Milton's could have produced—from so slight an incident as that which occurred at Ludlow Castle when the poet was its guest—a dramatic poem (*Comus*) so replete with beautiful imagery, and so lustrous with the graces of style? Here are a few lines :—

Can any mortal mixture of earth's mould
Breathe such divine, enchanting ravishment?
Sure something holy lodges in that breast,
And with these raptures moves the vocal air,
To testify his hidden residence :
How sweetly did they float upon the wings
Of silence, through the empty vaulted night,
At every fall smoothing the raven down
Of darkness, till it smiled !

*　　*　　*

So dear to heaven is saintly chastity,
That when a soul is found sincerely so,
A thousand liveried angels lacquey her,
Driving far off each thing of sin and guilt,
And, in clear dream and solemn vision,
Tell her of things that no gross ear can hear,
Till oft converse with heavenly habitants
Begin to cast a beam on th' outward shape,
The unpolluted temple of the mind,
And turns it by degrees to the soul's essence,
Till all be made immortal.

*　　*　　*

The Epilogue closes with these beautiful words :—

> Mortals, that would follow me,
> Love Virtue,—she alone is free :
> She can teach ye how to climb
> Higher than the sphery chime ;
> Or if Virtue feeble were,
> Heaven itself would stoop to her.

Here is an example of his famous *L'Allegro* :—

> Haste thee, nymph, and bring with thee
> Jest, and youthful Jollity,
> Quips, and cranks, and wanton wiles,
> Nods, and becks, and wreathèd smiles,
> Such as hang on Hebe's cheek,
> And love to live in dimple sleek ;
> Sport that wrinkled Care derides,
> And Laughter holding both his sides.
> Come, and trip it, as you go,
> On the light fantastic toe ;
> And in thy right hand lead with thee
> The mountain nymph, sweet Liberty ;
> And, if I give thee honour due,
> Mirth, admit me of thy crew,
> To live with her, and live with thee,
> In unreprovèd pleasures free ;
> To hear the lark begin his flight,
> And, singing, startle the dull night,
> From his watch-tower in the skies,
> Till the dappled dawn doth rise ;
> Then to come, in spite of sorrow,
> And at my window bid good-morrow.
>   *   *   *

What a dewy freshness and fragrance breathe from his lines on *May Morning* :—

> Now the bright morning star, day's harbinger,
> Comes dancing from the east, and leads with her
> The flowery May, who from her green lap throws
> The yellow cowslip and the pale primrose.
> Hail, beauteous May! that dost inspire
> Mirth, and youth, and warm desire;
> Woods and groves are of thy dressing,
> Hill and dale doth boast thy blessing.
> Thus we salute thee with our early song,
> And welcome thee, and wish thee long.

We are all familiar with Milton's majestic *Morning Hymn* : how grandly it opens :—

> These are thy glorious works, Parent of good :
> Almighty, thine this universal frame,
> Thus wondrous fair; Thyself how wondrous then!
> Unspeakable, who sitt'st above these heavens
> To us invisible, or dimly seen
> In these thy lowest works; yet these declare
> Thy goodness beyond thought, and power divine.
> Speak, ye who best can tell, ye sons of light,
> Angels! for ye behold Him, and with songs
> And choral symphonies, day without night,
> Circle His throne rejoicing; ye in heaven,
> On earth,—join all ye creatures to extol
> Him first, Him last, Him midst, and without end!

*   *   *

No less beautiful is his description of *Evening* in Paradise :—

Now came still evening on, and twilight gray
Had in her sober livery all things clad ;

Silence accompanied ; for beast and bird,
They to their grassy couch, these to their nests
Were slunk, all but the wakeful nightingale ;
She all night long her amorous descant sung :
Silence was pleased : now glowed the firmament
With living sapphires ; Hesperus, that led
The starry host, rode brightest, till the moon,
Rising in clouded majesty, at length
Apparent queen, unveiled her peerless light,
And o'er the dark her silver mantle threw !

What a rich collection of little gems might be gathered from the
brilliant pages of this great poet, had we space for the garnering.
Here are two or three, caught at random :—

From *Comus* :—

> How charming is divine philosophy !
> Not harsh and crabbed, as dull fools suppose ;
> But musical as is Apollo's lute,
> And a perpetual feast of nectared sweets,
> Where no crude surfeit reigns.

From *L'Allegro* :—

> Lap me in soft Lydian airs,
> Married to immortal verse,
> Such as the meeting soul may pierce
> In notes, with many a winding bout
> Of linked sweetness long drawn out.

From *Lycidas* :—

> Fame is the spur that the clear spirit doth raise
> (That last infirmity of noble mind)
> To scorn delights, and live laborious days ;
> But the fair guerdon when we hope to find,
> And think to burst out into sudden blaze,
> Comes the blind Fury with the abhorred shears,
> And slits the thin-spun life.

How much the world is indebted to the " blind old master of English song," it would be impossible to compute ; for not only has he enriched our literature with the vast resources of a mind pre-eminently endowed, but he was among the foremost of the pioneers of civil and religious liberty. His able and authoritative pen served as efficiently in that noble emprise, as legions of armed soldiers in the field. As the champion of human freedom, he was necessarily obnoxious to the opposing party ; accordingly, on the accession of Charles II., Milton became the object of bitter hostility : to such an extent, indeed, that in order to save his valuable life, his very existence had for a time to be kept secret. It is said that his friends spread a report that he was dead, and, assembling a mournful procession, followed his pretended remains to the grave. The king, some time afterwards discovering the trick, commended his policy "in escaping death by a seasonable show of dying." It is related of the Duke of York, that when, on one occasion, he visited Milton, and he was asked whether he did not regard the loss of his eyesight as a judgment inflicted on him for what he had written against the late king? he replied, "If your highness thinks that the calamities which befall us here are indications of the wrath of Heaven, in what manner are we to account for the fate of the late king, your father? the displeasure of Heaven must, upon this supposition, have been much greater upon him than upon me, for I have only lost my eyes, but he has lost his head!" Despised and persecuted as this illustrious man was for his political faith, he stood calmly and grandly forth, in the majesty and integrity of truth, amidst all; and his posterity has not forgotten his noble service. John Milton's great spirit left the world on Sunday, the eighth of November, 1674; and his sacred dust reposes near the chancel of St. Giles's, Cripplegate;—a shrine, whither tend many pilgrim feet from all parts of the civilized world. It is a note-worthy fact, that while the greatest of English poets (the bard of Avon alone excepted) received only the trifling sum of five pounds for the first edition of his great epic, one of his editors, Newton, received six hundred guineas for his annotations upon it.

The following vigorous and impressive stanzas are by BYRD :—

> My mind to me a kingdom is;
>   Such perfect joy therein I find,
> As far exceeds all earthly bliss
>   That God or nature hath assigned.
> Though much I want, that most would have,
> Yet still my mind forbids to crave.

Content I live; this is my stay,
   I seek no more than may suffice;
I press to bear no haughty sway;
   Look, what I lack, my mind supplies.
Lo! thus I triumph like a king,
Content with that my mind doth bring.

      *   *   *

Some have too much, yet still they crave;
   I little have, yet seek no more;
They are but poor, though much they have,
   And I am rich with little store.
They poor, I rich; they beg, I give;
They lack, I lend; they pine, I live.

      *   *   *

My wealth is health and perfect ease;
   My conscience clear, my chief defence;
I never seek by bribes to please,
   Nor by desert to give offence.   .
This is my choice; for why? I find
No wealth is like a quiet mind.

CHAMBERLAYNE, a poet but little known, but of evident genius, is the author of this beautiful description of a summer morning :—

The morning hath not lost her virgin blush,
Nor step, but mine, soiled the earth's tinselled robe.
How full of heaven this solitude appears,
This healthful comfort of the happy swain;
Who from his hard but peaceful bed roused up,
In's morning exercise saluted is
By a full quire of feathered choristers,
Wedding their notes to the enamoured air!

72

Here Nature, in her unaffected dress,
Plaited with valleys, and embossed with hills
Enchased with silver streams, and fringed with woods,
Sits lovely in her native russet.

Who is not charmed with the rich quaintness of worthy GEORGE
HERBERT? Here is his fine piece, entitled *Virtue* :—

Sweet day, so cool, so calm, so bright,
   The bridal of the earth and sky !
The dew shall weep thy fall to-night ;
     For thou must die.

Sweet rose, whose hue, angry and brave,
   Bids the rash gazer wipe his eye !
Thy root is ever in its grave—
     And thou must die.

Sweet Spring, full of sweet days and roses,
    A box where sweets compacted lie!
My music shows ye have your closes,
    And all must die.

Only a sweet and virtuous soul,
    Like seasoned timber, never gives;
But though the whole world turn to coal,
    Then chiefly lives.

These are the opening stanzas of his *Man's Medley* :—

Hark! how the birds do sing,
    And woods do ring:
All creatures have their joy, and man hath his:
    Yet if we rightly measure,
    Man's joy and pleasure
Rather hereafter, than in present, is.

To this life things of sense
    Make their pretence;
In th' other angels have a right by birth;
    Man ties them both alone,
    And makes them one,
With th' one touching heaven—with th' other, earth.

There is a charm about Herbert's poetry, notwithstanding the
strange conceits with which it abounds; as in the following lines,
entitled *Life* :—

I made a posie, while the day ran by:
Here will I smell my remnant out, and tie
    My life within this band.
But Time did beckon to the flowers, and they
By noon most cunningly did steal away,
    And wither'd in my hand.

My hand was next to them, and then my heart ;
I took, without more thinking, in good part
      Time's gentle admonition ;
Who did so sweetly death's sad taste convey,
Making my minde to smell my fatall day,
      Yet sugaring the suspicion.

Farewell, dear flowers ; sweetly your time ye spent,
Fit, while ye liv'd, for smell or ornament,
      And after death for cures.
I follow straight without complaints or grief,
Since, if my scent be good, I care not if
      It be as short as yours.

Addison, it may be remembered, thus refers to a brother bard in
the following couplet :—

    " Nor, DENHAM, must we e'er forget thy strains,
      While *Cooper's Hill* commands the neighboring plains."

It was this DENHAM that wrote that celebrated quartette—which
seems to have been a poetic inspiration :—

    Oh ! could I flow like thee, and make thy stream
    My great example, as it is my theme !
    Though deep, yet clear ; though gentle, yet not dull ;
    Strong without rage ; without o'erflowing, full !

ANDREW MARVELL, the friend of Milton, wrote these glowing
lines *On a Drop of Dew* :—

    See how the orient dew,
      Shed from the bosom of the morn,
    Into the blowing roses,
      Yet careless of its mansion new,
    For the clear region where 'twas born,

Round in itself encloses;
And in its little globe's extent,
Frames as it can its native element.

How it the purple flower does slight!
  Scarce touching where it lies;
  But giving back upon the skies,
Shines with a mournful light,
Like its own tear, because so long divided from the sphere,
Restless it rolls and insecure, trembling lest it grow impure,
  Till the warm sun pities its pain,
  And to the skies exhales it back again.

So the soul—that drop, that ray
Of the clear fountain of eternal day,
Could it within the human flower be seen,
  Remembering still its former height,
Shuns the sweet leaves and blossoms green,
  And recollecting its own light,
Does in its pure and circling thoughts express
The greater heaven in a heaven less.

DRYDEN's magnificent Ode, *On the Power of Music*, written in
1697, for the festival of St. Cecilia's day, is by many considered his
masterpiece. It is pronounced unequalled by any thing of its kind
since classic times; and is the best illustration of the pliancy of our
English extant. He wrote this grand Ode at Burleigh House,
where his translation of Virgil was partly executed. One morning
Lord Bolingbroke chanced to call on Dryden, whom he found in
unusual agitation. On inquiring the cause, "I have been up all
night," replied the bard; "my musical friends made me promise to
write them an Ode for the Feast of St. Cecilia: I have been so
struck with the subject which occurred to me, that I could not
leave it till I had completed it: here it is, finished at one sitting."

The poem is designed to exhibit the different passions excited by Timotheus in the mind of Alexander, feasting a triumphant conqueror in Persepolis. The grandeur of the poem can only be appreciated by perusing it entire, and more fully, indeed, on even a second perusal. Here is the opening stanza :—

'Twas at the royal feast, for Persia won
    By Philip's warlike son :
Aloft in awful state the god-like hero sate
    On his imperial throne ;

His valiant peers were placed around,
Their brows with roses and with myrtle bound ;
So should desert in arms be crown'd.
   The lovely Thais by his side
   Sat, like a blooming Eastern bride,
   In flower of youth and beauty's pride :

Happy, happy, happy pair !—
None but the brave, none but the brave,
None but the brave deserves the fair.

Timotheus, placed on high
Amid the tuneful quire,
With flying fingers touched the lyre ;
And trembling notes ascend the sky,
And heavenly joys inspire !

*   *   *

As instances of Dryden's lighter verse, we present the following :—

I feed a flame within, which so torments me,
That it both pains my heart, and yet contents me ;
'Tis such a pleasing smart, and so I love it,
That I had rather die than once remove it.
Yet he for whom I grieve shall never know it ;
My tongue does not betray, nor my eyes show it.
Not a sigh, nor a tear, my pain discloses,
But they fall silently, like dew on roses.
Thus, to prevent my love from being cruel,
My heart's the sacrifice, as 'tis the fuel ;
And while I suffer this, to give him quiet,
My faith rewards my love, though he deny it.
On his eyes will I gaze, and there delight me ;
Where I conceal my love, no frown can fright me :
To be more happy, I dare not aspire :
Nor can I fall more low, mounting no higher.

––––––

O, lull me, lull me, charming air !
My senses rock with wonder sweet !
Like snow on wool thy fallings are ;
Soft, like a spirit's, are thy feet.

Grief who need fear
That hath an ear?
Down let him lie,
And slumbering die,
And change his soul for harmony.

———

Ah, how sweet it is to love!
Ah, how gay is young Desire!
And what pleasing pains we prove
  When we first approach Love's fire!
    Pains of love be sweeter far
    Than all other pleasures are.
Sighs which are from lovers blown,
  Do but gently heave the heart;
E'en the tears they shed alone,
  Cure, like trickling balm, their smart.
    Lovers, when they lose their breath,
    Bleed away in easy death.

*   *   *

Dryden happening to pass an evening at the Duke of Bucking-
ham's, where were assembled Lord Dorset, the Earl of Rochester,
and other distinguished men, the conversation chanced to turn upon
literary topics. After some debate, it was agreed that each person
present should improvise some lines on any subject his fancy might
suggest, and that the contributions should be placed under the
candlestick. Dryden was excepted, but the office of umpire was
assigned to him. Some of the company were at more than ordi-
nary pains to outrival their competitors; but Lord Dorset was
noticed to write his two or three lines with the most tranquil unconcern. All the wits having contributed their effusions, Dryden
proceeded to unfold the leaves of their literary destiny. He discovered deep emotion during the process, and at length exclaimed,

" I must acknowledge that there are abundance of fine things in my hands, and such as do honour to the personages who penned them; but I am under the indispensable necessity of giving the preference to Lord Dorset. I must request you will hear it yourselves, gentlemen, and I believe you will all then approve my judgment:—'*I promise to pay to John Dryden, Esq., or order, on demand, the sum of Five hundred pounds.—Dorset.*' I must confess," continued Dryden, "that I am equally charmed with the style and the subject; and I flatter myself, gentlemen, that I stand in need of no argument to induce you to acquiesce in opinion, even against yourselves. This style of writing excels any other, ancient or modern : it is not the essence, but the quintessence of language, and is, in fact, reason and argument surpassing every thing in letters." Of course, the company cordially concurred with the bard, and complimented the superior penetration of the noble donor.

When Dryden was a boy at Westminster School, he was put, with others, to write a copy of verses on the miracle of the conversion of water into wine. Being a great truant, he had not time to compose his verses; and when brought up, he had only made one line of Latin, and two of English :—

> "*Vidit et erubuit lympha pudica Deum !*" [1]

> "The modest water, awed by power divine,
> Beheld its God, and blushed itself to wine ;"

which so pleased the master, that instead of being angry, he said it was a presage of future greatness, and gave the youth a crown on the occasion. What a contrast this first outburst of poetic power presents with the closing days of his literary career! when in his seventieth year he complains that, " worn out with study, and oppressed with fortune, he was compelled to contract with his publisher to furnish ten thousand verses at sixpence per line !"

Macaulay thus writes of Dryden :—" His command of language was immense. With him died the secret of the old poetic diction

---

[1] This may be a plagiarism from Crashaw's—" *Nympha pudica Deum vidit, et erubuit.*"

of England,—the art of producing rich effects by familiar words. On the other hand, he was the first writer under whose skilful management the scientific vocabulary fell into natural and pleasing verse :—

> 'The varying verse, the full-resounding line,
> The long majestic march, and energy divine.' "

Warton says, the most splendid and sublime passage that Dryden ever wrote is the following :—

> So when of old the Almighty Father sate
> In council, to redeem our ruin'd state,
> Millions of millions, at a distance round,
> Silent the sacred consistory crown'd,
> To hear what mercy, mix'd with justice, could propouna :
> All prompt, with eager pity, to fulfil
> The full extent of their Creator's will.
> But when the stern conditions were declared,
> A mournful whisper through the host was heard,
> And the whole hierarchy, with heads hung down,
> Submissively declin'd the ponderous proffer'd crown.
> Then, not till then, the Eternal Son from high
> Rose in the strength of all the Deity :
> Stood forth to accept the terms, and underwent
> A weight which all the frame of Heaven had bent,
> Nor He himself could bear, but as Omnipotent !

      *   *   *

ADDISON'S poetry is generally considered cold and artificial, although his graver productions are harmonious and beautiful ; they are, indeed, accepted as his best compositions. His well-known *Hymn*, says Thackeray, "shines like the stars." Here it is :—

> The spacious firmament on high,
> With all the blue ethereal sky,

And spangled heavens, a shining frame,
Their great Original proclaim.
The unwearied sun, from day to day,
Does his Creator's power display,
And publishes to every land
The work of an Almighty hand.

Soon as the evening shades prevail,
The moon takes up the wondrous tale,
And nightly, to the listening earth,
Repeats the story of her birth ;
While all the stars that round her burn,
And all the planets, in their turn,

Confirm the tidings as they roll,
And spread the truth from pole to pole.

What, though in solemn silence all
Move round this dark terrestrial ball ?
What, though no real voice, nor sound,
Amid their radiant orbs be found ?
In Reason's ear they all rejoice,
And utter forth a glorious voice ;
Forever singing, as they shine,
" The hand that made us is Divine."

One of Addison's best pieces is that written at the tomb of
Virgil, in 1741 : he also achieved a dramatic triumph in his celebrated tragedy of *Cato*.   Let us rehearse his grand soliloquy :—

It must be so.   Plato, thou reason'st well !
Else, whence this pleasing hope, this fond desire,
This longing after immortality ?
Or, whence this secret dread, and inward horror,
Of falling into naught ?   Why shrinks the soul
Back on herself, and startles at destruction ?
'Tis the Divinity that stirs within us :
'Tis Heaven itself that points out an hereafter,
And intimates—Eternity to man !
Eternity !—thou pleasing, dreadful thought !
Through what variety of untried being—
Through what new scenes and changes must we pass !
The wide, th' unbounded prospect lies before me ;
But shadows, clouds, and darkness rest upon it.
Here will I hold.—If there's a power above us
(And that there is, all nature cries aloud
Through all her works), He must delight in virtue ;
And that which He delights in, must be happy.

    *   *   *

The soul, secured in her existence, smiles
At the drawn dagger, and defies its point.
The stars shall fade away, the sun himself
Grow dim with age, and nature sink in years;
But thou shalt flourish in immortal youth,
Unhurt amidst the war of elements,
The wreck of matter, and the crush of worlds!

POPE was a precocious genius; for when only in his thirteenth
year, he wrote these pleasing lines on *Solitude* :—

Happy the man whose wish and care
    A few paternal acres bound,
Content to breathe his native air
      In his own ground.

Whose herds with milk, whose fields with bread,
    Whose flocks supply him with attire,
Whose trees in summer yield him shade,
      In winter fire.

Blest, who can unconcern'dly find
    Hours, days, and years slide soft away,
In health of body, peace of mind,
      Quiet by day,

Sound sleep by night; study and ease,
    Together mixt; sweet recreation;
And innocence, which most does please
      With meditation.

Thus let me live unseen, unknown,
    Thus unlamented let me die,
Steal from the world, and not a stone
      Tell where I lie.

He tells us that he sought the solace of poesy to beguile his hours
of physical suffering. At the age of sixteen he wrote his *Pastorals*;
and two or three years later, his *Messiah*, and *Essay on Criticism*.
Pope's bodily infirmity caused him to be at times very irascible;
and on one occasion his long-tried friend, Bishop Atterbury, in
pleasantry, described the poet as *Mens curva in corpore curvo*.¹ His
Essay on Man is replete with nervous and picturesque passages; it
is, however, occasionally tinctured with the heresies of his friend
Bolingbroke. Subjoined are a few fine passages from his famous
Essay on Man :—

Hope humbly then—with trembling pinions soar ;
Wait the great teacher, Death ; and God adore.
What future bliss, He gives not thee to know,
But gives that hope to be thy blessing now.
Hope springs eternal in the human breast,—
Man never is, but always to be blest.
The soul, uneasy and confined from home,
Rests and expatiates in a life to come.
Lo ! the poor Indian ! whose untutor'd mind
Sees God in clouds, or hears Him in the wind :
His soul, proud science never taught to stray
Far as the solar walk or Milky-way ;
Yet simple nature to his hope has given
Behind the cloud-topped hill a humbler heaven ;
Some safer world in depth of woods embraced,
Some happier island in the watery waste,
Where slaves once more their native land behold,
Nor fiends torment, nor Christians thirst for gold.
To be, contents his natural desire,
He asks no angel's wing, no seraph's fire ;

In justice to the poet, however, we ought to cite his noble couplet on his friend :—

" How pleasing Atterbury's softer hour !
How shined his soul unconquered in the Tower !"

He thinks, admitted to that equal sky,
His faithful dog shall bear him company.

   *   *   *

What a grand conception of his is this closing passage :—

All are but parts of one stupendous whole,
Whose body nature is, and God the soul ;
That, changed through all, and yet in all the same :
Great in the earth, as in th' ethereal frame ;
Warms in the sun, refreshes in the breeze,
Glows in the stars, and blossoms in the trees ;
Lives through all life, extends through all extent ;
Spreads undivided, operates unspent ;
Breathes in our soul, informs our mortal part,
As full, as perfect, in a hair as heart ;

As full, as perfect, in vile man that mourns,
As the rapt seraph, that adores and burns;
To Him no high, no low, no great, no small;
He fills, He bounds, connects, and equals all.
Cease then, nor order imperfection name:
Our proper bliss depends on what we blame.
Know thy own point: this kind, this due degree
Of blindness, weakness, Heaven bestows on thee.
Submit.—In this, or any other sphere,
Secure to be as blest as thou canst bear:
Safe in the hand of one disposing Power,
Or in the natal, or the mortal hour.
All nature is but art, unknown to thee;
All chance, direction, which thou canst not see;
All discord, harmony, not understood;
All partial evil, universal good.

The *Rape of the Lock*, which Johnson styles "the most airy, ingenious, and delightful of all Pope's compositions," was occasioned by a frolic of gallantry. Here are two passages; one portraying the mysteries of the toilet, and the other the heroine of the story:—

And now, unveiled, the toilet stands displayed,
Each silver vase in mystic order laid.
First, robed in white, the nymph intent adores,
With head uncovered, the cosmetic powers;
A heavenly image in the glass appears,
To that she bends, to that her eyes she rears:
The inferior priestess, at her altar's side,
Trembling begins the sacred rites of pride.
Unnumbered treasures ope at once, and here
The various offerings of the world appear;
From each she nicely culls with curious toil,
And decks the goddess with the glittering spoil.

This casket India's glowing gems unlocks,
And all Arabia breathes from yonder box.
The tortoise here and elephant unite,
Transformed to combs, the speckled and the white.
Here files of pins extend their shining rows,
Puffs, powders, patches, bibles, billet-doux.
Now awful beauty puts on all its arms;
The fair each moment rises in her charms,
Repairs her smiles, awakens every grace,
And calls forth all the wonders of her face;
Sees by degrees a purer blush arise,
And keener lightnings quicken in her eyes.
The busy Sylphs surround their darling care,
These set the head, and those divide the hair,
Some fold the sleeve, whilst others plait the gown;
And Betty's praised for labours not her own.

Fair nymphs and well-dressed youths around her shone,
But every eye was fixed on her alone.
On her white breast a sparkling cross she wore,
Which Jews might kiss, and infidels adore.
Her lively looks a sprightly mind disclose,
Quick as her eyes, and as unfixed as those;
Favours to none, to all she smiles extends;
Oft she rejects, but never once offends.
Bright as the sun, her eyes the gazers strike,
And, like the sun, they shine on all alike.
Yet graceful ease, and sweetness void of pride,
Might hide her faults, if belles had faults to hide:
If to her share some female errors fall,
Look on her face, and you'll forget them all.
This nymph, to the destruction of mankind,
Nourished two locks, which graceful hung behind

In equal curls, and well conspired to deck
With shining ringlets the smooth, ivory neck.
Love in these labyrinths his slaves detains,
And mighty hearts are held in slender chains.

* * *

Fair tresses man's imperial race insnare,
And beauty draws us with a single hair.
Th' adventurous baron the bright locks admired;
He saw, he wished, and to the prize aspired.

The poetry of Pope has been compared to mosaic work,—full of thoughts familiar to most minds, but draped in elegant metaphor. There is an absence of passion and emotion in his writings; he seldom excites a smile, and as seldom touches the sympathies by pathos. His " mellifluence," as Johnson expresses it, has the defect of monotony; but he possessed the faculty of making " sound an echo to the sense" in an eminent degree. Witness these lines:—

Soft is the strain when zephyr gently blows,
And the smooth stream in smoother numbers flows;
But when loud surges lash the sounding shore,
The hoarse rough verse should like the torrent roar.
When Ajax strives some rocks' vast weight to throw,
The words, too, labor, and the lines move slow:
Not so, when swift Camilla scours the plain,
Flies o'er the unbending corn, and skims along the main.

* * *

A needless Alexandrine ends the song,
That, like a wounded snake, drags its slow length along.

PARNELL's *Hermit*, familiar to most readers, and which Pope pronounced " very good," commences thus:—

Far in a wild, unknown to public view,
From youth to age a reverend hermit grew;

The moss his bed, the cave his humble cell,
His food the fruits, his drink the crystal well ;
Remote from men, with God he passed his days,
Prayer all his business, all his pleasure, praise.
A life so sacred, such serene repose,
Seemed heaven itself, till one suggestion rose—

That vice should triumph, virtue vice obey ;
This sprung some doubt of Providence's sway ;
His hopes no more a certain prospect boast,
And all the tenor of his soul is lost.
So, when a smooth expanse receives imprest
Calm nature's image on its watery breast,
Down bend the banks, the trees depending grow,
And skies beneath with answering colours glow ;

But, if a stone the gentle sea divide,
Swift ruffling circles curl on every side,
And glimmering fragments of a broken sun,
Banks, trees, and skies, in thick disorder run.
To clear this doubt, to know the world by sight,
To find if books, or swains, report it right—
For yet by swains alone the world he knew,
Whose feet came wandering o'er the nightly dew—
He quits his cell; the pilgrim staff he bore,
And fixed the scallop in his hat before;
Then, with the rising sun, a journey went,
Sedate to think, and watching each event.

*   *   *

THOMSON'S *Castle of Indolence*, the latest of his productions, seems to have been a labour of love with the poet. The sketch of himself is interesting, although he tells us, that all except the first line was written by a friend :—

A bard here dwelt, more fat than bard beseems,
    Who, void of envy, guile, and lust of gain,
On virtue still, and nature's pleasing themes,
    Poured forth his unpremeditated strain ;
    The world forsaking with a calm disdain,
Here laughed he careless in his easy seat,—
    Here quaff'd, encircled with the joyous train,
Oft moralizing sage, his ditty sweet,—
He loathèd much to write, he carèd to repeat.

There is a great charm about this poem ; its numbers seem to lull one into a dreamy sense of pleasure ; note this stanza :—

A pleasing land of drowsy herd it was,
    Of dreams that wave before the half-shut eye ;

And of gay castles in the clouds that pass,
  Forever flashing round a summer sky :
  There eke the soft delights, that witchingly
Instil a wanton sweetness through the breast,
  And the calm pleasures always hovered nigh ;
  But whate'er smacked of noyance or unrest,
Was far, far off expelled from that delicious nest.

                *   *   *

Here is a beautiful passage :—

  I care not, Fortune, what you me deny ;
    You cannot rob me of free Nature's grace,
  You cannot shut the windows of the sky,
    Through which Aurora shows her bright'ning face :
    You cannot bar my constant feet to trace
  The woods and lawns, by living stream, at eve :
    Let health my nerves and finer fibres brace,
  And I their toys to the great children leave ;
Of fancy, reason, virtue, naught can me bereave.

We should scarcely have expected that this lover of luxurious
ease, who used to linger a-bed, sometimes, till two of the afternoon,
could have given us such a burst of inspiration on early rising as
this :—

  Falsely luxurious ! will not man, awake,
  And springing from the bed of sloth, enjoy
  The cool, the fragrant, and the silent hour
  To meditation due, and sacred song ?
  For is there aught in sleep can charm the wise ?
  To lie in dead oblivion, losing half
  The fleeting moments of too short a life ?
  Total extinction of the enlightened soul ;
  Or else to feverish vanity alive,

Wilder'd and tossing through distempered dreams ?
Who would in such a gloomy state remain
Longer than nature craves ; when every muse,
And every blooming pleasure, wait without,
To bless the wildly-devious morning walk ?

Like others of the illustrious brotherhood, our poet lived for the
present, and seldom indulged any anxiety about the future ; the
consequence was, that his purse was not unfrequently exhausted.
On a certain occasion he was surprised by an unexpected visit from
Quin, the comedian, whom he had known only by reputation.
Puzzled to think what could have induced such a visit, he pressed
the question, when Quin replied, " Why, I will tell you. Soon
after I had read your *Seasons*, I took it into my head, that as I had
something to leave behind me when I died, I would make my will.
Among the rest of my legatees, I set down the author of the *Seasons*
for a hundred pounds : and this day, hearing that you were in this
house, I thought I might as well have the pleasure of paying the
money myself as order my executors to pay it, when perhaps you
might have less need of it ; and this, Mr. Thomson, is the object
of my visit."

The " poet of the *Seasons*" did much to improve the poetic taste
of his day. Campbell justly remarks : " Habits of early admiration
teach us all to look back upon this poet as the favourite companion
of our solitary walks, and as the author who has first, or chiefly,
reflected back to our minds a heightened and refined sensation of
the delight which rural scenery affords us." Thomson's sketches
are *Claude*-like,—full of pastoral beauty and sunshine. Here is a
beautiful burst of song, descriptive of summer dawn :—

The meek-eyed Morn appears, mother of dews,
At first faint-gleaming in the dappled east :
Till far o'er ether spreads the widening glow ;
And, from before the lustre of her face,

White break the clouds away. With quicken'd step
Brown night retires. Young day pours in apace,
And opens all the lawny prospect wide.
The dripping rock, the mountain's misty top,
Swell on the sight, and brighten with the dawn.
Blue, through the dusk, the smoking currents shine;

And from the bladed field the fearful hare
Limps, awkward; while along the forest glade
The wild deer trip, and often turning, gaze
At early passenger. Music awakes
The native voice of undissembled joy;
And thick around the woodland hymns arise.
Roused by the cock, the soon-clad shepherd leaves
His mossy cottage, where with peace he dwells;
And from the crowded fold, in order, drives
His flock, to taste the verdure of the morn.

After describing the traveller lost in the snow, the poet thus continues :—

> In vain for him the officious wife prepares
> The fire fair blazing, and the vestment warm ;
> In vain his little children, peeping out
> Into the mingling storm, demand their sire
> With tears of artless innocence.   Alas !
> Nor wife nor children more shall he behold,
> Nor friends, nor sacred home.   On every nerve
> The deadly winter seizes, shuts up sense,
> And o'er his inmost vitals creeping cold,
> Lays him along the snows a stiffened corpse,
> Stretched out, and bleaching on the northern blast !

As long as human passions shall animate or disturb the world, COLLINS's masterly *Ode* will doubtless be perused and prized : yet the gifted author suffered from neglect and poverty, and ultimately became the victim of mental disease.   Some evil genius seemed to have presided over his destiny, for in early life he fell in love with a fair damsel, who was born a day before himself, and she refused to respond to his appeals.   " Your case is a hard one," said a friend. " It is so indeed," replied Collins, " for I came into the world a day after the fair."   When at Magdalen College, Oxford, he was entertaining a few friends at tea.   Hampton, the translator of *Polybius*, unexpectedly entered, and finding no one disposed to dispute with him, deliberately upset the tea-table, scattering its contents across the room.   Collins, although constitutionally somewhat choleric, was so utterly confounded at the unexpected demonstration, that he took no notice of the aggressor, but calmly began picking up the broken pieces of china, mildly quoting this line of Horace :—

> " *Invenias etiam disjecti membra poetæ.*"

Now for his masterly *Ode* :—

When Music, heavenly maid, was young,
While yet in early Greece she sung,
The Passions oft, to hear her shell,
Thronged around her magic cell,
Exulting, trembling, raging, fainting,
Possest beyond the muse's painting;
By turns they felt the glowing mind
Disturbed, delighted, raised, refined;
Till once, 'tis said, when all were fired,
Filled with fury, rapt, inspired,
From the supporting myrtles round,
They snatched her instruments of sound;
And, as they oft had heard apart
Sweet lessons of her forceful art,
Each (for madness ruled the hour)
Would prove his own expressive power.

First Fear his hand, its skill to try,
 Amid the chords, bewildered laid,
And back recoiled, he knew not why,
 Even at the sound himself had made.

Next Anger rushed, his eyes on fire,
 In lightnings owned his secret stings;
In one rude clash he struck the lyre,
 And swept with hurried hand the strings.

With woful measures wan Despair,
 Low, sullen sounds his grief beguiled;
A solemn, strange, and mingled air;
 'Twas sad by fits, by starts 'twas wild.

But thou, oh Hope, with eyes so fair,
 What was thy delighted measure?
 Still it whispered promised pleasure,
And bade the lovely scenes at distance hail!

Still would her touch the strain prolong;
And from the rocks, the woods, the vale,
She called on Echo still, through all the song;
And, where her sweetest theme she chose,
A soft responsive voice was heard at every close,
And Hope enchanted smiled, and waved her golden hair.

And longer had she sung;—but, with a frown,
Revenge impatient rose;
He threw his blood-stained sword, in thunder, down,
And, with a withering look,
The war-denouncing trumpet took,
And blew a blast so loud and dread,
Were ne'er prophetic sounds so full of woe!
And, ever and anon, he beat
The double drum with furious heat;
And though sometimes, each dreary pause between,
Dejected Pity at his side,
Her soul-subduing voice applied,
Yet still he kept his wild, unaltered mien,
While each strained ball of sight seemed bursting from his head.

   *   *   *

With eyes upraised, as one inspired,
Pale Melancholy sat retired;
And, from her wild, sequestered seat,
In notes by distance made more sweet,
Poured through the mellow horn her pensive soul;
And, dashing soft from rocks around,
Bubbling runnels joined the sound;
Through glades and glooms the mingled measure stole,
Or o'er some haunted stream, with fond delay,
Round an holy calm diffusing,
Love of peace and lonely musing,
In hollow murmurs died away.

But O! how altered was its sprightlier tone,
  When Cheerfulness, a nymph of healthiest hue,
Her bow across her shoulder flung,
  Her buskins gemmed with morning dew,
Blew an inspiring air, that dale and thicket rung,
  The hunter's call, to Faun and Dryad known!
The oak-crowned Sisters, and their chaste-eyed queen,
  Satyrs and Sylvan Boys, were seen,
  Peeping from forth their alleys green:
  Brown Exercise rejoiced to hear;
And Sport leapt up, and seized his beechen spear.

  Last came Joy's ecstatic trial:
  He, with viny crown advancing,
First to the lively pipe his hand address;
  But soon he saw the brisk, awakening viol,
Whose sweet entrancing voice he loved the best:
They would have thought, who heard the strain,
  They saw, in Tempè's vale, her native maids,
  Amidst the festal sounding shades,
  To some unwearied minstrel dancing,
While, as his flying fingers kissed the strings,
  Love framed with Mirth, a gay fantastic round:
  Loose were her tresses seen, her zone unbound;
  And he, amidst his frolic play,
  As if he would the charming air repay,
Shook thousand odours from his dewy wings.

  Oh, Music! sphere-descended maid,
  Friend of Pleasure, Wisdom's aid!
  Why, goddess! why to us denied,
  Lay'st thou thy ancient lyre aside?
  As in that loved Athenian bower,
  You learned an all-commanding power;

Thy mimic soul, oh, nymph endeared,
Can well recall what then it heard.
Where is thy native simple heart,
Devote to Virtue, Fancy, Art?
Arise, as in that elder time,
Warm, energetic, chaste, sublime!
Thy wonders in that godlike age
Fill thy recording Sister's page.
'Tis said, and I believe the tale,
Thy humblest reed could more prevail,
Had more of strength, diviner rage,
Than all which charms this laggard age;
Even all at once together found,
Cecilia's mingled world of sound.
Oh! bid your vain endeavors cease,
Revive the just designs of Greece;
Return in all thy simple state;
Confirm the tales her sons relate!

Collins's grand lines, *The Patriot's Grave*, are among the finest of their class :—

How sleep the brave, who sink to rest,
By all their country's wishes blest!
When Spring, with dewy fingers cold,
Returns to deck their hallowed mould,
She there shall dress a sweeter sod
Than Fancy's feet have ever trod.
By fairy hands their knell is rung,
By forms unseen their dirge is sung;
There Honor comes, a pilgrim gray,
To bless the turf that wraps their clay;
And Freedom shall awhile repair,
To dwell a weeping hermit there.

SHENSTONE'S highest effort was his *Schoolmistress*. Here is an extract :—

In every village marked with little spire,
　　Embowered in trees, and hardly known to fame,
There dwells, in lowly shed and mean attire,
　　A matron old, whom we schoolmistress name,
　　Who boasts unruly brats with birch to tame ;
They grieven sore, in piteous durance pent,
　　Awed by the power of this relentless dame ;
And oft-times, on vagaries idly bent,
For unkempt hair, or task unconned, are sorely shent.

And all in sight doth rise a birchen tree,
　　Which Learning near her little dome did stowe ;
Whilom a twig of small regard to see,
　　Though now so wide its waving branches flow,
　　And work the simple vassals mickle woe :
For not a wind might curl the leaves that blew,
　　But their limbs shuddered, and their pulse beat low :
And as they looked, they found their horror grew,
And shaped it into rods, and tingled at the view.

Near to this dome is found a patch so green,
　　On which the tribe their gambols do display ;
And at the door imprisoning board is seen,
　　Lest weakly wights of smaller size should stray,
　　Eager, perdie, to bask in sunny day !
The noises intermixed, which thence resound,
　　Do learning's little tenement betray ;
Where sits the dame, disguised in look profound,
And eyes her fairy throng, and turns her wheel around.

Her cap, far whiter than the driven snow,
　　Emblem right meet of decency does yield ;

Her apron dyed in grain, as blue, I trow,
  As is the hare-bell that adorns the field :
  And in her hand, for sceptre, she does wield

Tway birchen sprays ; with anxious fear entwined,
  With dark distrust, and sad repentance filled ;
And steadfast hate, and sharp affliction joined,
And fury uncontrolled, and chastisement unkind.

A russet stole was o'er her shoulders thrown ;
  A russet kirtle fenced the nipping air ;

'Twas simple russet, but it was her own ;
  'Twas her own country bred the flock so fair !
  'Twas her own labour did the fleece prepare ;
And, sooth to say, her pupils, ranged around,
  Through pious awe, did term it passing rare ;
For they in gaping wonderment abound,
And think, no doubt, she been the greatest wight on ground.

    *   *   *

In elbow-chair (like that of Scottish stem,
  By the sharp tooth of cankering eld defaced,
In which, when he receives his diadem,
  Our sovereign prince and liefest liege is placed)
  The matron sat ; and some with rank she graced
('The source of children's and of courtiers' pride !),
  Redressed affronts, for vile affronts there passed ;
And warned them not the fretful to deride,
But love each other dear, whatever them betide.

      *   *

Unlike most other poets, YOUNG preferred to dilate upon themes connected with the shady side of life, rather than its cheerful aspects. This gloomy proclivity of his pen is the more remarkable from the fact that he was, even to old age, far from being insensible to worldly influences and enjoyments. Schlegel thinks that he was affected in his misanthropy, and unnatural in his pathos. The following incident does not seem to conflict with that opinion :—

Young was one day walking in his garden at Welwyn, in company with two ladies (one of whom he afterwards married) ; the servant came to acquaint him that a gentleman wished to speak with him. "Tell him," said the doctor, "I am too happily engaged to change my situation." The ladies insisted he should go, as his visitor was a man of rank, his patron and his friend ; but as persuasion had no effect, one took him by the right arm and the other by the left, and led him to the garden gate ; when, finding resistance

vain, he bowed, laid his hand upon his heart, and improvised the
following lines :—

> Thus Adam looked, when from the garden driven,
> And thus disputed orders sent from heaven :
> Like him, I go, but yet to go I'm loath ;
> Like him, I go, for angels drove us both :
> Hard was his fate, but mine still more unkind,—
> *His Eve went with him, but mine stays behind !*

Notwithstanding the morbid spirit which pervades and oversha-
dows most of his poetry, depriving it of much of its potency, yet it
abounds with grand imagery, and is sustained by splendor of conception. The genius of Christianity is the patron of all that is joyous ;
she gilds the pathway of the present life with Heaven's own brightness, and makes even the clouds and darkness which hang over the
grave, luminous with the rainbow of Hope. If the poet and moralist
had but infused a little starlight into his *Night Thoughts*, they would
have possessed a tenfold charm. It is said that his friend, the Duke
of Wharton, sent him a human skull with a candle fixed in it, as
the most fitting lamp for him during his nocturnal lucubrations.
But we must cull a few passages from our author : and here is an
apostrophe to *Night :*—

> O majestic night !
> Nature's great ancestor ! day's elder-born !
> And fated to survive the transient sun !
> By mortals and immortals seen with awe '
> A starry crown thy raven brow adorns,
> An azure zone thy waist ; clouds, in heaven's loom
> Wrought through varieties of shape and shade,
> In ample folds of drapery divine,
> Thy flowing mantle form, and, heaven throughout,
> Voluminously pour thy pompous train :

Thy gloomy grandeurs—nature's most august,
Inspiring aspect!—claim a grateful verse ;
And, like a sable curtain starred with gold,
Drawn o'er my labours past, shall clothe the scene.

Here are his impressive lines on *Procrastination* :—

Be wise to-day : 'tis madness to defer ;
Next day the fatal precedent will plead :
Thus on, till wisdom is pushed out of life.
Procrastination is the thief of time ;
Year after year it steals, till all are fled,
And to the mercies of a moment leaves
The vast concerns of an eternal scene.
If not so frequent, would not this be strange ?
That 'tis so frequent, this is stranger still !
Of man's miraculous mistakes, this bears
The palm,—that all men are about to live—
Forever on the brink of being born :
All pay themselves the compliment to think
They one day shall not drivel, and their pride
On this reversion takes up ready praise.

*   *   *

There are some noble thoughts in the following passage :—

How poor, how rich, how abject, how august,
How complicate, how wonderful is man !
How passing wonder He who made him such !
Who centred in our make such strange extremes,
From different natures marvellously mixt,
Connection exquisite of distant worlds !
Distinguished link in being's endless chain !
Midway from nothing to the Deity !

A beam ethereal, sullied and absorpt !
Though sullied and dishonoured, still divine !
Dim miniature of greatness absolute !
An heir of glory—a frail child of dust !

       *   *   *

One more passage, for the sake of its striking metaphor :—

    Hearts wounded, like the wounded air,
Soon close ; where passed the shaft no trace is found,
As from the wing no stain the air retains.

       *   *   *

Our last selection is from his *Love of Fame*, which Johnson so highly eulogizes :—

What will not men attempt for sacred praise ?
The love of praise, howe'er concealed by art,
Reigns more or less, and glows in every heart :
The proud, to gain it, toils on toils endure ;
The modest shun it but to make it sure.
O'er globes and sceptres, now on thrones it swells—
Now trims the midnight lamp in college cells.

       *   *

It aids the dancer's heel, the writer's head,
And heaps the plain with mountains of the dead :
Nor ends with life, but nods in sable plumes,
Adorns our hearse, and flatters on our tombs.

Thus conclude we our second evening's entertainment with the Minstrels ; and since it has been questioned, from his gravity, whether the author of *The Night Thoughts* was ever *Young*, we shall regard him as the last of the *old* poets. With regret we bid adieu, then, to these great masters of the lyre, whose magnificent melodies, quaint imagery, and rich cadences, fall upon the ear like a benediction—

> " Or like those maiden showers
> Which, by the peep of day, do strew
> A baptism o'er the flowers."

Justly has it been said, that with them " the imaginative ruled and reigned ; poetry lived much in the upper air, and, like the lark, sang best as it soared to heaven." A high, chivalrous spirit marked the Elizabethan age of song ; its pomp of diction and stateliness of measure often challenging the curious interest of the reader, by the subtle obscurity and inversion of its style, as well as by its rich cadences. What a galaxy of illustrious names then shed lustre upon literature and life ! It was, indeed, the golden age of letters, with its registered glories in philosophy, science, and song. It was the age of contemplation and devotion to study, as ours is of action. Although poets are mortal, poetry is immortal ; the muse's priesthood still lives in a line of illustrious succession, " to enrich her galleries with glowing and beautiful creations, embodied in deathless and glorified forms :" and the noble inheritance is ours to stimulate us in the highways of wisdom and virtue. We need not, therefore,

> " Sigh the old heroic ages back ;
> These worthies were but brave and honest men ;
> Let us their spirit catch,—pursue their track ;—
> Striving, not sighing, brings them back again."

THIRD
EVENING.

Gray, Akenside,

Jones, Berkeley. Irving, Allston,

Dana, Percival, Sigourney, Pierpont, Drake,

Sprague, Brooks, Payne, Burgoyne, Darwin. Woodworth,

Goldsmith, Cowper, Burns, Darley. Sheridan,

Logan, Leyden, Beattie, Chatterton,

Wolfe, Wilde. Halleck.

G RAY, who was "saturated with the finest essence of the Attic muse," has given us some grand stanzas, in his *Ode* founded upon the Welsh tradition, that when Edward the First conquered Wales, he ordered the bards to be put to death. These are the opening stanzas :—

" Ruin seize thee, ruthless king !
    Confusion on thy banners wait ;
  Though fann'd by Conquest's crimson wing,
    They mock the air with idle state

Helm, nor hauberk's twisted mail,
Nor e'en thy virtues, Tyrant, shall avail
To save thy secret soul from nightly fears,
From Cambria's curse, from Cambria's tears!"
Such were the sounds that o'er the crested pride
    Of the first Edward scattered wild dismay,
As down the steep of Snowden's shaggy side
    He wound with toilsome march his long array.
Stout Glo'ster stood aghast in speechless trance;
"To arms!" cried Mortimer, and couch'd his quiv'ring lance.

On a rock, whose haughty brow
    Frowns o'er old Conway's foaming flood,
Robed in the sable garb of woe,
    With haggard eyes the poet stood;
(Loose his beard, and hoary hair
Stream'd like a meteor to the troubled air;)
And with a master's hand, and prophet's fire,
Struck the deep sorrows of his lyre.
" Hark, how each giant-oak, and desert-cave,
    Sighs to the torrent's awful voice beneath!
O'er thee, oh King! their hundred arms they wave,
    Revenge on thee in hoarser murmurs breathe:
Vocal no more, since Cambria's fatal day
To high-born Hoel's harp, or soft Llewellyn's lay!"

      *   *   *

Both Campbell and Rogers were much charmed with Gray's
writings: the latter used to carry a copy of them in his pocket, to
read during his morning walks, till at length, he says, he could repeat
them all. Byron considered Gray's *Elegy* the corner-stone of his
glory. Tuckerman, with all a poet's appreciation, thus refers to this
remarkable production:—" Almost every line is a select phrase, not
to be improved by taste or ingenuity. The subject is one of the

happiest in the range of poetry. Who has not strayed at sunset into the quiet precincts of a country churchyard? Who has not sought the spot where ' the rude forefathers of the hamlet sleep?' Who has not felt a melancholy pleasure steal upon his soul, as he has stood among the graves, and received the solemn teachings of the scene 'amid the lingering light?' The spirit of such reveries, the tone and hues of such a landscape, Gray has caught, and enshrined forever in his verse."

Listen to the sweet, mournful music of some of the stanzas :—

> The curfew tolls the knell of parting day,
> The lowing herd winds slowly o'er the lea,
> The ploughman homeward plods his weary way,[1]
> And leaves the world to darkness and to me.
>
> Now fades the glimmering landscape on the sight,
> And all the air a solemn stillness holds,
> Save where the beetle wheels his droning flight,
> And drowsy tinklings lull the distant folds :
>
> Save that from yonder ivy-mantled tower,
> The moping owl does to the moon complain
> Of such as, wand'ring near her secret bower,
> Molest her ancient solitary reign.
>
>   *   *   *
>
> Beneath those rugged elms, that yew-tree's shade,
> Where heaves the turf in many a mould'ring heap,
> Each in his narrow cell forever laid,
> The rude forefathers of the hamlet sleep.
>
> The breezy call of incense-breathing morn,
> The swallow twitt'ring from the straw-built shed,

---

[1] This line admits of eighteen different transpositions, without destroying the sense or rhyme.

The cock's shrill clarion, or the echoing horn,
   No more shall rouse them from their lowly bed.

For them no more the blazing hearth shall burn,
   Or busy housewife ply her evening care:
No children run to lisp their sire's return,
   Or climb his knees the envied kiss to share.

*   *   *

Let not ambition mock their useful toil,
   Their homely joys, and destiny obscure;
Nor grandeur hear with a disdainful smile
   The short and simple annals of the poor.

The boast of heraldry, the pomp of power,
   And all that beauty, all that wealth e'er gave,
Await alike th' inevitable hour:
   The paths of glory lead but to the grave!

Nor you, ye proud, impute to these the fault
   If Memory o'er their tomb no trophies raise,
Where through the long-drawn aisle and fretted vault
   The pealing anthem swells the note of praise.

Can storied urn, or animated bust,
   Back to its mansion call the fleeting breath?
Can honour's voice provoke the silent dust,
   Or flatt'ry soothe the dull cold ear of death?

Perhaps in this neglected spot is laid
   Some heart once pregnant with celestial fire:
Hands, that the rod of empire might have swayed,
   Or waked to ecstasy the living lyre.

*   *   *

Full many a gem of purest ray serene,
   The dark, unfathomed caves of ocean bear;
Full many a flower is born to blush unseen,
   And waste its sweetness on the desert air.

       *   *   *

For who, to dumb forgetfulness a prey,
   This pleasing anxious being e'er resign'd,
Left the warm precincts of the cheerful day,
   Nor cast one longing, lingering look behind?

       *   *   *

On some fond breast the parting soul relies,
   Some pious drops the closing eye requires;
Ev'n from the tomb the voice of Nature cries,
   Even in our ashes live their wonted fires.

It is said that on the evening preceding the memorable battle of the Plains of Abraham, General Wolfe repeated the noble line, "The paths of glory lead but to the grave!" which must have seemed at such a time fraught with mournful meaning; and turning to his officers, said: "Now, gentlemen, I would rather be the author of that poem than take Quebec!"

There are two manuscripts of the *Elegy* in existence; and they were recently (in 1854) sold at auction—one for one hundred pounds, and the other—which contained five additional stanzas, never printed in the published editions—for one hundred and thirty pounds. The old tower of Upton church (Gray's "ivy-mantled tower") is still a most picturesque object, although fast falling into decay. The memory of the bard is, however, even more closely associated with another locality—that of Stoke. It was here he wrote, wandered, and died; and here, all that was mortal of him sleeps, under the yew-tree's shade.

Gray, with a friend, once attended an auction sale of books, where he saw an elegant book-case, filled with a choice collection of French classics, handsomely bound; the price being one hundred guineas. He had a great longing for this lot, but could not then afford to buy it. The conversation between the poet and his friend being overheard by the Duchess of Northumberland, who was acquainted with the latter, she took the opportunity of ascertaining who his friend was, and was told it was Gray, the poet. Upon their retiring, she bought the book-case, with its contents, and sent it to Gray's lodgings, with a note, importing that she " was ashamed of sending so small an acknowledgment for the infinite pleasure she had received in reading the *Elegy in a Country Churchyard*,—of all others her most favourite poem."

Gray was remarkably fearful of fire, and kept a ladder of ropes in his bed-room. On one occasion, some of his mischievous companions at Cambridge roused him at midnight with the cry of fire, saying the staircase was in flames. Up went the window, and the poet hastened down his rope-ladder as quickly as possible, but into a tub of cold water placed at the bottom to receive him. This practical joke extinguished his fear of fire, but he would not forgive the trick, and immediately changed his college.

That oft-quoted line, " Where ignorance is bliss, 'tis folly to be wise," we derive from Gray's *Ode to Eton College :*—

> Yet ah ! why should they know their fate,
> Since sorrow never comes too late,
>   And happiness too swiftly flies ?
> Thought would destroy their paradise
> No more : where ignorance is bliss,
>   'Tis folly to be wise.

Turning reluctantly, however, from this our favourite bard, let us carry with us, like a lingering strain of sweet and solemn music, the opening lines of his beautiful *Hymn to Adversity :*—

> Daughter of Jove, relentless power,
> Thou tamer of the human breast,

Whose iron scourge and tort'ring hour
  The bad affright, afflict the best !
Bound in thy adamantine chain,
The proud are taught to taste of pain,
And purple tyrants vainly groan
With pangs unfelt before, unpitied and alone.

When first thy sire to send on earth
  Virtue, his darling child, design'd,
To thee he gave the heavenly birth,
  And bade to form her infant mind.
Stern, rugged nurse ! thy rigid lore
With patience many a year she bore :
What sorrow was thou bad'st her know,
And from her own she learn'd to melt at others' woe.

       *   *   *

Here is a beautiful passage by AKENSIDE, written in the last year
of his life :—

                O ye dales
Of Tyne, and ye most ancient woodlands ; where,
Oft as the giant flood obliquely strides,
And his banks open and his lawns extend,
Stops short the pleasèd traveller to view,
Presiding o'er the scene, some rustic tower
Founded by Norman or by Saxon hands ;
O ye Northumbrian shades, which overlook
The rocky pavement and the mossy falls
Of solitary Wensbeck's limpid stream !
How gladly I recall your well-known seats,
Beloved of old, and that delightful time
When, all alone, for many a summer's day,
I wandered through your calm recesses, led
In silence by some powerful hand unseen.

Nor will I e'er forget you ; nor shall e'er
The graver tasks of manhood, or the advice
Of vulgar wisdom, move me to disclaim
Those studies which possessed me in the dawn

Of life, and fixed the colour of my mind
For every future year ; whence even now
From sleep I rescue the clear hours of morn,
And, while the world around lies overwhelmed
In idle darkness, am alive to thoughts
Of honourable fame, of truth divine
Or moral, and of minds to virtue won
By the sweet magic of harmonious verse.

There are some noble thoughts in the celebrated *Ode* by Sir
William Jones, the Orientalist.   Here are some of the lines :—

What constitutes a State ?
Not high-raised battlement or laboured mound,
Thick wall or moated gate ;

Not cities proud, with spires and turrets crowned ;
　　Not bays and broad-armed ports,
Where, laughing at the storm, rich navies ride ;
　　Not starr'd and spangled courts,
Where low-browed baseness wafts perfume to pride.

　　　　*　　　*　　　*

　　Men who their duties know,
But know their rights, and, knowing, dare maintain ;
　　Prevent the long-aimed blow,
And crush the tyrant, while they rend the chain :
　　These constitute a State.

Bishop BERKELEY's memorable lines, prophetic of planting the arts in the New World, are of enduring interest to us ; these are the closing stanzas :—

There shall be sung another golden age,
　　The rise of empire and of arts,
The good and great inspiring epic rage,
　　The wisest heads and noblest hearts.
Not such as Europe breeds in her decay ;
　　Such as she bred when fresh and young,
When heavenly flame did animate her clay,
　　By future poets shall be sung.
Westward the course of empire takes its way ;
　　The first four acts already past,
A fifth shall close the drama of the day ;
　　Time's noblest offspring is the last.

This poem was written when the author was residing at New-port, Rhode Island. To prove that the prophecy has been in great measure verified, we need but refer to the record of noble names in science, history, philosophy, and song, which adorn our American annals. Among the earlier American poets were BARLOW, TRUM-

BULL, FRENEAU, and ALLSTON, who was also a renowned painter. While residing in Europe, Allston enjoyed the friendship of Southey, Coleridge, and Lamb; as well as of Washington Irving, who expresses a reverence and affection for his pure and noble character, no less than for his genius. While referring to IRVING, we cannot refrain from adding to the world's applause our humble but grateful tribute of regard, as well for the memory of his beautiful character as for his imperishable productions. His name ought undoubtedly to be classed in the category of poets, since much of his charming prose is essentially poetry. He rarely wrote in verse; but there is a little waif of his extant, which he improvised at the instance of his friend Stuart Newton, to accompany his picture of an old philosopher reading from a folio to a young beauty asleep on a chair opposite. Here it is, quaint and characteristic :—

> Frostie age, frostie age! vain all thy learning;
> Drowsie page, drowsie page evermore turning.
>> Young head no lore will heed,
>>> Young heart's a reckless rover;
>> Young beautie, while you read—
>>> Sleeping, dreams of absent lover.

ALLSTON's principal poem is his *Sylphs of the Seasons*; but his lines on *Boyhood* are short and sweet :—

> Ah, then how sweetly closed those crowded days!
> The minutes parting one by one, like rays
>> That fade upon a summer's eve.
> But, oh! what charm, or magic numbers,
> Can give me back the gentle slumbers
>> Those weary, happy days did leave?
>> When by my bed I saw my mother kneel,
> And with her blessing took her nightly kiss;
> Whatever Time destroys, he cannot this—
>> E'en now that nameless kiss I feel.

His noble *Address to England*, which was first printed in Coleridge's *Sibylline Leaves*, 1810, commences with this stanza :—

> All hail, thou noble land! our fathers' native soil!
> Oh, stretch thy mighty hand, gigantic grown by toil,
>   O'er the vast Atlantic wave to our shore!
>   For thou with magic might
>   Canst reach to where the light
>   Of Phœbus travels bright
>   The world o'er.

*   *   *

The poem thus ends :—

> While the manners, while the arts, that mould a nation's soul,
> Still cling around our hearts,—between let ocean roll,
>   Our joint communion breaking with the sun :
>   Yet still from either beach
>   The voice of blood shall reach,
>   More audible than speech—
>   We are one!

DANA's principal poem, *The Buccaneer*, is considered a fine production: it is a tale of crime and remorse. The opening stanzas are finely descriptive :—

> The island lies nine leagues away; along its solitary shore,
> Of craggy rock and sandy bay, no sound but ocean's roar,
>   Save where the bold, wild sea-bird makes her home,
>   Her shrill cry coming through the sparkling foam.
> But when the light winds lie at rest, and on the glassy, heaving sea,
> The black duck, with her glossy breast, sits swinging silently,
>   How beautiful! no ripples break the reach,
>   And silvery waves go noiseless up the beach.

119

And inland rests the green, warm dell ; the brook comes tinkling
    down its side ;
From out the trees the Sabbath bell rings cheerful, far and wide,
    Mingling its sound with bleatings of the flocks,
    That feed about the vale among the rocks :
Nor holy bell, nor pastoral bleat, in former days within the vale ;
Flapped in the bay the pirate's sheet ; curses were on the gale ;
    Rich goods lay on the sand, and murdered men ;
    Pirate and wrecker kept their revels then.

*   *   *

Dana's *Little Beach-Bird* may be indicated as one of his happiest
efforts :—

    Thou little bird, thou dweller by the sea,
    Why takest thou its melancholy voice ?
And with that boding cry o'er the waves dost thou fly ?
O ! rather, bird, with me through the fair land rejoice !

    Thy flitting form comes ghostly dim and pale,
    As driven by a beating storm at sea ;
Thy cry is weak and scared, as if thy mates had shared
The doom of us : thy wail—what does it bring to me ?

*   *   *

PERCIVAL thus interprets to us *The Language of Flowers* :—

    In Eastern lands they talk in flowers,
    And they tell in a garland their loves and cares ;
    Each blossom that blooms in their garden bowers,
    On its leaves a mystic language bears.

    The Rose is a sign of joy and love—
    Young blushing love in its earliest dawn ;
    And the mildness that suits the gentle dove,
    From the Myrtle's snowy flower is drawn.

Innocence shines in the Lily's bell,
    Pure as the light in its native heaven ;
Fame's bright star and glory's swell,
    In the glossy leaf of the Bay are given.

The silent, soft, and humble heart,
    In the Violet's hidden sweetness breathes ;
And the tender soul that cannot part,
    A twine of Evergreen fondly wreathes.

The Cypress, that daily shades the grave,
    Is sorrow that mourns her bitter lot ;
And Faith, that a thousand ills can brave,
    Spea s in thy blue leaves, Forget-me-Not.
Then g. ther a wreath from the garden bowers,
And tell the wish of thy heart in flowers.

Here is the commencement of his fine poem, *The Coral Grove* :—

Deep in the wave is a coral grove,
Where the purple mullet and the gold-fish rove ;

Where the sea-flower spreads its leaves of blue,
That never are wet with falling dew,
But in bright and changeful beauty shine
Far down in the green and glassy brine.

The floor is of sand, like the mountain drift,
   And the pearl-shells spangle the flinty snow ;
From coral rocks the sea-plants lift
   Their boughs, where the tides and billows flow ;
The water is calm and still below,
   For the winds and waves are absent there,
And the sands are bright as the stars that glow
   In the motionless fields of the upper air.
There, with its waving blade of green,
   The sea-flag streams through the silent water,
And the crimson leaf of the dulse is seen
   To blush, like a banner bathed in slaughter.

       *   *   *

MRS. SIGOURNEY'S productions, mostly didactic, have long enjoyed a deserved popularity.   Her lines, *To an early Blue-Bird*, form a pleasing picture :—

Blue-bird ! on yon leafless tree,
Dost thou carol thus to me,
" Spring is coming—Spring is here ?"
Say'st thou so, my birdie dear ?
What is that in misty shroud
Stealing from the darkened cloud ?
Lo, the snow-flake's gathering mound
Settles o'er the whitened ground,
Yet thou singest blithe and clear,
" Spring is coming—Spring is here !"
Strik'st thou not too bold a strain ?
Winds are piping o'er the plain,

Clouds are sweeping o'er the sky,
With a black and threatening eye;
Urchins, by the frozen rill,
Wrap their mantles closer still;
Yon poor man, with doublet old,
Doth he shiver at the cold?
Hath he not a nose of blue?
Tell me, birdling, tell me true.

There are some beautiful and pathetic lines by PIERPONT, entitled *Passing Away*, commencing:—

Was it the chime of a tiny bell,
    That came so sweet to my dreaming ear,
Like the silvery tones of a fairy's shell
    That he winds on the beach so mellow and clear,
When the winds and the waves lie together asleep,
And the moon and the fairy are watching the deep,
    She dispensing her silvery light,
    And he his notes, as silvery quite,
While the boatman listens and ships his oar,
To catch the music that comes from the shore?—
    Hark! the notes, on my ear that play,
    Are set to words: as they float, they say,
        "Passing away! passing away!"
                *   *   *

His lines on the loss of his Child are full of natural pathos:—

I cannot make him dead! His fair, sunshiny head
    Is ever bounding round my study chair:
Yet, when my eyes grow dim with tears, I turn to him,
    The vision vanishes—he is not there!
I walk my parlour floor, and, through the open door,
    I hear a foot-fall on my chamber stair;

I'm stepping toward the hall to give the boy a call;
　　And then bethink me that—he is not there!
I thread the crowded street; a satchelled lad I meet,
　　With the same beaming eyes and coloured hair:
And, as he's running by, follow him with my eye,
　　Scarcely believing that—he is not there!

*　　　*　　　*

I cannot make him dead! When passing by the bed,
　　So long watched over with parental care,
My spirit and my eye seek him inquiringly,
　　Before the thought comes that—he is not there!

*　　　*　　　*

DRAKE has enriched American literature by a remarkable poem, *The Culprit Fay;* which discovers exquisite fancy and rare poetic beauty. The scene is laid in the Highlands of the Hudson, and the subject is a fairy story, decked with all the dainty accessories of Fairyland and forest scenery. The origin of the poem is traced to a conversation with Cooper, the novelist, and Halleck, the poet, who, speaking of the Scottish streams and their romantic associations, insisted that our own rivers were unsusceptible of the like poetic uses. Drake thought otherwise, and, to make his position good, produced, in three days after, this exquisite fairy tale. The opening passage of the poem is a description of moonlight on the Highlands of the Hudson:—

'Tis the middle watch of a summer's night—
The earth is dark, but the heavens are bright:
Naught is seen in the vault on high
But the moon, and the stars, and the cloudless sky,
And the flood which rolls its milky hue,
A river of light on the welkin blue.
The moon looks down on old Crónest,
She mellows the shades on his shaggy breast,

And seems his huge gray form to throw
In a silver cone on the wave below:
His sides are broken by spots of shade,
By the walnut-bough and the cedar made:
And through their clustering branches dark,
Glimmers and dies the fire-fly's spark,—
Like starry twinkles that momently break
Through the rifts of the gathering tempest's rack!

The stars are on the moving stream,
   And fling, as its ripples gently flow,
A burnished length of wavy beam
   In an eel-like, spiral line below;
The winds are whist, and the owl is still,
   The bat in the shelvy rock is hid,
And naught is heard on the lonely hill
But the cricket's chirp, and the answer shrill
   Of the gauze-winged katy-did;
And the plaint of the wailing whip-poor-will,
   Who moans unseen, and ceaseless sings
Ever a note of wail and woe,
   Till morning spreads her rosy wings,
And earth and sky in her glances glow.
       *   *   *

Here we have introduced to us the *Fairy culprit*:—

Wrapt in musing stands the sprite:
'Tis the middle wane of night.
       *   *   *
He cast a saddened look around,
   But he felt new joy his bosom swell,
When, glittering on the shadowed ground,
   He saw a purple muscle-shell;

Thither he ran, and he bent him low,
He heaved at the stern and he heaved at the bow,
And he pushed her over the yielding sand,
Till he came to the verge of the haunted land.
　　She was as lovely a pleasure-boat
　　　As ever fairy had paddled in,
　　For she glowed with purple paint without,
　　　And shone with silvery pearl within;
　　A sculler's notch in the stern he made,
　　An oar he shaped of the bootle-blade;
　　Then sprung to his seat with a lightsome leap,
　　And launched afar, on the calm, blue deep!
　　　　　*　　　*　　　*

No American can forget that to Drake we are indebted for our
National Ode, which commences,—

　　　When Freedom, from her mountain height,
　　　　Unfurled her standard to the air,
　　　She tore the azure robe of night,
　　　　And set the stars of glory there!

She mingled with its gorgeous dyes
The milky baldric of the skies,
And striped its pure, celestial white
With streakings of the morning light;
Then, from his mansion in the sun,
She called her eagle bearer down,
And gave into his mighty hand
The symbol of her chosen land.

Another of our American bards, SPRAGUE, has given us the following sweet bird-song: suggested by seeing two swallows flying into a church in Boston :—

Gay, guiltless pair, what seek ye from the fields of heaven?
Ye have no need of prayer, ye have no sins to be forgiven.
Why perch ye here, where mortals to their Maker bend?
Can your pure spirits fear the God ye never could offend?
Ye never knew the crimes for which we come to weep.
Penance is not for you, bless'd wanderers of the upper deep.
To you 'tis given to wake sweet nature's untaught lays;
Beneath the arch of heaven to chirp away a life of praise.

*   *   *

The poem by which this author is most known, entitled *Curiosity*, has a singular history. Griswold states that it was published in Calcutta a few years ago as an original production by a British officer, with no other alterations than the omission of a few American names, and the insertion of others in their places; and in this form it was reprinted in London, where it was much praised.

Now listen to the following song :—

Day, in melting purple dying,
Blossoms, all around me, sighing,
Fragrance, from the lilies straying,
Zephyr, with my ringlets playing,
   Ye but waken my distress;
   I am sick of loneliness.

127

*   *   *

Save thy toiling, spare thy treasure,
All I ask is friendship's pleasure;
Let the shining ore lie darkling,
Bring no gems in lustre sparkling:
    Gifts and gold are naught to me,
    I would only look on thee!

Tell to thee the high-wrought feeling,
Ecstasy but in revealing:
Paint to thee the deep sensation,
Rapture in participation,—
    Yet but torture, if comprest
    In a lone, unfriended breast.

*   *   *

These glowing stanzas, from MRS. BROOKS's *Zophiel*,—an exquisite story of a Jewish exiled maiden and her lovers,—exhibit the style of the authoress, whom Southey designated, in *The Doctor*, as "the most impassioned and imaginative of poetesses."

Turn we for a moment to a sweet, familiar ditty—known to all lovers of lyric verse,—'tis about the little sanctuary of *Home*:—

'Mid pleasures and palaces though we may roam,
Be it ever so humble, there's no place like home:
A charm from the skies seems to hallow it there,
Which, go through the world, you'll not meet elsewhere.
    Home, home, sweet home!
    There's no place like home!

*   *   *

Every person knows that sweet household lyric; but it is not every one who has heard the life-story of its author. That immortal song, so brim-full of tender pathos and natural feeling, would cause many to drop a tear of sympathy over the sad fate of its author, HOWARD PAYNE, were they to be told that,—an American adventurer in the heart of Paris, Vienna, and London, while hearing

128

'Mid pleasures & palaces, though we may roam
Be it ever so humble, there's no place like Home!
A charm from the sky seems to hallow us there
Which, seek through the world is ne'er met with elsewhere!

    Home, home! sweet, sweet Home!
     There's no place like Home!
     There's no place like Home!

An exile from Home, splendour dazzles in vain! —
Oh, give me my lowly thatch'd cottage again! —
— The birds singing gaily, that came at my call —
Give me them! — and the peace of mind dearer than all!

          John Howard Payne.

persons singing his own beautiful lines on the pleasures of home,—
he was not only denied the possession of one himself, but was even
destitute of the necessaries of life.

The following beautiful little lyric is from the pen of GENERAL
BURGOYNE, of our Revolutionary annals :—

> When first this humble roof I knew,
>   With various care I strove ;
> My grain was scarce, my sheep were few,
>   My all of life was love.
>
> By mutual toil our board was dressed,
>   The spring our drink bestowed ;
> But when her lip the brim had pressed,
>   The cup with nectar flowed !
>
> Content and peace the dwelling shared,
>   No other guest came nigh ;
> In them was given, though gold was sparer,
>   What gold could never buy.
>
> No value has a splendid lot,
>   But as the means to prove,
> That from the castle to the cot,
>   The all of life is—love.

Here is DARWIN's sweet *Song to May :*—

> Born in yon blaze of orient sky,
>   Sweet May ! thy radiant form unfold ;
> Unclose thy blue voluptuous eye,
>   And wave thy shadowy locks of gold.
>
> For thee the fragrant zephyrs blow,
>   For thee descends the sunny shower ;
> The rills in softer murmurs flow,
>   And brighter blossoms gem the bower.

Light graces decked in flowery wreaths,
   And tiptoe joys their hand combine,
And Love his sweet contagion breathes,
   And, laughing, dances round thy shrine.

Warm with new life, the glittering throng,
   On quivering fin and rustling wing,
Delighted join their votive song,
   And hail thee Goddess of the Spring!

This charming American song, the *Old Oaken Bucket*, is by
WOODWORTH :—

How dear to this heart are the scenes of my childhood,
   When fond recollection presents them to view ;

The orchard, the meadow, the deep-tangled wild-wood,
  And every loved spot which my infancy knew:
The wide-spreading pond, and the mill which stood by it,
  The bridge and the rock where the cataract fell;
The cot of my father, the dairy-house nigh it,
  And e'en the rude bucket which hung in the well.
    The old oaken bucket, the iron-bound bucket,
    The moss-covered bucket which hung in the well.

That moss-covered vessel I hailed as a treasure;
  For often, at noon, when returned from the field,
I found it the source of an exquisite pleasure—
  The purest and sweetest that nature can yield.
How ardent I seized it, with hands that were glowing,
  And quick to the white-pebbled bottom it fell;
Then soon, with the emblem of truth overflowing,
  And dripping with coolness, it rose from the well,—
    The old oaken bucket, the iron-bound bucket,
    The moss-covered bucket arose from the well.

*   *   *

Reverting again in imagination to one of the " nooks and corners"
of Old England, yclept the " Grecian Coffee-House," let us endeavour to recall from the buried past, that once famous rendezvous
of the wits, poets, and playwrights. It was here that a somewhat
portly personage, of ungainly gait, but of good-tempered face, was
wont to meet with his cosy companions, and while away many an
hour consecrated to poetry, politics, and potations. We refer to
" poor Goldy," as he was familiarly called; and a more generous-
hearted, gifted man,—one so studious of the happiness of others,
and as strangely indifferent to his own,—it would not be easy to
instance. His eccentricities of character have imparted to his history a romantic interest, rarely found in the record of a scholar's
life. A restless love of adventure, combined with an incorrigible

imprudence, perpetually involved him in difficulties; so that while the powers of his genius provoked the admiration of the world, his ludicrous inconsistencies of conduct no less excited its ridicule. Our smiles and tears are alike provoked by his mad exploits, his College career, his flight to Cork, his utter destitution, and also his unconquerable passion for roaming over Europe on foot,—beguiling his troubles and replenishing his purse, meanwhile, by means of his flute: or, as we follow him to his infelicitous, though brief, apprenticeship to "the poor chemist,"—from which condition his good friend and patron, Johnson, not only released him, but introduced him to the world of letters. Speaking of GOLDSMITH, Johnson remarked, that "no man was more foolish than he was when he had not a pen in his hand, or none more wise when he had." The Doctor was, indeed, a true friend to the author of *The Vicar of Wakefield*, in a time of especial need,—that critical dilemma with his landlady.

GOLDSMITH was a hard worker with his brain. He considered four lines a day, good work. Occasionally he read much at night, in bed; and when he wished to extinguish his candle, it is said he used to throw his slipper at it,—for, like Thomson and others, he was afflicted with a very indolent body. He was greatly astonished when Dodsley, his publisher, offered five shillings a couplet for his *Deserted Village*, when each line was fairly worth as many pounds; for it took him seven years in beating out its pure gold. Of all his poems, this bears the palm for finished excellence; and our interest in it is not lessened by knowing that it describes scenes in which he was, in early life, himself an actor. Auburn, the poetical name for the village of Lissoy, is situated in the county of Westmeath; the name of the schoolmaster was Paddy Burns, "a man severe to view;" and the ale-house, with its large spreading hawthorn bush, has also been identified,—where

> Imagination fondly stoops to trace
> The parlour splendours of that festive place.

OLIVER GOLDSMITH.

The church which tops the neighbouring hill, the mill, and the
brook, all remain the same as when his brother was the officiating
clergyman.   Mark how gracefully the poem opens :—

> Sweet Auburn ! loveliest village of the plain,
> Where health and plenty cheer'd the labouring swain
> Where smiling Spring its earliest visit paid,
> And parting Summer's lingering blooms delayed ;
> Dear lovely bowers of innocence and ease,
> Seats of my youth, when every sport could please ;
> How often have I loitered o'er thy green,
> Where humble happiness endeared each scene !
> How often have I paused on every charm,
> The sheltered cot, the cultivated farm,
> The never-failing brook, the busy mill,
> The decent church that topped the neighbouring hill,
> The hawthorn bush, with seats beneath the shade,
> For talking age, and whispering lovers made !
> How often have I blest the coming day,
> When toil remitting lent its turn to play,
> And all the village train, from labour free,
> Led up their sports beneath the spreading tree ;
> While many a pastime circled in the shade,
> The young contending as the old survey'd ;
> And many a gambol frolick'd o'er the ground,
> And sleights of art and feats of strength went round ;
> And still, as each repeated pleasure tired,
> Succeeding sports the mirthful band inspired ;
> The dancing pair that simply sought renown,
> By holding out, to tire each other down ;
> The swain, mistrustless of his smutted face,
> While secret laughter tittered round the place ;
> The bashful virgin's sidelong looks of love,
> The matron's glance, that would those looks reprove ;

These were thy charms, sweet village! sports like these,
With sweet succession, taught e'en toil to please;
These round thy bowers their cheerful influence shed,
These were thy charms,—but all those charms are fled.

Now let us con over his tribute to Retirement :—

O blest Retirement! friend to life's decline,
Retreats from care, that never must be mine,
How blest is he who crowns, in shades like these,
A youth of labour with an age of ease:

Who quits a world where strong temptations try,
And, since 'tis hard to combat, learns to fly !
For him no wretches, born to work and weep,
Explore the mine, or tempt the dangerous deep ;
No surly porter stands in guilty state,
To spurn imploring famine from the gate :
But on he moves to meet his latter end,
Angels around befriending virtue's friend ;
Sinks to the grave with unperceived decay,
While resignation gently slopes the way :
And, all his prospects brightening to the last,
His heaven commences ere the world be past.

      *   *   *

He thus picturesquely portrays the clergyman of the village :—

Thus to relieve the wretched was his pride,
And e'en his failings leaned to virtue's side ;
But in his duty prompt at every call,
He watched and wept, he prayed and felt for all :
And, as a bird each fond endearment tries,
To tempt its new-fledged offspring to the skies,
He tried each art, reproved each dull delay,
Allured to brighter worlds, and led the way.

      *   *   *

E'en children followed, with endearing wile,
And plucked his gown, to share the good man's smile
His ready smile a parent's warmth expressed,
Their welfare pleased him, and their cares distrest.
To them his heart, his love, his griefs, were given,
But all his serious thoughts had rest in heaven.
As some tall cliff that lifts its awful form,
Swells from the vale, and midway leaves the storm,

Though round its breast the rolling clouds are spread,
Eternal sunshine settles on its head.

What a grand simile is that contained in the closing lines!

His *Traveller* opens with this beautiful tribute to Home :—

Remote, unfriended, melancholy, slow,
Or by the lazy Scheld, or wandering Po ;
Or onward, where the rude Carinthian boor
Against the houseless stranger shuts the door :
Or where Campania's plain forsaken lies,
A weary waste expanding to the skies ;
Where'er I roam, whatever realms to see,
My heart, untravelled, fondly turns to thee :
Still to my brother turns, with ceaseless pain,
And drags at each remove a lengthening chain.

Eternal blessings crown my earliest friend,
And round his dwelling guardian saints attend.
Blest be that spot, where cheerful guests retire
To pause from toil, and trim their evening fire ;
Blest that abode, where want and pain repair,
And every stranger finds a ready chair ;
Blest be those feasts, with simple plenty crown'd,
Where all the ruddy family around
Laugh at the jests or pranks that never fail,
Or sigh with pity at some mournful tale ;
Or press the bashful stranger to his food,
And learn the luxury of doing good.

Gray, who, when dying, had the *Deserted Village* read to him,
exclaimed, "That man *is* a poet." Among the peculiarities of
Goldsmith was his thirst for notoriety : wherever he went, he was
desirous of being the object of attention. On a summer's excursion to the Continent, he accompanied a lady and her two beautiful

daughters, and often expressed a little displeasure at perceiving that more attention was paid to them than to himself. On their entering the town of Antwerp, the populace surrounded the door of the hotel at which they alighted, and expressed a desire to welcome the ladies in a demonstrative manner; and on their appearing at the balcony to acknowledge the compliment, the poet went with them. He soon discovered, however, that it was at the shrine of beauty the people did homage.

The characteristic excellence of Goldsmith's poetry is its truthfulness to nature, and it is this all-pervading charm that has embalmed his memory in the common heart. "The new spirit which had penetrated all departments of human thought and action, and which was evoked with the opening of the present century, told more immediately on poetry than on any other kind of literature, and recast it into manifold and more original forms. The breadth and volume of that poetic outburst can only be fully estimated by looking back to the narrow and artificial channels in which English poetry, since the days of Milton, had flowed. In the hands of Dryden and Pope, that which was a natural, free-wandering river, became a straight-cut, uniform canal. Or, without figure, poetry was withdrawn from country life, and made to live exclusively in town and affect the fashion. Forced to appear in courtly costume, it dealt with the artificial manners and outside aspects of men, and lost sight of the one human heart, which is the proper haunt and main region of song."[1]

Pass we now from the poet of nature to the poet of the affections, Cowper,—the poet who "has brought the muse, in her most attractive form, to sit down by our hearths, and has breathed a sanctity over the daily economy of our existence." He not only restored natural emotion and the language of life to song; but his poetry "influences the feelings as a summer-day affects the body— and the reader has a sense of enjoyment, calm, pure, and lasting:

---

[1] North British Review.

the tasteful read him for his grace, the serious for his religion."
Physically feeble and sensitive, he never engaged in the active pur-
suits of life, but early devoted himself to his muse.   Although constitutionally predisposed to melancholy, he yet possessed a vivid
perception of the ludicrous, as his inimitable *John Gilpin* sufficiently
attests.   Not merely a humorist, he was eminently a master
of pathos; witness his exquisite lines to his *Mother's Portrait*,—
lines so familiar to us all, but so choice as to extort from Southey
the confession that he would willingly barter all he had written—
and that was not little, as the world knows—for its authorship.
" I would forgive a man for not reading Milton," once said Charles
Lamb, " but I would not call that man my friend who should be
offended with the divine chit-chat of Cowper."

What grace and harmony are combined in the following passage
from *The Task*, descriptive of the scenery of the River Ouse :—

> Nor rural sights alone, but rural sounds,
> Exhilarate the spirit, and restore
> The tone of languid nature.   Mighty winds,
> That sweep the skirt of some far-spreading wood
> Of ancient growth, make music, not unlike
> The dash of ocean on his winding shore,
> And lull the spirit while they fill the mind ;—
> Unnumbered branches waving in the blast,
> And all their leaves fast fluttering all at once.
> Nor less composure waits upon the roar
> Of distant floods, or on the softer voice
> Of neighbouring fountain, or of rills that slip
> Through the cleft rock, and chiming as they fall
> Upon loose pebbles, lose themselves at length
> In matted grass, that with a livelier green
> Betrays the secret of their silent course.
> Nature inanimate displays sweet sounds,
> But animated nature sweeter still.

To soothe and satisfy the human ear.
Ten thousand warblers cheer the day, and one
The livelong night : nor these alone whose notes
Nice-fingered art must emulate in vain,
But cawing rooks, and kites that swim sublime
In still-repeated circles, screaming loud,
The jay, the pie, and even the boding owl,
That hails the rising moon, have charms for me.
Sounds inharmonious in themselves and harsh,
Yet heard in scenes where peace forever reigns,
And, only there, please highly for their sake.

       *   *   *

O Winter! ruler of the inverted year,
Thy scattered hair with sleet like ashes filled,
Thy breath congealed upon thy lips, thy cheeks
Fringed with a beard made white with other snows
Than those of age, thy forehead wrapped in clouds,
A leafless branch thy sceptre, and thy throne

A sliding car, indebted to no wheels,
But urged by storms along its slippery way,
I love thee, all unlovely as thou seem'st,
And dreaded as thou art!

Cowper's poetry is replete with sententious gems of thought:
such as the following :—

Knowledge is proud that he has learned so much;
Wisdom is humble that he knows no more.
*   *   *
The path of sorrow, and that path alone,
Leads to the land where sorrow is unknown.
*   *   *
A soul without reflection, like a pile
Without inhabitants, to ruin runs!
*   *   *
'Tis pleasant, through the loop-holes of Retreat,
    To peep at such a world:
To see the stir of the great Babel, and not feel the crowd:
To hear the roar she sends through all her gates,
At a safe distance, where the dying sound
Falls a soft murmur on th' uninjured ear.

That favourite poem, *The Sofa*, owes its existence to Lady Aus-
ten's suggestion, as she and the poet were conversing together on
the sofa. It presents a variety both of subject and style, without
the violation of order and harmony, while it breathes a spirit of the
purest and most exalted morality. Campbell says, It glides like a
river, which, rising from a playful little fountain, gathers beauty and
magnitude as it proceeds.

While the sweet melodies of Cowper were filling English hearts
and homes with music, a rustic peasant in the North was tuning his
reed to *A Mountain Daisy*, or singing his love-plaints to some fairy-
footed nymph beside a Scottish stream. The minstrelsy of BURNS

has stirred the hearts of all classes and degrees among men; but especially for the sons of Scotia has he enshrined in his verse the sentiments, tastes, and feelings, as well as the old heroic traditions of her glory, in strains " so simple, yet so sublime, that the world stood still to listen." That such a gifted one should have arisen from the ploughshare to become a great national poet, may well provoke astonishment; but that his personal career should have proved so inauspicious, no less stirs our sympathy and regret. A strange and significant contrast is exhibited between the lowly birthplace of Burns and his costly mausoleum.[1]

Scott, when young, met Burns; and he tells us the poet's eye, " which indicated the poetic temperament and character, was large, and of a dark cast; it glowed—I say, literally glowed—when he spoke with feeling or interest: I never saw such another eye in a human head, though I have seen the most distinguished men of my time." A brother poet thus tenders a loving tribute :—

> " The simple bard, unbroke by rules of art,
> He pours the wild effusions of his heart;
> And if inspired,—'tis Nature's powers inspire,—
> Hers all the melting thrill, and hers the kindling fire !"

True, " thoughtless follies laid him low, and stained his name ;" but here draw the mantle of charity, and let pity drop the tributary tear over his sorrows and sufferings; for he was bereft of sympathy and succour when most he needed their aid. Need we then wonder that he sang thus plaintively :—

> Pleasures are, like poppies, spread—
> You seize the flower, its bloom is fled :
> Or, like the snow-falls on the river,
> A moment white, then melts forever :

---

[1] It is in the form of a Grecian temple : in the basement story are placed the hut of the poet, and the Bible he gave to his Highland Mary, fastened to one of the covers of which is a lock of her golden hair.

141

Or like the borealis race,
That flit ere you can point their place :
Or like the rainbow's lovely form,
Evanishing amid the storm.

What a beautiful homily on that queenliest of graces, Charity, does he here offer us :—

Then gently scan your brother man ; still gentler, sister woman ;
Though they may gang a kennin wrang, to step aside is human.
One point must still be greatly dark, the moving why they do it ;
But just as tamely can we mark how far, perhaps, they rue it.

Wha made the heart, 'tis He alone decidedly can try us ;
He knows each chord, its various tone ; each spring, its various bias.
Then at the balance let's be mute, we never can adjust it ;
What's done, we partly may compute, but know not what's resisted.

Burns was little more than sixteen when he wrote some of his most remarkable effusions ; and the brief limit of thirty-seven years made up the poet's short span of life—a life so prolific of pleasure to the world ; so checkered and unpropitious to himself.

"Of his humorous pieces, the *Tam o' Shanter* is his best ; though there are traits of infinite merit in *Scotch Drink*, the *Holy Fair*, the *Hallow E'en*, and several of the songs ; in all of which, it is very remarkable that he rises occasionally into a strain of beautiful description or lofty sentiment, far above the pitch of his original conception. The poems of observation on life and characters are the *Twa Dogs*, and the various epistles—all of which show very extraordinary sagacity and powers of expression."[1] The exquisite description of *The Cotter's Saturday Night* affords, perhaps, the finest example of pathos and humour combined. Independent of its admirable fidelity to details of Scottish peasant-life of his day, Burns has cast

---

[1] Edinburgh Review.

over the poem a feeling of such gushing tenderness and peaceful sunshine, that, in spite of the occasional obscurity of its language, it is impossible for any one to read it unmoved :—

> November chill blaws loud wi' angry sugh ;
> The short'ning winter-day is near a close ;
> The miry beasts retreating frae the pleugh ;
> The black'ning trains o' craws to their repose.

> The toil-worn cotter frae his labour goes,
> This night his weekly moil is at an end,
> Collects his spades, his mattocks, and his hoes,
> Hoping the morn in ease and rest to spend,
> And weary, o'er the moor, his course does hameward bend.

At length his lonely cot appears in view,
   Beneath the shelter of an aged tree ;
Th' expectant wee-things, toddlin', stacher through
   To meet their dad, wi' flichterin' noise an' glee.
His wee bit ingle, blinkin' bonnily,
   His clean hearth-stane, his thriftie wifie's smile,
The lisping infant prattling on his knee,
   Does a' his weary kiaugh and care beguile,
An' maks him quite forget his labour an' his toil.

        *   *   *

With joy unfeigned, brothers and sisters meet,
   An' each for other's welfare kindly spiers ;
The social hours, swift-winged, unnoticed fleet,
   Each tells the unco's that he sees or hears ;
The parents, partial, eye their hopeful years ;
   Anticipation forward points the view.
The mother, wi' her needle an' her shears,
   Gars auld claes look amaist as weel's the new ;
The father mixes a' wi' admonition due.

        *   *   *

Observe how delicately he approaches the dainty little Daisy :—

Wee, modest, crimson-tippèd flower,
Thou'st met me in an evil hour,
For I maun crush amang the stoure
    Thy slender stem ;
To spare thee now is past my power,
    Thou bonnie gem.

Alas ! it's no thy neebor sweet,
The bonnie lark, companion meet !
Bending thee 'mang the dewy weet,
    Wi' spreckled breast,
When upward-springing, blithe, to greet
    The purpling east.

Cauld blew the bitter-biting north
Upon thy early, humble birth;
Yet cheerfully thou glinted forth
    Amid the storm,
Scarce reared above the parent earth
    Thy tender form.

The flaunting flowers our gardens yield,
High sheltering woods and wa's maun shield;
But thou, beneath the random bield
    O' clod or stane,
Adorns the histie stibble-field,
    Unseen, alane.
      *   *   *

Scott was so charmed with Burns's song, *Ae fond kiss, and then we sever*, that he said on one occasion, it was worth a thousand romances. Here are the first and last stanzas :—

Ae fond kiss—and then we sever!
Ae farewell—alas, forever!
Deep in heart-wrung tears I'll pledge thee;
Warring sighs and groans I'll wage thee.
      *   *   *
Had we never loved sae kindly,
Had we never loved sae blindly,
Never met—or never parted,
We had ne'er been broken-hearted.

Burns's beautiful lines addressed to *Mary in Heaven*, were composed under the following circumstances :—" My Highland lassie," he writes, " was a warm-hearted, charming young creature as ever blessed a man with generous love. After a pretty long trial of the most ardent reciprocal attachment, we met by appointment, on the second Sunday of May, in a sequestered spot by the banks of Ayr, where we spent the day in taking a farewell, before she should

embark for the West Highlands to arrange matters among her
friends for our projected change of life. At the close of Autumn
following, she crossed the sea to meet me at Greenock; where she
had scarce landed when she was seized with a malignant fever,
which hurried my dear girl to the grave in a few days! before I
could even hear of her illness." We learn from four of his biog-
raphers, that this adieu was performed with all those simple and
striking ceremonials which rustic sentiment has devised to prolong
tender emotions and to inspire awe. The lovers stood on each
side of a small purling brook—they laved their hands in its limpid
stream, and, holding a Bible between them, pronounced their vows
to be faithful to each other. They parted—never to meet again!
The anniversary of Mary Campbell's death (for that was her name)
awakening in the sensitive mind of Burns the most lively emotion,
he retired from his family, then residing on the farm of Ellisland,
and wandered, solitary, on the banks of the Nith, and about the
farm-yard, in the extremest agitation of mind, nearly the whole of
the night. His excitement was so great, that he threw himself on
the side of a corn-stack, and there conceived his sublime and tender
Elegy; which, although so well known, we shall, nevertheless,
present :—

> Thou ling'ring star, with less'ning ray,
>   That lov'st to greet the early morn,
> Again thou usherest in the day
>   My Mary from my soul was torn.
> O Mary! dear departed shade!
>   Where is thy place of blissful rest?
> Seest thou thy lover lowly laid?
>   Hear'st thou the groans that rend his breast?
>
> That sacred hour can I forget,
>   Can I forget the hallowed grove,
> Where by the winding Ayr we met,
>   To live one day of parting love?

146

ROBERT BURNS.

Eternity cannot efface
   Those records dear of transports past ;
Thy image at our last embrace ;
   Ah ! little thought we 'twas our last !

Ayr, gurgling, kiss'd his pebbled shore,
   O'erhung with wild woods, thick'ning, green ;
The fragrant birch, and hawthorn hoar,
   Twined amorous round the raptured scene ;
The flowers sprang wanton to be prest,
   The birds sang love on every spray,
Till too, too soon, the glowing west
   Proclaim'd the speed of wingèd day.

Still o'er these scenes my memory wakes,
   And fondly broods with miser care !
Time but the impression deeper makes,
   As streams their channels deeper wear.
My Mary ! dear departed shade !
   Where is thy place of blissful rest ?
Seest thou thy lover lowly laid ?
   Hear'st thou the groans that rend his breast ?

The muse of the poet-lover of the Highland Mary owed much of its inspiration to the sex. He tells us that when he desired to feel the pure spirit of poetry, and obey successfully its impulse, he put himself on a regimen of admiring a fine woman. Burns was possessed of deep emotions and delicate sensibilities, and he was easily subdued by the sweetest of human influences. " My heart," he says in one of his letters, " was complete tinder, and eternally lighted up by some goddess or other."

During the three years he spent at Ellisland, Burns was so deeply engaged in the labours of his farm, and those connected with his appointment in the Excise, that he had little of either time or inclination for the cultivation of his poetical gift. Yet, even in this

busy time, he contrived to celebrate the charms of one or two local
divinities. One of these was Miss Jeffrey, daughter of the minister
of Lochmaben. Spending an evening at the manse, he was greatly
pleased with this young lady, who did the honours of the table; and
he next morning presented at breakfast the lines which have made
her immortal :—

I gaed a waefu' gate yestreen, a gate, I fear, I'll dearly rue ;
I gat my death frae twa sweet een, twa lovely een o' bonnie blue.
'Twas not her golden ringlets bright, her lips like roses wat wi' dew,
Her heaving bosom, lily white—it was her een sae bonnie blue.

She talked, she smiled, my heart she wiled, she charmed my soul, I
    wist nae how ;
And aye the stound, the deadly wound, cam frae her een sae bonnie
    blue.
       *   *   *

GEORGE DARLEY wrote this *Song of the Summer Winds* :—

Up the dale and down the bourne, o'er the meadow swift we fly ;
Now we sing, and now we mourn, now we whistle, now we sigh.
By the grassy-fringèd river, through the murmuring reeds we sweep;
Mid the lily-leaves we quiver, to their very hearts we creep.

Now the maiden rose is blushing at the frolic things we say,
While aside her cheek we're rushing, like some truant bees at play.
Through the blooming groves we rustle, kissing every bud we pass,
As we did it in the bustle, scarcely knowing how it was.

Down the glen, across the mountain, o'er the yellow heath we roam,
Whirling round about the fountain, till its little breakers foam.
Bending down the weeping willows, while our vesper hymn we sigh ;
Then unto our rosy pillows, on our weary wings we hie.
There of idlenesses dreaming, scarce from waking we refrain,
Moments long as ages deeming, till we're at our play again.

From the same author we have this charming lyric :—

Down the dimpled greensward dancing bursts a flaxen-headed bevy,
Bud-lipt boys and girls advancing, Love's irregular little levy.

Rows of liquid eyes in laughter, how they glimmer, how they quiver!
Sparkling one another after, like bright ripples on a river.
Tipsy band of rubious faces, flushed with Joy's ethereal spirit,
Make your mocks and sly grimaces at Love's self, and do not
      fear it

The following fine songs are from SHERIDAN's play of *The Duenna* :—

Oh, had my love ne'er smiled on me,
   I ne'er had known such anguish ;
But think how false, how cruel she,
   To bid me cease to languish :
To bid me hope her hand to gain,
   Breathe on a flame half perish'd ;
And then, with cold and fixed disdain,
   To kill the hope she cherish'd.

Not worse his fate, who on a wreck,
   That drove as winds did blow it,
Silent had left the shatter'd deck,
   To find a grave below it.
Then land was cried—no more resign'd,
   He glow'd with joy to hear it ;
Not worse his fate, his woe, to find
   The wreck must sink ere near it !

———

Soft pity never leaves the gentle breast
Where love has been received a welcome guest ;
As wandering saints poor huts have sacred made,
He hallows every heart he once has swayed ;
And when his presence we no longer share,
Still leaves compassion as a relic there.

LOGAN's " magical stanzas of picture, melody, and sentiment," which Burke so much admired, addressed to the *Cuckoo*, are now before us :—

Hail, beauteous stranger of the grove ! thou messenger of Spring !
Now heaven repairs thy rural seat, and woods thy welcome sing.
What time the daisy decks the green, thy certain voice we hear ;
Hast thou a star to guide thy path, or mark the rolling year ?

Delightful visitant! with thee I hail the time of flowers,
And hear the sound of music sweet from birds among the bowers.
The schoolboy wandering through the wood, to pull the primrose gay,
Starts, the new voice of Spring to hear, and imitates thy lay.

What time the pea puts on the bloom, thou fliest thy vocal vale,
An annual guest in other lands, another Spring to hail.
Sweet bird! thy bower is ever green, thy sky is ever clear;
Thou hast no sorrow in thy song, no winter in thy year!

Oh, could I fly, I'd fly with thee! we'd make, with joyful wing,
Our annual visit o'er the globe,—companions of the Spring.

LEYDEN's celebrated *Ode to an Indian Gold Coin*, has attracted
the especial notice and commendation of Colton and other critics.
This remarkable poem was written in Cherical, Malabar; the author having left his native land, Scotland, in quest of a fortune in
India. He died shortly afterwards in Java :—

Slave of the dark and dirty mine!
    What vanity has brought thee here?
How can I love to see thee shine
    So bright, whom I have bought so dear?
    The tent-ropes flapping lone I hear
For twilight converse, arm in arm;
    The jackal's shriek bursts on mine ear
When mirth and music wont to cheer.

By Chérical's dark, wandering streams,
    Where cane-tufts shadow all the wild,
Sweet visions haunt my waking dreams
    Of Teviot loved, while still a child,
    Of castled rocks, stupendous piled,
By Esk or Eden's classic wave;
    Where loves of youth and friendship smiled,
Uncursed by thee, vile yellow slave!

Fade, day-dreams sweet, from memory fade!
  The perished bliss of youth's first prime,
That once so bright on fancy played,
  Revives no more in after-time.
  Far from my sacred natal clime,
I haste to an untimely grave;
  The daring thoughts that soared sublime
Are sunk in ocean's southern wave.

Slave of the mine! thy yellow light
  Gleams baleful as the tomb-fire drear:
A gentle vision comes by night
  My lonely, widowed heart to cheer:
  Her eyes are dim with many a tear,
That once were guiding-stars to mine;
  Her fond heart throbs with many a fear:
I cannot bear to see thee shine!

For thee, for thee, vile yellow slave,
  I left a heart that loved me true!
I crossed the tedious ocean-wave,
  To roam in climes unkind and new.
  The cold wind of the stranger blew
Chill on my withered heart: the grave
  Dark and untimely met my view,—
And all for thee, vile yellow slave!

Ha! com'st thou now so late to mock
  A wanderer's banished heart forlorn,
Now that his frame the lightning shock
  Of sun-rays tipt with death has borne?
  From love, from friendship, country, torn,
To memory's fond regrets the prey,
  Vile slave, thy yellow dross I scorn!—
Go, mix thee with thy kindred clay!

Another of Leyden's fine lyrics is that to the *Evening Star :*—

How sweet thy modest light to view, fair star, to love and lovers dear!
While trembling on the falling dew, like beauty shining through a
    tear.
           *   *   *
Thine are the soft, enchanting hours when twilight lingers o'er the
    plain,
And whispers to the closing flowers, that soon the sun will rise again.
Thine is the breeze, that, murmuring bland as music, wafts the
    lover's sigh,
And bids the yielding heart expand in love's delicious ecstasy.
Fair star! though I be doom'd to prove that rapture's tears are mix'd
    with pain,
Ah, still I feel 'tis sweet to love! but sweeter to be loved again!

BEATTIE's fine stanzas, descriptive of a morning landscape, commence thus :—

    But who the melodies of morn can tell ?—
        The wild brook babbling down the mountain side ;
    The lowing herd, the sheepfold's simple bell,
        The pipe of early shepherd dim descried
        In the lone valley, echoing far and wide,
    The clamorous horn along the cliffs above,
        The hollow murmur of the ocean tide,
    The hum of bees, the linnet's lay of love,
And the full choir that wakes the universal grove.

    The cottage curs at early pilgrim bark ;
        Crowned with her pail, the tripping milkmaid sings ;
    The whistling ploughman stalks a-field ; and, hark !
        Down the rough slope the ponderous wagon rings ;
        Through rustling corn the hare, astonished, springs ;
    Slow tolls the village clock the drowsy hour,
        The partridge bursts away on whirring wings,

Deep mourns the turtle in sequestered bower,
And the shrill lark carols clear from her aërial tour!

This sketch of English pastoral life reproduces, with daguerreotype effect, the scenes of half a century ago, before the rail-track
had superseded the rustic country road and the slow stage-coach.
The following stanza was a favorite with Dr. Chalmers:—

Oh! how canst thou renounce the boundless store
Of charms which nature to her votary yields!
The warbling woodland, the resounding shore,

154

The pomp of groves, the garniture of fields :
All that the genial ray of morning gilds,
And all that echoes to the song of even—
All that the mountain's sheltering bosom shields,
And all the dread magnificence of Heaven,—
Oh, how canst thou renounce, and hope to be forgiven?

CHATTERTON, "that marvellous boy who perished in his pride," was amusing himself one day, in company with a friend, reading the epitaphs in St. Pancras Churchyard. He was so deep in thought, that as he walked on, not perceiving a grave that was just dug, he tumbled into it. His friend, observing his situation, ran to his assistance, and, as he helped him out, told him, in a jocular manner, he was happy in assisting at the resurrection of genius. Poor Chatterton smiled, and, taking his companion by the arm, replied, " My dear friend, I feel the sting of a speedy dissolution. I have been at war with the grave for some time, and find it not so easy to vanquish it as I imagined. We can find an asylum to hide from every creditor but that." His friend endeavoured to divert his thoughts from the gloomy reflection : but what will not melancholy and adversity combined subjugate ? In three days after, this neglected and disconsolate youth of genius put an end to his existence by poison, or, as some think, his miseries were completed by starvation.

When only fourteen years of age, he published his first production in a newspaper; it purported to be from manuscripts by one Rowley, a monk of the fifteenth century. Horace Walpole detected the fabrication, and the exposure of the literary fraud entailed upon poor Chatterton neglect and severe exposure to want and suffering. His remarkable genius was unaccompanied by moral principle, and hence his desertion, and the melancholy termination of his brief and hapless career. In his native city, Bristol, as if to atone for this neglect, a splendid monument has been recently erected to his memory.

As a specimen of his antique verse, we extract the following lines on *Spring*, modernized in the orthography :—

155

The budding floweret blushes at the light,
  The meads be sprinkled with the yellow hue,
In daisied mantles is the mountain dight,
  The fresh young cowslip bendeth with the dew;
The trees enleafèd, into heaven straught,
When gentle winds do blow, to whistling din is brought.

The evening comes, and brings the dews along,
  The ruddy welkin shineth to the eyne,
Around the ale-stake minstrels sing the song,
  Young ivy round the door-posts doth entwine;
I lay me on the grass; yet, to my will,
Albeit all is fair, there lacketh something still.

The *Lines on the Burial of Sir John Moore*, by the Rev. CHARLES
WOLFE, Byron on one occasion pronounced little inferior to the
best Odes the age had produced. This noble poem found its way
to the press without the knowledge of its author: it was recited to
a friend in Ireland, who was so much impressed with its force and
beauty, that he requested a copy, which he sent to a local newspaper, with the author's initials. It soon created a great sensation,
and for a long time its authorship was a matter of much speculation.
Here are the stanzas :—

Not a drum was heard, not a funeral note,
  As his corse to the rampart we hurried;
Not a soldier discharged his farewell shot
  O'er the grave where our hero we buried

We buried him darkly, at dead of night,
  The sods with our bayonets turning;
By the struggling moonbeam's misty light,
  And the lantern dimly burning.

No useless coffin enclosed his breast,
  Not in sheet or in shroud we wound him;

But he lay like a warrior taking his rest,
  With his martial cloak around him.

Few and short were the prayers we said,
  And we spoke not a word of sorrow ;
But we steadfastly gazed on the face of the dead,
  And we bitterly thought of the morrow.

We thought, as we hollowed his narrow bed,
  And smoothed down his lonely pillow,
That the foe and the stranger would tread o'er his head,
  And we far away on the billow !

Lightly they'll talk of the spirit that's gone,
  And o'er his cold ashes upbraid him ;
But little he'll reck, if they let him sleep on
  In the grave where a Briton has laid him.

But half of our heavy task was done,
  When the clock struck the hour for retiring ;
And we heard the distant and random gun
  That the foe was sullenly firing.

Slowly and sadly we laid him down,
  From the field of his fame fresh and gory ;
We carved not a line, we raised not a stone,
  But we left him alone with his glory !

R. H. WILDE is the author of this clever sonnet to *The Mocking-Bird* :—

  Wing'd mimic of the woods ! thou motley fool !
    Who shall thy gay buffoonery describe ?
  Thine ever-ready notes of ridicule
    Pursue thy fellows still with jest and gibe.
    Wit, sophist, songster, *Yorick* of thy tribe,
  Thou sportive satirist of Nature's school ;

To thee the palm of scoffing we ascribe,
Arch-mocker, and mad Abbot of Misrule!
For such thou art by day—but all night long

Thou pour'st a soft, sweet, pensive, solemn strain,
    As if thou didst, in this thy moonlight song,
Like to the melancholy *Jaques*, complain,
    Musing on falsehood, folly, vice, and wrong,
And sighing for thy motley coat again.

FITZ-GREENE HALLECK is the well-known author of that effec-
tive and artistic poem, *Marco Bozzaris*,—the hero who fell in an
attack upon the Turkish camp, on the site of the ancient Platæa, and

expired in the moment of victory, exclaiming, " To die for Liberty is a pleasure, not a pain !"   Here are some of the lines :—

> At midnight, in his guarded tent,
>   The Turk was dreaming of the hour
> When Greece, her knee in suppliance bent,
>   Should tremble at his power.
> *   *   *
> They fought—like brave men, long and well :
>   They piled that ground with Moslem slain ;
> They conquered—but Bozzaris fell,
>   Bleeding at every vein.
> His few surviving comrades saw
> His smile—when rang their proud hurrah,
>   And the red field was won ;
> Then saw in death his eyelids close
> Calmly, as to a night's repose,
>   Like flowers at set of sun.
> *   *   *
> Bozzaris ! with the storied brave
>   Greece nurtured in her glory's time,
> Rest thee—there is no prouder grave,
>   Even in her own proud clime.
> *   *   *
> For thou art Freedom's now, and Fame's ;
> One of the few, the immortal names
>   That were not born to die !

HALLECK'S fine *Elegy on Burns* abounds with impassioned and glowing beauties.   We extract a few stanzas :—

> His is that language of the heart,
>   In which the answering heart would speak,
> Thought, word, that bids the warm tear start,
>   Or the smile light the cheek ;

And his that music, to whose tone
　　The common pulse of man keeps time,
In cot or castle's mirth or moan,
　　In cold or sunny clime.
　　　　＊　　　　＊　　　　＊
What sweet tears dim the eyes unshed,
　　What wild vows falter on the tongue,
When "Scots wha hae wi' Wallace bled,"
　　Or "Auld Lang Syne," is sung?

Pure hopes, that lift the soul above,
　　Come with his Cotter's Hymn of praise;
And dreams of youth, and truth, and love,
　　With Logan's banks and braes.

And when he breathes his master-lay
　　Of Alloway's witch-haunted wall,
All passions in our frames of clay
　　Come thronging at his call.
　　　　＊　　　　＊　　　　＊
And consecrated ground it is,
　　The last, the hallowed home of one
Who lives upon all memories,
　　Though with the buried gone.

Such graves as his are pilgrim-shrines,
　　Shrines to no code or creed confined,—
The Delphian vales, the Palestines,
　　The Meccas of the mind!

FOURTH
EVENING.

Brainard,

Pinkney, Read, Cutter,

Prentice, Cist, Gallagher, Perkins, Byron,

Crabbe, Scott, Hogg, Lamb, White, Montgomery,

Coleridge, Poe, Hemans, Southey, Moore,

Bryant, Hunt, Welby, Nichois,

Bot'a.

THAT the stupendous cataract of Niagara, with its picturesque associations, should have inspired the homage of many a gifted votary of the muse, need not provoke surprise. Yet any attempt to depict a scene so essentially august and sublime,—transcending, indeed, the limits of the loftiest intellect adequately to portray,— must of necessity fail to present it in all its stateliness and grandeur. Our poet BRAINARD'S lines are, we think, among the best that have appeared on the subject :—

> The thoughts are strange that crowd into my brain,
> While I look upward to thee! It would seem
> As if God poured thee from His " hollow hand,"
> And hung His bow upon thine awful front ;
> And spoke in that loud voice, which seemed to him
> Who dwelt in Patmos for his Saviour's sake,
> " The sound of many waters ;" and had bade
> Thy flood to chronicle the ages back,
> And notch His centuries in the eternal rocks.
> Deep calleth unto deep. And what are we,
> That hear the question of that voice sublime!
> Oh, what are all the notes that ever rung
> From war's vain trumpet, by thy thundering side!
> Yea, what is all the riot man can make,
> In his short life, to thy unceasing roar!
> And yet, bold babbler, wnat art thou to Him
> Who drowned a world, and heaped the waters far
> Above its loftiest mountains ?—a light wave,
> That breaks, and whispers of its Maker's might.

Brainard is not unknown to fame by his fine poem, *The Connecticut River;* which commences thus :—

> From that lone lake, the sweetest of the chain,
> That links the mountain to the mighty main,
> Fresh from the rock and swelling by the tree,
> Rushing to meet, and dare, and breast the sea—
> Fair, noble, glorious river! in thy wave
> The sunniest slopes and sweetest pastures lave :

The mountain torrent, with its wintry roar,
Springs from its home and leaps upon thy shore :
The promontories love thee—and for this
Turn their rough cheeks, and stay thee for thy kiss.

*   *   *

The young oak greets thee at the water's edge,
Wet by the wave, though anchored in the ledge.
'Tis there the otter dives, the beaver feeds,
Where pensive osiers dip their willowy weeds,
And there the wild-cat purs amid her brood,
And trains them, in the sylvan solitude,
To watch the squirrel's leap, or mark the mink
Paddling the water by the quiet brink ;
Or to outgaze the gray owl in the dark,
Or hear the young fox practising to bark.
Dark as the frost-nipp'd leaves that strew'd the ground,
The Indian hunter here his shelter found ;
Here cut his bow and shaped his arrows true,
Here built his wigwam and his bark canoe,
Spear'd the quick salmon leaping up the fall,
And slew the deer without the rifle-ball :
Here his young squaw her cradling-tree would choose,
Singing her chant to hush her swart pappoose :
Here stain her quills and string her trinkets rude,
And weave her warrior's wampum in the wood.
No more shall they thy welcome waters bless,
No more their forms thy moonlit banks shall press,
No more be heard, from mountain or from grove,
His whoop of slaughter, or her song of love.

*   *   *

Something of the Promethean fire of the Elizabethan age seems
to glow in the following lines by PINKNEY, of Maryland :—

165

I fill this cup to one made up of loveliness alone,
A woman, of her gentle sex the seeming paragon;
To whom the better elements and kindly stars have given
A form so fair, that, like the air, 'tis less of earth than heaven.
Her every tone is music's own, like those of morning birds,
And something more than melody dwells ever in her words;
The coinage of her heart are they, and from her lips each flows
As one may see the burthened bee forth issue from the rose.
Affections are as thoughts to her, the measures of her hours;
Her feelings have the fragrancy—the freshness of young flowers.

*   *   *

Her health! and would on earth there stood some more of such a
     frame,
That life might be all poetry, and weariness a name!

CUTTER, one of the poets of the West, is the author of this
striking poem, entitled *The Song of Steam*:—

> Harness me down with your iron bands,
>   Be sure of your curb and rein,
> For I scorn the power of your puny hands,
>   As the tempest scorns a chain.
> How I laughed, as I lay concealed from sight
>   For many a countless hour,
> At the childish boast of human might,
>   And the pride of human power!
>
> When I saw an army upon the land,
>   A navy upon the seas,
> Creeping along, a snail-like band,
>   Or waiting the wayward breeze;
> When I marked the peasant faintly reel
>   With the toil which he daily bore,
> As he feebly turned the tardy wheel,
>   Or tugged at the weary oar;

When I measured the panting courser's speed,
   The flight of the carrier-dove,
As they bore the law a king decreed,
   Or the lines of impatient love ;—
I could but think how the world would feel,
   As these were outstripped afar,
When I should be bound to the rushing keel,
   Or chained to the flying car.

Ha, ha, ha ! they found me at last,
   They invited me forth at length ;
And I rushed to my throne with a thunder-blast,
   And laughed in my iron strength.

        *   *   *

The following graceful little melody is from the pen of GEORGE
D. PRENTICE :—

In Southern seas there is an isle,
Where earth and sky forever smile ;
Where storms cast not their sombre hue
Upon the welkin's holy blue ;
Where clouds of blessèd incense rise
From myriad flowers of myriad dyes,
And strange bright birds glance through the bowers,
Like mingled stars, or mingled flowers.

Oh, dear one ! would it were our lot
To dwell upon that lovely spot,
To stray through woods with blossoms starred,
Bright as the dreams of seer or bard ;
To hear each other's whispered words
Mid the wild notes of tropic birds,
And deem our lives, in those bright bowers,
One glorious dream of love and flowers !

These pleasing lines, on *Olden Memories*, are by CIST, of Cincinnati :—

They are jewels of the mind ; they are tendrils of the heart,
That with our being are entwined—of our very selves a part.
They the records are of youth, kept to read in after-years :
They are manhood's well of truth, filled with childhood's early tears.
Like the low and plaintive moan of the night-wind through the trees,
Sweet to hear, though sad and lone, are those olden memories !

    *   *   *

In our days of mirth and gladness, we may spurn their faint control,
But they come, in hours of sadness, like sweet music, to the soul :
And in sorrow, o'er us stealing with their gentleness and calm,
They are leaves of precious healing, they are fruits of choicest balm.
Ever till, when life departs, death from dross the spirit frees,
Cherish in thine heart of hearts, all thine olden memories.

Now let us in imagination turn our gaze towards the magnificent spectacle of an iceberg, which our American bard, BUCHANAN READ, so well portrays :—

A fearless shape of brave device, our vessel drives through mist and
  rain,
Between the floating fleets of ice—the navies of the northern main.
These Arctic ventures, blindly hurled, the proofs of Nature's olden
  force,
Like fragments of a crystal world long shattered from its skyey
  course.

These are the buccaneers that fright the middle sea with dream of
  wrecks,
And freeze the south winds in their flight, and chain the Gulf-stream
  to their decks.
At every dragon prow and helm there stands some Viking as of yore ;
Grim heroes from the boreal realm where Odin rules the spectral
  shore.

And oft beneath the sun or moon their swift and eager falchions
    glow,
While, like a storm-vexed wind, the rune comes chafing through
    some beard of snow.
And when the far North flashes up with fires of mingled red and
    gold,
They know that many a blazing cup is brimming to the absent
    bold.

Up signal there, and let us hail yon looming phantom as we pass!
Note all her fashion, hull and sail, within the compass of your glass.
See at her mast the steadfast glow of that one star of Odin's
    throne ;
Up with our flag, and let us show the Constellation on our own.

           *   *   *

No answer, but the sullen flow of ocean heaving long and vast ;
An argosy of ice and snow, the voiceless North swings proudly past.

Very sweet and refreshing are his liquid lines to the *Wayside Spring* :—

Fair dweller by the dusty way—bright saint within a mossy shrine,
The tribute of a heart to-day, weary and worn, is thine.
The earliest blossoms of the year, the sweet-brier and the violet,
The pious hand of Spring has here upon thy altar set,
And not alone to thee is given the homage of the pilgrim's knee,
But oft the sweetest birds of heaven glide down and sing to thee.
Here daily from his beechen cell the hermit squirrel steals to drink,
And flocks, which cluster to their bell, recline along thy brink.

         *   *   *

And oft the beggar, masked with tan, in rusty garments, gray with
    dust,
Here sits and dips his little can, and breaks his scanty crust ;
And, lulled beside thy whispering stream, oft drops to slumber
    unawares,
And sees the angel of his dream upon celestial stairs.
Dear dweller by the dusty way, thou saint within a mossy shrine,
The tribute of a heart to-day, weary and worn, is thine!

The following exquisite lines are from the same source :—

She came, as comes the summer wind, a gust of beauty to my heart ;
Then swept away, but left behind emotions which shall not depart.
Unheralded she came and went, like music in the silent night—
Which, when the burthened air is spent, bequeathes to memory its
    delight.
Or like the sudden April bow that spans the violet-waking rain,
She bade those blessed flowers to grow which may not fall or fade
    again,
For sweeter than all things most sweet, and fairer than all things
    most fair,
She came, and passed with footsteps fleet, a shining wonder in the air!

GALLAGHER's fine poem on the *Miami Woods* contains this glowing picture of *Indian Summer*. This poet of the West seems to have caught inspiration from the bold, primeval aspects of Nature :—

> What a change hath passed upon the face
> Of Nature, where the waving forest spreads,
> Once robed in deepest green! All through the night
> The subtle frost hath plied its mystic art ;
> And in the day, the golden sun hath wrought
> True wonders ; and the winds of morn and even
> Have touched with magic breath the changing leaves.
> And now, as wanders the dilating eye
> Across the varied landscape, circling far,
> What gorgeousness, what blazonry, what pomp
> Of colors, bursts upon the ravished sight !
> Here, where the maple rears its yellow crest,
> A golden glory; yonder, where the oak
> Stands monarch of the forest, and the ash
> Is girt with flame-like parasite, and broad
> The dogwood spreads beneath, a rolling flood
> Of deepest crimson ; and afar, where looms
> The gnarlèd gum, a cloud of bloodiest red !

*   *   *

The two following extracts are from the same source :—

> When last the maple-bud was swelling,
>   When last the crocus bloomed below,
> Thy heart to mine its love was telling,
>   Thy soul with mine kept ebb and flow :
> Again the maple-bud is swelling—
>   Again the crocus blooms below—
> In heaven thy heart its love is telling,
>   But still our hearts keep ebb and flow.

When last the April bloom was flinging
   Sweet odours on the air of Spring,
In forest-aisles thy voice was ringing,
   Where thou didst with the red-bird sing;
Again the April bloom is flinging
   Sweet odours on the air of Spring,—
But now in heaven thy voice is ringing,
   Where thou dost with the angels sing.

———

Broad plains—blue waters—hills and valleys,
   That ring with anthems of the free!
Brown-pillared groves, and green-arched alleys,
   That Freedom's holiest temples be!
These forest-aisles are full of story:
   Here many a one of old renown
First sought the meteor-light of glory,
   And mid its transient flash—went down.

Historic names forever greet us,
   Where'er our wandering way we thread;
Familiar forms and faces meet us,
   As, living, walk with us the dead.
Man's fame, so often evanescent,
   Links here with thoughts and things that last;
And all the bright and teeming Present
   Thrills with the great and glorious Past!

      *   *   *

PERKINS, another of the woodland minstrels of the West, thus gilds his verse with sunshine:—

Oh! merry, merry be the day, and bright the star of even,—
   For 'tis our duty to be gay, and tread in holy joy our way;
Grief never came from heaven, my love, it never came from heaven.

Then let us not, though woes betide, complain of fortune's spite,
  As rock-encircled trees combine, and nearer grow and closer
    twine,
So let our hearts unite, my love, so let our hearts unite.

And though the circle here be small of heartily approved ones,
  There is a home beyond the skies, where vice shall sink and
    virtue rise,
Till all become the loved ones, love, till all become the loved ones.

Then let your eye be laughing still, and cloudless be your brow;
  For in that better world above, O! many myriads shall we love,
As one another now, my love, as one another now.

BYRON, notwithstanding all his errors of creed and conduct, seems to have been possessed of fine sensibilities, as the following incident will prove :—On a certain occasion, when in London, he was solicited to subscribe for a volume of poems, by a young lady of good education, whose connections were impoverished by reverses. He listened to her sad story, and, while conversing with her, wrote something on a piece of paper; he then, handing it to her, said, " This is my subscription, and I heartily wish you success." On reaching the street, she found it to be a check for fifty pounds.

That Byron was endowed with brilliant powers, none will deny; but all do not as readily admit that those gifts were sadly perverted. It is not true, as his false morality teaches, that great crimes imply great qualities, and that virtue is a slavery : it is in the converse of the proposition that truth rests. No wonder that Byron should have recorded, in this sad refrain, his own bitter experience :—

    " My days are in the yellow leaf;
        The fruits and flowers of love are gone,—
    The worm, the canker, and the grief,
        Are mine alone."

What a magnificent picture does he give us in these descriptive
lines, one of the finest passages in all poetry :—

Roll on, thou deep and dark blue ocean—roll!
Ten thousand fleets sweep over thee in vain;
Man marks the earth with ruin—his control

Stops with the shore ;—upon the watery plain
The wrecks are all thy deed, nor doth remain
A shadow of man's ravage, save his own,
When, for a moment, like a drop of rain,
He sinks into thy depths with bubbling groan,
Without a grave, unknell'd, uncoffin'd, and unknown.

His steps are not upon thy paths,—thy fields
   Are not a spoil for him,—thou dost arise
And shake him from thee; the vile strength he wields
   For earth's destruction, thou dost all despise,
   Spurning him from thy bosom to the skies,
And send'st him, shivering, in thy playful spray,
   And howling, to his gods, where haply lies
His petty hope in some near port or bay,
And dashest him again to earth: there let him lay.

The armaments which thunder-strike the walls
   Of rock-built cities, bidding nations quake,
And monarchs tremble in their capitals;
   The oak leviathans, whose huge ribs make
   Their clay creator the vain title take
Of lord of thee, and arbiter of war;
   These are thy toys, and as the snowy flake,
They melt into thy yeast of waves, which mar
Alike the Armada's pride, or spoils of Trafalgár.

Thy shores are empires, changed in all save thee—
   Assyria, Greece, Rome, Carthage, what are they?
Thy waters wasted them while they were free,
   And many a tyrant since; their shores obey
   The stranger, slave, or savage; their decay
Has dried up realms to deserts:—not so thou,
   Unchangeable save to thy wild waves' play—
Time writes no wrinkle on thine azure brow—
Such as creation's dawn beheld, thou rollest now.

Thou glorious mirror, where the Almighty's form
   Glasses itself in tempests; in all time,
Calm or convulsed—in breeze, or gale, or storm,
   Icing the pole, or in the torrid clime
   Dark-heaving;—boundless, endless, and sublime—

The image of Eternity—the throne
   Of the Invisible ; even from out thy slime
The monsters of the deep are made ; each zone
Obeys thee ; thou goest forth, dread, fathomless, alone.

   And I have loved thee, Ocean ! and my joy
      Of youthful sports was on thy breast to be
Borne, like thy bubbles, onward : from a boy
      I wanton'd with thy breakers—they to me
      Were a delight ; and if the freshening sea
Made them a terror—'twas a pleasing fear,
  . For I was as it were a child of thee,
And trusted to thy billows far and near,
And laid my hand upon thy mane—as I do here.

      *   *   *

The foregoing suggests another beautiful passage,—*The Ship-wreck*,—in *Don Juan* :—

Then rose from sea to sky the wild farewell—
   Then shriek'd the timid, and stood still the brave,—
Then some leap'd overboard with dreadful yell,
   As eager to anticipate their grave ;
And the sea yawn'd around her like a hell,
   And down she suck'd with her the whirling wave,
Like one who grapples with his enemy,
And strives to strangle him before he die.

And first one universal shriek there rush'd,
   Louder than the loud ocean, like a crash
Of echoing thunder : and then all was hush'd,
   Save the wild wind and the remorseless dash
Of billows ; but at intervals there gush'd,
   Accompanied with a convulsive splash,
A solitary shriek, the bubbling cry
Of some strong swimmer in his agony.

Another vivid picture is that of an Alpine storm :—

> The sky is changed!—and such a change! O night,
>   And storm, and darkness, ye are wondrous strong :
> Yet lovely in your strength, as is the light
>   Of a dark eye in woman! Far along,
>   From peak to peak, the rattling crags among,
> Leaps the live thunder! Not from one lone cloud,
>   But every mountain now hath found a tongue,
> And Jura answers, through her misty shroud,
> Back to the joyous Alps, who call to her aloud!
>
> And this is in the night :—Most glorious night!
>   Thou wert not sent for slumber! let me be
> A sharer in thy fierce and far delight,—
>   A portion of the tempest and of thee!
>   How the lit lake shines, a phosphoric sea,
> And the big rain comes dancing to the earth!
>   And now again 'tis black,—and now the glee
> Of the loud hills shakes with its mountain-mirth,
> As if they did rejoice o'er a young earthquake's birth.

.

Here is another fine allusion to the grandeur of Alpine scenery :—

> Above me are the Alps,
>   The palaces of Nature, whose vast walls
> Have pinnacled in clouds their snowy scalps,
>   And throned eternity in icy halls
>   Of cold sublimity, where forms and falls
> The avalanche,—the thunderbolt of snow!
>   All that expands the spirit, yet appals,
> Gathers around these summits, as to show
> How earth may pierce to heaven, yet leave vain man below.
>
> *   *   *

Byron's power is seen in the following passage, because it admirably exemplifies the union of great simplicity, both in conception and expression, with true poetic sublimity. The scene which excites the emotion is the memorable plain of Marathon, situated between a range of mountains on the one side, and the sea on the other :—

The mountains look on Marathon, and Marathon looks on the sea ;
And musing there an hour alone, I dreamed that Greece might still
    be free ;
      For, standing on the Persian's grave,
      I could not deem myself a slave.

A king sat on the rocky brow which looks o'er sea-born Salamis ;
And ships, by thousands, lay below, and men in nations ; all were his !
      He counted them at break of day ;
      And when the sun set,—where were they ?

Campbell used to say, that the lines which first convinced him that Byron was a true poet, were these, from the *Childe*[1] *Harold :*—

    Yet are thy skies as blue, thy crags as wild ;
      Sweet are thy groves, and verdant are thy fields,
    Thine olive ripe as when Minerva smiled,
      And still his honeyed wealth Hymettus yields ;
      There the blithe bee his fragrant fortress builds,
    The free-born wanderer of thy mountain air ;
      Apollo still thy long, long summer gilds,
    Still in his beam Mendali's marbles glare ;
    Art, glory, freedom fail, but Nature still is fair !

The *Childe Harold*, which appeared at various intervals, is generally supposed to be a narration of the author's life and travels. Shall we cite more of the brilliant passages which sparkle over its

---

[1] *Childe* is the old word for Knight.

pages *i* Rogers thought Byron's finest passage was that on Solitude, in the second canto of the poem :—

> To sit on rocks, to muse o'er flood and fell,
>> To slowly trace the forest's shady scene,
> Where things that own not man's dominion dwell,
>> And mortal foot hath ne'er, or rarely, been ;
>> To climb the trackless mountain all unseen,
> With the wild flock that never needs a fold ;
>> Alone o'er steeps and foaming falls to lean ;
> This is not solitude ; 'tis but to hold
> Converse with Nature's charms, and see her stores unroll'd.
>
> But midst the crowd, the hum, the shock of men,
>> To hear, to see, to feel, and to possess,
> And roam along, the world's tired denizen,
>> With none who bless us, none whom we can bless ;
>> Minions of splendour shrinking from distress !
> None that, with kindred consciousness endued,
>> If we were not, would seem to smile the less,
> Of all that flattered, followed, sought, and sued :
> This is to be alone ; this, this is solitude !

— — —

Here are his moral reflections on a skull :—

> Look on its broken arch, its ruined wall,
>> Its chambers desolate, and portals foul :
> Yes, this was once ambition's airy hall,
>> The dome of thought, the palace of the soul :
>> Behold through each lack-lustre, eyeless hole,
> The gay recess of wisdom and of wit,
>> And passion's host, that never brook'd control :
> Can all saint, sage, or sophist ever writ,
> People this lonely tower, this tenement refit ?

179

How vividly he presents to us .the scene of a Spanish bull-fight :—

> The lists are oped, the spacious area cleared,
>   Thousands on thousands piled are seated round ;
> Long ere the first loud trumpet's note is heard,
>   No vacant space for lated wight is found ;
>   Here dons, grandees, but chiefly dames, abound,

> Skill'd in the ogle of a roguish eye,
>   Yet ever well inclined to heal the wound :
> None through their cold disdain are doom'd to die,
> As moon-struck bards complain, by love's sad archery.

> Hushed is the din of tongues—on gallant steeds,
>   With milk-white crest, gold spur, and light-poised lance,
> Four cavaliers prepare for venturous deeds,
>   And lowly bending to the lists, advance ·
>   Rich are their scarfs, their chargers featly prance :

If in the dangerous game they shine to-day,
    The crowd's loud shout and ladies' lovely glance,
Best prize of better acts, they bear away,
And all that kings or chiefs e'er gain, their toils repay.

In costly sheen and gaudy cloak arrayed,
    But all a-foot, the light-limb'd Matadore
Stands in the centre, eager to invade
    The lord of lowing herds; but not before
    The ground, with cautious tread, is traversed o'er,
Lest aught unseen should lurk to thwart his speed:
    His arms a dart, he fights aloof, nor more
Can man achieve without the friendly steed,—
Alas! too oft condemn'd for him to bear and bleed.

Thrice sounds the clarion; lo! the signal falls,
    The den expands, and Expectation mute
Gapes round the silent circle's peopled walls.
    Bounds with one lashing spring the mighty brute,
    And, wildly staring, spurns, with sounding foot,
The sand, nor blindly rushes on his foe:
    Here, there, he points his threatening front, to suit
His first attack, wide waving to and fro
His angry tail; red rolls his eye's dilated glow.

Sudden he stops: his eye is fix'd: away,
    Away, thou heedless boy! prepare the spear:
Now is thy time to perish, or display
    The skill that yet may check his mad career.
    With well-timed croupe the nimble coursers veer;
On foams the bull, but not unscathed he goes;
    Streams from his flank the crimson torrent clear;
He flies, he wheels, distracted with his throes;
Dart follows dart; lance, lance; loud bellowings speak his woes.

*   *   *

Foiled, bleeding, breathless, furious to the last,
   Full in the centre stands the bull at bay,
Mid wounds and clinging darts, and lances brast,
   And foes disabled in the brutal fray ;
   And now the Matadores around him play,
Shake the red cloak, and poise the ready brand :
   Once more through all he bursts his thundering way—
Vain rage ! the mantle quits the conynge hand,
Wraps his fierce eye—'tis past—he sinks upon the sand !

*   *   *

Byron was a facile writer,—he composed his *Bride of Abydos* in
a single night, and, it is said, without once mending his pen : this is
not improbable, since his chirography was not remarkably distinct.
The Corsair, which has been thought by some critics his best production, was written in three weeks. Byron is said to have received
from Murray, his publisher, for the entire copyrights of his works,
upwards of thirty thousand guineas.

Among the numerous fine images which adorn Byron's poetry,
Wordsworth considered the two following the most felicitous :—

Yet, Freedom ! yet thy banner, torn, but flying,
Streams like the thunder-storm *against* the wind!

For Freedom's battle, once begun,
Bequeathed by bleeding sire to son,
Though baffled oft, is ever won!

Here are some more beautiful gems :—

Between two worlds life hovers like a star,
   'Twixt night and morn, upon the horizon's verge :
How little do we know that which we are !
   How less what we may be ! The eternal surge

Of time and tide rolls on, and bears afar
　　Our bubbles ; as the old burst, new emerge,
Lash'd from the foam of ages ; while the graves
Of empires heave but like some passing waves.

There is a pleasure in the pathless woods,
　　There is a rapture on the lonely shore,
There is society, where none intrudes,
　　By the deep sea, and music in its roar :
　　I love not Man the less, but Nature more,
From these our interviews, in which I steal
　　From all I may be, or have been before,
To mingle with the Universe, and feel
What I can ne'er express, yet cannot all conceal.

The *Rainbow* :—
　　　　　　A heavenly chameleon,
　　The airy child of vapour and the sun,
Brought forth in purple, cradled in vermilion,
　　Baptized in molten gold, and swathed in dun,
Glittering like crescents o'er a Turk's pavilion,
　　And blending every colour into one.

Poetry has been sometimes styled the " flower of experience ;"
and we have an illustration of this in the case of CRABBE, who so
well knew, from his own early struggles and privations, both how
to pity and portray those of others.　He was the poet of the poor,
and for the fidelity of his sketches has been called "the Hogarth
of verse."　Well might Washington Irving—referring to the numerous instances in which the poetic gift has been cradled in obscurity
and poverty—quaintly remark, "Genius delights to nestle its off-

spring in strange places!" Let us read a few lines addressed by Crabbe to a *Library* :—

> Wisdom loves
> This seat serene, and virtue's self approves :
> Here come the grieved, a change of thought to find,—
> The curious here, to feed a craving mind ;
> Here the devout their peaceful temple choose,
> And here the poet meets his favourite muse.
> With awe, around these silent walks I tread,—
> These are the lasting mansions of the dead :
> "The dead !" methinks a thousand tongues reply—
> "These are the tombs of such as cannot die !
> Crowned with eternal fame, they sit sublime,
> And laugh at all the little strife of time !"

*   *

SIR WALTER SCOTT, who has been styled " the potent wizard of romance, at the waving of whose wand came trooping on the stage of life again, gallant knights and ladies fair, foaming chargers and splendid tournaments, with their flashing armour and blazoned shields," was also the poet who loved to sing of knightly deeds of valour and old traditional love-lays.

He was endowed with a wonderful facility of composition. His brain has been compared to a high-pressure engine, the steam of which was "up" as soon as he entered his study, which was generally at six o'clock in the morning. After three hours' labour came breakfast, and after that he resumed his studies till dinner-time.

Scott is believed to have acquired over half a million of pounds sterling by his various literary labours,—an amount altogether unapproached by any other author of ancient or modern times. His own life-story, so full of vicissitude and surprising incident, has been styled a greater marvel than any of his romantic fictions.

SIR WALTER SCOTT.

His severe literary toils were not intermitted even amid the heavy financial disasters which overtook him in connection with the failure of his publishers; but with heroic determination he persevered in the noble purpose of discharging these obligations. Having accomplished the herculean task, his physical strength began to fail; and after a tour to Italy, he returned to Abbotsford, totally exhausted. When he arrived there, his dogs came about his knees, and he sobbed over them till he was reduced to a state of stupefaction. After lingering for two months, his mind became more clear, when he would ask to be placed at his desk, but the fingers refused to grasp the pen, and he sunk back, weeping. On the 21st of September, 1832, Sir Walter breathed his last.

Not long before he died, he said: " I have been, perhaps, the most voluminous author of the day, and it *is* a comfort to me to think that I have tried to unsettle no man's faith, to corrupt no man's principles, and that I have written nothing which, on my death-bed, I should wish blotted."

Melrose he has consecrated by his genius, *Abbotsford* by his living presence, and *Dryburgh* is made sacred by his sleeping dust: while Nature herself may be said, in his own beautiful lines, to do homage to the memory of his muse :—

> Call it not vain; they do not err,
>   Who say that when the poet dies,
> Mute Nature mourns her worshipper,
>   And celebrates his obsequies :
> Who say,—tall cliff and cavern lone,
> For the departed bard make moan :
> That mountains weep in crystal rill,—
> That flowers in tears of balm distil,—
> Through his loved groves that breezes sigh,
> And oaks in deeper groan reply;
> And rivers teach the rushing wave
> To murmur dirges round his grave.

In his *Rokeby* we have this fine song :—

> Allen-a-Dale has no fagot for burning,
> Allen-a-Dale has no furrow for turning,
> Allen-a-Dale has no fleece for the spinning,
> Yet Allen-a-Dale has red gold for the winning.
> Come, read me my riddle ; come, hearken my tale !
> And tell me the craft of bold Allen-a-Dale.

The Baron of Ravensworth prances in pride,
And he views his domains upon Arkindale side.
The mere for his net, and the land for his game,
The chase for the wild, and the park for the tame ;
Yet the fish of the lake, and the deer of the vale,
Are less free to Lord Dacre than Allen-a-Dale.

Allen-a-Dale was ne'er belted a knight,
Though his spur be as sharp, and his blade be as bright ;
Allen-a-Dale is no baron or lord,
Yet twenty tall yeomen will draw at his word ;
And the best of our nobles his bonnet will vail,
Who at Rere-cross on Stanmore meets Allen-a-Dale.

Allen-a-Dale to his wooing is come ;
The mother, she asked of his household and home :
" Though the Castle of Richmond stands fair on the hill,
My hall," quoth bold Allen, " shows gallanter still ;
'Tis the blue vault of heaven, with its crescent so pale,
And with all its bright spangles,"—said Allen-a-Dale.

The father was steel, and the mother was stone ;
They lifted the latch, and they bade him begone ;
But loud, on the morrow, their wail and their cry !
He had laughed on the lass with his bonnie black eye,
And she fled to the forest to hear a love-tale,
And the youth it was told by was—Allen-a-Dale !

Let us now note the interview of the *Last Minstrel* with the
Duchess :—

He passed where Newark's stately tower
Looks out from Yarrow's birchen bower :
The Minstrel gazed with wistful eye—
No humbler resting-place was nigh.

With hesitating step at last
The embattled portal-arch he passed,
Whose pond'rous grate and massy bar
Had oft rolled back the tide of war,
But never closed the iron door
Against the desolate and poor.

The Duchess marked his weary pace,
His timid mien, and reverend face,
And bade her page the menials tell,
That they should tend the old man well:
For she had known adversity,
Though born in such a high degree ;—
In pride of power, in beauty's bloom,
Had wept o'er Monmouth's bloody tomb !

       *   *   *

The aged Minstrel audience gained.
But when to tune his harp he tried,
His trembling hand had lost the ease
Which marks security to please ;
And scenes long past, of joy and pain,
Came wildering o'er his aged brain——
He tried to tune his harp in vain.

The pitying Duchess praised its chime,
And gave him heart, and gave him time,
Till every string's according glee
Was blended into harmony.

And then, he said, he would full fain
He could recall an ancient strain
He never thought to sing again.
It was not framed for village churls,
But for high dames and mighty earls :

He had played it to King Charles the Good,
When he kept court in Holyrood ;
And much he wished, yet feared to try
The long-forgotten melody.

Hear his tribute to the *Worth of Woman* :—

O woman ! in our hours of ease,
Uncertain, coy, and hard to please,
And variable as the shade
By the light quivering aspen made,
When pain and anguish wring the brow,
A ministering angel thou !

We all remember his fine lines on *Patriotism* :—

Breathes there the man, with soul so dead,
Who never to himself hath said,
    This is my own, my native land ?
Whose heart hath ne'er within him burned,
As home his footsteps he hath turned,
    From wandering on a foreign strand ?
If such there be, go, mark him well ;
For him no minstrel's raptures swell ;
High though his titles—proud his name,
Boundless his wealth as wish can claim ;—
Despite those titles, power, and pelf,
The wretch, concentred all in self,
Living, shall forfeit fair renown,
And doubly dying, shall go down
To the vile dust from whence he sprung,
Unwept, unhonoured, and unsung.

Scattered through his prose writings, we occasionally meet with some of his little songs: here is an admonitory one, from *The Antiquary*, on *Time*:—

> " Why sitt'st thou by that ruined hall,
>   Thou aged carle, so stern and gray?
> Dost thou its former pride recall,
>   Or ponder how it passed away?"

> " Know'st thou not me?" the Deep Voice cried;
>   " So long enjoyed, so oft misused—
> Alternate, in thy fickle pride,
>   Desired, neglected, and accused!

> " Before my breath, like blazing flax,
>   Man and his marvels pass away;
> And changing empires wane and wax,
>   Are founded, flourish, and decay.

> " Redeem mine hours—the space is brief—
>   While in my glass the sand-grains shiver,
> And measureless thy joy or grief,
>   When Time and thou shalt part forever!"

Now for a dainty little Serenade, from *The Pirate*:—

> Love wakes and weeps, while Beauty sleeps!
>   O for Music's softest numbers,
> To prompt a theme for Beauty's dream,
>   Soft as the pillow of her slumbers!

> Through groves of palm sigh gales of balm,
>   Fire-flies on the air are wheeling;
> While through the gloom comes soft perfume,
>   The distant beds of flowers revealing.

O wake and live ! No dream can give
A shadowed bliss the real excelling ;
No longer sleep, from lattice peep,
And list the tale that love is telling !

His *Marmion* is replete with glowing and picturesque passages, stirring descriptions, and the tumult and clash of arms. When Captain Ferguson was serving in the Peninsular war, a copy of this work reached him; and while his men were lying prostrate on the ground, and he kneeling at their head, he read aloud the description of the battle in the sixth canto,—the listening soldiers interrupting him only by a joyous huzza whenever the French shot struck the banks close above them. This incident presents one of the most remarkable instances on record of the power of verse. Listen to a brief extract, full of the action and excitement of the field ;—it is just when twilight falls upon the scene of conflict :—

But naught distinct they see :
While raged the battle on the plain ;
Spears shook, and falchions flashed amain ;
Fell England's arrow-flight like rain ;
Crests rose, and stooped, and rose again,
Wild and disorderly.

*　　*　　*

But as they left the darkening heath,
More desperate grew the strife of death.
The English shafts in volleys hailed,
In headlong charge their horse assailed ;
Front, flank, and rear, the squadrons sweep,
To break the Scottish circle deep,
That fought around their king.
But yet, though thick the shafts as snow,
Though charging knights like whirlwinds go,
Though bill-men ply the ghastly blow,
Unbroken was the ring.

The stubborn spearmen still made good
Their dark, impenetrable wood,
Each stepping where his comrade stood
   The instant that he fell.
No thought was there of dastard flight ;
Linked in the serried phalanx tight,
Groom fought like noble, squire like knight,
   As fearless and as well :
Till utter darkness closed her wing
O'er their thin host and wounded king.

     *   *   *

A yet more stirring passage is that of the death-scene of the hero,
which closes thus :—

The war, that for a space did fail,
Now, trebly thundering, swelled the gale,
   And " Stanley !" was the cry :
A light on Marmion's visage spread,
   And fixed his glazing eye :
With dying hand, above his head
He shook the fragment of his blade,
   And shouted " Victory !"
" Charge, Chester, charge ! On, Stanley, on !"
Were the last words of Marmion.

Hogg, the " Ettrick shepherd," has written many beautiful lyrics :
we select two of his most admired. The first is entitled, *When the
Kye come hame.* This is the latest version of this very beautiful
pastoral song :—

Come all ye jolly shepherds that whistle through the glen,
I'll tell ye of a secret that courtiers dinna ken,—
What is the greatest bliss that the tongue o' man can name ?
'Tis to woo a bonnie lassie when the kye come hame.

When the kye come hame, when the kye come hame,
'Tween the gloamin' and the mirk, when the kye come hame.

'Tis not beneath the burgonet, nor yet beneath the crown,
'Tis not on couch of velvet, nor yet on bed of down—
'Tis beneath the spreading birch, in the dell without a name,
Wi' a bonnie, bonnie lassie, when the kye come hame.

Then the eye shines so bright, the hale soul to beguile,
There's love in every whisper, and joy in every smile ;
O, wha wad choose a crown, wi' its perils and its fame,
And miss a bonnie lassie, when the kye come hame ?

See yonder pawkie shepherd, that lingers on the hill,
His ewes are in the fauld, and his lambs are lying still :
Yet he downa gang to bed, for his heart is in a flame—
To meet his bonnie lassie, when the kye come hame.

Awa' wi' fame and fortune—what comfort can they gi'e ?
And a' the arts that prey upon man's life and liberty :
Gi'e me the highest joy that the heart o' man can frame—
My bonnie, bonnie lassie, when the kye come hame.

His *Skylark* is a general favorite, for its rich melody :—

Bird of the wilderness, blithesome and cumberless,
    Sweet be thy matin o'er moorland and lea !
Emblem of happiness, blest is thy dwelling-place—
    O to abide in the desert with thee !

Wild is thy lay and loud, far in the downy cloud,
    Love gives it energy, love gave it birth.
Where, on thy dewy wing, where art thou journeying ?
    Thy lay is in heaven, thy love is on earth.

O'er fell and fountain sheen, o'er moor and mountain green,
    O'er the red streamer that heralds the day,
Over the cloudlet dim, over the rainbow's rim,
    Musical cherub, soar, singing away !

Then, when the gloaming comes, low in the heather blooms
    Sweet will thy welcome and bed of love be !
Emblem of happiness, blest is thy dwelling-place—
    O to abide in the desert with thee !

LAMB—the gentle, genial "Elia"—thus soliloquizes upon the loss of friends :—

I have had playmates, I have had companions,
In my days of childhood, in my joyful school-days ;
    All, all are gone, the old familiar faces !
I have been laughing, I have been carousing,
Drinking late, sitting late, with my bosom cronies ;
    All, all are gone, the old familiar faces !

      *   *   *

Ghost-like I paced round the haunts of my childhood ;
Earth seemed a desert I was bound to traverse,
    Seeking to find the old familiar faces.
Friend of my bosom, thou more than a brother,
Why wert not thou born in my father's dwelling ?
    So might we talk of the old familiar faces :
How some they have died, and some they have left me,
And some are taken from me ; all are departed ;
    All, all are gone—the old familiar faces !

The genius of KIRKE WHITE, which elicited the beautiful tribute of Byron, is seen in the following lines, addressed to *An Early Primrose* :—

Mild offspring of a dark and sullen sire !
Whose modest form, so delicately fine,
Was nursed in whirling storms, and cradled in the winds :

Thee, when young Spring first questioned Winter's sway,
And dared the sturdy blusterer to the fight,
Thee on this bank he threw, to mark his victory.

In this low vale, the promise of the year,
Serene, thou openest to the nipping gale,
Unnoticed and alone, thy tender elegance.

So virtue blooms, brought forth amid the storms
Of chill adversity; in some lone walk
Of life she rears her head, obscure and unobserved;

While every bleaching breeze that on her blows,
Chastens her spotless purity of breast,
And hardens her to bear serene the ills of life.

Hear MONTGOMERY's glowing apostrophe to *Home*:—

There is a spot of earth supremely blest—
A dearer, sweeter spot than all the rest—
Where man, creation's tyrant, casts aside
His sword and sceptre, pageantry and pride;
While in his softened looks benignly blend
The sire, the son, the husband, brother, friend;
Here woman reigns,—the mother, daughter, wife,—
Strews with fresh flowers the narrow way of life;
In the clear heaven of her delighted eye,
An angel-guard of loves and graces lie;
Around her knees domestic duties meet,
And fireside pleasures gambol at her feet.

*   *   *

The beautiful lines which he wrote upon Burns, will win a welcome from every reader:—

What bird, in beauty, flight, or song, can with the Bard compare,
Who sang as sweet, and soared as strong, as ever child of air?
His plume, his note, his form, could Burns for whim or pleasure
     change;
He was not one, but all by turns, with transmigration strange:—
The blackbird, oracle of Spring, when flowed his moral lay;
The swallow, wheeling on the wing, capriciously at play;

The humming-bird, from bloom to bloom, inhaling heavenly balm ;
The raven, in the tempest's gloom, the halcyon in the calm :

      *   *   *

The woodlark in his mournful hours, the goldfinch in his mirth ;
The thrush, a spendthrift of his powers, enrapturing heaven and
    earth ;
The swan, in majesty and grace, contemplative and still :
But roused—no falcon in the chase could like his satire kill ;
The linnet, in simplicity ; in tenderness, the dove ;
But more than all beside was he the nightingale in love.

Oh ! had he never stooped to shame, nor lent a charm to vice,
How had devotion loved to name that bird of paradise !
Peace to the dead ! In Scotia's choir of minstrels great and small,
He sprang from his spontaneous fire, the phœnix of them all !

One of the most spirit-stirring poems in the language is Montgomery's *Patriot's Pass-word.* It is founded on the heroic achieve-
ment of Arnold de Winkelried, at the battle of Sempach, in which
the Swiss insurgents secured the freedom of their country against
the despotic power of Austria, in the fourteenth century :—

In arms the Austrian phalanx stood,—
A living wall,—a human wood !
Impregnable their front appears,
All horrent with projected spears,
Whose polished points before them shine,
From flank to flank, one brilliant line,
Bright as the breakers' splendors run
Along the billows to the sun.
Opposed to these, a hovering band
Contended for their fatherland.

      *   *   *

Marshalled once more at Freedom's call,
They came to conquer, or to fall,—

Where he who conquered, he who fell,
Was deemed a dead or living Tell.
Such virtue had that patriot breathed,
So to the soil his soul bequeathed,
That wheresoe'er his arrows flew,
Heroes in his own likeness grew,
And warriors sprang from every sod
Which his awakening footstep trod.
And now the work of life and death
Hung on the passing of a breath;
The fire of conflict burned within,
The battle trembled to begin;
Yet while the Austrians held their ground,
Point for assault was nowhere found;
Where'er the impatient Switzers gazed,
The unbroken line of lances blazed;
That line 'twere suicide to meet,
And perish at their tyrants' feet:
How could they rest within their graves,
To leave their homes the haunts of slaves?
Would they not feel their children tread,
With clanking chains, above their head?
It must not be;—this day, this hour,
Annihilates the invader's power;
All Switzerland is in the field,
She will not fly, she cannot yield,—
She must not fall; her better fate
Here gives her an immortal date.
Few were the numbers she could boast,
Yet every freeman was a host,
And felt as 'twere a secret known,
That one should turn the scale alone,
While each unto himself was he
On whose sole arm hung victory!

It did depend on one indeed ;
Behold him—Arnold Winkelried !
There sounds not to the trump of fame
The echo of a nobler name.

Unmarked he stood amidst the throng,
In rumination deep and long,
Till you might see, with sudden grace,
The very thought come o'er his face,
And by the motion of his form
Anticipate the bursting storm,
And by the uplifting of his brow

Tell where the bolt would strike, and how.
But 'twas no sooner thought than done !
The field was in a moment won :—
" Make way for Liberty !" he cried,
Then ran, with arms extended wide,
As if his dearest friend to clasp ;—
Ten spears he swept within his grasp ;—
" Make way for Liberty !" he cried ;
Their keen points crossed from side to side ;
He bowed amidst them like a tree,
And thus made way for Liberty !

Swift to the breach his comrades fly ;
" Make way for Liberty !" they cry,
And through the Austrian phalanx dart,
As rushed the spears through Arnold's heart,
While, instantaneous as his fall,
Rout, ruin, panic seized them all ;
An earthquake could not overthrow
A city with a surer blow.
Thus Switzerland again was free,—
Thus death made way for Liberty !

It was remarked by Wordsworth, that many great men of this
age had done wonderful *things*, but that COLERIDGE was the only
wonderful *man* he ever knew : and this opinion was shared by many
others who visited the author of *The Ancient Mariner*. His character has been compared to a vast unfinished cathedral or palace,—
beautiful in its decoration and gigantic in its proportions, but in-
complete. Coleridge is said to have left behind him a prodigious
amount of treatises—unfinished. Lamb informs us that, two days
before his death, he wrote to a bookseller, proposing an epic poem,
on *The Wanderings of Cain*, to be in twenty-four books. His early
devotion to metaphysical studies continued with him through life, as

well as his love of poesy, which he tells us had been to him "its own exceeding great reward." This is seen, indeed, in the gush of poetic joy which pervades the following beautiful retrospect :—

Verse, a breeze mid blossoms straying,
     Where Hope clung feeding, like a bee,—
Both were mine ! Life went a-Maying
     With nature, hope, and poesy,
          When I was young !

When I was young ?—Ah, woful when !
Ah ! for the change 'twixt now and then !
This breathing house not built with hands,
     This body that does me grievous wrong,
O'er aëry cliffs and glittering sands,
     How lightly then it flashed along ;
Like those trim skiffs, unknown of yore,
     On winding lakes and rivers wide,
That ask no aid of sail or oar,
     That fear no spite of wind or tide !
Naught cared this body for wind or weather
When Youth and I lived in't together.

Flowers are lovely ; love is flower-like ;
     Friendship is a sheltering tree ;
Oh, the joys that came down shower-like,
     Of friendship, love, and liberty,
          Ere I was old !

Ere I was old ?—Ah, woful ere !
Which tells me, Youth's no longer here !
O Youth ! for years so many and sweet
     'Tis known that thou and I were one ;
I'll think it but a fond conceit—
     It cannot be that thou art gone !

Thy vesper-bell hath not yet toll'd—
And thou wert aye a masker bold.
What strange disguise hast now put on,
To make believe that thou art gone?
I see these locks in silvery slips,
   This drooping gait, this altered size:
But spring-tide blossoms on thy lips,
   And tears take sunshine from thine eyes!
Life is but thought; so think I will,
That Youth and I are house-mates still.

Coleridge was an impressive talker. On one occasion he asked Charles Lamb if he ever heard him preach? " I never heard you do any thing else," was his reply. His changeful career exhibits many phases of character; but to us he is most interesting as a poet. After leaving the Lakes—the neighbourhood of Southey, and the birth-place of *Christabel*—he took up his abode at Highgate, near London, ostensibly for medical treatment of his passion for opium, an indulgence for which he paid a fearful penalty. This habit of intoxication accounts for the strange mystery of his poetry; which has caused him, indeed, to be styled "a magnificent dreamer." Yet his wildest and most mystic poems are so thoughtful, dulcet, and fascinating, that they hold us spell-bound. His *Ancient Mariner*, *Christabel*, and *Kubla Khan*, are of this class. The last named, which is so remarkable for its rich delicacy of colouring, as well as its melody, owes its origin to the following incident :—The author relates that, in the summer of 1797, he was residing in a lonely farm-house, where, being unwell, he took an anodyne, from the effects of which he fell asleep in his chair, at the moment he was reading the following sentence in *Purchas's Pilgrims:*—"Here the Khan Kubla commanded a palace to be built, and a stately garden thereunto; and thus ten miles of fertile ground were enclosed with a wall." He continued asleep for three hours, during which he vividly remembered having composed from two to three hundred lines, and this without any consciousness of effort. On awaking, he remembered the whole, and, taking his pen, began instantly and eagerly to commit it to paper. He had written as far as the published fragment, when he was interrupted by some person on urgent business, which detained him about an hour. On resuming his pen, he was mortified to find that, with the exception of a few lines, all had vanished from his memory.

Coleridge's sweet and simple lines, written in early life, *To Genevieve*, evince a beautiful delicacy of sentiment :—

Maid of my love, sweet Genevieve !
    In beauty's light you glide along :
Your eye is like the star of eve,
    And sweet your voice as seraph's song.
Yet not your heavenly beauty gives
    This heart with passion soft to glow ;
Within your soul a voice there lives—
    It bids you hear the tale of woe.
When, sinking low, the sufferer wan
    Beholds no hand outstretched to save ;
Fair as the bosom of the swan,
    That rises graceful o'er the wave,
I've seen your breast with pity heave,
And therefore love I you, sweet Genevieve !

Coleridge had extraordinary power of summoning up images in his own mind ; a remarkable instance of this is, his poem purporting to be " composed in the Vale of Chamouni," since he never was at Chamouni, or near it, in his life, as we learn from Wordsworth. The origin of the *Ancient Mariner*, as related by Wordsworth, is somewhat humorous. " It arose," he says, " out of the want of five pounds which Coleridge and I needed to make a tour together in Devonshire. We agreed to write, jointly, a poem, the subject of which Coleridge took from a dream which a friend of his had once dreamt concerning a person suffering under a dire curse from the commission of some crime. I supplied the crime, the shooting of the Albatross, from an incident I had met with in one of Shelvocke's voyages. We tried the poem conjointly for a day or two, but we pulled different ways, and only a few lines of it are mine." This fascinating poem is familiar to us all.

Coleridge's exquisite stanzas, entitled *Love*, were originally preceded by the following beautiful lines :—

O leave the lily on its stem ; O leave the rose upon the spray ;
O leave the elder bloom, fair maids ! and listen to my lay.
A cypress and a myrtle bough this morn around my harp you twined,
Because it fashioned mournfully its murmurs in the wind.

And now a tale of love and woe, a woful tale of love I sing ;
Hark, gentle maidens ! hark, it sighs, and trembles on the string.
But most, my own dear Genevieve, it sighs and trembles most for
     thee !
O come, and hear the cruel wrongs befell the Dark Ladie.

Then follow the well-known stanzas, which were intended to form part of a projected poem, entitled *The Dark Ladie* :—

All thoughts, all passions, all delights, whatever stirs this mortal
     frame,
All are but ministers of Love, and feed his sacred flame.
Oft in my waking dreams do I live o'er again that happy hour,
When midway on the mount I lay beside the ruined tower.
The moonshine, stealing on the scene, had blended with the lights
     of eve ;
And she was there, my hope, my joy,—my own dear Genevieve !

She leaned against the armèd man,—the statue of the armèd knight ;
She stood and listened to my lay, amid the lingering light.

Few sorrows hath she of her own, my hope, my joy, my Genevieve!
She loves me best whene'er I sing the songs that make her grieve.

I played a soft and doleful air, I sang an old and moving story,—
An old, rude song, that suited well that ruin wild and hoary.
She listened with a flitting blush, with downcast eyes and modest
      grace ;
For well she knew, I could not choose but gaze upon her face.

           *   *   *

Here is introduced the story of the knight ; after which the poet
continues :—

But when I reached that tenderest strain of all the ditty,
My faltering voice and pausing harp disturbed her soul with pity.
She wept with pity and delight—she blushed with love and virgin
      shame ;
And, like the murmur of a dream, I heard her breathe my name.

Her bosom heaved, she stepped aside ; as conscious of my look, she
      stepped ;
Then suddenly, with timorous eye, she fled to me and wept.
She half enclosed me with her arms—she pressed me with a meek
      embrace ;
And bending back her head, looked up, and gazed upon my face.

'Twas partly love and partly fear, and partly 'twas a bashful art,
That I might rather feel than see the swelling of her heart.
I calmed her fears, and she was calm, and told her love with virgin
      pride,
And so I won my Genevieve,—my bright and beauteous bride !

The following playful lines were recently found on the back of
one of the manuscripts of Coleridge :—

Love's Burial-place: a Madrigal.

Lady.   If Love be dead—(and you aver it!)
        Tell me, Bard, where Love lies buried.
Poet.   Love lies buried where 'twas born:
        Ah, faithless nymph! think it no scorn,
        If in my fancy I presume
        To call thy bosom poor Love's tomb.
        And on that tomb to read the line,—
        " Here lies a Love that once seemed mine,
        But took a chill, as I divine,
        And died at length of a decline !"

Coleridge thus condenses *Courtship* into a couple of stanzas :—

We pledged our hearts, my love and I,
  I in my arms the maiden clasping ;
I could not tell the reason why,
  But, oh ! I trembled like an aspen.

Her father's love she bade me gain ;
  I went, but shook like any reed !
I strove to act the man—in vain !
  We had exchanged our hearts indeed.

EDGAR A. POE, whose minstrelsy sounds like the "echoes of strange, unearthly music," is best known by that remarkable production, *The Raven*, which, like *The Ancient Mariner*, holds the reader spell-bound by its mystic fascination. His song of *Annabel Lee* is a general favourite :—

It was many and many a year ago, in a kingdom by the sea,
That a maiden lived, whom you may know by the name of Annabel Lee :

And this maiden she lived with no other thought than to love, and
    be loved by me.

I was a child and she was a child, in this kingdom by the sea ;
But we loved with a love that was more than love, I and my An-
    nabel Lee,—
With a love that the winged seraphs of heaven coveted her and me.

And this was the reason that, long ago, in this kingdom by the sea,
A wind blew out of a cloud, chilling my beautiful Annabel Lee :
So that her high-born kinsman came, and bore her away from me,
To shut her up in a sepulchre in this kingdom by the sea.

           *   *   *

But our love it was stronger by far than the love of those who were
    older than we,
    Of many far wiser than we ;

And neither the angels in heaven above, nor the demons down under
    the sea,
Can ever dissever my soul from the soul of the beautiful Annabel Lee.

For the moon never beams without bringing me dreams of the beau-
    tiful Annabel Lee ;
And the stars never rise, but I feel the bright eyes of the beautiful
    Annabel Lee.
    And so all the night-tide I lie down by the side
    Of my darling, my darling, my life and my bride,
In the sepulchre there by the sea, in her tomb by the sounding sea !

Poe's *Bells* are full of ringing melody.   Listen :—

Hear the sledges with the bells—silver bells !
What a world of merriment their melody foretells !
How they tinkle, tinkle, tinkle, in the icy air of night !
      While the stars that oversprinkle
All the heavens, seem to twinkle with a crystalline delight ;
Keeping time, time, time, in a sort of Runic rhyme,
To the tintinnabulation that so musically wells
      From the bells, bells, bells,
From the jingling and the tinkling of the bells.

Hear the mellow wedding-bells—golden bells !
What a world of happiness their harmony foretells !
Through the balmy air of night how they ring out their delight !
From the molten golden notes, and all in tune,
      What a liquid ditty floats
To the turtle-dove that listens, while she gloats on the moon !
Oh, from out the sounding cells what a gush of euphony volumi-
    nously wells !
How it swells ! how it dwells on the future, how it tells
      Of the rapture that impels

To the swinging and the ringing of the bells, bells, bells,
To the rhyming and the chiming of the bells!

Hear the loud alarum-bells—brazen bells!
What a tale of terror, now, their turbulency tells!
In the startled ear of night how they scream out their affright;
Too much horrified to speak, they can only shriek, shriek, out of
       tune,
In a clamorous appealing to the mercy of the fire,
In a mad expostulation with the deaf and frantic fire,
Leaping higher, higher, higher, with a desperate desire,
And a resolute endeavour, now, now to sit, or never,
    By the side of the pale-faced moon.
Oh, the bells, bells, bells! what a tale their terror tells of despair!
How they clang, and clash, and roar! what a horror they outpour
    On the bosom of the palpitating air!

            *   *   *

MRS. HEMANS'S poetry has been compared to a cathedral chant—
deep, solemn, and impressive; entrancing rather than exciting the
spirit. The feeling of gloom and sadness which characterizes many
of her fine poems, causes little surprise to those who are familiar
with the history of her domestic sorrows and sufferings. Her
numerous productions, it is well known, are marked by religious
purity and womanly tenderness and grace. The last contribution of
her muse was a fine sonnet on *The Sabbath*,—a "soul-full effusion"
of despondency and aspiration, written three weeks before she died.
Her death was serene, and illustrative of one of her own beautiful
dirges,—fittingly, indeed, inscribed over her tomb :—

    Calm on the bosom of thy God,
      Fair Spirit, rest thee now;
    Even while with us thy footsteps trod,
      His seal was on thy brow.

Dust to its narrow house beneath,
　　Soul to its place on high!
They that have seen thy look in death,
　　No more may fear to die.

How full of touching beauty is her poem entitled *The Hour of Death!*—

Leaves have their time to fall,
And flowers to wither at the north wind's breath,
　　And stars to set; but all,
Thou hast all seasons for thine own, O Death!

Day is for mortal care,
Eve for glad meetings round the joyous hearth,
　Night for the dreams of sleep, the voice of prayer;
But all for thee, thou mightiest of the earth!

　　　　＊　　　　＊　　　　＊

What a charming description has she given us of the *Homes of England*:—

The stately homes of England, how beautiful they stand!
Amidst their tall ancestral trees, o'er all the pleasant land.
The deer across their greensward bound through shade and sunny
　　gleam,
And the swan glides past them, with the sound of some rejoicing
　　stream.

The merry homes of England! Around their hearths by night,
What gladsome looks of household love meet in the ruddy light!
There woman's voice flows forth in song, or childhood's tale is told,
Or lips move tunefully along some glorious page of old.

　　　　＊　　　　＊　　　　＊

Among her best productions we class her *Greek Song of Exile*,
Treasures of the Deep, and *The Forest Sanctuary;* but they must be
perused entire, to enjoy their touching beauty.

Familiar as they are to us, from their home interest, yet we never grow weary of her admirable stanzas on the *Landing of the Pilgrims* :—

The breaking waves dashed high on a stern and rock-bound coast,
And the woods against a stormy sky their giant branches tossed :
And the heavy night hung dark the hills and waters o'er,
When a band of exiles moored their bark on the wild New England
    shore.

Not as the conqueror comes, they, the true-hearted, came,
Not with roll of stirring drums, and the trumpet that sings of fame :
Not as the flying come, in silence and in fear,—
They shook the depths of the desert's gloom with their hymns of
    lofty cheer.

Amidst the storm they sang, and the stars heard and the sea !
And the sounding aisles of the dim woods rang to the anthem of
    the free !
The ocean eagle soared from his nest by the white wave's foam,
And the rocking pines of the forest roared—this was their welcome
    home !

There were men with hoary hair amidst that pilgrim band—
Why had *they* come to wither there, away from their childhood's
    land ?
There was woman's fearless eye, lit by her deep love's truth ;
There was manhood's brow, serenely high, and the fiery heart of
    youth.

What sought they thus afar ? bright jewels of the mine ?
The wealth of seas, the spoils of war ?—they sought a faith's pure
    shrine !
Ay, call it holy ground, the soil where first they trod ;
They have left unstained, what there they found—freedom to wor-
    ship God !

Mrs. Hemans thus gracefully enshrines in verse a beautiful Indian legend from Chateaubriand's *Souvenirs d'Amerique* :—

> We saw thee, O Stranger, and wept !
> We looked for the youth of the sunny glance,
> Whose step was the fleetest in chase or dance !
> The light of his eye was a joy to see,
> The path of his arrows a storm to flee !
> But there came a voice from a distant shore :
> He was call'd—he is found midst his tribe no more !
> He is not in his place when the night-fires burn,
> We look for him still—he will yet return !
> His brother sat with a drooping brow
> In the gloom of the shadowing cypress bough :
> We roused him—we bade him no longer pine,
> For we heard a step—but the step was thine.
>
> We saw thee, O stranger, and wept !
> We looked for the maid of the mournful song—
> Mournful, though sweet—she hath left us long !
> We told her the youth of her love was gone,
> And she went forth to seek him—she passed alone :
> We hear not her voice when the woods are still,
> From the bower where it sang, like a silvery rill.
> The joy of her sire with her smile is fled,
> The winter is white on his lonely head,
> He hath none by his side when the wilds we track
> He hath none when we rest—yet she comes not back !
> We looked for her eye on the feast to shine,
> For her breezy step—but the step was thine !
>
> We saw thee, O Stranger, and wept !
> We looked for the chief who hath left the spear
> And the bow of his battles forgotten here !

We looked for the hunter, whose bride's lament
On the wind of the forest at eve is sent ;
We looked for the first-born, whose mother's cry
Sounds wild and shrill through the midnight sky !
Where are they ?—thou'rt seeking some distant coast—
O ask of them, Stranger !—send back the lost !
Tell them we mourn by the dark blue streams,
Tell them our lives but of them are dreams !
Tell how we sat in the gloom to pine,
And to watch for a step—but the step was thine !

Another exquisite poem, *The Messenger-Bird*, by the same gifted
poetess, is founded upon a tradition among the Brazilian tribes, to
the effect, that this bird is a messenger sent by their deceased rela-
tives with news from the other world.

SOUTHEY, one of the most voluminous of writers (exceeding
Scott in this respect), is said to have destroyed more verses between
his twentieth and thirtieth year than he published during his whole
life.   His books were his most cherished and constant companions:
as he, indeed, tells us in one of his poems :—

My days among the dead are passed ; around me I behold
Where'er these casual eyes are cast, the mighty minds of old :
        My never-failing friends are they,
        With whom I converse night and day.

With them I take delight in weal, and seek relief in woe ;
And, while I understand and feel how much to them I owe,
        My cheeks have often been bedewed
        With tears of thoughtful gratitude.

       *   *   *

It is a mournful fact to add, also, that for nearly three years preceding his death, he sat amongst these silent " companions " in hope-

less vacuity of mind, unable to hold further "converse" with them: yet it is stated by Wordsworth, that even then he found him patting his books with both hands, affectionately, like a child.

He died, thus in eclipse, at Keswick, and his body now sleeps "amid the stillness and grandeur of his old Cumberland hills."

The following refrain seems tinged with his own sorrow :—

> The days of infancy are all a dream ;
> How fair, but, oh ! how short they seem—
>   'Tis life's sweet opening Spring !
> The days of youth advance ;
> The bounding limb, the ardent glance,
>   The kindling soul they bring—
> It is life's burning Summer-time.
> Manhood, matured with wisdom's fruit,
> Reward of learning's deep pursuit,
> Succeeds, as Autumn follows Summer's prime.
> And that, and that, alas ! goes by ;
> And what ensues ?—the languid eye,
> The failing frame, the soul o'ercast ;
> 'Tis Winter's sickening, withering blast,
> Life's blessèd season—for it is the last.

It is thus he moralizes on the *Holly-tree* :—

O reader ! hast thou ever stood to see the holly-tree ?
The eye that contemplates it well perceives its glossy leaves,
   Ordered by an Intelligence so wise
   As might confound the Atheist's sophistries.

Below a circling fence its leaves are seen, wrinkled and keen ;
No grazing cattle through their prickly round, can reach to wound ;
   But as they grow where nothing is to fear,
   Smooth and unarmed the pointless leaves appear.

I love to view these things with curious eyes, and moralize ;
And in this wisdom of the holly-tree can emblems see
    Wherewith, perchance, to make a pleasant rhyme,
    One which may profit in the after-time.

Thus, though abroad, perchance, I might appear harsh and austere,
To those who on my leisure would intrude, reserved and rude ;
    Gentle at home, amid my friends, I'd be,
    Like the high leaves upon the holly-tree.

            *   *   *

And as, when all the summer trees are seen so bright and green,
The holly leaves their fadeless hues display less bright than they ;
    But when the bare and wintry woods we see,
    What then so cheerful as the holly-tree ?

So serious should my youth appear among the thoughtless throng,
So would I seem amid the young and gay, more grave than they,
    That in my age as cheerful I might be
    As the green winter of the holly-tree.

His sweet lyric, on the immortality of *Love*, is universally admired :—

        They sin, who tell us love can die :
        With life all other passions fly,
          All others are but vanity :
        In heaven ambition cannot dwell,
        Nor avarice in the vaults of hell ;—
        Earthly these passions as of earth,
        They perish where they have their birth :
          But love is indestructible,—
        Its holy flame forever burneth—
        From heaven it came, to heaven returneth :

Too oft on earth a troubled guest,
At times deceived, at times oppressed,
  It here is tried and purified,—
Then hath in heaven its perfect rest :
It soweth here with toil and care,
But the harvest-time of love is there.

MOORE'S *Lake of the Dismal Swamp*, written at Norfolk, in Virginia, is founded on the following legend :—"A young man who lost his mind upon the death of a girl he loved, and who, suddenly disappearing from his friends, was never afterwards heard of. As he had frequently said, in his ravings, that the girl was not dead, but gone to the *Dismal Swamp*, it is supposed he had wandered into that dreary wilderness, and had died of hunger, or been lost in some of its dreadful morasses :"—

" They made her a grave too cold and damp
    For a soul so warm and true ;
And she's gone to the Lake of the Dismal Swamp,
Where, all night long, by a fire-fly lamp,
    She paddles her white canoe.

" And her fire-fly lamp I soon shall see,
    And her paddle I soon shall hear ;
Long and loving our life shall be,
And I'll hide the maid in a cypress tree,
    When the footstep of Death is near."

Away to the Dismal Swamp he speeds—
    His path was rugged and sore,
Through tangled juniper, beds of reeds,
Through many a fen, where the serpent feeds,
    And man never trod before.

And when on the earth he sank to sleep,
    If slumber his eye-lids knew,
He lay where the deadly vine doth weep
Its venomous tear, and nightly steep
    The flesh with blistering dew !

And near him the she-wolf stirred the brake,
    And the copper-snake breathed in his ear,
Till he starting cried, from his dream awake,
" Oh ! when shall I see the dusky Lake,
    And the white canoe of my dear ?"

He saw the Lake, and a meteor bright
    Quick over its surface played,—
" Welcome !" he said, " my dear one's light !"
And the dim shore echoed, for many a night,
    The name of the death-cold maid.

Till he hollowed a boat of the birchen bark,
    Which carried him off from shore ;
Far, far he followed the meteor-spark,
The wind was high and the clouds were dark,
    And the boat returned no more.

But oft, from the Indian hunter's camp,
    This lover and maid so true
Are seen, at the hour of midnight damp,
To cross the Lake by a fire-fly lamp,
    And paddle their white canoe !

"Anacreon Moore," as the author of the *Irish Melodies* has been called, like Byron, was a poet of passion, rather than of profound thought.   His imagery, dazzling and gorgeous with Oriental splendour, as well as the rich melody of his verse, combine to render the *Lalla Rookh* and *Loves of the Angels* works of rare fascination.   They may be said to be fragrant with Oriental odours.   Moore wrote the former in his cottage, near Dove-dale ; here he also composed many of his lyrics.

He received for his *Lalla Rookh* three thousand guineas ; the copyright of his several poems produced to him over thirty thousand pounds.   Here is a passage from the work last named :—

False flew the shaft, though pointed well :
The tyrant lived, the hero fell !
Yet marked the Peri where he lay,
    And when the rush of war was past,
Swiftly descending on a ray
    Of morning light, she caught the last—
Last glorious drop his heart had shed,
Before its free-born spirit fled.
" Be this," she cried, as she winged her flight,
" My welcome gift at the Gates of Light :

THOMAS MOORE.

Though foul are the drops that oft distil
  On the field of warfare, blood like this,
  For Liberty shed, so holy is,
It would not stain the purest rill
  That sparkles among the bowers of bliss !
Oh, if there be on this earthly sphere
A boon, an offering Heaven holds dear,
'Tis the last libation Liberty draws
From the heart that bleeds and breaks in her cause !"

Moore wrote those undying lines, the *Canadian Boat-Song*, during his passage of the St. Lawrence, from Kingston. He pencilled the lines, nearly as they stand in his works, in the blank page of a book which happened to be in his canoe. Some thirty years afterwards, a friend showed this original draught to Moore, when he recalled his youthful days, and alluded in a touching manner to his passage down the rapids of life.

His prelude to *The Loves of the Angels* is very beautiful :—

'Twas when the world was in its prime,
  When the fresh stars had just begun
Their race of glory, and young Time
  Told his first birth-days by the sun :
When, in the light of nature's dawn,
  Rejoicing men and angels met
On the high hill and sunny lawn,—
Ere Sorrow came, or Sin had drawn
  'Twixt man and heaven her curtain yet !
When earth lay nearer to the skies
  Than in these days of crime and woe,
And mortals saw, without surprise,
In the mid-air, angelic eyes
  Gazing upon this world below.
*   *   *

219

One of Moore's fine heroic songs commences :—

As by the shore, at break of day, a vanquished chief expiring lay,
Upon the sands, with broken sword, he traced his farewell to the free;
And there, the last unfinished word he, dying, wrote, was—"Liberty!"

      *   *   *

Another no less striking, we all remember it, beginning—

The harp that once through Tara's halls the soul of music shed,
Now hangs as mute on Tara's walls as if that soul had fled.
So sleeps the pride of former days—so glory's thrill is o'er,
And hearts that once beat high for praise, now feel that pulse no
    more.

      *   *   *

The following lyrics possess great beauty :—

    Let Fate do her worst, there are relics of joy,—
    Bright dreams of the past, which she cannot destroy :
    And they come in the night-time of sorrow and care,
    To bring back the features that joy used to wear.

    Long, long be my heart with such memories filled !
    Like the vase in which roses have once been distilled ;
    You may break, you may ruin the vase if you will,
    But the scent of the roses will hang round it still.

Oft in the stilly night, ere slumber's chain has bound me,
Fond memory brings the light of other days around me ;
    The smiles, the tears of boyhood's years,
      The words of love then spoken ;
    The eyes that shone, now dimmed and gone,
      The cheerful hearts now broken !

When I remember all the friends, so linked together,
I've seen around me fall, like leaves in wintry weather,

I feel like one who treads alone
   Some banquet hall deserted,
Whose lights are fled, whose garland's dead,
   And all but he departed !
Thus in the stilly night, ere slumber's chain has bound me,
Sad memory brings the light of other days around me.

     ——— —

Believe me, if all those endearing young charms,
   Which I gaze on so fondly to-day,
Were to change by to-morrow, and fleet in my arms,
   Like fairy gifts fading away,
Thou wouldst still be adored, as this moment thou art,
   Let thy loveliness fade as it will,
And around the dear ruin each wish of my heart
   Would entwine itself verdantly still.

It is not while beauty and youth are thine own,
   And thy cheeks unprofaned by a tear,
That the fervour and faith of a soul can be known,
   To which time will but make thee more dear ;
No, the heart that has truly loved never forgets,
   But as truly loves on to the close,
As the sun-flower turns on her god, when he sets,
   The same look which she turned when he rose.

We should honour any poet who gives utterance to so brave a
sentiment as the following :—

   Yes, 'tis not helm nor feather—
   For ask yon despot, whether
His plumèd bands could bring such hands
   And hearts as ours together.

   Leave pomps to those who need 'em,
   Give man but heart and freedom,

And proud he braves the gaudiest slaves
 That crawl where monarchs lead 'em.

The sword may pierce the beaver,
 Stone walls in time may sever,
'Tis mind alone, worth steel and stone,
 That keeps men free forever !

The following lines illustrate Moore's exquisite taste and skill :—

Oh, what a pure and sacred thing is Beauty curtained from the sight
Of the gross world, illumining one only mansion with her light !
Unseen by man's disturbing eye, the flower that blooms beneath the
  sea,
Too deep for sunbeams, doth not lie hid in more chaste obscurity.
A soul, too, more than half divine, where, through some shades of
  earthly feeling,
Religion's softened glories shine, like light through summer foliage
  stealing,
  Shedding a glow of such mild hue,
  So warm, and yet so shadowy too,
  As makes the very darkness there
  More beautiful than light elsewhere !

Our national bard, BRYANT, like Wordsworth, is eminently a
poet of nature, for he eloquently interprets to us her beautiful lessons. Calm and meditative are his varied productions ; and while
they are characterized by classic elegance and grace, they also
breathe a spirit of pure and exalted philosophy. The *Lines to a
Waterfowl*, one of his earlier poems, and one of his most justly
admired, is now before us :—

  Whither, midst falling dew,
 While glow the heavens with the last steps of day,
 Far, through their rosy depths, dost thou pursue
  Thy solitary way ?

Vainly the fowler's eye
Might mark thy distant flight to do thee wrong,
As, darkly seen against the crimson sky,
    Thy figure floats along.

Seek'st thou the plashy brink
Of weedy lake, or marge of river wide,
Or where the rocky billows rise and sink
    On the chafed ocean side?

There is a Power whose care
Teaches thy way along that pathless coast,—
The desert and illimitable air,—
    Lone wandering, but not lost.

All day thy wings have fanned,
At that far height, the cold, thin atmosphere,
Yet stoop not, weary, to the welcome land,
    Though the dark night is near.

And soon that toil shall end ;
Soon shalt thou find a summer home and rest,
And scream among thy fellows ; reeds shall bend,
    Soon, o'er thy sheltered nest.

'Thou'rt gone, the abyss of heaven
Hath swallowed up thy form ; yet, on my heart
Deeply hath sunk the lesson thou hast given,
    And shall not soon depart.

He who, from zone to zone,
Guides through the boundless sky thy certain flight,
In the long way that I must tread alone,
    Will lead my steps aright.

That noble poem, *Thanatopsis*, so full of Miltonic grandeur and
harmony, was composed by Mr. Bryant, in his eighteenth year.
Listen to its majestic lines :—

To him who, in the love of Nature, holds
Communion with her visible forms, she speaks
A various language ; for his gayer hours
She has a voice of gladness, and a smile
And eloquence of beauty, and she glides
Into his darker musings, with a mild
And healing sympathy, that steals away
Their sharpness ere he is aware.   When thoughts
Of the last bitter hour come like a blight
Over thy spirit, and sad images
Of the stern agony, and shroud and pall,
And breathless darkness, and the narrow house,
Make thee to shudder, and grow sick at heart :
Go forth under the open sky, and list
To nature's teachings.
          *   *   *

WILLIAM CULLEN BRYANT.

What can be finer than the closing passage :—

> So live, that, when thy summons comes to join
> The innumerable caravan, which moves
> To that mysterious realm, where each shall take
> His chamber in the silent halls of death,
> Thou go not, like the quarry-slave at night
> Scourged to his dungeon, but, sustained and soothed
> By an unfaltering trust, approach thy grave,
> Like one who wraps the drapery of his couch
> About him, and lies down to pleasant dreams.

A playful fancy pervades the following beautiful lines addressed to a bird, known to us by the name *Bob-o-link* :—

> Merrily swinging on brier and weed,
>   Near to the nest of his little dame,
> Over the mountain-side or mead,
>   Robert of Lincoln is telling his name :
> " Bob-o-link, bob-o-link, spink, spank, spink ;
> Snug and safe is that nest of ours,
> Hidden among the summer flowers :
>   Chee, chee, chee."

> Robert of Lincoln is gayly drest,
>   Wearing a bright black wedding-coat ;
> White are his shoulders and white his crest ;
>   Hear him call in his merry note,
> " Bob-o-link, bob-o-link, spink, spank, spink ;
> Look, what a nice new coat is mine,
> Sure there was never a bird so fine—
>   Chee, chee, chee."

> Robert of Lincoln's Quaker wife,
>   Pretty and quiet, with plain brown wings,

Passing at home a patient life,
   Broods in the grass while her husband sings—
" Bob-o-link, bob-o-link, spink, spank, spink :
Brood, kind creature ; you need not fear
Thieves and robbers while I am here—
               Chee, chee, chee."

Modest and shy as a nun is she ;
   One weak chirp is her only note.
Braggart, and prince of braggarts is he,
   Pouring boasts from his little throat :
" Bob-o-link, bob-o-link, spink, spank, spink :
Never was I afraid of man ;
Catch me, cowardly knaves, if you can—
               Chee, chee, chee."

      *   *   *

The *Prairies* :—

These are the gardens of the Desert, these
The unshorn fields, boundless and beautiful,
For which the speech of England has no name—
The Prairies.   I behold them for the first,
And my heart swells, while the dilated sight
Takes in the encircling vastness.   Lo ! they stretch
In airy undulations, far away,
As if the ocean, in his gentlest swell,
Stood still, with all his rounded billows fixed,
And motionless forever.   Motionless ?—
No— they are all unchained again.   The clouds
Sweep over with their shadows, and, beneath,
The surface rolls and fluctuates to the eye ;
Dark hollows seem to glide along and chase
The sunny ridges.   Breezes of the South !
Who toss the golden and the flame-like flowers,
226

And pass the prairie-hawk that, poised on high,
Flaps his broad wings, yet moves not—ye have played
Among the palms of Mexico and vines
Of Texas, and have crisped the limpid brooks
That from the fountains of Sonora glide
Into the calm Pacific—have ye fanned
A nobler or a lovelier scene than this?

    *   *   *

The following stanzas form part of his poem, entitled, *The Battle-field* :—

Soon rested those who fought ; but thou,
  Who minglest in the harder strife
For truths which men receive not now,
  Thy warfare only ends with life.

A friendless warfare ! lingering long
  Through weary day and weary year.
A wild, and many-weaponed throng
  Hang on thy front, and flank, and rear.

Yet nerve thy spirit to the proof,
  And blench not at thy chosen lot.
The timid good may stand aloof,
  The sage may frown—yet faint thou not.

Nor heed the shaft too surely cast,
  The foul and hissing bolt of scorn ;
For with thy side shall dwell, at last,
  The victory of endurance born.

Then follows the oft-cited, magnificent verse,—

Truth, crushed to earth, shall rise again ;
  The eternal years of God are hers ;
But Error, wounded, writhes with pain,
  And dies among his worshippers !

227

The *Hunter of the Prairies* is another fine poem :—

Ay, this is freedom !—these pure skies
    Were never stained with village smoke :
The fragrant wind, that through them flies,
    Is breathed from wastes by plough unbroke.

Here, with my rifle and my steed,
    And her who left the world for me,
I plant me, where the red deer feed
    In the green desert—and am free.
For here the fair savannas know
    No barriers in the bloomy grass ;
Wherever breeze of heaven may blow,
    Or beam of heaven may glance, I pass.
In pastures, measureless as air,
    The bison is my noble game ;
228

"What plant we with this apple tree?
Sweets for a hundred flowery springs
To load the May wind's restless wings,
When, from the orchard row, he pours
Its fragrance through our open doors.
A world of blossoms for the bee,
Flowers for the sick girl's silent room,
For the glad infant sprigs of bloom,
We plant with the apple tree."

William Cullen Bryant

Roslyn, L. I. July 12th 1875

The bounding elk, whose antlers tear
  The branches, falls before my aim.
Mine are the river-fowl that scream
  From the long stripe of waving sedge ;
The bear, that marks my weapon's gleam,
  Hides vainly in the forest's edge ;
In vain the she-wolf stands at bay ;
  The brinded catamount, that lies
High in the boughs to watch his prey,
  Even in the act of springing, dies.
With what free growth the elm and plane
  Fling their huge arms across my way,
Gray, old, and cumbered with a train
  Of vines, as huge, and old, and gray !
            *   *

Here, from dim woods, the aged past
  Speaks solemnly ; and I behold
The boundless future in the vast
  And lonely river, seaward rolled.
        *   *   *

Another of Mr. Bryant's most admired productions is his *Forest
Hymn*, commencing :—

The groves were God's first temples.   Ere man learned
To hew the shaft, and lay the architrave,
And spread the roof above them,—ere he framed
The lofty vault, to gather and roll back
The sound of anthems ; in the darkling wood,
Amid the cool and silence, he knelt down,
And offered to the Mightiest solemn thanks
And supplication.   For his simple heart
Might not resist the sacred influences
Which, from the stilly twilight of the place,
And from the gray old trunks that high in heaven

Mingled their mossy boughs, and from the sound
Of the invisible breath that swayed at once
All their green tops, stole over him, and bowed
His spirit with the thought of boundless power
And inaccessible majesty. Ah, why
Should we, in the world's riper years, neglect
God's ancient sanctuaries, and adore
Only among the crowd, and under roofs
That our frail hands have raised ? Let me, at least,
Here, in the shadow of this aged wood,
Offer one hymn—thrice happy, if it find
Acceptance in His ear.

*   *

" The name of LEIGH HUNT," says Smiles, " is associated in
our minds with all manner of kindness, love, beauty, and gentleness. He has given us a fresh insight into nature, made the flowers
seem gayer, the earth greener, the skies more bright, and all things
more full of happiness and blessing." He has given us some fine
poems. Here is one about the *Flowers*, with a touch of the quaintness of the elder poets :—

We are the sweet flowers, born of sunny showers,
    (Think, whene'er you see us, what our beauty saith) ;
Utterance mute and bright, of some unknown delight,
    We fill the air with pleasure by our simple breath :
All who see us, love us—we befit all places ;
Unto sorrow we give smiles,—and to graces, graces.
Mark our ways, how noiseless all, and sweetly voiceless,
    Though the March winds pipe to make our passage clear ;
Not a whisper tells where our small seed dwells,
    Nor is known the moment green when our tips appear.
We thread the earth in silence, in silence build our bowers,—
And leaf by leaf in silence show, till we laugh a-top, sweet flowers !

Take also the following, as examples of his style :—

Abou Ben Adhem (may his tribe increase !)
Awoke one night from a deep dream of peace,
And saw within the moonlight in his room,
Making it rich and like a lily in bloom,
An Angel writing in a book of gold :
Exceeding peace had made Ben Adhem bold,
And to the Presence in the room he said—
" What writest thou ?" The vision raised its head,
And, with a look made of all sweet accord,
Answered—" The names of those who love the Lord."
" And is mine one ?" said Abou ; " Nay, not so,"
Replied the Angel. Abou spoke more low,
But cheerly still ; and said, " I pray thee, then,
Write me as one that loves his fellow-men."
The Angel wrote, and vanished. The next night
It came again, with a great wakening light,
And showed the names whom love of God had blessed—
And, lo ! Ben Adhem's name led all the rest.

May :—

May, thou month of rosy beauty,
Month when pleasure is a duty ;
Month of bees and month of flowers,
Month of blossom-laden bowers ;
May, thy very name is sweet !
I no sooner write the word,
Than it seems as though it heard,
And looks up and laughs at me,
Like a sweet face, rosily ;
Like an actual colour bright,
Flushing from the paper's white.

231

If the rains that do us wrong
Come to keep the winter long,
And deny us thy sweet looks,
I can love thee, sweet, in books:
Love thee in the poet's pages,
Where they keep thee green for ages;
May's in Milton, May's in Prior,
May's in Chaucer, Thomson, Dyer;
May's in all the Italian books;
She has old and modern nooks,
Where she sleeps with nymphs and elves,
In happy places they call shelves,
With a drapery thick with blooms,
And will rise and dress your rooms.
Come, ye rains, then, if you will,
May's at home, and with me still;
But come, rather, thou, good weather,
And find us in the fields together!

One evening Leigh Hunt was the bearer of some good news to Carlyle, when the wife of the latter, who was also present, was so delighted, that she impulsively sprang from her chair and kissed the poet. The following morning he sent to her a bouquet of flowers, with these lines :—

Jenny kissed me when we met, jumping from the chair she sat in;
Time, you thief! who love to get sweets into your book,—put
that in :
Say I'm weary—say I'm sad—say that health and wealth have
missed me,—
Say I'm growing old—but add, *Jenny kissed me!*

AMELIA WELBY, of Kentucky, is the author of the following sweet lines :—

Sweet warblers of the sunny hours, forever on the wing,
I love them as I love the flowers, the sunlight, and the Spring.
They come like pleasant memories in Summer's joyous time,
And sing their gushing melodies as I would sing a rhyme.
In the green and quiet places, where the golden sunlight falls,
We sit with smiling faces to list their silver calls.
And when their holy anthems come pealing through the air,
Our hearts leap forth to meet them with a blessing and a prayer.

*   *

Like shadowy spirits seen at eve, among the tombs they glide,
Where sweet pale forms, for which we grieve, lie sleeping side by
side.
They break with song the solemn hush where peace reclines her
head,
And link their lays with mournful thoughts that cluster round the
dead.

*   *   *

Another poetess, MRS. NICHOLLS, of Cincinnati, thus beautifully
moralizes on *Indian Summer* :—

It is the Indian Summer-time, the days of mist, and haze, and
glory,
And on the leaves, in hues sublime, the Autumn paints poor Summer's story :
" She died in beauty," sing the hours, " and left on earth a glorious
shadow ;"
" She died in beauty, like her flowers," is painted on each wood and
meadow ;
She perished like bright human hopes, that blaze awhile upon life's
altar ;
And o'er her green and sunny slopes the plaintive winds her dirges
falter.

It is the Indian Summer-time! the crimson leaves like coals are
  gleaming,
The brightest tints of every clime are o'er our Western forests
  streaming;
How bright the hours! yet o'er their close the moments sigh in
  mournful duty,
And redder light around them glows, like hectic on the cheek of
  beauty!

*   *   *

MADAME BOTTA's fine lines, *On a Library*, will form a fitting
peroration to our Fourth Evening with the Minstrels :—

Speak low—tread softly through these halls,—here Genius lives
  enshrined!
Here reign, in silent majesty, the monarchs of the mind!
A mighty spirit-host they come from every age and clime ;
Above the buried wrecks of years, they breast the tide of Time,
And in their presence-chamber here they hold their regal state,
And round them throng a noble train,—the gifted and the great.
O, child of earth! when round thy path the storms of life arise,
And when thy brothers pass thee by with stern, unloving eyes,
Here shall the poets chant for thee their sweetest, holiest lays,
And prophets wait to guide thy steps in wisdom's pleasant ways.
Come, with these God-anointed kings be thou companion here,
And in the mighty realm of mind thou shalt go forth a peer.

FIRST
EVENING.

Pollok. Morris,

Rogers, Boies, Campbell, Osgood,

Hood, Maclean, Eastman, Elliott, Blanchard, Moir,

Spencer, Wordsworth, Shelley, Keats, Whittier, Keble,

Burbidge, Eliza Cook, Milman, Swain, Mrs. Norton, Hervey, Tuckerman,

Bowles, Praed, Linen, Motherwell, Mrs. Browning, Barbauld,

Lover, Peabody, Sterling, Jones, Wilson,

Mackay, Vedder, Cooke, Willis,

Clarke, Smith.

PLEASANT were many
scenes, but most to me
The solitude of vast extent, untouched
By hand of art, where Nature sowed herself,
And reaped her crops; whose garments were the clouds;
Whose minstrels, brooks; whose lamps, the moon and stars;
Whose organ-choir, the voice of many waters;

Whose banquets, morning dews ; whose heroes, storms ;
Whose warriors, mighty winds ; whose lovers, flowers ;
Whose orators, the thunderbolts of God ;
Whose palaces, the everlasting hills ;
Whose ceiling, heaven's unfathomable blue ;
And from whose rocky turrets battled high,
Prospect immense spread out on all sides round,—
Lost now beneath the welkin and the main,
Now walled with hills that slept above the storms.
Most fit was such a place for musing men,
Happiest sometimes when musing without aim.
It was, indeed, a wondrous sort of bliss
The lovely bard enjoyed, when forth he walked—
Unpurposed—stood, and knew not why ; sat down,
And knew not where ; arose, and knew not when ;
Had eyes, and saw not ; ears, and nothing heard ;
And sought—sought neither heaven nor earth—sought naught ;
Nor meant to think ; but ran, meantime, through vast
Of visionary things ; fairer than aught
That was ; and saw the distant tops of thoughts,
Which men of common stature never saw,
Greater than aught that largest worlds could hold,
Or give idea of, to those who read.

This bold and beautiful conception of Nature, and her influences upon a heart and intellect attuned to her ministries, is from POL-LOK's *Course of Time*. The author, like Kirke White, became an early victim of his devotion to the Muse ; for the same year that he gave his epic to the world, he had himself to bid adieu to it.

MORRIS's song, *Woodman, spare that Tree!* has not only taken its place among our household lyrics, but is not unknown abroad. It owes its existence to the following incident :—The author, some years since, was riding out with a friend in the suburbs of New

York city, and when near Bloomingdale, they observed a cottager in the act of sharpening his axe under the shadow of a noble ancestral tree. His friend, who was once the proprietor of the estate on which the tree stood, suspecting that the woodman intended to cut it down, remonstrated against the act, and accompanying the protest with a ten-dollar note, succeeded in preserving from destruction this legendary memorial of his earlier and better days. Now for the song :—

Woodman, spare that tree !—touch not a single bough !
In youth it sheltered me, and I'll protect it now.
'Twas my forefather's hand that placed it near his cot ;
There, woodman, let it stand,—thy axe shall harm it not.
That old familiar tree, whose glory and renown
Are spread o'er land and sea,—and wouldst thou cut it down ?
Woodman ! forbear thy stroke ! cut not its earth-bound ties ;
Oh, spare that aged oak, now towering to the skies !

When but an idle boy, I sought its grateful shade ;
In all their gushing joy, here, too, my sisters played ;
My mother kissed me here, my father pressed my hand,—
Forgive this foolish tear ; but let that old oak stand !
My heart-strings round thee cling, close as thy bark, old friend !
Here shall the wild-bird sing, and still thy branches bend.
Old tree ! the storm still brave ; and, woodman, leave the spot ;
While I've a hand to save, thy axe shall harm it not.

This lyric is also by the same author :—

To me the world's an open book, of sweet and pleasant poetry ;
I read it in the running brook that sings its way towards the sea.
It whispers in the leaves of trees, the swelling grain, the waving
    grass,
And in the cool, fresh evening breeze, that crisps the wavelets as
    they pass.

The flowers below, the stars above, in all their bloom and brightness
    given,
Are, like the attributes of love, the poetry of earth and heaven.
Thus Nature's volume, read aright, attunes the soul to minstrelsy,
Tinging life's clouds with rosy light, and all the world with poetry.

ROGERS seems to have imbibed much of the spirit of Goldsmith
in his poetry, as Campbell did that of Rogers. There is not only
an analogy between *The Pleasures of Hope* and *The Pleasures of
Memory*, beyond the mere titles; it is also observable in the style
and structure of the poems. Rogers was engaged for nine years
upon his first poem, and nearly the same space of time upon his
Human Life, while his *Italy* was not completed in less than sixteen
years. He was a princely patron of poor poets and artists, and
had "learned the luxury of doing good,"—but he was possessed
of ample means for the gratification of his noble purpose, as well
as his artistic taste. His house in St. James's Place—a costly mu-
seum of art—was, for many years, the resort of the most eminent
men of letters from all parts of the world. He expended upwards
of twenty thousand pounds upon the illustrated edition of his works,
the beautiful engravings of which have scarcely to this day been
surpassed.

The life of this remarkable man was extended beyond the average
term of human existence. When more than ninety, and a prisoner
in his chair, he still delighted to watch the changing colours of
the evening sky—to repeat passages of his favourite poets—or to
dwell on the merits of the great painters whose works adorned his
walls.

There is such quiet, pensive music in his *Pleasures of Memory*,
that it would be difficult to select a passage that would fail to please :
here is one :—

    Ethereal power ! whose smile of noon, of night,
    Recalls the far-fled spirit of delight ;

Instils that musing, melancholy mood,
Which charms the wise, and elevates the good ;—
Blest Memory, hail !

      *   *

Lulled in the countless chambers of the brain,
Our thoughts are linked by many a hidden chain ;
Awake but one, and, lo, what myriads rise !
Each stamps its image as the other flies :
Each, as the varied avenues of sense
Delight or sorrow to the soul dispense,
Brightens or fades, yet all, with magic art,
Control the latent fibres of the heart.

      *   *   *

There is a favourite passage from his *Human Life*, too good to pass over :—

The lark has sung his carol in the sky,
The bees have hummed their noontide harmony ;
Still in the vale the village-bells ring round,
Still in Llewellyn-Hall the jests resound :
For now the caudle-cup is circling there,
Now, glad at heart, the gossips breathe their prayer,
And, crowding, stop the cradle to admire
The babe, the sleeping image of his sire.
A few short years, and then these sounds shall hail
The day again, and gladness fill the vale ;
So soon the child a youth, the youth a man,
Eager to run the race his fathers ran.
Then the huge ox shall yield the broad sirloin ;
The ale now brewed, in floods of amber shine ,
And, basking in the chimney's ample blaze,
Mid many a tale told of his boyish days,
The nurse shall cry, of all her ills beguiled,

" 'Twas on these knees he sate so oft, and smiled."
And soon again shall music swell the breeze ;
Soon, issuing forth, shall glitter through the trees
Vestures of nuptial white, and hymns be sung,
And violets scattered round ; and old and young,
In every cottage-porch, with garlands green,
Stand still to gaze, and, gazing, bless the scene :
While, her dark eyes declining, by his side
Moves in her virgin-veil the gentle bride.
And once, alas ! nor in a distant hour,
Another voice shall come from yonder tower :
When in dim chambers long black weeds are seen,
And weepings heard where only joy has been ;
When by his children borne, and from his door,
Slowly departing, to return no more,
He rests in holy earth, with them that went before !
And such is human life ; so gliding on,
It glimmers like a meteor, and is gone !

Rogers's *Lines to a Butterfly* are replete with grace and beauty :—

Child of the sun ! pursue thy rapturous flight,
Mingling with her thou lov'st in fields of light ;
And, where the flowers of Paradise unfold,
Quaff fragrant nectar from their cups of gold.
There shall thy wings, rich as an evening sky,
Expand and shut with silent ecstasy !
Yet wert thou once a worm, a thing that crept
On the bare earth, then wrought a tomb and slept.
And such is man : soon from his cell of clay
To burst a seraph in the blaze of day.

We might cull many pearls of thought from this poet, but we
have only space for the following :—

The soul of music slumbers in the shell
Till waked and kindled by the master's spell ;
And feeling hearts, touch them but rightly, pour
A thousand melodies unheard before !

A guardian angel o'er his life presiding,
Doubling his pleasures, and his cares dividing.

The good are better made by ill,
As odours crushed are sweeter still.

Far from the joyless glare, the maddening strife,
And all the dull impertinence of life.

Let us turn now, with LAURA A. BOIES, to a sweet domestic
study—that of *Little Children :*—

There is music, there is sunshine, where the little children dwell,—
In the cottage, in the mansion, in the hut, or in the cell ;
There is music in their voices, there is sunshine in their love,
And a joy forever round them, like a glory from above.
There's a laughter-loving spirit glancing from the soft blue eyes,
Flashing through the pearly tear-drops, changing like the summer
        skies :
Lurking in each roguish dimple, nestling in each ringlet fair ;
Over all the little child-face gleaming, glancing everywhere.
They all win our smiles and kisses in a thousand pleasant ways,
By the sweet, bewitching beauty of their sunny, upward gaze ;
And we cannot help but love them, when their young lips meet our
        own,
And the magic of their presence round about our hearts is thrown.

When they ask us curious questions in a sweet confiding way,
We can only smile in wonder, hardly knowing what to say ;
As they sit in breathless silence, waiting for our kind replies,
What a world of mystic meaning dwells within the lifted eyes !
When the soul, all faint and weary, falters in the upward way,
And the clouds around us gather, shutting out each starry ray ;
Then the merry voice of childhood seems a soft and soothing
      strain,
List we to its silvery cadence, and our hearts grow glad again.
Hath this world of ours no angels ?   Do our dimly shaded eyes
Ne'er behold the seraph's glory in its meek and lowly guise ?
Can we see the little children, ever beautiful and mild,
And again repeat the story—nothing but a little child ?

    The same facile American pen thus daintily discourses on the
Rain :—

Like a gentle joy descending, to the earth a glory lending,
      Comes the pleasant rain :
    Fairer now the flowers are growing,
    Fresher now the winds are blowing,
      Gladder waves the grain :
    Grove and forest, field and mountain,
    Bathing in the crystal fountain,
Drinking in the inspiration, offer up a glad oblation—
    All around, about, above us,
    Things we love, and things that love us,
      Bless the gentle rain.

Beautiful, and still, and holy, like the spirit of the lowly,
      Comes the quiet rain :
'Tis a fount of joy distilling, and the lyre of earth is trilling,—
      Swelling to a strain :
Nature opens wide her bosom, bursting buds begin to blossom,

To her very soul 'tis stealing, all the springs of life unsealing,
Singing stream and rushing river drink it in, and praise the Giver
      Of the blessed rain.

We have already luxuriated over passages from the *Pleasures of Imagination*, and lingered lovingly amid the sweet images bodied forth by Rogers in the *Pleasures of Memory*: shall we now hold colloquy with CAMPBELL, and catch some glimpses of his bright visions of *Hope*? He thus announces his beautiful theme :—

At summer eve, when Heaven's ethereal bow
Spans with bright arch the glittering hills below,
Why to yon mountain turns the musing eye,
Whose sun-bright summit mingles with the sky?
Why do those cliffs of shadowy tint appear
More sweet than all the landscape smiling near?
'Tis distance lends enchantment to the view,
And robes the mountain in its azure hue.
Thus, with delight, we linger to survey
The promised joys of life's unmeasured way,
Thus, from afar, each dim-discovered scene
More pleasing seems than all the past hath been,
And every form, that Fancy can repair
From dark oblivion, glows divinely there.

      *   *   *

With thee, sweet Hope! resides the heavenly light,
That pours remotest rapture on the sight;
Thine is the charm of life's bewildered way,
That calls each slumbering passion into play.

      *   *   *

Auspicious Hope! in thy sweet garden grow
Wreaths for each toil, a charm for every woe.

      *   *   *

Here is a fine apostrophe to *Domestic Love* :—

> Who hath not paused while Beauty's pensive eye
> Asked from his heart the homage of a sigh ?
> *   *   *
> And say, without our hopes, without our fears,
> Without the home that plighted love endears,
> Without the smile from partial beauty won,
> Oh, what were man ?—a world without a sun.
> Till Hymen brought his love-delighted hour,
> There dwelt no joy in Eden's rosy bower !
> In vain the viewless seraph, lingering there,
> At starry midnight charmed the silent air ;
> In vain the wild bird carolled on the steep,
> To hail the sun, slow wheeling from the deep ;
> In vain, to soothe the solitary shade,
> Aërial notes in mingling measure played :
> The summer wind that shook the spangled tree,
> The whispering wave, the murmur of the bee ;—
> Still slowly passed the melancholy day,
> And still the stranger wist not where to stray.
> The world was sad ! the garden was a wild !
> And man, the hermit, sighed—till woman smiled !
> *   *   *

This beautiful passage closes the poem :—

> Eternal Hope ! when yonder spheres sublime
> Pealed their first notes to sound the march of Time,
> Thy joyous youth began—but not to fade.
> When all the sister planets have decayed ;
> When, rapt in fire, the realms of ether glow,
> And Heaven's last thunder shakes the world below ;
> Thou, undismayed, shalt o'er the ruins smile,
> And light thy torch at Nature's funeral pile !
> *   *   *

Moir says, " I do not think I overrate the merits of the *Pleasures of Hope*, whether taking it in its parts or as a whole, in preferring it to any didactic poem of equal length in the English language. It is like a long fit of inspiration." Campbell wrote it at Edinburgh when he was but twenty-one ; and so prolonged was its popularity, that it ultimately brought to its author the sum of four thousand five hundred pounds. His patriotic Odes are so heroic and stirring, and his more serious poems are so inspiring and impressive, that it is no wonder they should have become to us as " household words." What fire and energy characterize those grand naval Odes, *The Battle of the Baltic*, and *Ye Mariners of England;* and how sublimely roll out the stanzas of his *Last Man, What's Hallowed Ground?* and *The Rainbow !*

Irving thought Campbell's *Hohenlinden* contained more grandeur and moral sublimity than is to be found anywhere else in the same compass of English poetry. This, like most of his descriptive poems, Campbell seems to have written under the very inspiration of the scene.

Campbell's lyrics have an exquisite grace and delicacy of touch about them ; for example, the following :—

> Withdraw not yet those lips and fingers,
>   Whose touch to mine is rapture's spell ;
> Life's joy for us a moment lingers,
>   And death seems in that word—farewell !
> The hour that bids us part and go,
> It sounds not yet—oh no, no, no !
>
> Time, whilst I gaze upon thy sweetness,
>   Flies, like a courser nigh the goal :
> To-morrow where shall be his fleetness,
>   When thou art parted from my soul ?
> Our hearts shall beat, our tears shall flow,
> But not together—oh no, no !

the stone is laid over my head, how can literary fame appear to me, to any one, but as nothing? I believe, when I am gone, justice will be done to me in this way—that I was a pure writer. It is an inexpressible comfort, at my time of life, to be able to look back and feel that I have not written one line against religion or virtue." Is not this claim, which has been in his case well attested by the public censorship, the highest meed of praise that can be awarded to genius?

Campbell's funeral was a grand spectacle. As the solemn procession moved towards the open grave in Poet's Corner, Westminster Abbey, every voice was hushed, except that of the clergyman echoing along the vaulted aisles of the venerable pile—"I am the resurrection and the life." As the sad groups gathered around the grave, the solemn stillness was broken by a sweet strain of rich melody, alternating with grand bursts of chorus from the organ: it was the *Dead March in Saul.*

A touching incident occurred just as the corpse was about being sprinkled with its native earth;—a Polish officer came forward with a handful of dust, brought for the occasion from the tomb of Kosciuzko, and scattered it upon the coffin. It was a worthy tribute of affectionate regard to the memory of him who had done so much to immortalize the man and the cause.

This sweet lyric we derive from our American poetess, Mrs. Osgood:

She comes, in light, aërial grace; o'er Memory's glass the vision
    flies;
Her girlish form, her glowing face, her soft, black hair, her beaming
    eyes.
I think of all her generous love; her trustful heart, so pure and
    meek;
Her tears—an April shower—that strove with sunshine on her
    changing cheek.

She knows no worldly guile or art, but Love and Joy have made
   her fair :
And so I keep her in my heart, and bless her in my silent prayer.

Pass we now to the serio-comic Hood,—a poet whose memory
is "emblazoned with a halo of light-hearted mirth and pleasantry,"
but whose coruscations of wit and fancy do not more charm us, than
do the genial charities and deep human sympathies which characterize his graver productions.   If he was the "prince of punsters,"
he was also pre-eminently the poet of pathos; for, as a portrayer
of life in its various phases, his rich and graceful imagery, and vivid
descriptions of sorrow and suffering, were no less conspicuous than
the kindly spirit with which his sarcasms and satires are tempered,

so that while they cauterize, they cure. How much of human suffering has been mitigated, how many a home of sadness consoled, by the pleadings of his powerful pen! The spirit of his playful productions, so chaste, and so glittering with sportive gayety and humour, are yet enriched with the pure gold of wisdom, so that while they charm the imagination, they also benefit the heart.

Hood's fragile constitution was invaded, during his whole life, by a slow wasting disease, and it was terminated by protracted suffering. Referring to his own physical debility, he thus writes :—" That man who has never known a day's illness is a moral dunce,—one who has lost the greatest moral lesson in life,—who has skipped the finest lecture in that great school of humanity, the sick-chamber. Let him be versed in metaphysics, profound in mathematics, a ripe scholar in the classics, a bachelor of arts, or even a doctor in divinity,— yet he is one of those gentlemen whose education has been neglected. For all his college acquirements, how inferior he is in wholesome knowledge to the mortal who has had a quarter's gout, or a half-year of ague,—how infinitely below the fellow-creature who has been soundly taught his tic-douloureux, thoroughly grounded in rheumatism, and deeply *red* in the scarlet fever !"

It was while suffering from bodily sickness that poor Hood composed those touching and immortal poems,—*The Bridge of Sighs*, *The Lady's Dream*, *The Lay of the Labourer*, and *The Song of the Shirt*. It was the last-named that his wife at once pronounced one of the best things he ever wrote. Her verdict turned into a prophecy, for it obtained an immediate and long-continued popularity, and was also translated into several foreign languages :—

O, men, with sisters dear ! O, men, with husbands and wives !
It is not linen you're wearing out, but human creatures' lives !
  Stitch, stitch, stitch, in poverty, hunger, and dirt ;
Sewing at once, with a double thread, a shroud as well as a shirt !
But why do I talk of death—that phantom of grisly bone ?
I hardly fear his terrible shape, it seems so like my own ;

Work, work, work
              speed,

          That works for a daily feed —
     Nor time a tear to shed,

A little weeping would ease my heart,
   ~~But to ease my heart with tears~~
To ~~ease my heart with tears~~,
Oh, only for time to think & weep —
     But in these busy ld
My tears must stop for every drop
     Hinders needle & thread

     O but
Then give the soul sleep
    little
A leisure for love & hope
     Or only times, for grief.

It seems so like my own, because of the fasts I keep,—
Oh, God! that bread should be so dear, and flesh and blood so
  cheap!

          *   *   *

  What exquisite delicacy and force characterize his *Bridge of
Sighs* :—

          Alas! for the rarity of Christian charity
              Under the sun!
          Oh! it is pitiful! near a whole city full,
              House she had none!

              ❊   ❊   ❊

      The bleak wind of March made her tremble and shiver;
      But not the dark arch, or the black flowing river:
      Mad from life's history, glad of death's mystery,
          Swift to be hurled—
      Anywhere, anywhere out of the world!
      In she plunged boldly, no matter how coldly
          The rough river ran;
      Over the brink of it,— picture it, think of it,
          Dissolute man!
      Lave in it, drink of it, then, if you can!

              ❊   ❊   ❊

  Now two or three stanzas from the *Lady's Dream :*—

Of the hearts that daily break, of the tears that hourly fall,
Of the many, many troubles of life that grieve this earthly ball—
Disease, and hunger, and pain, and want; but now I dreamt of
    them all.
For the blind and the cripple were there, and the babe that pined
    for bread,
And the houseless man, and the widow poor, who begged—to bury
    the dead:

The naked, also, that I might have clad, the famished I might
    have fed!
The sorrow I might have soothed, and the unregarded tears;
For many a thronging shape was there, from long-forgotten years,
Ay, even the poor rejected Moor who raised my children's fears!
        *   *   *

The wounds I might have healed! the human sorrow and smart!
And yet it never was in my soul to play so ill a part:
But evil is wrought by want of thought, as well as want of heart!
        *   *   *

An illustration of the effect of antithesis, and grotesqueness of
fancy, we have in his *Ode* to his Son:—

    Thou happy, happy elf!
(But stop, first let me kiss away that tear—)
    Thou tiny image of myself!
(My love, he's poking peas into his ear!)
    Thou merry, laughing sprite!
    With spirits feather-light,
Untouched by sorrow, and unsoiled by sin,—
(Good heavens! the child is swallowing a pin!)
    Thou cherub-brat of earth!
Fit playfellow for fays, by moonlight pale,
    In harmless sport and mirth!
(That dog will bite him, if he pulls its tail;)
       *   *   *
Fresh as the morn, and brilliant as its star—
(I wish that window had an iron bar)—
Bold as the hawk, yet gentle as the dove—
    (I tell you what, my love,
I cannot write, unless he's sent above).

His *Dame Eleanor Spearing*, like his many other pieces, including
Young Ben, *Nelly Gray*, and *Ben Battle*, exhibit his irresistible fond-

ness for playing upon words. Here is a passage from the first-named :—

> She was deaf as a nail—that you cannot hammer
> A meaning into, for all your clamour—
> There never *was* such a deaf old Gammer '
> Deaf to sounds, as a ship out of soundings,
> Deaf to verbs, and all their compoundings,
> Adjective, noun, and adverb, and particle,
> Deaf to even the definite article—
> No verbal message was worth a pin,
> Though you hired an earwig to carry it in !
> Of course the loss was a great privation,
> For one of her sex—whatever her station—
> And none the less that the Dame had a turn
> For making all families one concern,
> And learning whatever there was to learn
> In the prattling, tattling Village of Tringham—
> As who wore silk ? and who wore gingham ?
> And what the Atkins' shop might bring 'em ?
> How the Smiths contrived to live ? and whether
> The fourteen Murphys all pigg'd together ?
> The wages per week of the Weavers and Skinners,
> And what they boiled for their Sunday dinners ?
>
>   ❋   ❋   ❋
>
> Was all a sealed book to Dame Eleanor Spearing ;
>   And often her tears would rise to their founts—
> Supposing a little scandal at play
> 'Twixt Mrs. O'Fie and Mrs. Au Fait—
>   That she couldn't audit the Gossips' accounts.

The *Dream of Eugene Aram* has been regarded as one of Hood's finest productions ; but a high critical authority thinks his *Haunted House* bears the palm, it is so wonderfully full of creative power.

" It required the finest mental apprehension, the white heat of imagination, the most sensitive perception, to take such a picture as this, wherein the indefinite is caught and fixed so definitely :— a living, lonely human being is thus isolated and suspended betwixt the spirit-world of the air overhead and the reptile-world of crumbling ruin at the feet :" [1]—

> The centipede along the threshold crept,
>   The cobweb hung across in mazy tangle,
> And in its winding-sheet the maggot slept,
>   At every nook and angle.
> The keyhole lodged the earwig and her brood,
>   The emmets of the steps had old possession,
> And marched in search of their diurnal food
>   In undisturbed procession.
> Such omens in the place there seemed to be,
>   At every crooked turn, or on the landing,
> The straining eye-ball was prepared to see
>   Some apparition standing !
> The dreary stairs, where with the sounding stress
>   Of every step so many echoes blended,
> The mind, with dark misgivings, feared to guess
>   How many feet ascended.

Even the ancestral portraits on the walls are filled with no mere simulated life,—

> Their souls were looking through their painted eyes
>   With awful speculation.

At the sound of the door creaking on its rusty hinges, it seems as though the murder would out at last. The screech-owl appears to " mock the cry that she had heard some dying victim utter :"—

---

[1] Quarterly Review.

A shriek that echoed from its joisted roof,
    And up the stair, and further still and further,
Till in some ringing chamber far aloof
    It ceased its tale of murther!
The wood-louse dropped and rolled into a ball,
    Touched by some impulse, occult or mechanic;
And nameless beetles ran along the wall,
    In universal panic.

The subtle spider, that from overhead
    Hung like a spy on human guilt and error,
Suddenly turned, and up its slender thread
    Ran with a nimble terror.
                *   *   *
O'er all there hung the shadow of a fear,
    A sense of mystery the spirit daunted,
And said, as plain as whisper in the ear,
    " The place is haunted!"
                *   *   *

Prophetic hints that filled the soul with dread,
  But through one gloomy entrance pointing mostly,
The while some secret inspiration said,
  " That chamber is the ghostly !"
Across the door no gossamer festoon
  Swung pendulous,—no web, no dusty fringes,
No silky chrysalis or white cocoon,
  About its nooks and hinges.
The spider shunned the interdicted room,
  The moth, the beetle, and the fly were banished,
And where the sunbeam fell athwart the gloom,
  The very midge had vanished.
One lonely ray that glanced upon a bed,
  As if with awful aim direct and certain,
To show the Bloody Hand, in burning red,
  Embroidered on the curtain.

Here is a sweet passage from *The Fairies :—*

Oh, these be Fancy's revellers by night !
  Stealthy companions of the downy moth—
Diana's motes, that flit in her pale light,
  Shunners of sunbeams in diurnal sloth :
  These be the feasters on night's silver cloth,—
The gnat, with shrilly trump, is their convener,
  Forth from their flowery chambers, nothing loath,
With lulling tunes to charm the air serener,
Or dance upon the grass, to make it greener.

These be the pretty genii of the flowers,
  Daintily fed with honey and pure dew—
Midsummer's phantoms in her dreaming hours,
  King Oberon, and all his merry crew,
  The darling puppets of Romance's view ;

Fairies and sprites, and goblin elves we call them,
    Famous for patronage of lovers true ;
No harm they act, neither shall harm befall them,
So do not thus with crabbed frowns appall them.
            *   *   *
For these are kindly ministers of nature
    To soothe all covert hurts and dumb distress ;
Pretty they be, and very small of stature,
    For mercy still consorts with littleness :
    Wherefore the sum of good is still the less,
And mischief grossest in this world of wrong :
    So do these charitable dwarfs redress
    The tenfold ravages of giants strong,
    To whom great malice and great might belong.

Here are two gems : —

We watched her breathing through the night, her breathing soft and
        low,
As in her breast the wave of life kept heaving to and fro.
So silently we seemed to speak, so slowly moved about,
As we had lent her half our powers to eke her living out.
Our very hopes belied our fears, our fears our hopes belied—
We thought her dying when she slept, and sleeping when she died.
For when the morn came, dim and sad, and chill with early showers,
Her quiet eyelids closed—she had another morn than ours.

———

Love thy mother, little one ! kiss and clasp her neck again,—
Hereafter she may have a son will kiss and clasp her neck in vain :
        Love thy mother, little one.

Gaze upon her living eyes, and mirror back her love for thee,—
Hereafter thou mayst shudder sighs to meet them when they cannot
        see :
        Gaze upon her living eyes !

Press her lips the while they glow with love that they have often
    told,—
Hereafter thou mayst press in woe, and kiss them till thine own
    are cold.
        Press her lips the while they glow !

       *   *   *

It is the glory of Hood, that he was not only a master poet, but
a philanthropist—he remembered the forgotten. It has been well
remarked, that his greatest work is that which his poems will do for
the poor. The critic already referred to remarks : " Hood was not
one of those lofty and commanding minds that rise but once in an
age, on the mountain ranges of which light first smiles and last
lingers. He does not keep his admirers standing at gaze in distant
reverence and awe. He is no cold, polished, statuesque idol of the
intellect, but one of the darlings of the English heart. You never
think of Hood as dead and turned to marble : statue or bust could
never represent him to the imagination. It is always a real human
being, with the quaintest, kindliest smile, that looks into your face,
and straightway your heart is touched to open and let him in. Few
names will call forth so tender a familiarity of affection as that of
rare Tom Hood." His last lines were these :—

      Farewell, Life ! my senses swim,
      And the world is growing dim ;
      Thronging shadows cloud the light,
      Like the advent of the night—
      Colder, colder, colder still,
      Upward steals a vapour chill ;
      Strong the earthy odour grows—
      I smell the mould above the rose !

      Welcome, Life ! the Spirit strives !
      Strength returns and hope revives ;

Cloudy fears and shapes forlorn
Fly like shadows at the morn.
O'er the earth there comes a bloom ;
Sunny light for sullen gloom,
Warm perfume for vapour cold—
I smell the rose above the mould!

The subjoined plaintive and beautiful lines are part of MRS.
MACLEAN'S (L. E. L.) poem on *Night at Sea* :—

The lovely purple of the noon's bestowing
  Has vanished from the waters, where it flung
A royal colour, such as gems are throwing
  Tyrian or regal garniture among.
'Tis night, and overhead the sky is gleaming ;
  Through the slight vapour trembles each dim star ;
I turn away—my heart is sadly dreaming
  Of scenes they do not light, of scenes afar.
My friends, my absent friends! do you think of me as I think
    of you ?
            *   *   *

The world, with one vast element omitted—
  Man's own especial element, the earth ;
Yet o'er the waters is his rule transmitted
  By that great knowledge wherein power has birth.
How oft, on some strange loveliness while gazing,
  Have I wished for you—beautiful as new,
The purple waves, like some wild army, raising
  Their snowy banners as the ship cuts through.
My friends, my absent friends! do you think of me as I think
    of you ?

Bearing upon its wings the hues of morning,
  Up springs the flying-fish, like life's false joy,

Which of the sunshine asks that frail adorning
  Whose very light is fated to destroy.
Ah, so doth genius, on its rainbow pinion,
  Spring from the depths of an unkindly world;
So spring sweet fancies from the heart's dominion—
  Too soon in death the scorched-up wing is furled.
My friends, my absent friends! whate'er I see is linked with
  thoughts of you.

　　　　*　　　　*　　　　*

EASTMAN, of Vermont, has given us, with daguerreotype fidelity,
a little domestic picture, that is a gem for its simple pastoral
beauty :—

The farmer sat in his easy chair, smoking his pipe of clay,
While his hale old wife with busy care was clearing the dinner away :
  A sweet little girl, with fine blue eyes,
  On her grandfather's knee was catching flies.
The old man laid his hand on her head, with a tear in his wrinkled
  face—
He thought how often her mother, dead, had sat in the self-same
  place :
  As the tear stole down from his half-shut eye,
  " Don't smoke," said the child, " how it makes you cry !"
The house-dog lay stretched out on the floor, where the shade after
  noon used to steal,
The busy old wife by the open door was turning the spinning wheel,
  And the old brass clock on the mantel-tree
  Had plodded along to almost three—
Still the farmer sat in his easy chair, while, close to his heaving
  breast,
The moistened brow, and the cheek so fair, of his sweet grandchild
  were press'd ;
  His head, bent down, on her soft hair lay—
  Fast asleep were they both, that summer day !

Here is a single specimen of the vigorous verse of EBENEZER ELLIOTT, the "poet of the poor:"—

GOD said—"Let there be light!" Grim darkness felt His might, and fled away :
Then startled seas, and mountains cold, shone forth, all bright in blue and gold, and cried, " 'Tis day—'tis day !"
" Hail, holy light !" exclaimed the thunderous cloud that flamed o'er daisies white ;
And lo ! the rose, in crimson drest, leaned sweetly on the lily's breast, and, blushing, murmured—" Light !"
Then was the skylark born ; then rose the embattled corn ; then floods of praise
Flowed o'er the sunny hills of noon ; and then, in silent night, the moon poured forth her pensive lays.
Lo ! heaven's bright bow is glad ! Lo ! trees and flowers, all clad in glory, bloom.

LAMAN BLANCHARD's beautiful lines, *The Mother's Hope*, glow with all the rich tenderness of the dainty theme :—

Is there, when the winds are singing in the happy summer-time,
When the raptured air is ringing with earth's music heavenward springing,
Forest chirp, and village chime,—is there, of the sounds that float
Unsighingly, a single note, half so sweet, and clear, and wild,
     As the laughter of a child ?

    *   *   *

Organ finer, deeper, clearer, though it be a stranger's tone,
Than the winds and waters dearer, more enchanting to the hearer,
     For it answereth to his own ;
But of all its witching words, those are sweetest, bubbling wild
     Through the laughter of a child.

There is a very touching poem by MOIR, entitled *Casa Wappy*, which was the self-conferred pet name of his infant son; we cite a portion of the verses :—

And hast thou sought thy heavenly home, our fond, dear boy—
The realms where sorrow dare not come, where life is joy?
    Pure at thy death as at thy birth,
    Thy spirit caught no taint from earth;
    Even by its bliss we mete our death,—Casa Wappy!

Despair was in thy last farewell, as closed thine eye;
Tears of our anguish may not tell when thou didst die;
    Words may not paint our grief for thee,
    Sighs are but bubbles on the sea
    Of our unfathomed agony,—Casa Wappy!

Thou wert a vision of delight, to bless us given;
Beauty embodied to our sight, a type of heaven:
    So dear to us thou wert, thou art
    Even less thine ownself than a part
    Of mine and of thy mother's heart,—Casa Wappy!

Thy bright brief day knew no decline, 'twas cloudless joy;
Sunrise and night alone were thine, beloved boy!
    This morn beheld thee blithe and gay,
    That found thee prostrate in decay,
    And ere a third shone—clay was clay,—Casa Wappy!

     *   *   *

The nursery shows thy pictured wall, thy bat, thy bow,
Thy cloak and bonnet, club and ball; but where art thou?
    A corner holds thine empty chair,
    Thy playthings, idly scattered there,
    But speak to us of our despair,—Casa Wappy!

Even to the last thy every word—to glad, to grieve—
Was sweet as sweetest song of bird on summer's eve:
 In outward beauty undecayed,
 Death o'er thy spirit cast no shade,
 And like the rainbow thou didst fade,—Casa Wappy!
    *   *   *

This favourite little lyric is by ROBERT C. SPENCER :—

Too late I stayed; forgive the crime; unheeded flew the hours;
How noiseless falls the foot of Time that only treads on flowers!
What eye with clear account remarks the ebbing of his glass,
When all its sands are diamond sparks, that dazzle as they pass?
Ah! who to sober measurement Time's happy swiftness brings,
When birds of Paradise have lent their plumage for his wings?

Here is a sweet pastoral sketch, by WORDSWORTH; let us, in
imagination, go a-nutting with the philosophic poet :—

               Among the woods,
And o'er the pathless rocks, I forced my way
Until, at length, I came to one dear nook
Unvisited, where not a broken bough
Drooped with its withered leaves, ungracious sign
Of devastation, but the hazels rose
Tall and erect, with milk-white clusters hung,
A virgin scene,—or beneath the trees I sate
Among the flowers, and with the flowers I played:
A temper known to those who, after long
And weary expectation, have been blest
With sudden happiness beyond all hope.
       ❊   ❊   ❊

    And I saw the sparkling foam,
And, with my cheek on one of those green stones

That, fleeced with moss, beneath the shady trees,
Lay round me, scattered like a flock of sheep,
I heard the murmur and the murmuring sound,
In that sweet mood when pleasure loves to pay
Tribute to ease : and, of its joys secure,

The heart luxuriates with indifferent things,
Wasting its kindliness on stocks and stones,
And on the vacant air.   Then up I rose,
And dragged to earth both branch and bough, with crash
And merciless ravage ; and the shady nook
Of hazels, and the green and mossy bower,
Deformed and sullied, patiently gave up

Their quiet being: and, unless I now
Confound my present feelings with the past,
Even then, when from the bower I turned away
Exulting, rich beyond the wealth of kings,
I felt a sense of pain when I beheld
The silent trees and the intruding sky.
Then, dearest maiden! move along these shades
In gentleness of heart; with the gentle hand
Touch—for there is a spirit in the woods.

Wordsworth, it has been said, "appealed to the universal spirit, and strove to sound sweeter strings, and deeper depths, than others had essayed to do; and sought to make poetry a melodious anthem of human life, with all its hopes, dreads, and passions." The apparent simplicity of his style is informed with an inner and subtle meaning, which pervades all he writes; and this characteristic is especially true of his *Lines on Tintern Abbey*, and his *Ode to Immortality*. Few poets were more ardent lovers of nature; he tells us as much in the following stanza:—

One impulse from a vernal wood may teach you more of man,
Of moral evil and of good, than all the sages can.

Many of his pastoral pieces are, consequently, fresh as the morning; as Coleridge has said, "they have the dew upon them." When once asked where his library was, he pointed to the woods and streams, saying, "These are my books." So fond was he of wandering over hill and dale, by fountain or fresh shade, that De Quincey estimates his entire perambulations at about one hundred and eighty thousand miles. His calm and beautiful life, so sequestered from the noise and tumult of the town, and so replete with eloquent and sagacious teaching to the world, was extended to eighty years.

The following beautiful tribute to *Woman's Worth* was originally addressed to his wife, three years after marriage:—

267

She was a phantom of delight
When first she gleamed upon my sight ;
A lovely apparition, sent
To be a moment's ornament ;
Her eyes as stars of twilight fair,—
Like twilight's, too, her dusky hair ;
But all things else about her drawn
From May-time and the cheerful dawn :
A dancing shape, an image gay,
To haunt, to startle, and waylay.
I saw her, upon nearer view,
A spirit, yet a woman too !
Her household motions light and free,
And steps of virgin liberty :
A countenance in which did meet
Sweet records, promises as sweet :
A creature not too bright or good
For human nature's daily food,—
For transient sorrows, simple wiles,
Praise, blame, love, kisses, tears, and smiles.
And now I see, with eye serene,
The very pulse of the machine :
A being breathing thoughtful breath—
A traveller 'twixt life and death :
The reason firm, the temperate will,
Endurance, foresight, strength, and skill,—
A perfect woman, nobly planned
To warm, to comfort, and command,—
And yet a spirit still and bright,
With something of an angel light !

His fine poem on *Tintern Abbey*, he tells us, was composed after crossing the Wye, and during a ramble of four or five days with his sister. Not a line of it was uttered, and not any part of it written down, till he reached Bristol. This is the choice passage from the poem; where he tells us, that to this practice he owed

> A gift
> Of aspect most sublime : that blessed mood
> In which the burden of the mystery,
> In which the heavy and the weary weight
> Of all this unintelligible world
> Is lightened : that serene and blessed mood
> In which the affections gently lead us on,
> Until the breath of this corporeal frame,
> And even the motion of our human blood,
> Almost suspended, we are laid asleep
> In body, and become a living soul :
> While, with an eye made quiet by the power
> Of harmony, and the deep power of joy,
> We seek into the life of things.

Few poems of Wordsworth have been more often cited than his grand *Ode on Immortality* ; here is a passage from it :—

> There was a time when meadow, grove, and stream,
> The earth, and every common sight, to me did seem
> Apparelled in celestial light—the glory and the freshness of a dream.
> It is not now, as it hath been of yore ;
> Turn wheresoe'er I may, by night or day,
> The things which I have seen, I now can see no more.
> The rainbow comes and goes, and lovely is the rose ;
> The moon doth with delight look round her when the heavens are
> bare ;
> Waters on a stormy night are beautiful and fair ;
> The sunshine is a glorious birth ; but yet I know, where'er I go,
> That there hath passed away a glory from the earth.

*   *   *

Our birth is but a sleep and a forgetting;
The soul that rises with us, our life's star,
Hath had elsewhere its setting, and cometh from afar.
Not in entire forgetfulness, and not in utter nakedness,
But trailing clouds of glory do we come
From God, who is our home.

Heaven lies about us in our infancy!
Shades of the prison-house begin to close upon the growing boy,
But he beholds the light, and whence it flows; he sees it in his joy.
The youth, who daily farther from the East
Must travel, still is Nature's priest,
And by the Vision splendid is on his way attended:
At length the man perceives it die away,
And fade into the light of common day.

* * *

Another of the admired poems of Wordsworth is that addressed to the *Daffodils* :—

I wandered lonely as a cloud, that floats on high o'er vales and hills,
When all at once I saw a crowd, a host of golden daffodils,
Beside a lake, beneath the trees,
Fluttering and dancing in the breeze.

Continuous as the stars that shine and twinkle on the Milky-way,
They stretched, in never-ending line, along the margin of a bay;
Ten thousand saw I at a glance,
Tossing their heads in sprightly dance.

The waves beside them danced; but they outdid the sparkling waves
in glee:
A poet could not but be gay in such a jocund company.
I gazed, and gazed, but little thought
What wealth the show to me had brought.

For oft when on my couch I lie, in vacant or in pensive mood,
They flash upon that inward eye which is the bliss of solitude ;
    And then my heart with pleasure fills,
    And dances with the daffodils.

The well-known tale of *Peter Bell* was founded upon an anecdote
the poet read in a newspaper, of an ass being found hanging his
head over a canal in a wretched posture. Upon examination, a dead
body was found in the water, which proved to be that of its master.

His poem of *The Brothers* arose out of the fact related to him, at
Ennerdale, that a shepherd had fallen asleep upon the top of the
rock called " the Pillar," and perished, as here described, his staff
being left midway on the rock.. It was of this poem that Southey,
writing to Coleridge, said, " God bless Wordsworth for that poem !"
And Coleridge also confessed that he " never read that model of
English pastoral with an unclouded eye."

In glancing over the illuminated pages of this great poet, we can
scarcely fail to be charmed with the roseate tints and aromatic
odours with which he delights to deck his themes. Professor Wilson said, he would rather have been the author of that sweet pastoral
lyric *To Lucy*, than of an innumerable swarm of what the vulgar
taste has called clever songs :—

She dwelt among the untrodden ways beside the springs of Dove,
A maid whom there were none to praise, and very few to love :
A violet by a mossy stone half hidden from the eye !
Fair as a star, when only one is shining in the sky.
She lived unknown, and few could know when Lucy ceased to be ;
But she is in her grave,—and oh ! the difference to me !
          *   *   *

We cull two or three more little brilliants ;—here they are :—

Sympathy with Nature :—

    My heart leaps up when I behold a rainbow in the sky :

So was it when my life began, so is it now I am a man,
So be it when I shall grow old—so let me die!
The child is father of the man:
And I would wish my days to be bound each to each by natural piety.

Thanks to the human heart by which we live,
Thanks to its tenderness, its joys and fears;
To me the meanest flower that blows can give
Thoughts that too often lie too deep for tears.

Fragrance of Good Deeds :—

More sweet than odours caught by him who sails
Near spicy shores of Araby the blest,—
A thousand times more exquisitely sweet,—
The freight of holy feeling which we meet,
In thoughtful moments, wafted by the gales
From fields where good men walk, or bowers wherein they rest.

One of Wordsworth's finest sonnets is that he composed upon Westminster Bridge, in the autumn of 1803; here it is:—

Earth has not any thing to show more fair:
Dull would he be of soul who could pass by
A sight so touching in its majesty:
This city now doth like a garment wear
The beauty of the morning; silent, bare,
Ships, towers, domes, theatres, and temples lie
Open unto the fields, and to the sky,
All bright and glittering in the smokeless air.
Never did sun more beautifully steep
In his first splendour valley, rock, or hill:
Ne'er saw I, never felt, a calm so deep.
The river glideth at its own sweet will:
Dear God! the very houses seem asleep;
And all that mighty heart is lying still!

In SHELLEY's *Queen Mab*, we have this beautiful apostrophe to *Night :—*

How beautiful this Night ! the balmiest sigh
Which vernal zephyrs breathe in morning's ear
Were discord to the speaking quietude

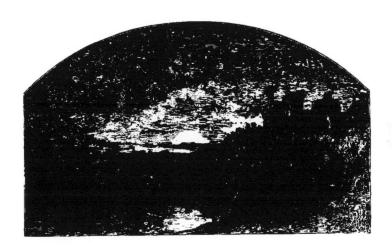

That wraps this moveless scene.　Heaven's ebon arch,
Studded with stars unutterably bright,
Through which the moon's unclouded splendour rolls,
Seems like a canopy which love has spread,
To curtain her sleeping world.

Among the most admired productions of Shelley are the lines to *The Cloud,* and the *Ode to the Skylark.* Judge of the rich quality of these compositions by the following extracts :—

The Cloud :—

I bring fresh showers for the thirsting flowers
    From the seas and the streams ;
I bear light shade for the leaves, when laid
    In their noon-day dreams.
From my wings are shaken the dews that waken
    The sweet birds every one,
When rocked to rest on their mother's breast,
    As she dances about the sun.
I wield the flail of the lashing hail,
    And whiten the green plains under ;
And then again I dissolve it in rain,
    And laugh as I pass in thunder.

        *   *

That orbèd maiden, with white fire laden,
    Whom mortals call the moon,
Glides glimmering o'er my fleece-like floor
    By the midnight breezes strewn ;
And wherever the beat of her unseen feet,
    Which only the angels hear,
May have broken the woof of my tent's thin roof,
    The stars peep behind her and peer :
And I laugh to see them whirl and flee,
    Like a swarm of golden bees,
When I widen the rent in my wind-built tent,
    Till the calm rivers, lakes, and seas,
Like strips of the sky fallen through me on high,
    Are each paved with the moon and these.
I bind the sun's throne with the burning zone,
    And the moon's with a girdle of pearl ;
The volcanoes are dim, and the stars reel and swim,
    When the whirlwinds my banner unfurl.

      *   *   *

I am the daughter of earth and water,
    And the nursling of the sky ;
I pass through the pores of the ocean and shores ;
    I change, but I cannot die.
For after the rain, when with never a stain
    The pavilion of heaven is bare,
And the winds and sunbeams, with their convex gleams,
    Build up the blue dome of air,
I silently laugh at my own cenotaph,
    And out of the caverns of rain,
Like a child from the womb, like a ghost from the tomb,
    I arise and unbuild it again.

To a Skylark :—

Hail to thee, blithe spirit ! bird thou never wert,
That from heaven, or near it, pourest thy full heart
In profuse strains of unpremeditated art !
Higher still and higher, from the earth thou springest
Like a cloud of fire ; the blue deep thou wingest,
And singing still dost soar, and soaring, ever singest.
In the golden lightning of the sunken sun,
O'er which clouds are brightening, thou dost float and run,
Like an unbodied joy whose race is just begun.
The pale purple even melts around thy flight ;
Like a star of heaven in the broad daylight,
Thou art unseen, but yet I hear thy shrill delight.
                *   *   *
All the earth and air with thy voice is loud,
As, when night is bare, from one lonely cloud
The moon rains out her beams, and heaven is overflowed.
What thou art we know not ; what is most like thee ?
From rainbow-clouds there flow not drops so bright to see,
As from thy presence showers a rain of melody.

Like a poet hidden in the light of thought,
Singing hymns unbidden, till the world is wrought
To sympathy with hopes and fears it heeded not :
Like a high-born maiden in a palace-tower,
Soothing her love-laden soul in secret hour
With music sweet as love, which overflows her bower :
Like a glow-worm golden in a dell of dew,
Scattering unbeholden its aërial hue
Among the flowers and grass, which screen it from the view.

   *   *   *

Teach us, sprite or bird, what sweet thoughts are thine :
I have never heard praise of love or wine
That panted forth a rapture so divine.
Chorus hymeneal, or triumphant chant,
Matched with thine would be all but an empty vaunt—
A thing wherein we feel there is some hidden want.

   *   *   *

We look before and after, and pine for what is not ;
Our sincerest laughter with some pain is fraught ;
Our sweetest songs are those that tell of saddest thought.

      *   *

Teach me half the gladness that thy brain must know,
Such harmonious madness from my lips would flow,
That the world should listen then, as I am listening now.

Note the brilliant fancy gleaming throughout these stanzas : few
poets, if any, since Spenser, have possessed such an exuberance of
beautiful imagery as Shelley and Keats. Had they not died so
young, it is impossible to conjecture what wonders they might have
achieved in the world of song.

Now let us gather a few fair flowers from Shelley's various
poems :—

Music, when soft voices die,
Vibrates in the memory ;
Odours, when sweet violets sicken,
Live within the sense they quicken.
Rose-leaves, when the rose is dead,
Are heaped for the belovèd's bed ;
And so thy thoughts, when thou art gone,
Love itself shall slumber on.

Sensitive Plant :—

A Sensitive Plant in a garden grew,
And the young winds fed it with silver dew ;
And it opened its fan-like leaves to the light,
And closed them beneath the kisses of night,
And the Spring arose on the garden fair,
Like the spirit of love felt everywhere :
And each flower and herb on earth's dark breast
Rose from the dreams of its wintry rest.
But none ever trembled and panted with bliss,
In the garden, the field, or the wilderness,
Like a doe in the noontide with love's sweet want,
As the companionless Sensitive Plant.

Autumn :—

The warm sun is failing, the bleak wind is wailing,
The bare boughs are sighing, the pale flowers are dying,
            And the year
On the earth her death-bed, in a shroud of leaves dead,
            Is lying ;

Come, months, come away, from November to May,
    In your saddest array ;
Follow the bier of the dead cold year,
And, like dim shadows, watch by her sepulchre.

The chill rain is falling, the nipt worm is crawling,
The rivers are swelling, the thunder is knelling
    For the year ;
The blithe swallows are flown, and the lizards each gone
    To his dwelling ;
Come, months, come away ; put on white, black, and gray,
    Let your light sisters play—
Up, follow the bier of the dead cold year,
And make her grave green with tear on tear.

Spring :—

O Spring ! of hope, and love, and youth, and gladness,
White-winged emblem ! brightest, best, and fairest !
Whence comest thou, when with dark Winter's sadness
The tears that fade in sunny smiles thou sharest ?
Sister of joy ! thou art the child who wearest
Thy mother's dying smile, tender and sweet ;
Thy mother Autumn, for whose grave thou bearest
Fresh flowers, and beams like flowers, with gentle feet
Disturbing not the leaves which are her winding-sheet.

A short time before poor KEATS's death, he told an artist-friend that he thought his intensest pleasure in life had been to watch the growth of flowers ; and not long before he died, he said, " I feel the flowers growing over me."

" His grave, at Rome, is marked by a little head-stone, on which are carved, somewhat rudely, his name and age, and the epitaph dictated by himself a few days previously—

    ' Here lies one whose name was writ in water.'

No tree or shrub has been planted near it, but the daisies, faithful to their buried lover, crowd his small mound with a galaxy of their innocent stars, more prosperous than those under which he lived."[1]

It is the prerogative of the poet to extract, by the alembic of his mind, beautiful thoughts and images from the minute and common, as well as the more rare and august aspects of nature. Few things win the poet's love and admiration so deeply as her rich garniture of flowers ; for instance, hear Keats's exquisite lines :—

> A thing of beauty is a joy forever—
> Its loveliness increases, it will never
> Pass into nothingness, but still will keep
> A bower quiet for us, and a sleep
> Full of sweet dreams, and health, and quiet breathing !
> Therefore, on every morrow are we wreathing
> A flowery band to bind us to the earth.

His most renowned poem is the *Eve of St. Agnes :* here are a few stanzas :—

> St. Agnes' eve—ah ! bitter chill it was !
>   The owl, for all his feathers, was a-cold ;
> The hare limped trembling through the frozen grass,
>   And silent was the flock in woolly fold ;
>   Numb were the Beadman's fingers, while he told
> His rosary, and while his frosted breath,
>   Like pious incense from a censer old,
> Seemed taking flight for heaven without a death,
> Past the sweet Virgin's picture, while his prayer he saith.
>
> *   *   *
>
> Full on the casement shone the wintry moon,
>   And threw warm gules on Madeline's fair breast,
> As down she knelt for heaven's grace and boon :

---

[1] J. R. Lowell.

Rose-bloom fell on her hands, together prest,
And on her silver cross soft amethyst,
And on her hair a glory, like a saint ;
She seemed a splendid angel, newly drest,
Save wings for heaven.

    *   *   *

A casement high and triple-arched it was,
All garlanded with carven imageries
Of fruits, and flowers, and bunches of knot-grass,
And diamonded with panes of quaint device,
Innumerable of stains and splendid dyes,
As are the tiger-moth's deep damask'd wings ;
And in the midst, 'mong thousand heraldries,
And twilight saints, and dim emblazonings,
A shielded scutcheon blush'd with blood of queens and kings.

Now let us turn to the pictorial pages of one of our most picturesque poets, WHITTIER, whose " lyre has been struck to many
a stirring note for freedom and human progress." We have the
highest authority for ascribing to his muse the attributes of " lyric
fervour and intensity combined with a tender and graceful fancy."

Our American bard is a true worshipper of Nature, as we see
from the following fine passage :—

The ocean looketh up to heaven, as 'twere a living thing ;
The homage of its waves is given in ceaseless worshipping.
They kneel upon the sloping sand, as bends the human knee,
A beautiful and tireless band, the priesthood of the sea !
They pour the glittering treasures out, which in the deep have birth,
And chant their awful hymns about the watching hills of earth.
The green earth sends its incense up from every mountain-shrine,
From every flower and dewy cup that greeteth the sunshine.
The mists are lifted from the rills, like the white wing of prayer ;
They lean above the ancient hills, as doing homage there.

JOHN G. WHITTIER.

The forest-tops are lowly cast o'er breezy hill and glen,
As if a prayerful spirit passed on nature as on men.
The clouds weep o'er the fallen world, e'en as repentant love,
Ere, to the blessed breeze unfurled, they fade in light above.
The sky is as a temple's arch, the blue and wavy air
Is glorious with the spirit-march of messengers at prayer.
The gentle moon, the kindling sun, the many stars are given,
As shrines to burn earth's incense on, the altar-fires of Heaven!

As the key-note of Whittier's poetry, we might take his own quaint
and beautiful lines : —

> I love the old melodious lays
>   Which softly melt the ages through,
> The songs of Spenser's golden days,
> Arcadia Sidney's silver phrase,
> Sprinkling o'er the noon of Time with freshest morning dew.

Whittier's style is characterized by its pure, strong Saxon : it is said
that he engenders his stirring and beautiful thoughts while walking
abroad, and subsequently commits them to paper. One of his graver
pieces, *The Reward*, commences thus : —

> Who, looking backward from his manhood's prime,
> Sees not the spectre of his misspent time ;

And, through the shade
Of funeral cypress, planted thick behind,
Hears no reproachful whisper on the wind
From his loved dead?

Who hears no trace of Passion's evil force?
Who shuns thy sting, O terrible Remorse?
Who would not cast
Half of his future from him, but to win
Wakeless oblivion for the wrong and sin
Of the sealed Past?

Alas! the evil, which we fain would shun,
We do, and leave the wished-for good undone;
Our strength to-day
Is but to-morrow's weakness, prone to fall;
Poor, blind, unprofitable servants all,
Are we alway.

Yet who, thus looking backward o'er his years,
Feels not his eyelids wet with grateful tears,
If he hath been
Permitted, weak and sinful as he was,
To cheer and aid, in some ennobling cause,
His fellow-men.

His *Dream of Summer* is eminently poetic:—

Bland as the morning breath of June the southwest breezes play,
And through its haze the winter noon seems warm as summer's day.
The snow-plumed angel of the North has dropped his icy spear;
Again the mossy earth looks forth, again the streams gush clear.
The fox his hill-side cell forsakes, the muskrat leaves his nook,
The blue-bird in the meadow-brakes is singing with the brook;
" Bear up, O mother Nature," cry bird, breeze, and streamlet free;
" Our winter voices prophesy of summer days to thee."

*   *

The Night is mother of the Day, the Winter of the Spring,
And ever upon old Decay the greenest mosses cling.
Behind the cloud the starlight lurks, through showers the sunbeams
      fall ;
For God, who loveth all His works, has left His hope with all.

What a grace and exquisite delicacy of touch characterize these
lines :—

A beautiful and happy girl, with step as soft as summer air,
      And fresh young lip and brow of pearl,
Shadowed by many a careless curl of unconfined and flowing hair :
A seeming child in every thing, save thoughtful brow and ripening
      charms,
As Nature wears the smile of Spring when sinking into Summer's
      arms.

A mind rejoicing in the light which melted through its graceful bower,
      Leaf after leaf serenely bright
And stainless in its holy white, unfolding like a morning flower :
A heart which, like a fine-toned lute, with every breath of feeling
      woke,
And, even when the tongue was mute, from eye and lip in music
      spoke.

How thrills once more the lengthening chain of memory at the
      thought of thee !—
      Old hopes which long in dust have lain,
Old dreams come thronging back again, and boyhood lives again in
      me ;
I feel its glow upon my cheek, its fulness of the heart is mine,
As when I leaned to hear thee speak, or raised my doubtful eye to
      thine.

I hear again thy low replies, I feel thy arm within my own,
      And timidly again uprise

The fringed lids of hazel eyes with soft brown tresses overblown.
Ah! memories of sweet summer eves, of moonlit wave and willowy
way,
Of stars, and flowers, and dewy leaves, and smiles and tones more
dear than they!

KEBLE'S lines on *The Lilies of the Field* are well worthy our
reciting :—

Sweet nurslings of the vernal skies, bathed with soft airs, and fed
with dew,
What more than magic in you lies, to fill the heart's fond view?
In childhood's sports, companions gay,
In sorrow, on life's downward way,
How soothing in our last decay,
Memorials prompt and true.

Relics ye are of Eden's bowers, as pure, as fragrant, and as fair,
As when ye crowned the sunshine hours of happy wanderers there.
Fallen all beside,—the world of life,
How is it stained with fear and strife!
In Reason's world what storms are rife,
What passions rage and glare!

But cheerful and unchanged the while your first and perfect form
ye show,
The same that won Eve's matron smile in the world's opening glow.
The stars of heaven a course are taught
Too high above our human thought;
Ye may be found if ye are sought,
And as we gaze, we know.

*　　　*　　　*

BURBIDGE'S lines on a *Mother's Love* are very charming :—

A little in the doorway sitting, the mother plied her busy knitting;
And her cheek so softly smiled,

Wherever through the ages rise
The altars of self-sacrifice,
Where love its arms has opened wide,
Or man for man has calmly died,
I see the same white wings outspread
That hovered o'er the Master's head
Up from undated time they come,
The martyr souls of heathendom,
And to His cross and passion bring
Their fellowship of suffering.

John G. Whittier

You might be sure, although her gaze was on the meshes of the lace,
    Yet her thoughts were with her child.
But when the boy had heard her voice, as o'er her work she did
    rejoice,
    His became silent altogether;
And slyly creeping by the wall, he seized a single plume, let fall
    By some wild bird of longest feather;
And all a-tremble with his freak, he touched her slightly on the
    cheek.
O what a loveliness her eyes gather in that one moment's space,
While peeping round the post she spies her darling's laughing face!
    O mother's love is glorifying—
    On the cheek like sunset lying,—
    In the eyes a moistened light,
    Softer than the moon at night!

Here is another sweet lyric of his :—

If I desire with pleasant songs to throw a merry hour away,
Comes Love unto me, and my wrongs in careful tale he doth display,
      And asks me how I stand for singing,
      While I my helpless hands am wringing.
And then another time, if I a noon in shady bower would pass,
Comes he, with stealthy gestures, sly, and flinging down upon the
    grass,
      Quoth he to me : My master dear,
      Think of this noontide such a year !
And if elsewhile I lay my head on pillow, with intent to sleep,
Love lies beside me on the bed, and gives me ancient words to
    keep ;
      Says he : These books, these tokens number—
      Maybe, they'll help you to a slumber.
So every time when I would yield an hour to quiet, comes he still ;
And hunts up every sign concealed, and every outward sign of ill !
      And gives me his sad face's pleasures,
      For merriment's, or sleep's, or leisure's.

ELIZA COOK's lyrics are well known, especially her song of the
Old Arm-chair, Nature's Gentleman, Washington, &c. Here is the
opening of her cheerful lines on *The World :*—

    Talk who will of the world as a desert of thrall,
      Yet, yet there is bloom on the waste ;
    Though the chalice of Life hath its acid and gall,
      There are honey-drops, too, for the taste :
    We murmur and droop, should a sorrow-cloud stay,
      And note all the shades of our lot ;
    But the rich rays of sunshine that brighten our way
      Are basked in, enjoyed, and forgot.
      *   ::   *

Now for the *Old Arm-chair* :—

> I love it! I love it! and who shall dare
> To chide me for loving that old arm-chair?
> I've treasured it long as a sainted prize,
> I've bedewed it with tears, and embalmed it with sighs;
> 'Tis bound by a thousand bands to my heart;
> Not a tie will break, not a link will start.
> Would ye learn the spell?—a mother sat there;
> And a sacred thing is that old arm-chair!
> In childhood's hour I lingered near
> The hallowed seat, with listening ear;
> And gentle words that mother would give,
> To fit me to die, and teach me to live:
> She told me shame would never betide—
> With truth for my creed, and God for my guide;
> She taught me to lisp my earliest prayer,
> As I knelt beside that old arm-chair.
>
>   *   *   *
>
> Say it is folly, and deem me weak;
> While the scalding drops start down my cheek;
> But I love it, I love it! and cannot tear
> My soul from a mother's old arm-chair.

MILMAN'S poetry is, for the most part, of a serious cast; yet he has given us the following light-hearted stanzas :—

> I would not from the wise require the lumber of their learned
>   lore;
> Nor would I from the rich desire a single counter of their store:
> For I have ease, and I have health, and I have spirits light as air;
>   And more than wisdom—more than wealth,—
>   A merry heart that laughs at care.

Like other mortals of my kind, I've struggled for Dame Fortune's
    favour;
And sometimes have been half inclined to rate her for her ill be-
    haviour;
But life was short,—I thought it folly to lose its moments in despair;
       So slipped aside from melancholy,
       With merry heart that laughed at care.

          *   *   *

So now from idle wishes clear, I make the good I may not find;
Adown the stream I gently steer, and shift my sail with every wind;
And, half by nature, half by reason, can still with pliant heart prepare
       The mind, attuned to every season,
       The merry heart, that laughs at care.

Yet, wrap me in your sweetest dream, ye social feelings of the mind;
Give, sometimes give your sunny gleam, and let the rest good-
    humour find;
Yes, let me hail, and welcome give to every joy my lot may share;
       And pleased and pleasing let me live,
       With merry heart that laughs at care.

SWAIN's lyrics are well known to lovers of music. His method
with coquettes is effectively given:—

Whatsoe'er she vowed to-day, ere a week had fled away,
       She'd refuse me!
And shall I her steps pursue—follow still, and fondly too?
       No—excuse me!
If she love me,—it were kind just to teach her her own mind;
       Let her lose me!
For no more I'll seek her side—court her favour—feed her pride;
       No—excuse me!
Let her frown—frowns never kill; let her shun me, if she will—
       Hate—abuse me:
Shall I bend 'neath her annoy,—bend—and make my heart her toy?
       No—excuse me!

Listen to his rhythmical lines to *Home Happiness:*—

Oh, there's a power to make each hour as sweet as Heaven de-
    signed it ;
Nor need we roam to bring it home, though few there be that
    find it ;
We seek too high for things close by, and lose what nature found us !
For life hath here no charm so dear as Home and friends around us !
We oft destroy the present joy for future hopes—and praise them ;
Whilst flowers as sweet bloom at our feet, if we'd but stoop to raise
    them.
For things afar still sweetest are, when youth's bright spell hath
    bound us ;
But soon we're taught that earth hath naught like Home and friends
    around us !

            *   *

Listen to our poet's delicate analysis of the Tender Passion ;—

Love ? I will tell thee what it is to love !
    It is to build with human thoughts a shrine,
Where Hope sits brooding like a beauteous dove ;
    Where Time seems young, and Life a thing divine.
All tastes, all pleasures, all desires combine
    To consecrate this sanctuary of bliss.
Above, the stars in cloudless beauty shine ;
    Around, the streams their flowery margins kiss ;
    And if there's heaven on earth, that heaven is surely this.
Yes, this is Love ; the steadfast and the true ;
    The immortal glory which hath never set ;
The best, the brightest boon the heart e'er knew ;
    Of all Life's sweets, the very sweetest yet !
    O ! who but can recall the eve they met
To breathe, in some green walk, their first young vow ?
    While summer flowers with moonlight dews were wet,

And winds sighed soft around the mountain's brow,
And all was rapture then, which is but memory now !

The *Quarterly Review*, referring to CAROLINE NORTON, styles
her the Byron of our modern poetesses, as she evinces much of
that intense personal passion by which his poetry is distinguished.
This is seen in her beautiful stanzas *To the Duchess of Sutherland*,
although they discover none of that poet's misanthropy. Here is
a passage :—

Thou gav'st me that the poor do give the poor,—
    Kind words, and holy wishes, and true tears ;
The loved, the near of kin could do no more,
    Who changed not with the gloom of varying years,
        But clung the closer when I stood forlorn,
        And blunted Slander's dart with their indignant scorn.
For they who credit crime, are they who feel
    Their own hearts weak to unresisted sin ;
Memory, not judgment, prompts the thoughts which steal
    O'er minds like these, an easy faith to win ;
        And tales of broken truth are still believed
        Most readily by those who have themselves deceived.

*   *   *

Great delicacy of fancy and feeling characterizes the verses of
T. K. HARVEY. In his lines on a *Convict Ship*, we have the following :—

'Tis thus with our life, while it passes along,
Like a vessel at sea, amidst sunshine and song !
Gayly we glide, in the gaze of the world,
With streamers afloat, and with canvas unfurled ;

All gladness and glory, to wandering eyes,
Yet chartered by sorrow, and freighted with sighs :
Fading and false is the aspect it wears,
As the smiles we put on just to cover our tears ;
And the withering thoughts which the world cannot know,
Like heart-broken exiles, lie burning below :
Whilst the vessel drives on to that desolate shore
Where the dreams of our childhood are vanished and o'er !

*   *   *

As specimens of the muse of our poet and essayist, TUCKERMAN,
we submit his beautiful lines *To the Eve, of Powers :*—

Ah, thine is not the woe of love forlorn,
   That Niobe's maternal anguish wears,
Nor yet the grief of sin, remorseful born,
   Canova's Magdalen so gently bears :
But the sad consciousness that through a wrong
   Conceived in self, and for a selfish end,
Immeasurable pain will now belong
   To unborn millions, with their life to blend ;
A heritage whereby sweet nature's face,
   So radiant with hope, and love's dear spell,
And all on earth that breathes of joy and grace,
   Shall know the tear, the shadow, and the knell ;
O Mother of our race !—Art does but image Fate
In thee, so fair and fond, and yet disconsolate.

The following fine sonnet was suggested by a proposition, on the
part of the New York Historical Society, that a new poetical name
should be given to North America :—

Worthy the patriot's thought and poet's lyre,
This second baptism of our native earth,

To consecrate anew her manhood's fire,
   By a true watchword all of mountain-birth ;
For to the hills has Freedom ever clung,
   And their proud name should designate the free ;

That when its echoes through the land are rung,
   Her children's breasts may warm to liberty !
My country ! in the van of nations thou
   Art called to raise Truth's lonely banner high ;
'Tis fit a noble title grace thy brow,
   Born of thy race, beneath thy matchless sky,
And Alps and Apennines resign their fame,
When thrills the world's deep heart with Alleghania's name !

BOWLES, whose poetry enjoys the distinction of " having delighted and inspired the genius of Coleridge,"—thus portrays, with " Dutch minuteness and perspicacity of colouring," *South American Scenery* :—

Beneath aërial cliffs and glittering snows,
The rush-roof of an aged warrior rose,
Chief of the mountain-tribes ; high overhead
The Andes, wild and desolate, were spread,
Where cold Sierras shot their icy spires,
And Chillan trailed its smoke and smouldering fires
A glen beneath—a lonely spot of rest—
Hung, scarce discovered, like an eagle's nest.
Summer was in its prime ; the parrot-flocks
Darkened the passing sunshine on the rocks ;
The chrysomel and purple butterfly,
Amid the clear blue light, are wandering by ;
The humming-bird, along the myrtle bowers,
With twinkling wing, is spinning o'er the flowers ;
The wood-pecker is heard with busy bill,
The mock-bird sings—and all beside is still.
And look, the cataract, that bursts so high
As not to mar the deep tranquillity,
The tumult of its dashing fall suspends,
And, stealing drop by drop, in mist descends ;
Through whose illumined spray and sprinkling dews
Shine to the adverse sun the broken rainbow hues.
Checkering, with partial shade, the beams of noon,
And arching the gray rock with wild festoon,
Here its gay network and fantastic twine
The purple cogul threads from pine to pine,
And oft as the fresh airs of morning breathe,
Dips its long tendrils in the stream beneath.
There, through the trunks, with moss and lichens white,
The sunshine darts its interrupted light,

And, mid the cedar's darksome bough, illumes,
With instant touch, the lori's scarlet plumes.

These lines on *Childhood* are by MACKWORTH PRAED:—

Once on a time, when sunny May
   Was kissing up the April showers,
I saw fair Childhood hard at play
   Upon a bank of blushing flowers;
Happy,—he knew not whence or how;
   And smiling,—who could choose but love him?
For not more glad was Childhood's brow
   Than the blue heaven that beamed above him.
Old Time, in most appalling wrath,
   That valley's green repose invaded;
The brooks grew dry upon his path,
   The birds were mute, the lilies faded;
But Time so swiftly winged his flight,
   In haste a Grecian tomb to batter,
That Childhood watched his paper kite,
   And knew just nothing of the matter.
      *   *   *
Then stepped a gloomy phantom up,
   Pale, cypress-crowned, Night's awful daughter,
And proffered him a fearful cup,—
   Full to the brim, of bitter water:
Poor Childhood bade her tell her name;
   And when the beldame muttered "Sorrow,"
He said—"Don't interrupt my game,—
   I'll taste it, if I must, to-morrow."
      *   *   *
Then Wisdom stole his bat and ball,
   And taught him, with most sage endeavour,
Why bubbles rise, and acorns fall,
   And why no toy may last forever:

She talked of all the wondrous laws
　　Which Nature's open book discloses,
And Childhood,—ere she made a pause,
　　Was fast asleep among the roses.
Sleep on, sleep on! Oh! Manhood's dreams
　　Are all of earthly pain or pleasure,
Of glory's toils, ambition's schemes,
　　Of cherished love, or hoarded treasure :
But to the couch where Childhood lies,
　　A more delicious trance is given,
Lit up by rays from Seraph eyes,
　　And glimpses of remembered heaven !

MOTHERWELL, the Scottish poet, sketched his beautiful outline of *Jeanie Morrison* when only fourteen years of age. His plaintive and picturesque poetry has attracted the admiration of many, and especially that of Prof. Wilson. List to one of his lyrics :—

Could love impart, by nicest art,
　　To speechless rocks a tongue, ·
Their theme would be, beloved, of thee,—
　　Thy beauty all their song.
And clerk-like, then, with sweet amen,
　　Would echo from each hollow
Reply all day ; while gentle fay,
　　With merry whoop, would follow.
Had roses sense, on no pretence
　　Would they their buds unroll ;
For, could they speak, 'twas from thy cheek
　　Their daintiest blush they stole.
Had lilies eyes, with glad surprise,
　　They'd own themselves outdone,
When thy pure brow and neck of snow
　　Gleamed in the morning sun.

Could shining brooks, by amorous looks,
Be taught a voice so rare,
Then, every sound that murmured round
Would whisper—" Thou art fair !"

* * *

His lines on *Summer* are beautifully expressed :—

They come ! the merry Summer months of Beauty, Song, and
Flowers ;
They come ! the gladsome months that bring thick leafiness to
bowers ;
Up, up, my heart, and walk abroad ; fling cark and care aside,
Seek silent hills, or rest thyself where peaceful waters glide ;
Or underneath the shadow vast of patriarchal tree,
Scan through its leaves the cloudless sky in rapt tranquillity.

* * *

There is no cloud that sails along the ocean of yon sky,
But hath its own winged mariners to give it melody ;
Thou seest their glittering fans outspread, all gleaming like red
gold ;
And hark ! with shrill pipe musical, their merry course they hold.
God bless them all, those little ones, who, far above this earth,
Can make a scoff of its mean joys, and vent a nobler mirth.

* * *

The *Gude-Wife*, a touching little poem, by JAMES LINEN, of
California, Mr. Bryant has pronounced not unworthy of *Burns :*—

I feel I'm growing auld, gude-wife—I feel I'm growing auld ;
My steps are frail, my een are bleared, my pow is unco bauld.
I've seen the snaws o' fourscore years o'er hill and meadow fa',
And, hinnie ! were it no' for you, I'd gladly slip awa'.
I feel I'm growing auld, gude-wife—I feel I'm growing auld ;
Frae youth to age I've keepit warm the love that ne'er turned cauld.

296

I canna bear the dreary thocht that we maun sindered be ;
There's naething binds my poor auld heart to earth, gude-wife, but
thee.

*   *   *

Here is a sweet, touching poem :—

Sleep on, baby on the floor, tired of all thy playing—
Sleep with smile the sweeter for that you dropped away in ;

On your curls' fair roundness stand golden lights serenely ;
One cheek, pushed out by the hand, folds the dimple inly—
Little head and little foot, heavy laid for pleasure :
Underneath the lids half-shut, plants the shining azure :

Open-souled in noon-day sun, so you lie and slumber;
Nothing evil having done, nothing can encumber.

       *   *   *

And God knows, who sees us twain, child at childish leisure,
I am all as tired of pain, as you are of pleasure.
Very soon, too, by His grace, gently wrapt around me,
I shall show as calm a face—I shall sleep as soundly—
Differing in this, that you clasp your playthings sleeping,
While my hand must drop the few given to my keeping,—
Differing in this, that I, sleeping, must be colder,
And, in waking presently, brighter to beholder,—
Differing in this beside,—(Sleeper, have you heard me?
Do you move, and open wide your great eyes toward me?)
That while I you draw withal from this slumber solely,
Me, from mine, an angel shall, trumpet-tongued and holy!

This is from the pen of one of the most gifted personages of modern times, MRS. E. BARRETT BROWNING, whose writings have been as warmly welcomed in our country as in England. Her life was one of prolonged bodily suffering, but her rare genius triumphed over all bodily infirmity. It was from her couch of pain that she sent forth those vigorous and beautiful productions that have crowned her as "the world's greatest poetess."

After her marriage with the poet Browning, Florence became their home; it was here she died. Among the many favourite poems of this eminent poetess, is that on *Sleep :* here are two or three of its beautiful stanzas :—

        Of all the thoughts of God that are
        Borne inward, unto souls afar,
           Along the Psalmist's music deep—
        Now, tell me if that any is,
        For gift or grace, surpassing this—
           " He giveth His beloved sleep?"

What would we give to our beloved?
The hero's heart, to be unmoved—
   The poet's star-tuned harp, to sweep—
The Senate's shout, to patriot vows—
The monarch's Crown, to light the brows?—
   " He giveth *His* beloved sleep."
      *   *   *

" Sleep soft, beloved "—we sometimes say,
But have no tune to charm away
   Sad dreams that through the eyelids creep;
But never doleful dream again
Shall break the happy slumber, when
   " He giveth His beloved sleep."
His dew drops mutely on the hill;
His cloud above it saileth still,
   Though on its slope men toil and reap!
More softly than the dew is shed,
Or cloud is floated overhead,
   " He giveth His beloved sleep."
      *   *   *

How prophetic of her own history were the closing lines :—

And friends, dear friends, when it shall be
That this low breath is gone from me,
   And round my bier ye come to weep;
Let one, most loving of ye all,
Say, " Not a tear must o'er her fall,—
   ' He giveth His beloved sleep!'"

Her fine poem on *Cowper* is one of the happiest illustrations of her power of pathos : witness these stanzas:—

Like a sick child, that knoweth not his mother while she blesses,
And drops upon his burning brow the coolness of her kisses;—

That turns his fevered eyes around—"My mother! where's my
   mother?"
As if such tender words and looks could come from any other!

The fever gone, with leaps of heart he sees her bending o'er him;
Her face all pale from watchful love, the unweary love she bore
   him!
Thus woke the poet from the dream his life's long fever gave him,
Beneath those deep, pathetic eyes, which closed in death to save him.

Thus! oh, not thus! no type of earth could image that awaking,
Wherein he scarcely heard the chant of seraphs round him breaking;
Or felt the new, immortal throb of soul from body parted;
But felt those eyes alone, and knew " *My* Saviour! *not* deserted!"

Wordsworth and Rogers much admired this stanza, in a poem on
Life, by Mrs. BARBAULD:—

> Life! we've been long together,
> Through pleasant and through cloudy weather;
> 'Tis hard to part when friends are dear;
> Perhaps 'twill cost a sigh, a tear;
> Then steal away, give little warning,
> Choose thine own time,
> Say not good-night, but in some brighter clime
> Bid me good-morning.

Her beautiful lines, on the *Death of the Virtuous*, were signally
illustrated by her own tranquil decease :—

Sweet is the scene when Virtue dies! when sinks a righteous soul
   to rest!
How softly beam the closing eyes, how gently heaves the expiring
   breast!
So fades a summer cloud away, so sinks the gale when storms are
   o'er,—

So gently shuts the eye of day, so dies the wave along the shore.
Triumphant smiles the victor brow, fanned by some angel's purple
    wing ;
Where is, O Grave ! thy victory now ? and where, insidious Death,
    thy sting ?

Here are LOVER's beautiful lines, founded upon the Irish conceit,
that when a child smiles in its sleep it is talking with the angels :—

A baby was sleeping,—its mother was weeping,
    For her husband was far on the wild raging sea ;
And the tempest was swelling round the fisherman's dwelling,
    And she cried, " Dermot, darling, oh, come back to me !"

Her beads while she numbered, the baby still slumbered,
    And smiled in her face as she bended her knee ;
" Oh, blest be that warning, my child, thy sleep adorning,
    For I know that the angels are whispering with thee !

" And while they are keeping bright watch o'er thy sleeping,
    Oh, pray to them softly, my baby, with me ;
And say thou wouldst rather they'd watch o'er thy father,
    For I know that the angels are whispering with thee !"

The dawn of the morning saw Dermot returning,
    And the wife wept for joy her babe's father to see :
And closely caressing her child with a blessing,
    Said, " I knew that the angels were whispering with thee !"

Our own poet PEABODY's description of *The Backwoodsman* is
very graphic and picturesque :—

The silent wilderness for me ! where never sound is heard,
Save the rustling of the squirrel's foot, and the flitting wing of bird,
Or its low and interrupted note, or the deer's quick, crackling tread,
And the swaying of the forest boughs, as the wind moves overhead.

Alone (how glorious to be free!), my good dog at my side,
My rifle hanging on my arm, I range the forests wide.
And now the regal buffalo across the plains I chase—
Now track the mountain stream, to find the beaver's lurking-place.

    *   *   *

My palace, built by God's own hand, the world's fresh prime hath
    seen,
While stretch its living halls away, pillared and roofed with green.
My music is the wind, that now pours loud its swelling bars,
Now lulls in dying cadences ; my festal lamps are stars.

    *   *   *

And in these solitary haunts, while slumbers every tree
In night and silence, God himself seems nearer unto me.
I *feel* His presence in these shades, like the embracing air,
And as my eyelids close in sleep, my heart is hushed in prayer.

STERLING, the friend of Carlyle, who placed a high estimate on
his genius, has not left us a large poetic legacy ; but here is one of
his poems, full of music and cheerful philosophy :—

Earth, of man the bounteous mother, feeds him still with corn and
    wine ;
He who best would aid a brother, shares with him these gifts divine.
Many a power within her bosom, noiseless, hidden, works beneath ;
Hence are seed, and leaf and blossom, golden ear and clustered
    wreath.
These to swell with strength and beauty is the royal task of man ;
Man's a king ; his throne is duty, since his work on earth began.
Bud and harvest, bloom and vintage—these, like man, are fruits of
    earth ;
Stamped in clay, a heavenly mintage, all from dust receive their
    birth.
Barn and mill, and wine-vat's treasures, earthly goods for earthly
    lives,—

These are Nature's ancient pleasures; these her child from her
   derives.
What the dream but vain rebelling, if from earth we sought to
   flee?
'Tis our stored and ample dwelling; 'tis from it the skies we see.
Wind and frost, and hour and season, land and water, sun and
   shade,
Work with these, as bids thy reason, for they work thy toil to aid.
Sow thy seed, and reap in gladness! man himself is all a seed;
Hope and hardness, joy and sadness—slow the plant to ripeness lead.

   ERNEST JONES is the author of the following stanzas; and very
beautiful they are :—

What stands upon the highland? what walks across the rise,
As though a starry island were sinking down the skies?

What makes the trees so golden? what decks the mountain-side,
Like a veil of silver folden round the white brow of a bride?
The magic moon is breaking, like a conqueror from the east,
The waiting world awaking to a golden fairy feast.

She works, with touch ethereal, by changes strange to see,
The cypress, so funereal, to a lightsome fairy tree ;
Black rocks to marble turning, like palaces of kings ;
On ruined windows burning a festal glory flings ;
The desert halls uplighting, with falling shadows glance,
Like courtly crowds uniting for the banquet or the dance :
With ivory wand she numbers the stars along the sky,
And breaks the billows' slumbers with a love-glance of her eye ;
Along the corn-fields dances, brings bloom upon the sheaf ;
From tree to tree she glances, and touches leaf by leaf ;
Wakes birds that sleep in shadows ; through their half-closed eyelids
    gleams ;
With her white torch through the meadows lights the shy deer to
    the streams.
The magic moon is breaking, like a conqueror from the east,
And the joyous world partaking of her golden fairy feast !

PROFESSOR WILSON is the author of the following beautiful
sonnet :—

A cloud lay cradled near the setting sun,
    A gleam of crimson tinged its braided snow ;
Long had I watched the glory moving on,
    O'er the still radiance of the lake below ;
    Tranquil its spirit seemed, and floated slow,
Even in its very motion there was rest ;
    While every breath of eve that chanced to blow
Wafted the traveller to the beauteous West :
    Emblem, methought, of the departed soul,
To whose white robe the gleam of bliss is given,
    And by the breath of Mercy made to roll
Right onward to the golden gates of heaven,
    Where to the eye of faith it peaceful lies,
    And tells to man his glorious destinies.

MACKAY's heroic tribute to *Valour* and *Virtue* is excellent :—

Who shall be fairest ? who shall be rarest ?
  Who shall be first in the songs that we sing ?
She who is kindest when fortune is blindest,
  Bearing through winter the blossoms of spring :
Charm of our gladness, friend of our sadness,
  Angel of life, when its pleasures take wing !
She shall be fairest, she shall be rarest,
  She shall be first in the songs that we sing !

Who shall be nearest, noblest, and dearest,
  Named but with honour and pride evermore ?
He, the undaunted, whose banner is planted
  On glory's high ramparts and battlements hoar ;
Fearless of danger, to falsehood a stranger,
  Looking not back when there's duty before !
He shall be nearest, he shall be dearest,
  He shall be first in our hearts evermore !

Much of Mackay's healthful verse is freighted with excellent counsel ; for instance, the following :—

What might be done if men were wise—
  What glorious deeds, my suffering brother,
Would they unite in love and right,
  And cease their scorn for one another !
Oppression's heart might be imbued
  With kindling drops of loving-kindness,
And knowledge pour, from shore to shore,
  Light on the eyes of mental blindness.
All slavery, warfare, lies, and wrongs,
  All vice and crime, might die together,
And wine and corn, to each man born,
  Be free as warmth in sunny weather.

The meanest wretch that ever trod,
　The deepest sunk in guilt and sorrow,
Might stand erect in self-respect,
　And share the teeming world to-morrow.
What might be done? *This* might be done,
　And more than *this*, my suffering brother—
More than the tongue e'er said or sung,
　If men were wise and loved each other.

PENDLETON' COOKE, another of our American bards, thus chants
his love-lay :—

I loved thee long and dearly, Florence Vane!
My life's bright dream and early hath come again;
I renew, in my fond vision, my heart's dear pain,
My hope and thy derision, Florence Vane.

The ruin lone and hoary, the ruin old,
Where thou didst mark my story, at even told,—
That spot—the hues Elysian of sky and plain—
I treasure in my vision, Florence Vane.

Thou wast lovelier than the roses in their prime;
Thy voice excelled the closes of sweetest rhyme;
Thy heart was as a river without a main.
Would I had loved thee never, Florence Vane!

But fairest, coldest wonder! Thy glorious clay
Lieth the green sod under—alas the day!
And it boots not to remember thy disdain—
To quicken love's pale ember, Florence Vane.

The lilies of the valley by young graves weep,
The pansies love to dally where maidens sleep;
May their bloom, in beauty vying, never wane
Where thine earthly part is lying, Florence Vane!

A Scottish bard, DAVID VEDDER, is the author of those sublime lines which Dr. Chalmers was so fond of rehearsing to his theological pupils :—

Talk not of temples—there is one built without hands, to mankind given :
Its lamps are the meridian sun, and all the stars of heaven.
Its walls are the cerulean sky, its floor the earth, serene and fair ;
The dome is vast immensity—all Nature worships there !
The Alps arrayed in stainless snow, the Andean ranges yet untrod,
At sunrise and at sunset, glow like altar-fires to God !
A thousand fierce volcanoes blaze, as if with hallowed victims rare ;
And thunder lifts its voice in praise—all Nature worships there !

   *   *   *

The cedar and the mountain pine, the willow on the fountain's brim,
The tulip and the eglantine, in reverence bend to Him ;
The song-birds pour their sweetest lays, from tower, and tree, and middle air ;
The rushing river murmurs praise—all Nature worships there !

One of N. P. WILLIS's masterpieces is his *Parrhasius*, yet the subject is not one that ministers pleasure to the reader. His *Melanie* must be perused entire in order to its due appreciation. The poem on *Idleness* is a fine illustration of poetic skill ; but we must content ourselves with his little cabinet picture of a *Child Tired of Play* :—

  " Tired of play ! Tired of play !"
  What hast thou done this livelong day ?
  The birds are silent, and so is the bee ;
  The sun is creeping up steeple and tree ;
  The doves have flown to the sheltering eaves,
  And the nests are dark with the drooping leaves ;
  Twilight gathers, and day is done—
  How hast thou spent it, restless one ?

" Playing ?"   But what hast thou done beside,
To tell thy mother at eventide ?
What promise of morn is left unbroken,—
What kind word to thy playmate spoken,—
Whom hast thou pitied, and whom forgiven,—
How with thy faults has duty striven ?
What hast thou learned by field and hill,
By greenwood path, and singing rill ?
There will come an eve to a longer day,
That will find thee tired—but not with play !

*　　*　　*

Very beautiful are his lines, commencing—

My mother's voice ! how often creep its accents on my lonely
hours !
Like healing sent on wings of sleep, or dew to the unconscious
flowers.
I can forget her melting prayer while leaping pulses madly fly,
But in the still, unbroken air, her gentle tones come stealing by.
And years, and sin, and folly flee,
And leave me at my mother's knee.

The evening hours, the birds, the flowers, the starlight, moonlight,—
all that's meet
For heaven, in this lost world of ours,—remind me of her teachings
sweet.
My heart is harder, and perhaps my thoughtlessness hath drunk up
tears ;
And there's a mildew in the lapse of a few swift and checkered
years—
But Nature's book is, even yet,
With all a mother's lessons writ.

*　　*　　*

His lines on *Dawn* are very choice—dewy and fragrant :—

> Throw up the window. 'Tis a morn for life
> In its most subtle luxury. The air
> Is like a breathing from a rarer world ;

> And the south wind is like a gentle friend,
> Parting the hair so softly on my brow.
> It has come over gardens, and the flowers
> That kissed it are betrayed : for as it parts,
> With its invisible fingers, my loose hair,

I know it has been trifling with the rose,
And stooping to the violet.   There is joy
For all God's creatures in it.   The wet leaves
Are stirring at its touch, and birds are singing
As if to breathe were music, and the grass
Sends up its modest odour with the dew,
Like the small tribute of humility.

     *   *   *

S. J. CLARKE ("Grace Greenwood") is the writer of these glowing stanzas on *Love's Sweet Memories* :—

Canst thou forget, beloved, our first awaking
   From out the shadowy calms of doubts and dreams,
To know Love's perfect sunlight round us breaking,
   Bathing our beings in its gorgeous gleams—
                    Canst thou forget ?

A sky of rose and gold was o'er us glowing,
   Around us was the morning breath of May ;
Then met our soul-tides, thence together flowing,
   Then kissed our thought-waves, mingling on their way :
                    Canst thou forget ?

     *   *   *

Canst thou forget the childlike heart-outpouring
   Of her whose fond faith knew no faltering fears ?
The lashes drooped to veil her eyes adoring,
   Her speaking silence, and her blissful tears—
                    Canst thou forget ?

Canst thou forget, though all Love's spells be broken,
   The wild farewell, which rent our souls apart ?
And that last gift, affection's holiest token,
   The severed tress, which lay upon thy heart—
                    Canst thou forget ?

     *   *   *

Here is CROLY's fine tribute to *Domestic Love* :—

> O, love of loves !—to thy white hand is given
>   Of earthly happiness the golden key !
> Thine are the joyous hours of winter's even,
>   When the babes cling around their father's knee ;
>   And thine the voice, that on the midnight sea
> Melts the rude mariner with thoughts of home,
>   Peopling the gloom with all he longs to see.
> Spirit ! I've built a shrine ; and thou hast come,
> And on its altar closed—forever closed thy plume !

We close our Fifth Poetic Evening with some of HORACE SMITH's pictorial stanzas, entitled *A Hymn to the Flowers* :—

> Day-stars ! that ope your eyes with morn, to twinkle
>   From rainbow galaxies of earth's creation,
> And dew-drops on her holy altars sprinkle,
>   As a libation !
>
> Ye matin-worshippers ! who, bending lowly
>   Before the uprisen sun, God's lidless eye,
> Throw from your chalices a sweet and holy
>   Incense on high !
>
> Ye bright mosaics ! that with storied beauty
>   The floor of Nature's temple tessellate,
> What numerous emblems of instructive duty
>   Your forms create !
>
> *   *   *
>
> Your voiceless lips, O Flowers ! are living preachers,
>   Each cup a pulpit, and each leaf a book,
> Supplying to my fancy numerous teachers
>   From loneliest nook !

Floral apostles ! that, in dewy splendour,
   "Weep without woe, and blush without a crime,"
O, may I deeply learn, and ne'er surrender,
          Your lore sublime !

      *   *   *

Ephemeral sages ! what instructors hoary
   For such a world of thought could furnish scope ?
Each fading calyx a *memento mori*,
          Yet fount of hope !

Posthumous glories ! angel-like collection !
   Upraised from seed or bulb interred in earth,
Ye are to me a type of resurrection
          And second birth.

315TH
EVENING

Longfellow, Chadwick,

Fields, Massey, Bulwer-Lytton, Holmes,

Emerson, R. Brown, E. Arnold, C. Young, Street,

H. Coleridge, Frances Brown, Proctor, R. Browning, A. Proctor,

Bailey, A. Smith, Saxe, Hinxman, Kingsley, B. Taylor, Robert Lowell,

Thackeray, Macaulay, Westwood, J. R. Lowell, R. B. Lytton,

A. C. Coxe, Aldrich, Tennyson, Stoddard, Stedman,

Cranch, Dickens, F. Tennyson, Allingham,

Winter, Boker. Ingelow.

UNDER a spreading chestnut-tree, the village smithy stands ;
 The smith, a mighty man is he, with large and sinewy hands ;
And the muscles of his brawny arms are strong as iron bands.
His hair is crisp, and black, and long ; his face is like the tan ;
His brow is wet with honest sweat ; he earns whate'er he can,
And looks the whole world in the face, for he owes not any man.

Week in, week out, from morn till night, you can hear his bellows
   blow ;
You can hear him swing his heavy sledge, with measured beat and
   slow ;
Like a sexton ringing the village bell, when the evening sun is low.
And children, coming home from school, look in at the open door ;
They love to see the flaming forge, and hear the bellows roar,
And catch the burning sparks that fly like chaff from a threshing-
   floor.
He goes on Sunday to his church, and sits among his boys ;
He hears the parson pray and preach ; he hears his daughter's voice
Singing in the village choir, and it makes his heart rejoice.
It sounds to him like her mother's voice, singing in Paradise !
He needs must think of her once more, how in the grave she lies ;
And with his hard, rough hand he wipes a tear out of his eyes.
Toiling,—rejoicing,—sorrowing, onward through life he goes ;
Each morning sees some task begin, each evening sees it close :
Something attempted, something done, has earned a night's repose.
Thanks, thanks to thee, my worthy friend, for the lesson thou hast
   taught !
Thus, at the flaming forge of life, our fortunes must be wrought ;—
Thus, on its sounding anvil, shaped each burning deed and thought !

LONGFELLOW, whose *Village Blacksmith* we have now introduced,
has been justly regarded, both at home and abroad, as one of the
representative poets of the age. His muse is characterized by rare
melody of versification and brilliancy of imagery ; while the beautiful
and delicate feeling of home affections that pervades his productions,
renders him an especial favourite with all fireside circles. His historical and descriptive poems possess a rich and quaint charm.
Nothing can exceed the exquisite finish of some of his shorter
poems,—it was some half-dozen of these that secured for him so
eminent a fame. Those poems which have already become classic
are his *Psalm of Life*, *The Old Clock on the Stairs*, *Village Blacksmith*,

The night shall be filled with music
And the cares, that infest the day
Shall fold their tents like the Arabs,
And as silently steal away.

Henry W. Longfellow

Excelsior, The Ladder of St. Augustine, and *The Footsteps of Angels,* although there are many later productions that merit, and must attain, a like distinction. Here are three noble verses from the *Psalm of Life :* —

> Art is long, and time is fleeting,
>   And our hearts, though stout and brave,
> Still, like muffled drums, are beating
>   Funeral marches to the grave.
>
>   ❊   ❊   ❊
>
> Lives of great men all remind us
>   We can make our lives sublime,
> And, departing, leave behind us
>   Footprints on the sands of time!
>
> Footprints! that perhaps another,
>   Sailing o'er life's solemn main,
> A forlorn and shipwrecked brother,
>   Seeing,—shall take heart again.

The *Song of Hiawatha* has perhaps been the most popular of any of his recent productions ; but that which is generally esteemed his greatest work is *Evangeline,* which possesses an additional interest for us, since it illustrates some of the stirring incidents of our early history. " I shall never forget," writes an English author, on his recent visit to the United States, "that I have been permitted to touch the hand, and to listen to the discourse—full of calm, and wise, and gentle things—of a noble American man,—of him who wrote the *Village Blacksmith* and *Evangeline,*—of him whose life has been blameless, whose record is pure, whose name is a sound of fame to all people—Henry Wadsworth Longfellow."

One of his recent poems, entitled " *Weariness,*" must conclude our selections from his works :—

> O little feet, that such long years
> Must wander on, through doubts and fears,
> Must ache and bleed beneath your load !

I, nearer to the wayside inn,
Where toil shall cease and rest begin,
    Am weary, thinking of your road.

O little hands, that, weak or strong,
Have still to serve or rule so long,
    Have still so long to give or ask !
I, who so much with book or pen
Have toiled among my fellow-men,
    Am weary, thinking of your task.

O little hearts, that throb and beat
With such impatient, feverish heat,
    Such limitless and strong desires !
Mine, that so long has glowed and burned,
With passions into ashes turned,
    Now covers and conceals its fires.

O little souls, as pure and white
And crystalline as rays of light
    Direct from heaven, their source divine !
Refracted through the mist of years,
How red my setting sun appears,
    How lurid looks this soul of mine !

Very touching is the pathos of these plaintive lines, by SHELDON
CHADWICK :—

Our baby lies under the snow, sweet wife, our baby lies under the
    snow,
Out in the dark with the night, while the winds so loudly blow.
As a dead saint thou art pale, sweet wife, and the cross is on thy
    breast ;
Oh, the snow no more can chill that little dove in its nest !
Shall we shut the baby out, sweet wife, while the chilling winds do
    blow ?
Oh, the grave is now its bed, and its coverlet is of snow.
Oh, our merry bird is snared, sweet wife, that a rain of music gave,
And the snow falls on our hearts, and our hearts are each a grave !
Oh, it was the lamp of our life, sweet wife, blown out in a night
    of gloom ;
A leaf from our flower of love, nipped in its fresh spring bloom.
But the lamp will shine above, sweet wife, and the leaf again shall
    grow,
Where there are no bitter winds, and no dreary, dreary snow !

FIELDS, the author-bookseller of Boston, wrote this refrain :—

Underneath the sod low-lying, dark and drear,
Sleepeth one who left, in dying, sorrow here.
Yes! they're ever bending o'er her eyes that weep ;
Forms that to the cold grave bore her, vigils keep.
When the Summer moon is shining, soft and fair,
Friends she loved, in tears are twining chaplets there.
Rest in peace, thou gentle spirit, throned above!
Souls like thine, with God inherit life and love!

As a specimen of the rich music of GERALD MASSEY'S verse, we
offer the two following brilliant extracts :—

Death of the Babe Christabel :—

In this dim world of clouding cares,
    We rarely know, till 'wildered eyes
    See white wings lessening up the skies,
The angels with us unawares!
And thou hast stolen a jewel, Death!
    Shall light thy dark up like a star—
    A beacon kindling from afar—
Our light of love and fainting faith.
        *   *   *
Our beautiful bird of light hath fled ;
    Awhile she sat, with folded wings,—
    Sang round us a few hoverings,—
Then straightway unto glory sped!
        *   *   *
Through childhood's morning-land, serene
    She walked betwixt us twain, like Love ;
    While, in a robe of light above,
Her better angel walked unseen,—

320

Till life's highway broke bleak and wild ;
  Then, lest her starry garments trail
  In mire, heart bleed, and courage fail—
The angel's arms caught up the child !
             *   *   *

God's ichor fills the hearts that bleed ;
  The best fruit loads the broken bough ;
  And in our minds our sufferings plough,
Immortal Love sows sovereign seed !

Ah ! 'tis like a tale of olden time, long, long ago ;
When the world was in its golden prime, and Love was lord below !
Every vein of Earth was dancing with the Spring's new wine !
'Twas the pleasant time of flowers when I met you, love of mine !
Ah ! some spirit sure was straying out of heaven that day,
When I met you, Sweet ! a-Maying in that merry, merry May
Little heart ! it shyly opened its red leaves' love lore,
Like a rose that must be ripened to the dainty, dainty core.
But its beauties daily brighten, and it blooms so dear,—
Though a many winters whiten, I go Maying all the year
And my proud heart will be praying blessings on the day
When I met you, Sweet, a-Maying, in that merry, merry May.

Very charming is the following from the pen of Sir E. Bulwer
Lytton :—

Hollow is the oak beside the sunny waters drooping ;
Thither came, when I was young, happy children trooping ;
Dream I now, or hear I now—far, their mellow whooping ?
Gay, below the cowslip bank, see the billow dances,
There I lay, beguiling time—when I lived romances ;
Dropping pebbles in the wave, fancies into fancies ;
Farther, where the river glides by the wooded cover,

Where the merlin singeth low, with the hawk above her,
Came a foot and shone a smile—woe is me, the lover!
Leaflets on the hollow oak still as greenly quiver,
Musical, amid the reeds, murmurs on the river;
But the footstep and the smile!—woe is me forever!

These beautiful lines are also by this eminent novelist and poet :—

When stars are in the quiet skies, then most I pine for thee;
Bend on me then thy tender eyes, as stars look on the sea.
For thoughts, like waves that glide by night, are stillest when they
    shine;
Mine earthly love lies hushed in light, beneath the heaven of thine.
There is an hour when angels keep familiar watch o'er men,
When coarser souls are wrapped in sleep; sweet Spirit, meet me then!
There is an hour when holy dreams through slumber fairest glide,
And in that mystic hour it seems thou shouldst be by my side.
My thoughts of thee too sacred are for daylight's common beam;
I can but know thee as my star, my angel, and my dream!
When stars are in the quiet skies, then most I pine for thee;
Bend on me then thy tender eyes, as stars look on the sea.

As a genial satirist, OLIVER WENDELL HOLMES is perhaps unsurpassed by any American writer; he is not only a humorist, but
a true poet of passion and pathos, although his *forte* is the grotesque :
witness the following extracts :—

But now his nose is thin, and it rests upon his chin
    Like a staff;
And a crook is in his back, and a melancholy crack
    In his laugh.
For I know it is a sin for me to sit and grin
    At him here;
But the old three-cornered hat, and the breeches, and all that,
    Are so queer!

Quite equal to the above is the following, entitled *My Aunt* :—

My aunt, my dear unmarried aunt ! Long years have o'er her flown ;
Yet still she strains the aching clasp that binds her virgin zone :
I know it hurts her—though she looks as cheerful as she can ;
Her waist is ampler than her life, for life is but a span !
My aunt, my poor deluded aunt ! her hair is almost gray ;
Why will she train that winter curl in such a spring-like way ?
How can she lay her glasses down, and say she reads as well,
When through a double convex lens she just makes out to spell ?

*   *

Holmes's *Wine Song* has been justly admired :—

Flash out a stream of blood-red wine!—
  For I would drink to other days ;
And brighter shall their memory shine,
  Seen flaming through its crimson blaze.
The roses die, the summers fade ;
  But every ghost of boyhood's dream
By nature's magic power is laid
  To sleep beneath this blood-red stream.
It filled the purple grapes that lay
  And drank the splendours of the sun,
Where the long Summer's cloudless day
  Is mirrored in the broad Garonne ;
It pictures still the bacchant shapes
  That saw their hoarded sunlight shed,—
The maidens dancing on the grapes,—
  Their milk-white ankles splashed with red.
Beneath these waves of crimson lie,
  In rosy fetters prisoned fast,
Those flitting shapes that never die,
  The swift-winged visions of the past.

Kiss but the crystal's mystic rim,
  Each shadow rends its flowery chain,
Springs in a bubble from its brim,
  And walks the chambers of the brain.

    *   *   *

Here, clad in burning robes, are laid
  Life's blossomed joys, untimely shed ;
And here those cherished forms have strayed
  We miss awhile, and call them dead.
What wizard fills the maddening glass ?
  What soil the enchanted clusters grew,
That buried passions wake, and pass
  In beaded drops of fiery dew ?

    *   *   *

Here is his graphic sketch of the *Ploughman* :—

Clear the brown path, to meet his coulter's gleam !
Lo ! on he comes, behind his smoking team,
With toil's bright dew-drops on his sunburnt brow,
The lord of earth, the hero of the plough !
First in the field, before the reddening sun,
Last in the shadows when the day is done.
Line after line, along the bursting sod,
Marks the broad acres where his feet have trod ;
Still, where he treads the stubborn clods divide,
The smooth, fresh furrow opens deep and wide ;
Matted and dense, the tangled turf upheaves,
Mellow and dark, the ridgy corn-field cleaves ;
Up the steep hill-side, where the labouring train
Slants the long track that scores the level plain ;
Through the moist valley, clogged with oozing clay,
The patient convoy breaks its destined way ;
At every turn the loosening chains resound,

The mossy marbles rest
On the lips that he has prest
   In their bloom,
And the names he loved to hear
Have been carved for many a year
   On the tomb.

   Oliver Wendell Holmes,
    Boston July 20th 1875

The swinging ploughshare circles glistening round,
Till the wide field one billowy waste appears,
And wearied hands unbind the panting steers.
These are the hands whose sturdy labour brings
The peasant's food, the golden pomp of kings:

This is the page whose letters shall be seen
Changed by the sun to words of living green;
This is the scholar whose immortal pen
Spells the first lesson hunger taught to men;
These are the lines that heaven-commanded Toil
Shows on his deed—the charter of the soil!

   *   *   *

One more extract from his charming compositions, and one of the best :—

We count the broken lyres that rest
  Where the sweet wailing singers slumber ;
But, o'er their silent sister's breast,
  The wild flowers, who will stoop to number ?
A few can touch the magic string,
  And noisy Fame is proud to win them ;
Alas ! for those that never sing,
  But die with all their music in them !
Nay, grieve not for the dead alone,
  Whose song has told their hearts' sad story ;
Weep for the voiceless, who have known
  The cross without the crown of glory !
Not where Leucadian breezes sweep
  O'er Sappho's memory-haunted billow,
But where the glistening night-dews weep,
  On nameless sorrow's churchyard pillow !
O hearts that break and give no sign,
  Save whitening lip and fading tresses,
Till Death pours out his cordial wine,
  Slow dropped from Misery's crushing presses :—
If singing breath, or echoing chord,
  To every hidden pang were given,
What endless melodies were poured,
  As sad as earth, as sweet as heaven.

EMERSON's fine lines, entitled *Each and All*, are now before us :—

Little thinks, in the field, yon red-cloaked clown
Of thee, from the hill-top looking down ;
The heifer that lows in the upland farm,
Far heard, lows not thy ear to charm ;
The sexton, tolling his bell at noon,

Deems not that great Napoleon
Stops his horse, and lists with delight,
Whilst his files sweep round yon Alpine height ;
Nor knowest thou what argument
Thy life to thy neighbour's creed has lent.
All are needed by each one—
Nothing is fair or good alone.

       *   *   *

The delicate shells lay on the shore ;
The bubbles of the latest wave
Fresh pearls to their enamel gave,
And the bellowing of the savage sea
Greeted their safe escape to me.
I wiped away the weeds and foam,-
I fetched my sea-born treasures home ;
But the poor, unsightly, noisome things
Had left their beauty on the shore,
With the sun, and the sand, and the wild uproar.
The lover watched his graceful maid,
As mid the virgin train she strayed ;
Nor knew her beauty's best attire
Was woven still by the snow-white choir.
At last she came to his hermitage,
Like the bird from the woodlands to the cage ;
The gay enchantment was undone—
A gentle wife, but fairy none.
Then I said, " I covet truth ;
   Beauty is unripe childhood's cheat—
I leave it behind with the games of youth."
   As I spoke, beneath my feet
The ground-pine curled its pretty wreath,
   Running over the club-moss burs ;
I inhaled the violet's breath ;
   Around me stood the oaks and firs ;

Pine-cones and acorns lay on the ground;
Over me soared the eternal sky,
Full of light and of Deity:
Again I saw, again I heard,—
The rolling river, the morning bird;
Beauty through my senses stole—
I yielded myself to the perfect whole.

His admired poem on the *Rhodora* commences thus :—

In May, when sea-winds pierced our solitudes,
I found the fresh Rhodora in the woods,
Spreading its leafless blooms in a damp nook,
To please the desert and the sluggish brook :
The purple petals fallen in the pool
   Made the black waters with their beauty gay ;
Here might the red-bird come his plumes to cool,
   And court the flower that cheapens his array.
Rhodora ! if the sages ask thee why
This charm is wasted on the marsh and sky,
Dear, tell them that if eyes were made for seeing,
Then beauty is its own excuse for being.

     *   *   *

ROWLAND BROWN has published some beautiful effusions, in which he has exhibited much delicacy of fancy. Here are his lines on *Love-Letters :*—

As snowdrops come to a wintry world like angels in the night,
And we see not the Hand who has sent us them, though they give
    us a strange delight ;
And strong as the dew to freshen the flower or quicken the slum-
    bering seed,
Are those little things called " letters of love," to hearts that com-
    fort need.

For alone in the world, midst toil and sin,
These still, small voices wake music within.
They come, they come, these letters of love, blessing and being
blest,
To silence fear with thoughts of cheer, that give to the weary rest!
A mother looks out on the angry sea with a yearning heart in vain,
And a father sits musing over the fire, as he heareth the wind and
the rain ;
And a sister sits singing a favourite song, unsung for a long, long
while,
Till it brings the thought, with a tear to her eye, of a brother's
vanished smile ;
And with hearts and eyes more full than all,
Two lovers look forth for these blessings to fall ;
And they come, they come, these letters of love, blessing and
being blest,
To silence fear with thoughts of cheer, that give to the weary rest!
Oh! never may we be so lonely in life, so ruined and lost to love,
That never an olive-branch comes to our ark of home from some
cherished dove ;
And never may we, in happiest hours, or when our prayers ascend,
Feel that our hearts have grown too cold for a thought on an absent
friend :
For, like summer rain to the fainting flowers,
They are stars to the heart in its darkest hours,
And they come, they come, these letters of love, blessing and being
blest,
To silence fear with thoughts of cheer, that give to the weary rest!

EDWIN ARNOLD, one of the sweetest of England's latest poets,
is the author of these delicate lines to the *Almond Blossom :—*

Blossom of the almond-trees,
April's gift to April's bees,

Birthday ornament of Spring,
Flora's fairest daughterling ;—
Coming when no flow'rets dare
Trust the cruel outer air ;
When the royal king-cup bold
Dares not don his coat of gold ;
And the sturdy blackthorn spray
Keeps his silver for the May ;
Coming when no flow'rets would,
Save thy lowly sisterhood,
Early violets, blue and white,
Dying for their love of light.
Almond blossom, sent to teach us
That the Spring-days soon will reach us,
Lest, with longing over-tried,
We die as the violets died—
Blossom, clouding all the tree
With thy crimson broidery,
Long before a leaf of green
On the bravest bough is seen ;
Ah ! when winter winds are swinging
All thy red bells into ringing,
With a bee in every bell,
Almond bloom, we greet thee well.

How daintily he dilates upon the charm of Woman's gentle
voice :—

Not in the swaying of the summer trees,
  When evening breezes sing their vesper hymn—
Not in the minstrel's mighty symphonies,
  Nor ripples breaking on the river's brim,
Is earth's best music ; these may have awhile
High thoughts in happy hearts, and carking cares beguile :

But even as the swallow's silken wings,
    Skimming the waters of the sleeping lake,
Stir the still silver with a hundred rings,
    So doth one sound the sleeping spirit wake
To brave the danger, and to bear the harm—
A low and gentle voice—dear Woman's chiefest charm.

An excellent thing it is! and ever lent
    To truth, and love, and meekness; they who own
This gift, by the All-gracious Giver sent,
    Ever by quiet step and smile are known:
By kind eyes that have wept, hearts that have sorrowed—
By patience never tired, from their own trials borrowed.

An excellent thing it is—when first in gladness
    A mother looks into her infant's eyes,—
Smiles to its smiles, and saddens to its sadness—
    Pales at its paleness, sorrows at its cries;
Its food and sleep, and smiles and little joys—
All these come ever blent with one low, gentle voice.

            *   *   *

The following lines, simple and homely, yet touchingly beautiful,
are by CHARLOTTE YOUNG :—

How like a tender mother, with loving thoughts beguiled,
Fond Nature seems to lull to rest each faint and weary child!
Drawing the curtain tenderly, affectionate and mild.

Hark to the gentle lullaby, that through the trees is creeping!
Those sleepy trees that nod their heads, ere the moon as yet comes
        peeping,
Like a tender nurse, to see if all her little ones are sleeping.

One little fluttering bird, like a child in a dream of pain,
Has chirped and started up, then nestled down again.
Oh, a child and a bird, as they sink to rest, are as like as any twain.

ALFRED B. STREET's picturesque sketches of American Forest Scenery are excellent. It is evident that he is a lover of the meadows, woods, and streams, as well as of the wildest and most romantic of Nature's solitudes. Shall we roam with him through one of our primeval wildernesses :—

A lovely sky, a cloudless sun,
   A wind that breathes of leaves and flowers,
O'er hill, through dale, my steps have won,
   To the cool forest's shadowy bowers :
One of the paths all round that wind,
   Traced by the browsing herds I choose,
And sights and sounds of human-kind
   In Nature's lone recesses lose :
The beech displays its marbled bark,
   The spruce its green tent stretches wide,
While scowls the hemlock, grim and dark,
   The maple's scalloped dome beside :
All weave on high a verdant roof,
That keeps the very sun aloof,
Making a twilight soft and green,
Within the columned vaulted scene.
Sweet forest-odours have their birth
From the clothed boughs and teeming earth ;
   Where pine-cones dropped, leaves piled and dead,
Long tufts of grass, and stars of fern,
With many a wild-flower's fancy urn,
   A thick, elastic carpet spread ;
Here, with its mossy pall, the trunk,
Resolving into soil, is sunk ;
There, wrenched but lately from its throne,
   By some fierce whirlwind circling past,
Its huge roots massed with earth and stone,
   One of the woodland kings is cast.

A narrow vista, carpeted
With rich green grass, invites my tread;
Here showers the light in golden dots,
There sleeps the shade in ebon spots,

So blended that the very air
Seems net-work as I enter there.
The partridge, whose deep-rolling drum
    Afar has sounded on my ear,
Ceasing his beatings as I come,
    Whirrs to the sheltering branches near;

The little milk-snake glides away,
The brindled marmot dives from day :
And now, between the boughs, a space
Of the blue, laughing sky I trace :
On each side shrinks the bowery shade ;
Before me spreads an emerald glade ;
The sunshine steeps its grass and moss,
That couch my footsteps as I cross :
Merrily hums the tawny bee,
The glittering humming-bird I see ;
Floats the bright butterfly along,
The insect choir is loud in song ;
A spot of light and life it seems,
A fairy haunt for fancy dreams.
Here stretched, the pleasant turf I press,
In luxury of idleness ;
Sun-streaks, and glancing wings, and sky,
Spotted with cloud-shapes, charm my eye ;
While murmuring grass, and waving trees,
Their leaf-harps sounding to the breeze,
And water-tones that tinkle near,
Blend their sweet music to my ear ;
And by the changing shades alone
The passage of the hours is known.

These fine lines, to *The Nightingale*, are by HARTLEY COLE-
RIDGE :—

'Tis sweet to hear the merry lark, that bids a blithe good-morrow;
But sweeter to hark in the twinkling dark to the soothing song of
      sorrow.
Oh, nightingale, what does she ail ? And is she sad or jolly ?
For ne'er on earth was sound of mirth so like to melancholy.
The merry lark, he soars on high, no worldly thought o'ertakes him ;

He sings aloud to the calm blue sky, and the daylight that awakes
    him.
As sweet a lay, as loud, as gay, the nightingale is trilling:
With feeling bliss, no less than his, her little heart is thrilling.
Yet ever and anon a sigh peers through her lavish mirth;
For the lark's bold song is of the sky, and hers is of the earth.
By night and day she tunes her lay, to drive away all sorrow;
For bliss, alas! to-night must pass, and woe may come to-morrow.

Some beautiful lines have been written by a blind Irish girl, named
FRANCES BROWN. We present the following extract, as a specimen; it is about the *Woodland Streams:*—

Your murmurs bring the pleasant breath of many a sylvan scene;
They tell of sweet and sunny vales, and woodlands wildly green;
Ye cheer the lonely heart of age, ye fill the exile's dreams
With hope, and home, and memory,—ye unforgotten streams.
         *   *   *
The bards—the ancient bards—who sang when thought and song
    were new,—
O, mighty waters! did they learn their minstrelsy from you?
For still, methinks, your voices blend with all their glorious themes,
That flow forever fresh and free as the eternal streams!
Well might the sainted seer of old, who trod the tearless shore,
Like many waters deem the voice the angel hosts adore!
For still, where deep the rivers roll, afar the torrent gleams,
Our spirits hear the voice of God, amid the rush of streams!

PROCTOR'S ("Barry Cornwall") poetry is characterized by graceful images, couched in glowing words. His lyrics are especially
choice; for instance, how glowing and voluptuous, yet how pure, is
the following description of *A Chamber Scene:*—

    Tread softly through these amorous rooms;
      For every bough is hung with life,

And kisses, in harmonious strife,
Unloose their sharp and winged perfumes !
From Afric, and the Persian looms,
  The carpet's silken leaves have sprung,
  And heaven, in its blue bounty, flung
Those starry flowers, and azure blooms.

Tread softly ! By a creature fair
  The deity of Love reposes,
  His red lips open, like the roses
Which round his hyacinthine hair
  Hang in crimson coronals ;
  And Passion fills the arched halls ;
And Beauty floats upon the air.

Tread softly—softly, like the foot
  Of Winter, shod with fleecy snow,
  Who cometh white, and cold, and mute,
  Lest he should wake the Spring below.
Oh, look ! for here lie Love and Youth,
  Fair spirits of the heart and mind ;
Alas ! that one should stray from truth,
  And one—be ever, ever blind !
          *   *   *

Hear his homily on the *Brevity of Life* :—

We are born,—we laugh, we weep, we love, we droop,—we die !
Ah ! wherefore do we laugh or weep ? why do we live or die ?
Who knows that secret deep ?—Alas ! not I.
Why doth the violet spring, unseen by human eye ?
Why do the radiant seasons bring sweet thoughts, that quickly fly ?
Why do our fond hearts cling to things that die ?
We toil through pain and wrong ; we fight—and fly ;
We love, we lose ; and then, ere long, stone-dead we lie !
O life ! is *all* thy song—endure, and—die ?

His song of *The Sea* is familiar to us all, commencing :—

> The sea! the sea! the open sea,—
> The blue, the fresh, the ever free!
> Without a mark, without a bound,
> It runneth the earth's wide regions round :
> It plays with the clouds ; it mocks the skies ;
> Or like a cradled creature lies.

How quaintly and feelingly he appeals to *Time :*—

> Touch us gently, Time! let us glide adown thy stream
> Gently, as we sometimes glide through a quiet dream!
> Humble voyagers are we—husband, wife, and children three—
> (One is lost—an angel fled to the azure overhead!)
>
> Touch us gently, Time! we've not proud nor soaring wings ;
> Our ambition, our content, lies in simple things.
> Humble voyagers are we o'er life's dim, unsounded sea,
> Seeking only some calm clime : touch us gently, gentle Time!

One of ROBERT BROWNING'S finest poems is that entitled *Evelyn Hope :*—

> Beautiful Evelyn Hope is dead!
>   Sit and watch by her side an hour.
> That is her book-shelf—this her bed ;
>   She plucked that piece of geranium flower,
> Beginning to die, too, in the glass.
>   Little has yet been changed, I think ;
> The shutters are shut, no light may pass,
>   Save two long rays through the hinge's chink.
> Sixteen years old when she died!
>   Perhaps she had scarcely heard my name,—
> It was not her time to love : beside,
>   Her life had many a hope and aim,

Duties enough and little cares,
  And now was quiet, now astir,
Till God's hand beckoned unawares,
  And the sweet white brow is all of her.
Is it too late, then, Evelyn Hope?
  What, your soul was pure and true,
The good stars met in your horoscope,
  Made you of spirit, fire, and dew,—
And, just because I was thrice as old,
  And our paths in the world diverged so wide,
Each was naught to each, must I be told?
  We were fellow-mortals, naught beside?
No, indeed! for God above
  Is great to grant, as mighty to make,
And creates the love to reward the love,—
  I claim you still, for my own love's sake!
            *   *   *
I loved you, Evelyn, all the while:
  My heart seemed full as it could hold;
There was place and to spare for the frank young smile,
  And the red young mouth, and the hair's young gold.
So, hush! I will give you this leaf to keep,—
  See, I shut it inside the sweet, cold hand.
There, that is our secret! go to sleep:
  You will wake, and remember, and understand.

The rich and varied qualities of Browning's genius are beautifully exemplified in his poem referred to; but here is another passage, from his *Dramatis Personæ* (*Among the Rocks*), of a different character, no less admirable:—

Oh, good, gigantic smile o' the brown old Earth,
  This Autumn morning! How he sets his bones
To bask i' the sun, and thrusts out knees and feet

For the ripple to run over in its mirth ;
   Listening the while, where on the heap of stones
The white breast of the sea-lark twitters sweet.

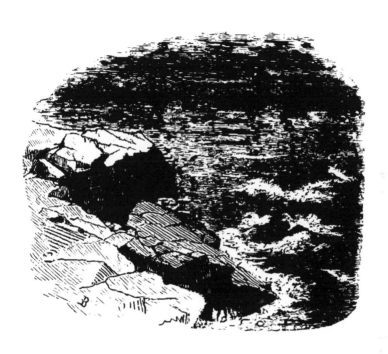

That is the doctrine, simple, ancient, true ;
   Such is life's trial, as old Earth smiles and knows.
If you loved only what were worth your love,
Love were clear gain, and wholly well for you :
   Make the low nature better by your throes !
Give Earth yourself, go up for gain above !
         *   *   *

We present two more of his fine lyrics :—

This is a spray the bird clung to, making it blossom with pleasure,
Ere the high tree-top she sprung to, fit for her nest and her treasure.
    O, what a hope beyond measure
  Was the poor spray's, which the flying feet hung to,—
  So to be singled out, built in, and sung to !

This is a heart the queen leant on, thrilled in a minute erratic,
Ere the true bosom she bent on, meet for Love's regal dalmatic.
    O, what a fancy ecstatic
  Was the poor heart's, ere the wanderer went on—
  Love, to be saved for it, proffered to, spent on.

        All June I bound the rose in sheaves ;
        Now, rose by rose, I strip the leaves,
        And strew them where Pauline may pass.
        She will not turn aside ? Alas !
        Let them lie. Suppose they die ?
        The chance was they might take her eye.
        How many a month I strove to suit
        These stubborn fingers to the lute !
        To-day I venture all I know.
        She will not hear my music ? So !
        Break the string—fold Music's wing.
        Suppose Pauline had bade me sing ?
          *   *   *

One of ADELAIDE PROCTOR'S best lyrics is that entitled *A Dream* :—

All yesterday I was spinning, sitting alone in the sun :
And the dream that I spun was so lengthy, it lasted till day was done.
I heeded not cloud or shadow that flitted over the hill,
Or the humming-bees or the swallows, or the trickling of the rill.

I took the threads for my spinning all of blue summer air,
And a flickering ray of sunlight was woven in here and there.
The shadows grew longer and longer, the evening wind passed by,
And the purple splendour of sunset was flooding the western sky.
But I could not leave my spinning, for so fair my dream had grown,
I heeded not, hour by hour, how the silent day had flown.
At last the gray shadows fell round me, and the night came dark
and chill,
And I rose and ran down the valley, and left it all on the hill.
I went up the hill this morning, to the place where my spinning lay—
There was nothing but glistening dew-drops remained of my dream
to-day.

BAILEY, the author of *Festus*, has written some exquisite little
songs : here is one :—

> For every leaf the loveliest flower
> Which beauty sighs for from her bower—
> For every star a drop of dew—
> For every sun a sky of blue—
> For every heart a heart as true !
> For every tear by pity shed
> Upon a fellow-sufferer's head,
> Oh ! be a crown of glory given—
> Such crowns as saints to gain have striven,
> Such crowns as seraphs wear in heaven.
> For all who toil at honest fame,
> A proud, a pure, a deathless name—
> For all who love, who loving bless,
> Be life one long, kind, close caress,
> Be life all love, all happiness !

There is great Miltonic vigour in the following extracts :—

> Keep thy spirit pure
> From worldly taint, by the repellent strength

Of virtue. Think on noble thoughts and deeds
Ever. Count o'er the rosary of truth ;
And practise precepts which are proven wise.
It matters not, then, what thou fearest ; walk
Boldly and fearlessly in the light thou hast :
There is a Hand above will lead thee on.

———

We live in deeds, not years ; in thoughts, not breaths ;
In feelings, not in figures on a dial.
We should count Time by heart-throbs. He most lives
Who thinks most, feels the noblest, acts the best.
And he whose heart beats quickest, lives the longest ;
Lives in one hour more than in years do some,
Whose fat blood sleeps as it slips along their veins.

ALEXANDER SMITH'S vigorous verse may be exampled by the
following brief passage on *Intellectual Beauty* :—

Beauty still walketh on the earth and air ;
   Our present sunsets are as rich in gold
   As ere the Iliad's music was out-rolled ;
The roses of the Spring are ever fair,
'Mong branches green still ringdoves coo and pair,
And the deep sea still foams its music old.
So, if we are at all divinely souled,
This beauty will unloose our bonds of care.
'Tis pleasant, when blue skies are o'er us bending,
Within old starry-gated Poesy,
To meet a soul, set to no worldly tune,
Like thine, sweet friend ! Oh, dearer this to me
Than are the dewy trees, the sun, the moon,
Or noble music with a golden ending !

Spes est Votis

I see, as parcel of a new creation,
  The beatific hour
When every bud of lofty aspiration
  Shall blossom into flower;

We are not mocked; it was not in derision
  God made our spirits free,
The Poet's dreams are but the dim prevision
  Of blessings that shall be,

When they who lovingly have hoped (trusted)
  (Despite some transient fears,-
Shall see Life's jarring elements adjust)
  And rounded into spheres!
            John G. Saxe.

He evinces great affluence of poetic beauty and grandeur of
thought in the following passage :—

> Sunset is burning like the seal of God
> Upon the close of day. This very hour
> Night mounts her chariot in the eastern glooms,
> To chase the flying Sun, whose flight has left
> Foot-prints of glory in the clouded west :
> Swift is she hailed by wingèd swimming steeds,
> Whose cloudy manes are wet with heavy dews,
> And dews are drizzling from her chariot-wheels
> Brainful of dreams, as summer hive with bees.
> And round her, in the pale and spectral light,
> Flock bats and grizzly owls on noiseless wings.
> The flying Sun goes down the burning west,
> Vast Night comes noiseless up the eastern slope,
> And so the eternal chase goes round the world.

Saxe, our American humorist, is worthy of his wide fame ;
listen to his premonitory indications of senescence :—

> My days pass pleasantly away ;
>   My nights are blest with sweetest sleep;
> I feel no symptoms of decay ;
>   I have no cause to mourn or weep ;
> My foes are impotent and shy ;
>   My friends are neither false nor cold ;
> And yet, of late, I often sigh—
>   I'm growing old !
>
> My growing talk of olden times,
>   My growing thirst for early news,
> My growing apathy to rhymes,
>   My growing love of easy shoes,

My growing hate of crowds and noise,
My growing fear of taking cold,
All whisper, in the plainest voice,
  I'm growing old !

I'm growing fonder of my staff ;
 I'm growing dimmer in the eyes ;
I'm growing fainter in my laugh ;
 I'm growing deeper in my sighs ;
I'm growing careless of my dress ;
 I'm growing frugal of my gold ;
I'm growing wise ; I'm growing—yes,
  I'm growing old !

  *   *   *

The following fine lines, entitled *Love's Impress*, are by E. HINX-
MAN :[1]—

Her light foot on a noble heart she set,
 And went again upon her heedless way,
Vain idol of so steadfast a regret
 As never but with life could pass away.

Youth, and youth's easy virtues, made her fair ;
 Triumphant through the sunny hours she ranged,
Then came the winter—bleak, unlovely, bare,
 Still ruled her image over one unchanged.

So, where some trivial creature played of old,
 The warm, soft clay received the tiny dint ;
We cleave the deep rock's bosom, and behold,
 Sapped in its core, the immemorial print.

[1] Fraser's Magazine.

Men marvel such frail record should outlive
The vanished forests and the hills o'er-hurled,
But high-souled Love can keep a type alive
Which has no living answer in the world.

CHARLES KINGSLEY'S poem, the *Three Fishers*, is a fine picture :—

Three fishers went sailing down to the west,
　Away to the west, as the sun went down ;
Each thought of the woman who loved him the best,
　And the children stood watching them out of the town :
　　For men must work, and women must weep,
　　And here's little to earn, and many to keep,
　　　Though the harbour bar be moaning.
Three wives sat up in the lighthouse tower,
　And trimmed the lamps as the sun went down ;
And they looked at the squall, and they looked at the shower,
　While the night rack came rolling up, ragged and brown :
　　For men must work, and women must weep,
　　Though storms be sudden and waters deep,
　　　And the harbour bar be moaning.
Three corpses lie out on the shining sands,
　In the morning gleam, as the tide went down,
And the women are weeping and wringing their hands,
　For those who will never come home to the town.
　　For men must work, and women must weep,
　　And the sooner it's over, the sooner to sleep,
　　　And good-by to the bar and its moaning.

We all remember his quaint lines in *Alton Locke*, commencing :—

O Mary, go and call the cattle home, and call the cattle home
　across the Sands o' Dee ;
The western wind was wild and dark wi' foam, and all alone
　went she.

Let us then read his fine *Song of the River*, which is equally
characteristic and beautiful:—

Clear and cool, clear and cool,
By laughing shallow and dreaming pool:
Cool and clear, cool and clear,
By shining shingle and foaming wear ;
Under the crag where the ouzel sings,
And the ivied wall where the church-bell rings,
Undefiled, for the undefiled ;
Play by me, bathe in me, mother and child.

Dank and foul, dank and foul,
By the smoke-grimed town in its murky cowl:
Foul and dank, foul and dank,
By wharf, and sewer, and slimy bank ;
Darker and darker the further I go,
Baser and baser the richer I grow ;
Who dare sport with the sin-defiled ?
Shrink from me, turn from me, mother and child.

Strong and free, strong and free,
The flood-gates are open, away to the sea :
Free and strong, free and strong,
Cleansing my streams as I hurry along
To the golden sands and the leaping bar,
And the taintless tide that awaits me afar,
As I lose myself in the infinite main, ·
Like a soul that has sinned and is pardoned again,
Undefiled, for the undefiled ;
Play by me, bathe in me, mother and child.

Here is another poetic gem from his pen :—

The world goes up, and the world goes down,
And the sunshine follows the rain ;

And yesterday's sneer and yesterday's frown
   Can never come over again,
   Sweet wife, can never come over again.
For woman is warm, though man be cold,
   And the night will hallow the day ;
Till the heart which at even was weary and old,
   Can rise in the morning gay,
   Sweet wife, can rise in the morning gay.

Here is a beautiful little waif, on the *Press*, by BAYARD TAYLOR :—

Oh ! the click of the type as it falls into line,
And the clank of the press, make a music divine !
'Tis the audible footfall of thought on the page—
The articulate beat of the heart of the age !
As the ebbing of ocean leaves granite walls bare,
And reveals to the world its great autograph there !

From the same popular writer we have another fine poem, *The Phantom*:—

Again I sit within the mansion, in the old, familiar seat ;
And shade and sunshine chase each other o'er the carpet at my feet ;
But the sweet-brier's arms have wrestled upward in the summers
    that are past,
And the willow trails its branches lower than when I saw them last.
They strive to shut the sunshine wholly from out the haunted room,—
To fill the house that once was joyful, with silence and with gloom.
And many kind, remembered faces within the doorway come,—
Voices that wake the sweeter music of one that now is dumb.
They sing, in tones as glad as ever, the songs she loved to hear ;
They braid the rose in summer garlands, whose flowers to her were
    dear.
And still her footsteps in the passage, her blushes at the door,
Her timid words of maiden welcome, come back to me once more.

And, all forgetful of my sorrow, unmindful of my pain,
I think she has but newly left me, and soon will come again.
She stays without, perchance, a moment, to dress her dark brown hair;
I hear the rustle of her garments—her light step on the stair !
O fluttering heart ! control thy tumult, lest eyes profane should see
My cheeks betray the rush of rapture her coming brings to me !
She tarries long—but lo ! a whisper beyond the open door—
And, gliding through the quiet sunshine, a shadow on the floor !
Ah ! 'tis the whispering pine that calls me, the vine whose shadow
    strays ;
And my patient heart must still await her, nor chide her long delays.
But my heart grows sick with weary waiting, as many a time before ;
Her foot is ever at the threshold,—yet never passes o'er.

ROBERT LOWELL'S beautiful poems evince great originality and
power : take, for instance, his lines entitled *Our Inland Summer
Nightfall* :—

Within the twilight came forth tender snatches
    Of birds' songs, from beneath their darkened eaves ;
But now a noise of poor ground-dwellers matches
    This dimness : neither loves, nor joys, nor grieves.
A piping, slight and shrill, and coarse, dull chirpings fill
    The ear, that all day's stronger, finer music leaves.
From this smooth hill, we see the vale below, there,
    And how the mists along the stream-course draw :
By day, great trees from other ages grow there,
    A white lake now, that daylight never saw.
It hugs in ghostly shape the Old Deep's shore and cape,
    As when, where night-hawks skim, swam fish with yawning maw.
All grows more cool, though night comes slowly over,
    And slowly stars stand out within the sky !
The trampling market-herd and way-sore drover
    Crowd past with seldom cries,—their halt now nigh.

From out some lower dark comes up a dog's short bark;
   There food and welcome rest, there cool, soft meadows lie.
The children, watching by the roadside wicket,
   Now houseward troop, for Blind-man's-Buff or Tag;
Here chasing, sidelong, fire flies to the thicket,
   There shouting, with a grass-tuft reared for flag.
They claim this hour from night :
But with a sure, still sleight,
   The sleep-time clogs their feet, and one by one they lag.

        *   *

And now the still stars make all heaven sightly :
   One, in the low west, like the sky ablaze;
The Swan, that with her shining Cross floats nightly,
   And Bears that slowly walk along their ways.
There is the golden Lyre, and there the Crown of fire :
   Thank God for nights so fair to these bright days !

THACKERAY's lines, *At the Church Gate*, are daintily put :—

Although I enter not, yet round about the spot
       Ofttimes I hover;
And, near the sacred gate, with longing eyes I wait,
       Expectant of her.
The minster-bell tolls out above the city's rout,
       And noise and humming.
They've hushed the minster-bell; the organ 'gins to swell;
       She's coming, she's coming !
My lady comes at last, timid, and stepping fast,
       And hastening hither,
With modest eyes downcast; she comes,—she's here,—she's past !
       May Heaven go with her !
Kneel undisturbed, fair saint ! pour out your praise or plaint
       Meekly and duly;

I will not enter there, to sully your pure prayer
    With thoughts unruly.
But suffer me to pace round the forbidden place,
    Lingering a minute,—
Like outcast spirits, who wait, and see, through Heaven's gate,
    Angels within it.

What a grand, heroic movement is there in MACAULAY's celebrated lay of the Huguenots, entitled *Ivry;* we can only give two
stanzas :—

Now glory to the Lord of Hosts, from whom all glories are !
And glory to our Sovereign Liege, King Henry of Navarre !

Now let there be the merry sound of music and of dance,
Through thy corn-fields green, and sunny vines, O pleasant land of
    France!
And thou, Rochelle, our own Rochelle, proud city of the waters,
Again let rapture light the eyes of all thy mourning daughters;
As thou wert constant in our ills, be joyous in our joy;
For cold, and stiff, and still are they who wrought thy walls' annoy.
Hurrah! hurrah! a single field hath turned the chance of war!
Hurrah! hurrah! for Ivry, and Henry of Navarre!

        *   *   *

Hurrah! the foes are moving.   Hark to the mingled din
Of fife, and steed, and trump, and drum, and roaring culverin.
The fiery duke is pricking fast across Saint André's plain,
With all the hireling chivalry of Guelders and Almayne.
Now by the lips of those ye love, fair gentlemen of France,
Charge for the golden lilies upon them with the lance!
A thousand spurs are striking deep, a thousand spears in rest,
A thousand knights are pressing close behind the snow-white crest;
And in they burst, and on they rushed, while, like a guiding star,
Amidst the thickest carnage, blazed the helmet of Navarre!

        *   *   *

One of Macaulay's noblest *Lays of Ancient Rome* is that of
Virginia, especially its closing lines, which are of wonderful beauty
and power.

T. WESTWOOD, one of the latest of the lyric poets of England,
gives us these sportive and beautiful stanzas:—

Under my window, under my window, all in the midsummer weather,
Three little girls with fluttering curls flit to and fro together:—
    There's Bell, with her bonnet of satin sheen,
    And Maud, with her mantle of silver green.
    And Kate, with her scarlet feather.

Under my window, under my window, leaning stealthily over,
Merry and clear, the voice I hear of each glad-hearted rover.
   Ah! sly little Kate, she steals my roses,
   And Maud and Bell twine wreaths and posies,
    As merry as bees in clover.

Under my window, under my window, in the blue midsummer
    weather,
Stealing slow, on a hushed tip-toe, I catch them all together:
   Bell, with her bonnet of satin sheen,
   And Maud, with her mantle of silver green,
   And Kate, with her scarlet feather.

Under my window, under my window, and off through the orchard
    closes;
While Maud she flouts, and Bell she pouts, they scamper and drop
    their posies:
   But dear little Kate takes naught amiss,
   And leaps in my arms with a loving kiss,
   And I give her all my roses.

Here are two other poems by the same author :—

   Do you remember how we used to pace
    Under the lindens, by the garden wall?
   It was a homely, but secluded place,
    Safe sheltered from the prying gaze of all.
   Deep in the azure distance loomed the tall,
    Grand, heathery hills, and one bluff-headland high
    Rose, rain-crowned, against the golden sky;—
   How lovingly around you seemed to fall
   Those linden shadows—when you laid aside
    Your hat, in the hot noon, and let the air
    Kiss cheek and forehead, while I fetched you rare

Red-coated peaches, or the purple pride
Of grapes, still glowing with the autumn sun!—
And we sipped other fruit too, little one.

Piped the blackbird on the beechwood spray :
" Pretty maid, slow wandering this way,
    What's your name ?" quoth he—
"What's your name ?   O stop and straight unfold,
Pretty maid, with showery curls of gold,"—
    " Little Bell,"—said she.

Little Bell sat down beneath the rocks—
Tossed aside her gleaming golden locks—
    " Bonny bird," quoth she,
" Sing me your best song before I go."
" Here's the very finest song I know,
    Little Bell," said he.

And the blackbird piped ; you never heard
Half so gay a song from any bird—
    Full of quips and wiles,
Now so round and rich, now soft and slow,
All for love of that sweet face below,
    Dimpled o'er with smiles.

And the while the bonny bird did pour
His full heart out freely o'er and o'er
    'Neath the morning skies,
In the little childish heart below,
All the sweetness seemed to grow and grow,
And shine forth in happy overflow
    From the blue bright eyes.

*   *   *

One of the finest of JAMES RUSSELL LOWELL'S poems is that entitled *The Vision of Sir Launfal*, *or*, *the Tradition of the* "*Holy Grail.*" Tennyson, in his *Sir Galabad*, and Longfellow, in his *Golden Legend*, have also made it the subject of poetic treatment. We select only a few lines, introductory to Lowell's poem :—

> Not only around our infancy
> Doth heaven with all its splendours lie ;
> Daily, with souls that cringe and plot,
> We Sinais climb, and know it not :
> Over our manhood bend the skies ;
>   Against our fallen and traitor lives
> The great winds utter prophecies ;
>   With our faint hearts the mountain strives ;
> Its arms outstretched, the Druid wood
>   Waits with its benedicite ;
> And to our age's drowsy blood
>   Still shouts the inspiring sea.

How buoyant and jocund is the following passage on *The Sweet Influences of Spring:*

> Joy comes, grief goes, we know not how :
> Every thing is happy now,—
>   Every thing is upward striving :
> 'Tis as easy now for the heart to be true,
> As for grass to be green or skies to be blue,—
>   'Tis the natural way of living :
> Who knows whither the clouds have fled ?
>   In the unscarred heaven they leave no wake,
> And the eyes forget the tears they have shed,
>   The heart forgets its sorrow and ache ,

JRLowell. 1st Aug, 1875

What figure more immovably august
Than that grave strength so patient & so pure,
Calm in good fortune, when it wavered. Sure,
That soul serene, impenetrably just,
Modelled on classic lines so noble they endure?
That soul so softly=radiant & so white
The track it left seems less of fire than light
And cold to such as love intemperature?

The soul partakes the season's youth,
And the sulphurous rifts of passion and woe
Lie deep 'neath a silence pure and smooth,
Like burnt-out craters healed with snow.

    *   *   *

Lowell's delicate lines on *Violets* are worthy of the dainty little
flower :—

Violets—sweet violets !
   Thine eyes are full of tears ;
Are they wet even yet
   With the thought of other years ?
Or with gladness are they full,
For the night so beautiful,
   And longing for those far-off spheres ?

Loved one of my youth thou wast,
   Of my merry youth,
And I see, tearfully,
All the fair and sunny past,
   All its openness and truth,
Ever fresh and green in thee,
As the moss is in the sea.

Thy little heart, that hath with love
Grown coloured like the sky above,
   On which thou lookest ever,—
Can it know all the woe
   Of hope for what returneth never,—
All the sorrow and the longing
To these hearts of ours belonging ?

One of the most touchingly beautiful of modern poems is Lowell's
First Snow-fall, written on the grave of his first-born ; here it is—
full of gushing tenderness :—

The snow had begun in the gloaming, and busily all the night
Had been heaping field and highway with a silence deep and white.
Every pine and fir and hemlock wore ermine too dear for an earl,
And the poorest twig on the elm-tree was ridged inch-deep with
    pearl.
             *   *   *
I stood and watched by the window the noiseless work of the sky,
And the sudden flurries of snow-birds like brown leaves whirling by.
I thought of a mound in sweet Auburn, where a little head-stone
    stood,
How the flakes were folding it gently, as did robins the babes in
    the wood.
             *   *   *
I remembered the gradual patience that fell from that cloud-like
    snow,
Flake by flake, healing and hiding the scar of that deep-stabbed woe.
And again to the child I whispered—"The snow that husheth all,
Darling, the merciful Father alone can make it fall."
Then, with eyes that saw not, I kissed her; and she, kissing back,
    could not know
That *my* kiss was given to her sister folded close under deepening
    snow.

His sparkling lines to the *Fountain* are full of beauty :—

        Into the sunshine, full of light,
        Leaping and flashing from morn till night ;
        Into the moonlight, whiter than snow,
        Waving so flower-like when the winds blow !
        Into the starlight, rushing in spray,
        Happy at midnight, happy by day !
        Ever in motion, blithesome and cheery,
        Still climbing heavenward, never a-weary :
        Glad of all weathers, still seeming best,
        Upward or downward, motion thy rest :

Full of a nature nothing can tame,
Changed every moment—ever the same :
Ceaseless aspiring, ceaseless content,
Darkness or sunshine thy element :
Glorious Fountain ! let my heart be
Fresh, changeful, constant, upward, like thee!

ROBERT BULWER LYTTON ("Owen Meredith") is the author
of these delicate lines, entitled *The Chess-Board :*—

My little love, do you remember—
(Ere we were grown so sadly wise)—
Those evenings in the bleak December,
Curtained warm from the snowy weather,
When you and I played chess together,
Checkmated by each other's eyes?

*   *   *

Ah me ! the little battle's done,
Dispersed is all its chivalry ;
Full many a move, since then, have we
Mid life's perplexing checkers made,
And many a game with Fortune played,—
What is it we have won ?

This, this at least,—if this alone ;—
That never, never, never more,
As in those old still nights of yore
(Ere we were grown so sadly wise),
Can you and I shut out the skies,
Shut out the world and wintry weather,
And, eyes exchanging warmth with eyes,
Play chess, as then we played, together !

ARTHUR CLEVELAND COXE, author of *Christian Ballads*, thus
pays tribute to historic Old England :—

Land of the rare old chronicle, the legend, and the lay,
Where deeds of fancy's dream are truths of all thine ancient day ;
Land where the holly-bough is green around the Druid's pile,
And greener yet the histories that wreathe his rugged isle ;
Land of old story—like thine oak, the aged, but the strong,
And wound with antique mistletoe, and ivy-wreaths of song.
Old isle and glorious—I have heard thy fame across the sea,
And know my fathers' homes are thine ; my fathers rest with thee !

*   *   *

And I have wooed thy poet-tide from fountain-head along,
From warbled gush to torrent roar, and cataract of song.
And thou art no strange land to me, from Cumberland to Kent,
With hills and vales of household name, and woods of wild event:
For tales of Guy and Robin Hood my childhood ne'er would tire,
And Alfred's poet story roused my boyhood to the lyre.

*   *   *

Fair isle! thy Dove's wild dale along with Walton have I roved,
And London, too, with all the heart of burly Johnson, loved.
Chameleon-like, my soul has ta'en its every hue from thine,
From Eastcheap's epidemic laugh to Avon's gloom divine.
All thanks to pencil and to page of graver's mimic art,
That England's panorama gave to picture up my heart:
That round my spirit's eye hath built thine old cathedral piles,
And flung the checkered window-light adown their trophied aisles.
I know thine abbey, Westminster, as sea-birds know their nest,
And flies my home-sick soul to thee, when it would find a rest;
Where princes and old bishops sleep, with sceptre and with crook,
And mighty spirits haunt around each Gothic shrine and nook.
I feel the sacramental hue of choir and chapel there,
And pictured panes that chasten down the day's unholy glare;
And dear it is, on cold gray stone, to see the sunbeams crawl,
In long-drawn lines of coloured light that streak the bannered wall.

*   *   *

I've seen thy beacon-banners blaze our mountain coast along,
And swelled my soul with memories of old romaunt and song;
Of Chevy-Chase, of Agincourt, of many a field they told;
Of Norman and Plantagenet, and all their fame of old!

*   *   *

Thy holy Church—the Church of God—that hath grown old in
     thee,
Since there the ocean-roving Dove came bleeding from the sea;
When pierced afar, her weary feet could find no home but thine,
Until thine altars were her nest, thy fanes her glory's shrine!

359

These opening stanzas of *The Ballad of Babie Bell*—describing a
little life that "was but three Aprils long"—is by our American
poet, ALDRICH :—

Have you not heard the poets tell
How came the dainty Babie Bell
   Into this world of ours?
The gates of heaven were left ajar :
   With folded hands and dreamy eyes
   Wandering out of Paradise,
She saw this planet, like a star,
Hung in the glistening depths of even—
   Its bridges, running to and fro,
   O'er which the white-winged angels go,
Bearing the holy Dead to Heaven !
She touched a bridge of flowers—those feet,
   So light they did not bend the bells
   Of the celestial asphodels !
They fell like dew upon the flowers,
Then all the air grew strangely sweet ;
And thus came dainty Babie Bell
   Into this world of ours !
She came, and brought delicious May !
   The swallows built beneath the eaves ;
   Like sunlight, in and out the leaves,
The robins went, the livelong day :
The lily swung its noiseless bell,
   And o'er the porch the trembling vine
   Seemed bursting with its veins of wine :
How sweetly, softly, twilight fell !
O, earth was full of singing-birds
   And opening Spring-tide flowers,
When the dainty Babie Bell
   Came to this world of ours !

The poet-laureate of England, ALFRED TENNYSON, whose *May-Queen*, *Idyls of the King*, and *In Memoriam*, have won for him such high fame, has also enriched our English poetry with numerous lyrics of exquisite beauty. That fine outburst of philosophy and feeling, *In Memoriam*, has been compared to "a stream of song and sorrow, flowing deeply and calmly, and in the light of peaceful memories and tranquil hopes." Here is the opening stanza :—

> This truth came borne with bier and pall,
> I felt it when I sorrowed most,
> 'Tis better to have loved and lost,
> Than never to have loved at all.

> *   *

His last poem of *Enoch Arden* is the most touchingly beautiful of all his later productions. It is a simple story of two rival suitors for the hand and heart of Annie Lee, who all grew up from childhood together. Enoch, the sailor, at length becomes the accepted lover : he marries her, and subsequently goes on a distant voyage. Years intervene, and no tidings of him reach his wife, who mourns him as dead. Philip, the miller, meanwhile becomes wealthy, seeks again his early love —Annie, who, after many delays, and misgivings as to the fate of Enoch,—

> At last, one night it chanced
> That Annie could not sleep, but earnestly
> Prayed for a sign, "My Enoch, is he gone?"
> Then, compassed round by the blind wall of night,
> Brooked not the expectant terror of her heart,
> Started from bed, and struck herself a light,
> Then desperately seized the Holy Book,
> Suddenly set it wide to find a sign,
> Suddenly put her finger on the text —
> "Under a palm-tree." That was nothing to her :
> No meaning there : she closed the Book and slept ;

When, lo! her Enoch sitting on a height,
Under a palm-tree, over him the Sun:
"He's gone," she thought—"he is happy; he is singing

' Hosanna in the highest :' yonder shines
The Sun of Righteousness, and these be palms,
Whereof the happy people strowing, cried
' Hosanna in the highest !' "   Here she woke,

ALFRED TENNYSON.

Resolved, sent for him, and said wildly to him—
" There is no reason why we should not wed."

     *   *   *

So these were wed, and merrily rang the bells—
Merrily rang the bells, and they were wed.

     *   *   *

After twelve long years, poor old Enoch returns to his native place from his shipwreck and exile on a desert isle ; he finds all things changed, and is told of his own death, of his wife's long sorrow, of Philip's friendship, and how that friendship was at last repaid,—by a kindly gossip of the village, who can see no trace of Enoch Arden in the bent, gray-haired, worn-out old man who seeks the shelter of her half-ruined roof. Bowed down by unspeakable sadness, one wish only is present to him,—to see *her* face once again, and " know that she is happy." He yields to the irresistible longing, and from Philip's garden he gains a sight of the comfort and the genial happiness of Philip's hearth :

Now when the dead man come to life beheld
His wife—his wife no more, and saw the babe—
Hers, yet not his—upon the father's knee,
And all the warmth, the peace, the happiness,
And his own children tall and beautiful,
And him—that other—reigning in his place,
Lord of his rights and of his children's love,—
Then he—though Miriam Lane had told him all,
Because things seen are mightier than things heard—
Staggered and shook, holding the branch, and feared
To send abroad a shrill and terrible cry,
Which in one moment, like the blast of doom,
Would shatter all the happiness of the hearth.
He therefore, turning softly, like a thief,
Lest the harsh shingle should grate underfoot,
And feeling all along the garden-wall,

Lest he should swoon, and tumble, and be found,—
Crept to the gate, and opened it, and closed,
As lightly as a sick man's chamber-door,
Behind him, and came out upon the waste.
And there he would have knelt, but that his knees
Were feeble, so that falling prone he dug
His fingers into the wet earth and prayed :—
" Too hard to bear! why did they take me thence?
O God Almighty, blessed Saviour! Thou
That didst uphold me on my lonely isle,
Uphold me, Father, in my loneliness
A little longer! Aid me, give me strength
Not to tell her, never to let her know.
Help me not to break in upon her peace.
My children too! must I not speak to these?
They know me not. I should betray myself.
Never : no father's kiss for me—the girl
So like her mother, and the boy, my son."

It would, indeed, be hard to parallel the homely and tragic pathos
of this picture.

Tennyson's muse is characterized by exquisite finish, rich colouring, and dramatic energy. How graceful and delicate is this sketch,
from the *Day-Dream* :—

Year after year unto her feet, she lying on her couch alone,
Across the purple coverlet the maiden's jet-black hair has grown,
On either side her tranced form forth streaming from a braid of
    pearl ;
The slumbrous light is rich and warm, and moves not on the
    rounded curl.
           *   *   *
She sleeps : her breathings are not heard in palace chambers far
    apart ;
The fragrant tresses are not stirred that lie upon her charmèd heart.

Ask me no more. The moon may draw the sea;
The cloud may stoop from heaven & take the shape,
With fold to fold, of mountain or of cape,
But, O too fond, when have I answer'd thee?
                    Ask me no more.

Tears, idle tears, I know not what they mean,
Tears from the depth of some divine despair
Rise in the heart & gather to the eyes
In looking on the happy Autumn fields,
And thinking on the days that are no more.

                    A Tennyson

She sleeps: on either side upswells the gold-fringed pillow lightly
    pressed ;
She sleeps, nor dreams, but ever dwells a perfect form in perfect rest.

            *   *   *

Take another instance of his power of condensation—that of
The Dead Warrior :—

Home they brought her warrior dead : she nor swooned nor uttered
    cry :
All her maidens, watching, said—" She must weep, or she will die."
Then they praised him, soft and low, called him worthy to be loved,
Truest friend and noblest foe ; yet she neither spoke nor moved.
Stole a maiden from her place, lightly to the warrior stepped,
Took the face-cloth from the face ; yet she neither moved nor wept.
Rose a nurse of ninety years, set his child upon her knee—
Like summer-tempest came her tears—" Sweet my child, I live for
    thee."

As a specimen of his grand heroic verse, his *Charge of the Light
Brigade* is an instance too well known to require comment.

R. H. STODDARD, of New York, has contributed many graceful
and beautiful lyrics ; the following are from his pen :—

      The wild November comes at last
        Beneath a veil of rain ;
      The night-wind blows its folds aside,
        Her face is full of pain.
      The latest of her race, she takes
        The Autumn's vacant throne :
      She has but one short month to live,
        And she must live alone.
      A barren realm of withered fields ;
        Bleak woods of fallen leaves ;

The palest morns that ever dawned ;
The dreariest of eves
It is no wonder that she comes,

Poor month ! with tears of pain ;
For what can one so hopeless do
But weep, and weep again?

There are gains for all our losses, there are balms for all our pain ;
But when youth—the dream—departs, it takes something from our
     hearts,
          And it never comes again.

We are stronger, and are better, under manhood's sterner reign :
Still we feel that something sweet followed youth with flying feet,
          And will never come again.

Something beautiful is vanished, and we sigh for it in vain ;
We behold it everywhere, on the earth and in the air,
　　　But it never comes again.

STEDMAN, of New York, who wields an artistic pen, thus in-
dites a song to the *Summer Rain :*—

　　　Yestermorn the air was dry
　　　As the winds of Araby,
　　　While the sun, with pitiless heat,
　　　Glared upon the glaring street,
　　　And the meadow fountains sealed,
Till the people everywhere, and the cattle in the field,
And the birds in middle air, and the thirsty little flowers,
Sent to heaven a fainting prayer for the blessed summer showers.
　　　Not in vain the prayer was said ;
　　　For at sunset, overhead,
　　　Sailing from the gorgeous West,
　　　Came the pioneers, abreast,
　　　Of a wondrous argosy—
　　　The Armada of the sky !
　　　Far along I saw them sail,
　　　Wafted by an upper gale ;
　　　Saw them, on their lustrous route,
　　　Fling a thousand banners out :
　　　Yellow, violet, crimson, blue,
　　　Orange, sapphire,—every hue
　　That the gates of heaven put on,
　　　To the sainted eyes of John,
　　　In that hallowed Patmian isle,
　　　Their skyey pennons wore ; and, while
　　　I drank the glory of the sight,
　　　Sunset faded into night.
　　　Then diverging far and wide,
　　　To the dim horizon's side,

Silently and swiftly there,
Every galleon of the air,
Manned by some celestial crew,
Out its precious cargo threw,
And the gentle summer rain
Cooled the fevered earth again.

*   *   *

C. P. CRANCH, one of our American bards, thus philosophizes:—

Thought is deeper than all speech, feeling deeper than all thought;
Souls to souls can never teach what unto themselves was taught.
We are spirits clad in veils; man by man was never seen;
All our deep communing fails to remove the shadowy screen.

*   *   *

Like the stars that gem the sky, far apart, though seeming near,
In our light we scattered lie; all is thus but starlight here.
What is social company but a babbling summer stream?
What our wise philosophy but the glancing of a dream?
Only when the sun of love melts the scattered stars of thought,
Only when we live above what the dim-eyed world hath taught,
Only when our souls are fed by the fount which gave them birth,
And by inspiration led which they never drew from earth,—
We, like parted drops of rain, swelling till they meet and run,
Shall be all absorbed again,—melting, flowing into one.

The Ivy-Green of DICKENS is a gem of the purest water:—

Oh! a dainty plant is the Ivy-green, that creepeth o'er ruins old!
Of right choice food are his meals, I ween, in his cell so lone and
   cold.
The walls must be crumbled, the stones decayed, to pleasure his
   dainty whim;

And the mould'ring dust that years have made is a merry meal for
him.

    Creeping where no life is seen,
    A rare old plant is the Ivy-green.

      *   *   *

Whole ages have fled, and their works decayed, and nations scat-
tered been,
But the stout old Ivy shall never fade from its hale and hearty
green.
The brave old plant in its lonely days shall fatten upon the past,
For the stateliest building man can raise is the Ivy's food at last.

    Creeping where no life is seen,
    A rare old plant is the Ivy-green.

Many other beautiful episodes are scattered throughout the productions of the world-renowned author of the *Pickwick Club*, such,
for example, as the description of Little Paul, in *Dombey and Son*.

FREDERICK TENNYSON, brother of the gifted Laureate, thus pays
beautiful tribute to Women and Children :—

    Oh ! if no faces were beheld on earth
      But toiling manhood and repining age,
    No welcome eyes of innocence and mirth
      To look upon us kindly, who would wage
    The gloomy battle for himself alone ?
      Or through the dark of the o'erhanging cloud
    Look wistfully for light ? Who would not groan
      Beneath his daily task, and weep aloud ?
    But little children take us by the hand,
      And gaze with trustful cheer into our eyes ;
    Patience and Fortitude beside us stand
      In woman's shape, and waft to heaven our sighs.

      *   *

ALLINGHAM, one of the living poets of Ireland, thus chants to us a moral :—

> What saith the river to the rushes gray ?
>   Rushes sadly bending, river slowly wending ?
> Who can tell the whispered things they say ?
>   Youth, and prime, and life, and time,
> Forever, ever fled away !
>   *   *   *
> Draw him tideward down ; but not in haste,
> Mouldering daylight lingers ; night with her cold fingers
> Sprinkles moonbeams on the dim sea-waste,
> Ever, ever fled away ! Vainly cherished, vainly chased.
>   *   *   *

Here are his pensive lines on *Autumn* :—

> Now Autumn's fire burns slowly along the woods,
>   And day by day the dead leaves fall and melt,
>   And night by night the monitory blast
>   Wails in the key-hole, telling how it passed
> O'er empty fields, or upland solitudes,
>   Or grim wide wave ; and now the power is felt
> Of melancholy, tenderer in its moods
>   Than any joy indulgent Summer dealt.
> Dear friends, together in the glimmering eve,
>   Pensive and glad, with tones that recognize
>   The soft, invisible dew on each one's eyes,
> It may be somewhat thus we shall have leave
>   To walk with Memory, when distant lies
> Poor Earth, where we were wont to live and grieve.

What a touching cabinet picture is here presented to us by W. WINTER, of New York :—

The apples are ripe in the orchard, the work of the reaper is done,
And the golden woodlands redden in the blood of the dying sun.

At the cottage-door the grandsire sits, pale, in his easy chair,
While the gentle wind of twilight plays with his silver hair.
A woman is kneeling beside him ; a fair young form is pressed,
In the first wild passion of sorrow, against his aged breast.
And, far from over the distance, the faltering echoes come
Of the flying blast of the trumpet, and the rattling roll of the drum.
Then the grandsire speaks, in a whisper, " The end no man can see ;
But we give him to his country, and we give our prayers to Thee !"
The violets star the meadows, the rosebuds fringe the door,
While over the grassy orchard the pink-white blossoms pour.
But the grandsire's chair is empty, the cottage is dark and still ;
There's a nameless grave on the battle-field, and a new one under
    the hill !
And a pallid, tearless woman by the cold hearth sits alone,
And the old clock in the corner ticks on with a steady drone.

Listen to this heroic *Dirge*, by G. H. BOKER, of Philadelphia :—

Close his eyes, his work is done !
    What to him is friend or foeman,
Rise of moon, or set of sun,
    Hand of man, or kiss of woman ?
        Lay him low, lay him low,
        In the clover or the snow !
        What cares he ? he cannot know :
        Lay him low !

As man may, he fought his fight,
    Proved his truth by his endeavour ;
Let him sleep in solemn night,
    Sleep forever and forever.
        Lay him low, lay him low,
        In the clover or the snow !
        What cares he ? he cannot know :
        Lay him low !

371

Fold him in his Country's stars,
　　Roll the drum and fire the volley!
What to him are all our wars,
　　What but death bemocking folly?
　　　　Lay him low, lay him low,
　　　　In the clover or the snow!
　　　　What cares he? he cannot know:
　　　　Lay him low!

Leave him to GOD's watching eye,
　　Trust him to the Hand that made him;
Mortal love weeps idly by:
　　GOD alone has power to aid him.
　　　　Lay him low, lay him low,
　　　　In the clover or the snow!
　　　　What cares he? he cannot know:
　　　　Lay him low!

JEAN INGELOW, one of the most original writers of our age, has acquired distinguished fame as a poetess. In her dramatic tale of *High Tide*, we have the following nervous lines:—

I sat and spun within the doore, my thread brake off, I raised myne
　　eyes,
The level sun, like ruddy ore, lay sinking in the barren skies;
　　　　And dark against day's golden death
　　　　She moved where Lindis wandereth—
　　　　My sonne's faire wife, Elizabeth.
"Cusha! Cusha! Cusha!" calling, ere the early dews were falling,
Farre away I heard her song, "Cusha! Cusha!" all along;
　　　　Where the reedy Lindis floweth, floweth, floweth,
　　　　From the meads where melick groweth,
　　　　Faintly came her milking song:—

"Cusha! Cusha! Cusha!" calling, "for the dews will soon be falling;
Leave your meadow-grasses mellow, mellow, mellow;

Quit your cowslips, cowslips yellow;
Come uppe Whitefoot, come uppe Lightfoot,
Quit the stalks of parsley hollow, hollow, hollow;
Come uppe Jetty, rise and follow, from the clovers lift your head;

Come uppe Whitefoot, come uppe Lightfoot,
Come uppe Jetty, rise and follow, Jetty to the milking shed."

         *   *   *

           Lo ! along the river's bed
A mighty eygre reared his crest, and uppe the Lindis raging sped.
    It swept with thunderous noises loud ;
    Shaped like a curling snow-white cloud,
    Or like a demon in a shroud.
And rearing Lindis, backward pressed, shook all her trembling bankes
    amaine,
Then madly at the eygre's breast flung uppe her weltering walls
    again.
    Then bankes came downe with ruin and rout—
    Then beaten foam flew round about—
    Then all the mighty floods were out.
So farre, so fast the eygre drove, the heart had hardly time to beat,
Before a shallow seething wave sobbed in the grasses at oure feet :
The feet had hardly time to flee before it brake against the knee,
    And all the world was in the sea.

         *   *   *

That flow strewed wrecks about the grass, that ebbe swept out the
    flocks to sea ;
A fatal ebbe and flow, alas ! to manye more than myne and me ;
    But each will mourn his own (she saith).
    And sweeter woman ne'er drew breath
    Than my sonne's wife Elizabeth.

         *   *   *

The following lyric illustrates the pictorial beauty of her style,
no less felicitously :—

    When the dimpled water slippeth,
    Full of laughter on its way,

And her wing the wagtail dippeth,
Running by the brink at play ;
When the poplar leaves atremble
Turn their edges to the light,
And the far-up clouds resemble
Veils of gauze most clear and white ;
And the sunbeams fall and flatter
Woodland moss and branches brown,
And the glossy finches chatter
Up and down, up and down :
Though the heart be not attending,
Having music of her own,
On the grass, through meadows wending,
It is sweet to walk alone.

*   *   *

\- —

Thus have we reached the terminus of our pleasure excursion
through the glorious realms of Poesy.   All along our course, has
the bright sunshine of song beautified and gladdened our hearts.
Right pleasurable, indeed, have been

" Those lyric feasts,
Where we such clusters had,
As made us nobly wild, not mad !"

In after-time shall we not recall with delight, from the store-
house of memory, the rich treasures of exalted thought and exquisite imagery which we have so lavishly enjoyed ?

" Blessings be with them and eternal praise,
The Poets, who on earth have made us heirs
Of truth and pure delights, by heavenly lays !"

375

For not only are they the "unacknowledged legislators of the world," they are among the foremost of its benefactors; and their magic numbers, flowing from "the happiest and best moments of the best and happiest minds," should be thus authoritative. Let us, then, ever cherish with affectionate regard the rich legacy they have bequeathed to us, as *lares* and *penates* near each household hearth. "True poems are caskets," wrote Irving, "which enclose in a small compass the wealth of the language,—its family jewels." Thus should we prize them, even as we do the precious metals,— nay, more—since gold will leave us at the grave, but the wealth of the mind

"Unto the heavens with us we have!"

Such glowing and beautiful utterances as the minstrels have left us find a ready response in the common heart of humanity, because they are the expression of its universal thought. Nor ever will their sweet voices be hushed or unheeded, in a world which the tuneful throng have made all resonant with the rich melodies of the ages.

"For doth not song to the whole world belong?
Is it not given wherever tears can fall,
Wherever hearts can melt, or blushes glow,
Or mirth or sadness mingle as they flow—
A heritage for all?"

Druck:
Customized Business Services GmbH
im Auftrag der KNV-Gruppe
Ferdinand-Jühlke-Str. 7
99095 Erfurt